ME, MYSELF
AND HIM

ME, MYSELF AND HIM

A NOVEL

E.N. JOY

URBAN CHRISTIAN

www.urbanchristianonline.net

Urban Books, LLC
1199 Straight Path
West Babylon, NY 11704

Me, Myself and Him © copyright 2008 E.N. Joy

ISBN-13: 978-1-60162-844-2
ISBN-10: 1-60162-844-7

First Trade Printing March 2008
First Mass Market Printing January 2010
Printed in the United States of America

10   9   8   7   6   5   4   3   2

*This is a work of fiction. Any references or similarities to ac-
tual events, real people, living, or dead, or to real locales are
intended to give the novel a sense of reality. Any similarity
in other names, characters, places, and incidents is entirely
coincidental.*

Submit Wholesale Orders to:
Kensington Publishing Corp.
C/O Penguin Group (USA) Inc.
Attention: Order Processing
405 Murray Hill Parkway
East Rutherford, NJ 07073-2316
Phone: 1-800-526-0275
Fax: 1-800-227-9604

Dedication

Aunt Gwen, it was you who took me to a place where I could get to know Christ and get the promise of eternal life, and I thank you for that. To this day, we walk this Christian walk together— there to help each other out along the way.

Victorious Life Christian Center, you were the place that introduced me to Christ. Your place of worship has kept me looking ahead, never looking back to wallow in my past, but only looking back to see where God has brought me from (. . . *a mighty long way!*).

Mother Darling, can you believe we are Christians now—not only in name, but in actions—true practicing Christians? As a little girl, we may not have taken walks together in the park, but this walk with Christ is one that I wouldn't trade for the world.

My husband, Nick (Bang), even though we praise differently, worship different and have our own personal relationships with God, thank you for letting me cover you with holy oil whenever I felt the need to—LOL (Well, it worked didn't it? Look at us now).

To my children: My two daughters, Little Joy and Henney, thank you for praying, reading the Bible, and for ministering God's Word through dance with me. I'm so truly blessed and honored to have been chosen by God to carry two little angels in my womb; my son, Randy, you are an awesome young man of God. It has been prophesized to me that you will become a mighty man of God. I can't wait to rejoice in that day with you and I pray every day for that manifestation. I'm truly blessed and honored to have been chosen by God to carry one of His messengers in my womb.

To Ayanna and Angie, thanks for understanding why a sista couldn't hang out at the bachelorette parties—LOL. But it was an honor to be there when God made you one with your soul mates. Your continued support for my work and my walk does not go unnoticed. You both mean so much to me and played such major parts in my life. I love you both with all my heart.

Martina, my little niece, you have been a divine little angel in my life and I love you as if our blood pumped the very same blood. . . . Wait a minute; it does—the blood of the lamb, in which we are both covered. We are connected and related through Christ—the ultimate DNA! Love ya!

Last but not least, to my Dad and my four sisters, I love having you here on earth to love and support me, but it's our eternal life together in heaven that I'm most looking forward to. I love you all.

Acknowledgments

Carl Weber, and Urban Books only knew me as an author who wrote secular novels that included street lit and erotica. When I informed him of the change in my life—the change in my walk—which ultimately resulted in a change in what I wrote, he never questioned my sincerity or capabilities. Instead, he provided the platform I needed to do just what I wanted to do with this book, which is to minister God's Word through my gift of written Word. Thank you, Mr. Weber.

All glory be to God for the wonderful guidance of Pastor Howard Williams and First Lady of Victorious Life Christian Center. In addition to all the other stones of the church, Pastor, I was one of the rolling stones. Thanks for making sure the church doors and your heart were open when it was time for me to roll back in and do God's will in the very place He called me to do it. And to my dear brothers and sisters in Christ at VLCC, thank you for all of your support and prayers.

Aunt Gwen, I had Uncle Johnny and Aunt Joy to care for my son when I had to dedicate my time to travels and writing. For my girls, I have you. Not only do you care for them, but you pick up where I left off when they leave my home and come to yours. You provide an atmosphere where God is still present. Not too many mommies can say that about the place where they drop their kids off to be cared for.

To my reading fans, especially those who knew me by my other writing names and works and yet still decided to support me in my spiritual writings (Namely, Women Empowered by Reading Book Club, who even made me an honorary member): you have no idea what a blessing you are to my heart. That right there is unconditional love. Not too many authors can claim that sort of victory from their readers. Most fans love writers to stick with the same program and give 'em what they want. But you have allowed me to do more than just please man, you have allowed me to please God. I'm convinced you will be blessed for that.

Granddaddy Edwards, who has read every single last one of my books, thank you for your undying love and support. I'll love you always and you'll always hold the record for being the only one in the family who has read every single work I've ever published (although my mother-in-law, Gwen Marsh, is running neck and neck ;-)

Miss Darlene, you bought a copy of the very first book I ever wrote when it was printed on 8½" x 11" sheets of paper. Years later you have still continued to support me beyond anything I could ever imagine. I don't know how long you have been saved . . . but you have always been an angel to me.

I must thank my dedicated reading team, who gave me their honest feedback before the book ever even reached my editor: Earth, Trini, and Shelia, your loving criticism was well received. Thank you for your kind and uplifting words, and more importantly, for supporting what I do. I love you all. Vanessa, my girl, you know God used you to help make sure that His Word didn't get lost in any unnecessary verbiage or drama. I can't thank you enough. And I can't forget Locksie of Arc Book Club. Girl, you are brutal, but honest. That's why you are highly respected for what you do. And thanks for letting me use your name (in both my books). Hope I did you proud.

To the Urban Christian authors, each and every one of you motivated me through your own works. Let's continue to lift each other in prayer as God continues to show us favor for being obedient and doing His will by ministering His Word through the written word.

I'm going to bring this acknowledgement full circle and acknowledge last, but not least, my editor, Martha Weber. You know you have a reputation in the Urban family for those fifteen and a half pages of editorial notes you produce; but God is simply using you to pull the writer out of writers. Nineteen published works later, I can finally say that, thanks to you, Martha Weber, I'm a writer!

Chapter 1

"God ain't into threesomes!" Mary scolded her niece.

Locksie looked up at her aunt in shock. "Aunt Mary," she blushed.

"Get your mind out of the gutter, girl," Mary said as she joined Locksie at the kitchen table with two cups of coffee in hand. She placed one in front of Locksie and the other to her peanut-butter-colored lips, which were an identical shade to her flawless skin complexion.

"Get my mind out of the gutter?" She folded her arms.

"Yes, because I'm not talking about *that* kind of threesome; the sexual kind," Mary explained. "I'm talking about intimacy, but not the type of intimacy your filthy mind has managed to wander off to."

Locksie chuckled as she took a sip of her hot beverage. "Well, what did you expect me to think? You're sitting here mentioning God, threesomes and intimacy all in the same breath. I didn't know ol' Jehovah got down like that." Locksie chuckled once again, but could tell by the way her aunt's eyebrows began to close in tight that she wasn't finding the humor in her comment.

"What I'm trying to say is that God wants to be intimate with you; not sexually, but spiritually." Mary looked her niece in the eyes as her voice softened and she hugged herself. "God wants to pull you in close. He wants you to rest on His bosom so that He can whisper in your ear the answer to all your problems. He wants to get so intimate with you that your soul intertwines with His." She entangled her fingers together for demonstration. "But like I said," she got serious again, "God ain't into threesomes. And He ain't into no quickies either."

Locksie threw her hands up. "Now, how do you expect me to get my mind out of the gutter if you keep putting it there? Now you're sitting here talking about God and quickies."

"Will you just listen already, nasty girl?" Mary said, playfully spanking her niece on the back of her hand.

"Ouch!"

"That didn't hurt . . . Now listen. When I said quickies, I meant those quick little prayers to God people sometimes squeeze into their busy schedule here and there, usually while the television is on or while they're sitting in their car listening to the radio. If you want to get intimate with God, it's just got to be you and Him—not you, Him, and Zenith. Not you, Him, and Hot 107. You know what I mean?"

"Yeah, yeah, yeah, Aunt Mary," Locksie said,

rolling her eyes, signaling that she had just about had enough of this conversation.

For the life of Locksie, she never could understand why she tolerated her Aunt Mary always preaching about God when she couldn't tolerate her own mother doing it. Maybe it was because she was older now and wasn't actually being forced to sit there and listen. When Locksie was young, her mother had robbed her of choice by making God and church mandatory, instilling a fear of hell and damnation in her mind. Aunt Mary hadn't used God and church to rob her of a normal childhood like Locksie felt her mother had done.

Mary shook her head and looked up to the heavens.

Locksie giggled at her aunt's dramatics. She always enjoyed having coffee with her favorite aunt—her only aunt—every morning before she headed in to work at the local Fiesta hair salon she managed. Although at the fifty-year mark in age, Aunt Mary could definitely keep up with her younger niece. A volunteer aerobics instructor for the Columbus Parks and Recreation Department, Mary's physique put Locksie's to shame. Not that Locksie was out of shape or anything; just not as in shape as Mary's four feet, eleven-inch petite, muscular frame.

With a five feet, seven-and-one-half-inch frame, Locksie's 158 pounds spread out evenly as not to make her look frumpy with the excess ten pounds that it wouldn't exactly hurt her to lose. But it was only in the buff that those extra few pounds made themselves known. Under the black smock she was required to wear at work, her body wasn't visible at all; only her pretty brown face that always bore flawlessly applied make-up.

A Mary Kay representative on the side, Locksie made sure to always be a walking campaign ad for the cosmetic line whose products seemed to be catering more and more to African Americans. Locksie sold at least one of her products daily, even if it was nothing more than a tube of lip gloss. That was a personal goal she had set for herself a year ago when she first paid the $100 fee to become a consultant.

"You're worried about me?" Locksie asked Mary. "You're the one talking about threesomes and quickies. Either God is off the chain, or you need to get you some." Locksie laughed, dodging another swat from her aunt.

"Cut it out. You know what I'm trying to say and you're just mad because I'm speaking the truth. Every morning you come over here with the same old complaints about you and Dawson." Dawson was Locksie's live-in boyfriend of three years. "And how something is missing from your relationship. Well, I'll tell you what's missing: God is." Mary rolled her eyes. "Over there living in sin together in that big ol' house of yours." Mary began to mumble under her breath as she took a sip from her cup.

"So how should I be living in sin, Aunt Mary? By my lonesome?"

"Damn right! By yourself! If you gon' choose to live in sin, why drag somebody else with you?"

"I see with all that going to church and praying you be doing, that ol' cursin' demon ain't let loose of your tongue yet," Locksie said sarcastically with a chuckle, sucking her teeth as she put her cup to her lips and swallowed. She realized that this was probably another reason why she could tolerate her aunt over her mother. Aunt Mary was funny. She wasn't ashamed to admit that although she was a Christian, she wasn't a perfect Christian; she still had stuff of her own to be delivered from. She wasn't telling everybody else they were going to hell, which is exactly what Locksie's mother used to always tell her.

Mary, on the other hand, knew that approach was everything. And although she admired how her sister had tried to instill the goodness of the Lord in her niece's heart, she couldn't wholeheartedly agree with her past methods.

"I'm working on that cursing thing," Mary admitted, "and I'm believing in God to deliver me from it; truly I am. But never you mind me." Mary pointed at her niece. "Think you slick trying to change the subject. Like I said before . . ." She took a sip of her coffee and then continued. "God ain't into no threesomes. It can't be you, Him and Dawson; you, Him, and your job; you, Him, and nobody or nothing else for that matter. God wants you to submit to Him and Him only. He wants your mind, your body, your heart, and your soul. And once He has that, you never know. Your assignment may be to bring Dawson's soul to Him. Or your test could be to let Dawson go. All I'm saying is just worry a little less about your man, and focus a little more on *the* man."

Locksie tilted her head and poked out her lips as if to suggest that Mary was overexaggerating Locksie's concerns about Dawson. "Stop adding yeast to my feelings about Dawson. You're mak-

ing it bigger than it seems. Besides, he's my man;
I'm supposed to please him. And I don't worry
any more about my man than the next woman
worries about hers."

"Yes, you do, and you know I ain't lying,"
Mary corrected her. "You come over here wanting
me to teach you how to cook a certain dish, trying
to make your man happy. If it isn't about cooking,
you need me to help you sew up his torn britches.
You've even come over here asking me to help
you pin up your hair before y'all go out. But
you've never once," Mary put her index finger
up, "not once, asked me to help you or teach you
how to do something that is going to make God
happy."

Locksie let out a sigh, wondering how was it
that lately Mary had managed to drag God into
every conversation they had. In a way, Locksie
understood where her aunt was coming from, but
Locksie couldn't see God; however, she could see
Dawson. Locksie couldn't hear God. She could
hear Dawson. She didn't want to waste her time
trying to please some man up in the sky who
might not even be real. Why should she, when
she had Dawson right there on Earth, in the flesh?

"There ain't a doubt in my mind that pleasing
Dawson isn't going to be a complete waste of
time," Locksie reasoned. "Besides, God ain't struck
me down with a bolt of lightening yet, so obviously He's cool with how I'm living. The wages of
sin is death, right?" Locksie looked herself up and
down and then wiggled her fingers. "Well, I ain't
dead, so I must be doing something right."

Mary just shook her head. "Well, I know the
last thing my Heavenly Father wants me to do is

sit here with you and get into a verbal battle about who He is and what He can do. Although I'm sure He appreciates my efforts, He doesn't need me to." Mary winked at Locksie, lifted her cup to her mouth, and while gazing at Locksie over the rim of her cup, said, "He'll show you Himself." After taking one last sip, Mary stood up and began to chuckle. "Yes, in-deedy. God don't need me, or any other man for that matter, to tell you who He is or what He can do . . . He'll show you Himself . . . and it's all in a matter of time."

Chapter 2

"Umm, baby," Locksie said as she rolled off Dawson and onto her side. "That felt so good it must be a sin." All Locksie wanted to do was bask in the arms of her lover. But she couldn't. It was Sunday morning, and she had something important to do.

Dawson rolled over behind Locksie. Intertwined, their matching brown skin made it hard to tell where hers began and his ended. Dawson pulled Locksie's brown- with-honey-highlights, shoulder-length hair behind her double-pierced ear and then pressed his thick lips against it. In his deep, baritone voice he whispered, "Then since we're just two sinners going to hell anyway, let's make it worthwhile." He began nibbling on Locksie's ear.

"Oh no, you don't." Locksie pulled away and stepped out of the bed. "You know I have to do Eve's hair this morning."

"It's Sunday, our only day off," Dawson whined. "How you gon' arrange to do somebody's naps?

You know how I look forward to my Sundays with you, Locks." Dawson called Locksie by his pet name for her. Not only was it short for Locksie, but he had told her that she had three locks on him; one on his heart, one on his mind and one on his body.

As Locksie's feet padded toward the master bath that adjoined their bedroom, which was so huge that the builders referred to it as "the owner's retreat," she turned to look at Dawson and smiled. She could tell just by looking at him how sincere he was. She loved it when he desired her. It made her feel good to be desired and loved, especially by a man as beautiful as Dawson. He was the spittin' image of The Ohio State University graduate and former professional NFL star, Eddie George. And the taste that fell in Locksie's mouth at just the mention of Dawson's name was delicious.

They had met three years ago at the gym where Locksie used to be a member and Dawson still worked. Dawson started off as her personal trainer, which was his licensed profession, and then he became her friend. It took approximately four dinner dates, two movie dates and two home-cooked meals for them to transition from friends to lovers.

"Baby, don't whine like that," Locksie said, playfully pouting her lips. "You know what your whining does to me."

"Then come here and let it do what it do." Dawson winked as he motioned with his index finger for Locksie to rejoin him in bed.

"You know I would if I could, but Eve is going to be here in a few. I'm sewing tracks in, and for all that hair she wants, we'd be at Fiesta all day long trying to get it done if I did it during my work hours. That's why I'm doing it here at the house. That way I can bank all the money. You know at Fiesta I'm on salary, so I'm not about to give them the money for all that work I have to do."

"Why doesn't she just buy a daggone wig?" Dawson huffed as he pulled the covers up to his neck in defeat.

"I'll make it up to you, I promise," Locksie said as she entered the bathroom.

"When? How?" Dawson asked with excitement, quickly sitting up at attention as he stared at Locksie's thick silhouette. Seconds later, every part of him was at attention.

"When? Tonight. How? However you want it, baby." Locksie licked her lips and let the door close shut in front of her, leaving a panting Dawson on the other side.

By the time she stepped into the shower and began washing the lathering suds down her body, it happened again; that feeling was revisiting her. She'd hoped that this time, after having sex, it wouldn't, but it had. Her smile, the aftermath of her lovemaking with Dawson, turned into a look of shame. She kept her head down and watched the water stream down the drain, realizing that the sin of fornication wouldn't so easily do the same.

Locksie had to catch her thoughts and ask herself when she had started referring to her and Dawson's lovemaking as fornication. She loved making love to him. She loved the way he made her feel. She loved him; the man she had vowed to love to eternity the first night the two of them exchanged those three words. As far as Locksie was concerned, Dawson was her Mr. Right. But for the life of her, she couldn't explain why everything was starting to feel so wrong.

Lately it seemed as though the wonderful feeling of having Dawson inside of her was becoming more and more short-lived. At first, Locksie tried to blame it on her recent discussions with her aunt Mary—that maybe all that talk about God, fornication, sin and death was starting, slowly but surely, to hinder Locksie's sex life. But she knew it was something deeper than that.

During their sexual encounter, Locksie could do nothing but enjoy and indulge, but now, only moments later, the pleasurable feeling of her climax was laced with guilt. What once made her feel like she was on top of a mountain was now making her feel as though she was in the lowest of valleys.

Just last week while she and Dawson were being intimate, she had closed her eyes and smiled as his lovin' took her to that next level, but then her eyes snapped open and she stared up at the ceiling as if there was a mirror there and she was watching herself. Only it felt as though it wasn't just her eyes that were watching her—that maybe someone else was watching her too. Feeling embarrassed at the thought that someone could actually see what was going on in her bedroom, Locksie had simply closed her eyes again and escaped back into the comfort of Dawson.

After failing to wash her sins down the drain, Locksie turned off the water and stepped out of the shower. Even though the bathroom was filled with warm steam, all of a sudden she felt a cold chill. She grabbed her towel, not because of the tender breeze that had just ripped through the bathroom, but because she felt that same feeling she had experienced last week. So she covered up quickly, not wanting to be exposed. She knew that no one else was in the bathroom, but still, the feeling that there was someone watching her was all too real to ignore.

"Argghhh!" Locksie screamed as the bathroom door flung open, startling the heck out of her.

"Sorry," Dawson said, entering the bathroom, now wearing a pair of fitted boxer briefs. "I didn't mean to scare you."

"Don't you knock?" Locksie snapped. "I mean, you knew I was in here. How you just gonna bust in like somebody wasn't even already in the bathroom?" Locksie, slightly shivering, clenched her towel around her.

"Dang, I'm sorry," Dawson said with a puzzled look on his face. He had never knocked before entering the bathroom when he knew she was in there. And Locksie had never once seemed to mind him invading her space so freely. Not once . . . up until now.

"And you should be sorry," Locksie said, heading out of the bathroom, brushing past Dawson, but making sure her body didn't touch his in even the slightest way. "Next time knock."

"What's with this change in you?" Dawson threw his hands up and let them flop back down to his side.

Locksie sighed and allowed her tense shoulders to relax. "Nothing," she said as she pulled the bathroom door closed behind her. "Nothing's changed," she mumbled a second time, in an attempt to convince herself. Locksie leaned against the door with her hand still on the knob and closed her eyes. She had just lied to Dawson. When he asked her what had changed, she told him nothing. But she knew very well that something had changed; she just couldn't put her finger on exactly what it was.

Chapter 3

The next day, Locksie was at work trying to focus on her client's hair, but instead, thoughts of her and Dawson lingered on her mind.

"You sure you okay today?" asked Hannah, one of Locksie's regular clients at Fiesta.

Locksie had been doing Hannah's hair for close to a year. Outside of the salon, they never talked to each other on the phone or went out together or anything, but in the salon, there was just this bond between them as if they'd been friends for years. It's funny how women have that certain relationship with their beauticians. They tell their hairstylists things they'd never tell their best friends, knowing that everything is going to stay right inside the shop; which is usually where their friendships stays as well.

Hannah was one of several clients who had followed Locksie from the beauty school to the hair salon. She was also one of Locksie's few white clients. Hannah wasn't 100% white, though. Born to a black mother and a white father, her father's genes dominated, especially in the fire-red hair and the red freckles sprinkled across Hannah's sugar-cookie-colored skin.

"Yeah, I'm good," Locksie replied, removing one of the bobby pins she had nestled between her lips. She was using them to keep Hannah's pin curls in place.

Hannah may have appeared to be a white girl, but her hairstyles were more typical of those worn by black women, letting the brothas know she had some chocolate drizzled over her sundae. This was how Elkan, her husband, knew he had a chance with her. As the fine, honey-dipped brotha he was, when Elkan saw Hannah up at Alumn Creek Beach with all those hips and booty hanging out of her swimsuit and her hair cornrowed down her back, he was convinced that she was the one white girl who could make him throw out his "never play in the snow" motto.

With a five feet, eleven-inch, 180-pound frame and looks that could land him any woman he wanted, Elkan definitely had been blessed with his share of women, but he vowed to himself that he would never disrespect the black woman by dating outside of his race; especially a white woman. He had contemplated a Latino Jennifer Lopez look-a-like who worked as a clerk at the law firm where he practiced civil law, but he came to the conclusion that no matter how dark her skin was, she still wasn't no sistah. Besides, what would his mama think, him bringing someone other than a black queen home? So whenever Elkan got attention from a white woman, his conscience would remind him that he didn't play in the snow. But the moment he laid eyes on Hannah, he silenced that little voice in his head and made a move.

There was something about Hannah that just stood out from all the women at the beach, especially since half of them were blatantly trying to get Elkan's attention, which was a complete turn off for him. He liked being the cat that chased the mouse and not the other way around. Hannah, on the other hand, had paid Elkan no mind at all. He comforted his ego by coming to the conclusion that Hannah just hadn't noticed him yet. As Elkan lay on his stomach with his chin rested on top of his hands, he was watching Hannah rub sunblock all over her body. He was certain she had noticed him when she got up and came strutting his way. He prepared a huge smile aimed just at her. But Hannah just walked right on by Elkan as if the slab of handsome wasn't even in her path. She didn't even turn back to apologize when she kicked sand in his face as she was dashing by him, headed for the water.

Not about to go unnoticed by Hannah, Elkan made his way to the waters and managed to strike up a conversation with the bathing beauty. They hit it off instantly, even sharing a soda on Elkan's bath mat after exiting the water. Lying there talking on the beach for hours, Hannah and Elkan ignored the friends they had come with. But what they couldn't ignore was the evil eye the sistahs were giving Elkan, and the looks of disgust the white men were giving Hannah.

The conversation was engaging and flowed easily. But it was as if Elkan had been holding his breath the entire time, and the moment Hannah told him that her mother was black, he could breathe again. He wanted to shout it out to all the sistahs on the beach who had been giving him the evil eye for choosing the pale girl over them, "She's black too! Her mother is black." Instead, he just smiled and thought, *Thank you, Jesus. This one can go home to Mama!*

Elkan compared Hannah to that chocolate-dipped ice cream cone from the Dairy Queen, only someone had just eaten all the chocolate covering off of her so she appeared like nothing more than a vanilla ice cream cone. But he knew she was black, and that was enough. At least that's what he tried to convince himself of, but Hannah could sense differently.

"You sure everything is good?" Hannah asked Locksie.

Locksie looked up at the picture of her and Dawson that was on her station. It had been taken two years ago, before he shaved off all of his hair. In the picture he had a goatee, but he had since shaved off all of his facial hair too.

"Yeah, positive . . . I guess."

"That means no," Hannah said as she spun around in the chair after Locksie had placed the last bobby pin in her hair.

Locksie relaxed her shoulders and sighed. "Seriously, Hannah, I guess everything is okay. I mean, I think it is. I don't know. It's just that lately with Dawson and me . . ." Locksie looked around the salon to make sure no one else was listening. Then she lowered her voice. "The sex—"

"Don't tell me," Hannah said, cutting Locksie off. "You ain't as into it anymore? That happened with Elkan and me, you know, after the incident where he cheated on me with that wench named

Peni. It just took a long time for my body to start craving him again, you know. And then there are those times when you just get sick of the same old—"

"It's not that." Locksie was quick to come to Dawson's defense in the lovemaking department. "It's good." Locksie smiled. "It's real good when we're getting down. It's afterward that I have a problem."

Hannah had a puzzled look on her face. "What is it?" She pondered for a second and then said, "Ahh. I get it. He throws in the towel afterward?"

Now Locksie had a puzzled look on her face. "Huh?"

"You know, throws in the towel after sex—for you to wipe yourself off." Hannah shook her head. "There is nothing more degrading than that. You give a man a special part of you and what does he do when y'all finished? Gets up, pisses, throws a towel at you to wipe yourself off with and then says, 'Yo babe, how 'bout making me something to eat?'"

Locksie laughed at Hannah's deep-voiced imitation of a man. She could tell she was speaking from experience.

"I'm serious, girl," Hannah said. "That's why I loved Elkan so much from the start. He wasn't anything like that. He was so considerate and passionate. From the first time we ever made love to the last, it's been nothing but a scene from a classic romance movie. That's why I don't understand why . . ."

Hannah's voice began to fade, and Locksie knew where her thoughts had gone—back to five years ago, when she found out that Elkan had not only cheated on her with a client of his, Peni Lampkin, but that a child was the result of the affair. It was the child Elkan and Hannah had been trying to conceive since their wedding night seven years ago, only Hannah hadn't been able to get pregnant.

Devastated, Hannah had moved in with her mother the night that Elkan sat her down with a tearful confession that she would never forget. He begged her not to leave him. He unpacked her things from the suitcase just as quickly as she was packing them.

"Baby, I'm sorry," Elkan had cried to her. "Peni meant nothing to me. It was one time. I swear to God. It was that night after I had won her lawsuit for her. I had to take her the paperwork to sign so that she could get her settlement. When I showed up, she had a nice little thank-you celebration set-up waiting. After one too many glasses of wine . . ."

"Let me guess," Hannah had interrupted him. "She thanked you for a job well done with a well done blow job?" Elkan put his head down in shame. "Oh, and then one thing led to another. Isn't that how the story always goes?"

"Sorry, Hannah. I wish I could take it back, but I can't. And now there is a child involved. A child she insists on giving birth to."

Tears Hannah had been able to hold throughout Elkan's miserable confession suddenly just poured out, accompanied by wails so loud that it took her a minute to realize that the horrendous sounds were coming from deep within her own soul. Elkan tried to hold her and console her, but she fought him off, slumping down to the ground like a melted candy bar on the cement on the hottest day of the summer.

"What color was she?" Hannah was finally able to ask once she stood up and got herself together.

"Huh?" Elkan had clearly heard her inquiry.

"Was she black?" Hannah yelled. "I mean all the way black? Black-mama-and-black-daddy kind of black?"

"Yes, she's black, but look, Hannah, that doesn't matter. What matters is that I cheated and I shouldn't have, no matter what color she is," Elkan reasoned.

"And she's going to have your baby. I'm your wife, but yet another woman is carrying your child." Hannah pointed at herself for clarification that she was his wife. That she should be the woman giving him his first born. Just hearing those words come out of her own mouth, reaffirming the situation at hand, sent Hannah back to the ground in a tearful fit. "God, why? Why are you doing this to me? To my life? This is a mean, mean, cruel joke, God. You are a mean, cruel God."

Even though Hannah had been saved as a teenager at the church where her uncle was a deacon, in her adult life, she hadn't been to church very much with the exception of an Easter Sunday here and there. The last time she had attempted to go to church was a couple years ago when Christmas had fallen on a Sunday. She had woken up that morning, and for the first time, felt the true meaning of Christmas brewing in her belly. She felt what pastors had been preaching about for centuries—that it wasn't about shop-

ping in overcrowded malls for overpriced gifts,
but that it was to remember the birth of Jesus.

Hannah had gotten dressed and hopped in her
car, heading to church. She had even adjusted her
radio dial to 106 Joy, the gospel station in Columbus, Ohio. When she arrived at the church door-
steps, she was disappointed to find that it was
closed. Some pastors across the country had decided to make the executive call that with Christmas falling on a Sunday, the attendance would be
too low to have service, since everyone would be
at home opening gifts. The church Locksie had
decided to go to that morning was one of them. *If
they won't even open up the church doors on the birth-
day of God's Son*, Hannah thought, *then why should
I even bother?* Disappointed, she turned away,
never to return to church again. She couldn't help
but think how God had closed the doors on her that
Sunday, and now, as she sat weeping on her bedroom floor, He had closed the door on her marriage too.

At the time, Elkan didn't know what to do for
his wife. He wanted to help her by just taking her
into his arms. But how ironic would it have been
for her to want to rest in the arms of the person
who had hurt her? For the first time ever, Elkan
now knew what Prince meant by the one line in
his song titled "Girlfriend": *Would you run to me if
somebody hurt you, even if the somebody was me?* Instead of running to Elkan, Hannah ran to her
mother and father.

It only took two weeks for Hannah's parents to
convince her that she shouldn't walk away from
her marriage without at least trying to work
things out. "God wouldn't have you marry a man

just to be hurt, wounded and left for dead," her mother told her.

"God ain't gonna bring you this far just to leave you," her father added. "This is just a test. He wants to see if you trust in Him to see you through all of this."

Although God was the last person Hannah wanted to put her trust in to fix the situation she felt He had let happen to her, she did believe Elkan was worth fighting for. And the last thing she wanted was for that hussy, Peni Lampkin, to live happily ever after with her man. So to this day, as far as Hannah was concerned, she had made the right decision by forgiving Elkan and giving their marriage another chance.

"Look, Hannah." Locksie interrupted her thoughts as she removed the cape from around Hannah's shoulders. "You know I love Dawson to death, and he loves me. My mind is just playing tricks on me is all. It's nothing, really. I'm just letting my aunt Mary get to me."

"Ohhhh," Hannah said, nodding her head. "I get it. Has your sanctified auntie been making you feel guilty about spreadin' without weddin'?" Hannah chuckled. "Trust me. I know what it's like. My mom and dad did the same thing with Elkan and me when we were only dating. It got so weird that I started hearing my parents' voice during sex. 'Your body is your temple . . . blah blah blah.' Pretty soon the aftermath of sex with Elkan was like the aftermath of eating an entire chocolate cake or pizza all by yourself. It was sho' nuff good while you were eating it, but then with all the guilt and weight you had to carry around as a result, you felt miserable and it just didn't seem worth it."

"Hmm, not even my aunt Mary has used that analogy—fornication and gluttony."

"Hey, they're both sins. I'm not a huge Bible reader, but I don't think anywhere in the Bible God puts any greater weight on one sin than He does the other. That's society's doing. You know how it is. We like to pick and choose our own sins. Some pick murder, some pick fornication, some pick gluttony. A sin is a sin. Anyway, I better get out of here. It's Elkan's son's weekend with us. His mother will be dropping him off at the house in a little bit and I need to be there."

"All right then, chick. Have a good weekend . . . Oh, wait. I need to ring you up."

The two women headed over to the register. Locksie had gotten so wrapped up in Hannah's words that she almost forgot to charge Hannah for her hair service. She wondered if it was possible, because of the life she was living with Dawson, that right now God was looking down on her with the same disgrace and disappointment as He would a murderer. Locksie hated the mere idea that God might feel like that about her. But, if He did, He'd have every right to. After all, Hannah couldn't have put it any better; a sin is a sin.

Chapter 4

"Hey, Ma," Locksie said through the phone receiver after looking down at the caller ID box. She had just walked in from work to a ringing phone.

"Praise the Lord," her mother replied. "In all thine ways acknowledge Him and He will direct thy path."

Locksie sighed and allowed her eyes to roll in her head. One day she just wished her mother would call her and have regular mother-daughter talks minus all the scripture. Thanks to her mother, Locksie would never have to read the Bible; her mother would have recited every verse after a few more phone calls.

"Hello to you too," Locksie said with traces of sarcasm in her tone. "How are you?"

"Blessed and highly favored."

"So how was your day?" Locksie reluctantly continued.

"This was the day that the Lord made, so I rejoiced and was glad in it."

"Look, Ma, is there something specific you needed? My job is on the other line," Locksie lied. She could tell that this phone call, like all the others, was going to be Bible study instead of a conversation. She didn't mind the fact that her mother loved the Lord; she just wished she wouldn't be so overzealous with it. Locksie believed in God. She just wasn't as into Him as her mother was, and didn't appreciate the fact that her mother continuously flaunted the love affair.

"Oh, no, honey. There's nothing specific that I wanted. I just hadn't talked to you in weeks and I don't think you've been back home here to Michigan since you left for college," her mother joked. "Just wanted to make sure you were still breathing. Although if you weren't, I know you'd be in a better place in the comfort of our Father. You might not understand now how the Lord Jesus Christ is your Savior, but I pray to God daily that by the time He calls you, you will have accepted Him into your heart."

Okay, now Ms. Martha Winters had fallen off her rocker and sank too far into the deep end for even Locksie to tolerate. "I gotta go, Ma. I'll talk to you later."

"God bless y—"

Locksie quickly hung up the phone. She grabbed her forehead and then made her way to her bedroom. "Gosh," she said as she flopped back onto the bed, spreading out her arms. "Now I know what that poor stringy-haired white girl in the movie, *Carrie*, was going through." Locksie shook her head. "And my mother wonders why I never come back home to visit her. Puhleez!"

Locksie sat up and picked up the phone by her

bed to call her aunt Mary. Aunt Mary might be a Christian, but she didn't wear it on her sleeve and try to beat Locksie upside the head with it in the same manner her mother did. Nor did she force her to commit the sin of gluttony by making her digest more Bible scriptures than she could chew by constantly shoving them down her throat. Aunt Mary had her ways about trying to get Locksie to convert from just believing in God to receiving Him, but they weren't nearly as badgering as her mother's ways. Aunt Mary knew when to quit.

"Hello," Mary answered the phone, sounding out of breath.

"Hey, Auntie, it's me," Locksie said. "You busy or something?"

"No, I was actually getting ready to close the door behind me when I heard the phone ring, so I ran back in to get it."

Locksie looked over at the clock and frowned. "It's almost seven o'clock. Your show is about to come on. Since when is anything more important than your favorite television show? If I went into labor with my first born during your show, you'd ask me to wait and have the baby until after it went off." Both women laughed.

"I know, child, but what's going on? Did you need something?"

"Nah, just got done talking to your crazy sister."

"Well, she's your mother. What did Martha do now?"

"Nothing. You know how she is. I mean, I can't even get a hello out of her without a 'Praise the Lord! Hallelujah!'" Locksie sounded frustrated.

Mary chuckled. "Well, I can't knock her. I know how it is to be in love with Jesus and just want to tell the world. Kind of like when you first met Dawson. You couldn't stop talking about that man. You wanted to walk up to strangers, tap them on the shoulder and tell them what a good man you had found. Well, once you get beyond just knowing of Jesus to really getting to know Jesus, then you can't help but fall in love with Him. And you'll want to tell the world about the love of your life every chance you get."

"Come on, though, Aunt Mary. You know Martha will Rodney King somebody with scripture." Aunt Mary burst out laughing. "But she will. She will beat you down with some Bible verses."

"Oooh, Locksie, stop it," Mary said, getting her laughter under control. "You a mess."

"No, she's a mess. You don't know what it was like growing up with her, going from church to church. It was awful. I mean, how did she expect me to get to know God if we never stayed at His house long enough for me to be formerly introduced?"

"I know. I used to tell her about that. That's why we had that big falling out and ain't really been that close since. I told her she just couldn't change churches every time God revealed to her that something wasn't right in one church. I mean, as far as she knows, God could have been revealing things to her about the church and the people in the church so that He could use her to help correct them. I mean, your mother is a powerful woman of God, Locksie. But sometimes she just wouldn't stand still and let God use her."

"Her? Stand still? Ha."

"Yeah, well, she's still your mother and she's still my sister. God knows her heart. But personally, I think there's a little more to why she's the way she is than just being in love with Jesus."

"Yeah?" Locksie said, curious at the sincere tone Mary had used. It was as if Mary knew something about her mother that she didn't.

"Yeah, but, hey, I gotta get going. I'll see you in the morning. Oh, and I have this new gourmet coffee I bought from TJ Maxx. You know how they be having all those neat little tea and coffee gift sets? The ones you would never buy for yourself but always give as gifts and appreciate when someone else buys it for you? Well, I finally broke down and bought some for myself."

"Goodie, I can't wait because I've always wanted to try those gourmet coffees, but like you said, it's just something you never treat yourself to."

"We are children of the King and we deserve it. All right then, Locksie boo, I'll see you tomorrow. Love you."

"Love you too, Auntie. Bye."

Locksie hung up the phone, meaning to have asked her aunt where she was going.

The beeping of the Brinks door chime let Locksie know that Dawson had arrived home. Every time one of the doors or windows in the house opened, the chime went off.

"Hey, baby," Dawson said to Locksie as he entered the room. He walked over and puckered his lips before planting a wet, juicy kiss on her.

Locksie stared him up and down, becoming slightly turned on by the way his sweatsuit was sticking to every muscle on his body. She then said, "Hey yourself."

Dawson paused, noticing the once-over his woman had given him. He licked his lips and then slowly bent down toward Locksie.

She immediately put her hands up to stop him in his tracks. "Don't even think about it with your sweaty, funky self."

"Come on, baby," he said, pressing against her hands, pushing her back on the bed. "You know how much I love making love to you. You gon' deny me due to a little sweat?" He leaned in closer, pressing up against Locksie's hands.

"Yuck! Stop it!" she exclaimed, turning her head from left to right as she let out giggles. Locksie used to wonder if Dawson really loved making love to her as much as he proclaimed, or if he just liked making love period. After all, she wasn't the ugliest woman in the world, but she wasn't the finest either, and she saw Dawson as the finest man in the world. So what was it about her that made him want her so much and so often? What was so special about her that made her so worthy of a man like Dawson? After a while, Locksie accepted the fact that, plain and simple, she had a good man who saw her for what she was, a good woman.

"We gon' get sweaty anyway," Dawson said as he kissed all over her neck after forcing his way through her resistance.

Dawson's skin was moist and cool, forcing his nylon workout suit to stick to him. Before Locksie could even try to fight him off again, she became seduced by and indulged in Dawson's wet, juicy kisses.

"Mmmm, you're right," Locksie said as she began to lift Dawson's sweat jacket over his head. "We gon' just get sweaty anyway."

He smiled and then placed a kiss delicately on her soft lips. After Locksie aided Dawson in peeling off the rest of his clothing, Dawson helped Locksie out of her clothes. She laid back as she took in all the man Dawson was willing to give her. And after what felt like a trip to the moon, Locksie lay there in the bed, feeling like she had just eaten that entire chocolate cake and pizza Hannah had spoken about.

Chapter 5

It was after one in the morning, and for the life of her, Hannah couldn't figure out who could be calling her husband on his cell phone at this hour. Her eyes hadn't been closed for very long after just watching an episode of *Cheaters*, so when Elkan's cell phone rang from the other room, it jarred her out of her light sleep.

Hannah used her cell phone for her business, for which she did advertising consulting from the home. She met with the owners of small businesses and entrepreneurs trying to get word out about their businesses and services, helping them put together feasible advertising packages. She gave them unique ideas that they could never have come up with on their own, then found companies who could bring the ideas to life. But even Hannah turned off her phone at night. She couldn't help but think that Elkan always left his on for some particular reason, or should she say one particular person—Peni, the baby momma from hell.

Peni seemed to enjoy pulling out the baby momma card whenever she pleased, calling Elkan at all hours to discuss matters of their son. Hannah knew she only did it to try to get up under her skin . . . and it worked.

Some mambo tune blazed from the living room coffee table, where Elkan had left his phone after talking with one of the firm partners about a case. Upon hearing it, Elkan, who must have also been in a light sleep, jumped up out of the bed and raced to answer it.

"What is it? Is everything okay?" are the only words Elkan said loud enough for Hannah to hear clearly. From that point on, his voice seemed to have gotten quieter, as if he was intentionally talking low or walking farther away from the bedroom so that Hannah couldn't hear his conversation.

Hannah could just picture Elkan pacing through their single-story ranch style home, talking sexy to his mistress in every corner of their house while his loving wife waited for him to return to bed. *God, I gotta stop this*, Hannah thought as she buried her head into her hands. She was tearing herself apart.

Hannah had forgiven Elkan for his single act of adultery, but she sure hadn't forgotten about it. Although she never threw it up in his face, it stayed on her mind constantly, eating away at her like a cancer, sometimes making her physically sick with stomach pains and headaches. When people complimented her for going from a size ten to a size eight, she just smiled and nodded, not wanting to take credit for the exercise and sacrifice most thought she had subjected herself to when she knew it was worry and stress alone that had suppressed her appetite.

"What do you mean it's not fair to you, Peni?" Hannah thought she heard Elkan say.

Hannah looked back over at the clock that read 1:19 A.M. There was no way Peni could be calling about their son at that hour unless something was wrong with him. Hannah got out of the bed and crept over to the door to see if she could hear a little better.

"Will you stop yelling before you wake up my son?" she heard Elkan grit.

Hannah had witnessed more than her share of her husband arguing with Peni on the other line. And she knew that their five-year-old love child, Elkan Junior, had heard enough one-sided phone arguments between his mother and father to last him a lifetime as well. Hannah knew that the last thing her husband wanted was for his son to be awakened in the middle of the night by his mother ranting and raving. Hannah couldn't believe all the times Peni had yelled and cursed Elkan out only for him to hear his son's small voice finally chime in in the background and ask his mother to stop.

"You mean you've been talking like this in front of my son?" Hannah would hear Elkan ask Peni. "You've been cursing and calling me out of my name with my child sitting right there? What kind of mother are you?"

Peni always took Elkan's query as the worst insult ever—someone questioning her parenting skills—and it would only fire her up even more. Any curse words or derogatory names she hadn't thrown at Elkan were surely balled up in her fist, about to be released. Eventually Elkan got to the point where he'd let the conversation go Peni's way if it meant his son wouldn't be subjected to that kind of talk. So, he refused to argue back at Peni.

Of course Hannah didn't see it the way Elkan tried to explain it to her. From what she could tell, her husband was weak when it came to Peni. Throughout their entire relationship, Elkan never had a problem standing up to Hannah and saying what was on his mind, so why didn't he show the same aggressiveness toward Peni?

Hannah was, in fact, a very passive person, but she would often wonder if the way Elkan stood up to her but not Peni had anything to do with the difference in their skin colors. Hannah had heard it as many times as the next black woman about their so-called dominating attitudes, always trying to put their men in check. She had been told by brothas that this was why some black men turned to white women. But Hannah didn't yell, point her finger or do the bobble head when she talked, and she was just as black as any other black woman. This meant to her that not all black women should be stereotyped as acting a certain way. But Hannah had to admit, when it came to Elkan, she wasn't so sure if these stereotypical characteristics that Peni displayed made him feel as though he was dealing with the so-called *real* black woman.

So many thoughts went through Hannah's mind as she stood in the doorway and listened to her husband soft-talk to the woman he had cheated with.

"Look, sweetie, we'll talk about it tomorrow at

a decent hour. Kiss my son for me. Good-bye," Elkan said.

Hannah quickly ran back into the bed with her heart beating a mile a minute. She hoped Elkan hadn't seen her or sensed that she had been eavesdropping. When she heard him enter the room, she tried to hold her breath. That little jog back to the bed was like a mini marathon, and she didn't want him to notice her breathing so heavily. She knew she couldn't play possum for long because she wanted so badly to ask Elkan about the phone call. Unless she called him on it, she wouldn't have been able to sleep. So, when he tried to slowly and softly climb back into the bed without waking her, she pretended that he had interrupted her sleep with his movement.

"What are you doing?" she asked.

"Oh, nothing. I didn't mean to wake you. Go back to sleep, sweetie."

No this fool did not just call me the same thing he called that heifer, Hannah thought. "Was that your cell phone I heard ringing?" *There, I said it. Now what you got to say? And you better come correct.* Hannah perhaps didn't talk with a whole lot of attitude, but she thought with it.

"Oh, uh, yeah, it was," Elkan said as he got comfortable under the cover. "Good night."

Good Night? Ha, yeah right. "Who was it?"

Yawning, Elkan said, "It was nobody."

Nobody. Well, since when do you hold conversations with nobody in the middle of the night? "So you mean they hung up?" *Please don't lie to me. When people lie they have something to hide. Don't let my husband be hiding something from me. I don't think I can take anymore trust issues. Please, don't let him lie.*

"Yeah, they hung up," he lied. It was his way of making a long story short, but it was a bad idea on his part.

A huge knot formed in Hannah's throat as her eyes began to water. She couldn't believe Elkan had allowed that lie to fall off his lips, as if lying was the easiest thing in the world for him to do. At first, Hannah didn't even have words for him; she was just going to cry herself to sleep like she had done plenty of nights before. But tonight she decided that she was not gon' cry. She was tired of crying. That never seemed to get her anywhere. Instead, she decided that if Elkan wanted to deal with a *black* woman, she was gon' give him *black* all right. Even if it was just some members of society's stupid, stereotypical definition of black, it was time for Elkan to receive every man's fantasy—role-play in the bedroom. Hannah was about to be somebody other than the sweet, non-confrontational Hannah he was used to. She was about to be a mad black woman!

"They hung up, huh?" Hannah sucked her teeth.

"Yeah, you heard me. I said they hung up. Now go to sleep, babe. You know I got an early trial in the morning."

"Well, why didn't you tell the person who called you that you had a trial in the morning?"

"Because they hung up. I told you."

"Well, let's call them back and tell them now." Hannah snatched the covers off with an attitude, got out of the bed and stomped toward the door.

Being that Elkan slept on the side of the bed closest to the door, he was able to jump up out of the bed so fast that he caught up with Hannah before she could make her way out the door. "Honey, what are you doing? It's one-thirty in the morning. It's not that serious. Besides, the person that called hung up."

"That's what caller ID is for. We'll look at the caller ID on your cell and see who it was that called, and we'll call 'em back. Plain and simple." Hannah brushed her hands together as if to suggest that the task would be as easy as taking out the trash.

"No, wait!" Elkan grabbed her arm.

"What, Elkan? We're going to go see who is calling your cell phone at one o'clock in the morning so we can tell them about themselves. I mean, after all, you have a court date in the morning. How rude." Once again Hannah tried to walk off, and Elkan tightened his grip. He stood there staring into Hannah's eyes—eyes that were relentless. Something told him that this time, unlike all the other times, Hannah wasn't going to just roll over and go to sleep on this one.

"Look, Hannah, I lied. It was Peni. But it's late. Can we just talk about this tomorrow? After my court hearing, I'll take you to lunch."

"You said you would never lie to me again, Elkan," Hannah told him. "You said you would never lie or cheat on me again."

"Come on, Hannah, darn it!" Elkan said as if he was the one who should be upset. "I'm not cheating on you, and I really didn't lie. I told you the person that called hung up. Well, they did hang up—after we finished talking. But I didn't lie because I was trying to hide anything. I lied to make a long story short. For heaven's sake, it's going on two in the morning and I knew if I told you it was Peni who had called, I'd have to explain it and be up all night and stuff. And like I said, I have to be in court."

"So you feel as though with all that you and that tramp have put me through, you don't owe me a little conversation no matter what time of night it is?"

"I knew it. I knew it. There it is!" Elkan balled his fist and punched the air.

"There what is?"

"It took a few years, but I knew eventually you'd start throwing the past back up in my face. You said that you forgave me for cheating on you, but I knew you really hadn't. I knew it, and that's why I always felt that I had to lie—to protect you."

Somehow Elkan had managed to turn the tables on tonight's events. The conversation was no longer about the fact that another woman had called him, but that Hannah had secretly been convicting him while making him think she had forgiven him.

"Elkan, that's not true," Hannah said. "When I said I forgave you, I really did. I haven't been suffocating you, wanting to know where you are and who you are with all the time, going through your pockets or none of that." Hannah tried to convince him by looking at him with sincere eyes. "I've done nothing but love you—love you and Little E. It was so hard to forgive you, but I did. And after all that, now you want to stand here and accuse me of being insincere?" Tears began to fall down Hannah's face.

"Oh, Hannah, I'm sorry," Elkan said, wrapping his arms around her and kissing her forehead. "Baby, I'm so sorry. I didn't mean to doubt your sincerity. I'm sorry, baby. I'm sorry for everything." Elkan kissed Hannah on the forehead again, then he lifted her face with his hands and began to place kisses on her lips. "Do you forgive me?" he asked between kisses that were starting to burn Hannah with passion. "Do you forgive me?"

"Yes, baby. Yes," Hannah said as she grabbed the back of his head and returned his kisses. "I'm sorry too. I just want us to be happy and love each other."

Intoxicated from the sweetness of Hannah's tongue, Elkan lifted her off her feet and carried her to bed. "Woman, I'm gonna love you right now."

Elkan laid Hannah in the middle of the bed and slowly, from the top, began to unbutton her silky avocado-colored gown. His tongue took a tour of the inside of her mouth like it was its first time ever being there.

Hannah began to unbutton her gown from the bottom, meeting her husband halfway in their joint effort. She poured out of her gown once it was all the way unbuttoned, and Elkan raised his head to stare at his wife. While he covered every inch of her in kisses, Hannah rubbed her hands through Elkan's low-cut, dark brown hair. Once his mouth found her mouth again, they became one inside each other. Being married had its struggles and hard work, but as Hannah melted underneath her husband, she could only focus on the pros.

When Hannah woke up the next morning, she felt like she had been to heaven and back. Her husband had made love to her like never before.

That little tiff about Peni's phone call was a night-mare long forgotten as far as Elkan was con-cerned. But unfortunately for Hannah, Peni was one of those nightmares that wasn't going to allow itself to be so easily forgotten.

Chapter 6

"I can't believe I'm asking my little brother for female advice." Dawson shook his head as he stood in position over his younger brother, Drake, spotting him on weights.

"Don't be embarrassed. Older doesn't always mean wiser, big bro," Drake managed to breathe out as he finished up his third set of lifts. "It's not your fault that God just so happened to have blessed me with a better understanding about the psyche of the female species." He let out a huge sigh after struggling to push up his very last lift. Dawson aided him in resting the barbell in its proper place. "I may only be twenty-five years old, but I'm beyond my years when it comes to the ladies." He winked at his brother.

"Don't go getting the big head," Dawson said as he sat on the bench next to Drake.

At least once or twice a month, the two brothers worked out at the gym together. This was the most time they could fit into their busy schedules. Although Dawson was eight years Drake's senior, they were still pretty close growing up. They didn't spend as much time together in their adulthood as they would have liked to, but the same brotherly love was still present whenever they were together.

They had different fathers, each bearing their own father's last name, yet looked more like twins. Their personalities, however, were total opposites. While Dawson had always enjoyed the company of a lovely lady, never able to settle down with one before meeting Locksie, Drake had always been the settling down type. But he was never lucky enough to find that one woman who was also willing to settle down—or attend church regularly like he did.

For some reason, Drake, as wholesome as he appeared, always attracted women who wanted to give it up after knowing him only a few days—sometimes after only a few hours. Then there were those women who were more interested in the kind of car he drove than they were in the fact that he had graduated in the top five percent of his class from Capital University.

Dawson had warned him that once women learned that he was the young entrepreneur featured throughout the city's local newspapers, who owned a graphics design business with the country's top businesses as clients, they wouldn't be able to see past that. Being one of the elite million-dollar condo owners in downtown Columbus added to his appeal as well.

"So Locksie is getting weird on you, huh?" Drake confirmed the statement his brother had made to him earlier about how Locksie seemed to be changing.

"Yeah, I mean all of a sudden she's acting like she's embarrassed for me to see her naked. She had a fit one day when I barged into the bathroom when she was getting out of the shower. And I don't want to get graphic here, but after sex, instead of feeling like I pleased her, I feel like I've raped her or something."

"Dang, man, is it like that?"

"And you know how much I love her. She's the first woman I've ever dated that I didn't cheat on. I would never force sex on on her."

"Has she told you that she feels like you're forcing her to have sex?"

"No, nothing like that. As a matter of fact, it's nothing she says that makes me feel this way, but it's everything she does. She used to have this smile on her face after we'd been intimate, but now she has this look of guilt and shame. I can't even lie; that's really starting to screw with my manhood. You know, bruh?"

"So, have you talked to her about it, or are you just talking to me?"

"What am I supposed to say? She hasn't talked to me about it. The only person she ever talks to is her aunt Mary." Dawson thought for a moment. "Matter of fact, it's probably because of her that Locksie's acting this way."

"Why do you say that?" Drake asked, wiping his forehead with his hand towel.

"Her aunt Mary is all into the church and stuff."

"So, what's that got to do with anything? I go to church too."

"Yeah, but you don't Bible-bash people and try to push religion and your beliefs on everybody else. You do you and let other people do them. Her aunt is slick about sneaking sin and fornication into a conversation. Trust me, I know. We've invited her over to dinner enough times for me to experience it firsthand."

Drake chuckled. "Yeah, well, don't hate on her auntie just because she wants her niece to live a life pleasing to God."

Dawson took offense and stood up. "So, what are you trying to say? That because of me, God doesn't like Locksie?"

"Calm down, man." Drake made a gesture with his hands for Dawson to lower his voice. "I ain't trying to get on a religious trip, nor do I have a heaven or a hell to put anybody in, but, man, God's Word is what it is. There is no exception. The wages of sin is death. And no, that doesn't mean that you are going to drop dead because you sinned. It means you might jeopardize eternal life with the Father. But our God is a good God. A God of second chances. A forgiving God. That's why He allows us to repent for our sins."

"This is why I don't even holler at you on stuff like this. We're too different. But now you're starting to change even more. Maybe I spoke too soon. Maybe it was only a matter of time before you started all that Jesus crap too."

Drake knew that his brother was right. Ever since he got invited to that Bible study on campus, he hadn't been the same. He had only been on campus for two months when his dormmate, whose mother was a minister, started a Bible study. Drake only went because his money was tight and his dormmate was serving food and refreshments. And although Drake had gone to feed his flesh with food, he ended up getting spiritually fed, and on that night, he gave his life to Christ. So again, Dawson was right; Drake hadn't been the same since—and he wasn't going to apologize for it.

"I wish you didn't feel that way, bro," Drake told Dawson, "but I ain't gonna apologize for the man I changed into. You know, in high school, I didn't have to worry about abstaining from sex. It wasn't like chicks were falling all over me. I was as skinny as a tree limb with a face full of acne. I wore pop bottle glasses."

"Thank goodness for Lasic eye surgery," Dawson jumped in with a snicker. "Now you don't have to wear those Steve Urkel glasses anymore.

"And thank God for Proactiv skin treatment," Drake added as he shared a slight chuckle with his brother.

"And what about me,"—Dawson flexed his muscles—"the dude responsible for helping you get that nice little build you got now?"

"Yes, and thank God for you. But anyway, back in high school, I was the epitome of a geek. I was on the chess team for crying out loud. I couldn't even get a girl to be my study partner, let alone sleep with me."

"Yeah, but by college, you was like a whole new dude," Dawson complimented.

"Still, I just couldn't see myself with a different chick every day of the week like I saw some of those other cats in college doing—getting chicks pregnant, having babies too soon and dropping out of college, paying for abortions, abortions gone bad and the girls never being able to have kids again. There were others going to the clinic every month to get rid of an STD—some they couldn't get rid of because a cure had yet to be found—or even worse, getting HIV." Drake sighed after rattling off his list. "I just couldn't be one of the brothers dating and sleeping with all kinds of women just because they could."

"Let me guess—you're referring to me." Dawson looked his brother up and down and sucked his teeth. "Dude, that was the past. I don't go through women like water anymore, and besides,"—he leaned in to whisper in his brother's ear—"it was just jock itch."

Drake shook his head as Dawson continued.

"You know I've changed since hooking up with Locks. But even still, don't trip. You done switched up on the ladies quite a few times yourself as I recall."

Drake was quick to defend himself. "Yeah, but that's because most of the time the ladies I meet, although dime-pieces, aren't sent to me to be my soul mate. Some of them portray themselves as godly women, but then they're the first ones trying to initiate physical contact—contact that they know what it's going to lead to. They ain't nothing but traps from the devil trying to keep me from being holy, if you know what I mean."

"No, I don't know what you mean. Shoot, I remember what I used to do when the ladies would throw themselves at me."

"What would you do?"

"Catch 'em, what else?" The brothers laughed. "Look, bruh, I'm sorry, man. I didn't mean to snap on you," Dawson apologized. "It's just that I gave up a whole other lifestyle to be with Locksie, and I don't want that to be in vain."

"It's cool," Drake said, standing, giving his brother some dap. "I know how much you love Locksie, but it sounds to me like the lifestyle you and Locksie are living is starting to bother her."

"So, you saying I should just live with my girl and not sex her up until she gets over all this mess?"

Drake chuckled. "It ain't that easy, man. I mean, when it comes to something like that, and again, I know you ain't trying to hear all this, but the Bible tells you exactly what to do when your flesh tries to take over. First Corinthians 6:17 says to flee fornication. It works for me."

"Negro, please," Dawson said, sucking his teeth. "So, you trying to tell me that when the ladies push up on you, you cut 'em loose?"

"That's what I'm telling you."

"Once again, another reason why I never talked about women with you." The two headed toward the locker room. "But I know even though you might be some dumb, you ain't plumb dumb. You ain't ran from all of the honeys you've hooked up with, otherwise you'd still be a . . ." Dawson's voice trailed off, and then he nudged his brother's shoulder with his own. "You know what I'm saying? And I don't care how much scripture you can quote, you can't make me believe you ain't never got you none."

Drake shrugged his shoulders. "Okay then, I won't try to convince you. Besides, it ain't you I have to convince; it's God." Drake took a few more steps until he was finally in the men's locker room. He had tried his best to ignore the curves of the women along his path, although there was a curve or two that caught his eye.

After following Drake into the locker room, Dawson stopped his little brother in his tracks by grabbing his shoulders. "You trying to tell me that you ain't never . . . that you are a . . ." Dawson couldn't even fix his lips to say it, so Drake helped him out.

"A virgin? Yep, that's exactly what I'm saying," Drake confirmed.

"Shhh," Dawson said, putting his hand over Drake's mouth and then looking around the locker room to make sure no one else had heard him. "You trying to have every dude up in here know you ain't never been with no chick? They liable to think me and you are . . . you know . . ."

Drake laughed as he walked over to his locker and opened it. Like a lot of patrons, he never brought a lock with him, so he just placed his items in a locker and hoped no one would want to bother stealing his clothes.

Drake felt a little guilty about letting his brother assume that for all these years he had at least had sex with one woman. But he knew the first thing his brother would think was that he was gay, or even put some pressure on him by teasing and taunting him. This might have made him want to conquer one woman after another just to prove a point—that he wasn't gay and could get any woman that he wanted to. And he probably could. He'd run into several women who flat out let him know that they wouldn't mind letting him please them in bed. But he just couldn't do it. With the fear of the Almighty in his heart, he chose to please God instead.

But Drake knew that he could no longer continue lying by omission to his brother—or any one else in the world, for that matter. A couple weeks ago, the pastor at his church had preached a Word about how Christians should openly share their walk with the Lord and their testimonies to others, so that they may be witnesses to God's work and what He can do. "If another person sees that He did it for you," the pastor had preached, "then they will think, *surely He can do it for me.*" It was time for Drake to be a witness; and who better to be a witness to than his own brother?

"I don't mind being a witness to someone else, so I don't care who hears me. By not being embarrassed about living according to God's Word, maybe I can make the next man want to do the same."

Dawson just stood there shaking his head. "I can't believe you ain't never got you no trim. And how come all this time I've never known? How come you never told me about your problem until now?"

"Trim?" Drake was too distracted by Dawson's initial comment to address his questions. "That's something you do to hedges, not a woman. See, brothers are too embarrassed to even say the words *make love.* That's why most of y'all just having sex." Drake continued on to answer Dawson's question. "And you've never known until now because you've never asked."

"Well, I just assumed that you were getting some tri—Look . . . call it what you want to, but you are definitely a better man than me. I couldn't go without sex. But then again, it's probably easier for you not to partake in something you've never had. You don't know what you're missing, so you don't miss it. But asking a man who has already gotten him a taste to just stop altogether . . . puhleez!"

"Easy my foot. I'm still a man," Drake reasoned. "Man, you think I didn't want to stop and holler at those women out there in the gym? Do you think that I'm so far gone that I don't notice them in those little leotards and Spandex shorts? Well, I do. But if I acted upon my feelings, that would be nothing more than my fleshly desires. And when I get with a woman, I don't want it to be about flesh. I want my spirit and my soul to crave her, not this." Drake pointed at his private area.

"My spirit and my soul do crave Locksie, but so does this." Dawson repeated Drake's action. "And I can't help that."

Drake smiled at his brother's sincerity. "You really love Locksie, don't you?"

"Yeah, man. I never thought I would ever say that about a woman, but I do. I love Locksie. That's my baby." A proud smile spread across Dawson's face as he thought about his woman.

"Well, I'm sure Locksie loves you just as much, but from the sound of things, I believe a change is about to occur in Locksie's walk. Trust me. I've heard enough testimonies from women who have turned their lives over to God to know so."

"Her walk?" Dawson had a puzzled look on his face.

"Yep. Her walk in life, and if I'm putting my finger on it correctly, her walk with Christ."

"So, what does that mean for us—me and her? What does that mean for me?"

Drake looked down at Dawson's sneakers. "It

means you gon' have to go out and invest in another pair of shoes if you plan on keeping up with her pace. Because trust me, once someone finally decides to take Christ's hand and allow Him to lead them through life's journey, for those who might try and block the path, it's keep up or be dragged." Drake looked over at his brother. "Or even worse, get left behind."

Chapter 7

"God's a jealous God," Mary told her niece as they sipped on a cup of the new gourmet coffee she had purchased. "And I honestly think that's why your mama acts the way she acts."

Locksie almost spit out the sip of coffee she had just taken. "Are you trying to tell me that my mother is so afraid that God will be jealous if she doesn't eat, sleep, drink, breathe or talk about Him twenty-four/seven that she'll go to hell?" Locksie was almost mad at herself for thinking that Mary's explanation would be something profound, not ridiculous.

"From past conversations I've had with your mama, I feel she believes God thought that she loved your father more than she loved Him. God got jealous and took your father away from her, and it was God who sent your daddy off to be with that other woman and her kids, never looking back at the family he already had."

Locksie quickly became serious as she continued to take sips of the delicious blend. "Non-sense," Locksie said. She was trying to convince herself that God didn't have the power to place or remove a person as He saw fit.

"Oh, now, don't think for one minute God can't take it away just as quickly as He gives it. Let Him bless a man with one of them fancy sports cars and watch what happens if that man starts to do more for, and with, that car than he does for God. See if that man can drive that car around on a nice sunny Sunday morning, but can't go to church and thank the Lord for it . . . or even just drop to his knees and give thanks. See how quickly God can take that car back and get that man's attention."

"He wouldn't," Locksie begged to differ.

"Child, I don't know what kind of God you pray to, but my God can, and will, do anything as He so pleases. You remember that line in *Diary of a Mad Black Woman*? The one where the woman's mother told her, 'God can come down and show you who's God'?"

Locksie, almost in a trance, nodded her head as she recalled the line her aunt was referring to.

"Trust me, you don't want God to come down and show you just how powerful He is. God respects no man. He is the King of kings and the Lord of lords." As if her aunt Mary had been touched by the Holy Spirit, Locksie watched her flinch, close her eyes and just barely mouth, "Thank you, Jesus."

Mary opened her eyes to see a frozen Locksie, who didn't know how to react, staring at her. "Anyway," Mary said, deciding to put her initial train of thought back on the track. "See, Locksie, your father wasn't really a God-fearing man. I mean, he wasn't an atheist, but he wasn't a saint neither." Aunt Mary chuckled as if she were reminiscing on some of Locksie's father's ways. "He couldn't see what it was that your mother saw in church and praying and whatnot. He was always complaining about how she spent more time in church than she did with him. And he'd have a fit when he'd get the bank statements and see how much money she was giving in tithes and offerings. If you ask me, he too, just like God, was jealous; only I think your father was more jealous of the preacher man than he was of God."

"Doesn't surprise me any," Locksie said. "I think Daddy was jealous of me. If mama spent too much time combing my hair, he got mad. But I still don't understand what any of that has to do with your sister being a holy roller."

"See, Locksie, what you need to understand is that God will remove things from your life that He feels are interfering with you submitting to Him . . . including people."

Just then a burst of thunder filled the air, which made Locksie jump out of her seat. "Is it raining?" she questioned, walking over to the window over the kitchen sink. "It can't be. The weatherman didn't say anything about a chance of rain, and it was clear as a bell when I drove over here." Locksie pulled the curtains back and she and Mary watched raindrops hit the window. She turned around and faced Mary. "I swear the sun was shining and everything on my way over."

"Guess that just goes to show who the weatherman really is." Downing the last of her coffee and then standing, Mary shrugged her shoulders and replied, "See how quickly God changes things?" She winked as she brushed by her niece to put her cup in the sink. "Come on, girl, let's get out of here." Mary couldn't help but laugh inside at the frightened look on Locksie's face and God's sense of humor.

Without saying a word, Locksie placed her cup in the sink and followed Mary to the door. Her aunt's words to her today were more intense than they had ever been. Although they weren't meant to scare Locksie, they had. *Perhaps this is what God-fearing means*, Locksie thought, looking outside at the rain that seemed to have just come out of nowhere—as if God was making a point. If she hadn't before, she certainly feared Him now.

Chapter 8

Locksie felt good to have a day off during the week. She had started it by going to the gym with Dawson, but that idea wasn't long-lived. After only ten minutes on the treadmill, Locksie was sweating and out of breath. She felt embarrassed because the woman Dawson was personally training, who had to be twenty years older than Locksie, didn't even seem fazed by the movements Dawson was prescribing for her.

"Look, babe, I'm going to head on out and knock my errands out of the way," Locksie told Dawson as he coached his client on some arm curls.

"Already?" he questioned then turned his attention to his client. "Five more. Four more . . ."

"Yeah, you go ahead and work. I'll see you this evening."

"You sure? I'll be done with Mrs. Wilson in about thirty, and then I'll have an hour before my next session. You can just ride the bike or something for the next half hour and then—"

"No, really, I'm fine," Locksie was quick to say. A whole half hour pedaling fast but going nowhere? An entire thirty minutes? One thousand, eight hundred seconds? *No, thank you*, Locksie thought.

"Love you." Locksie pecked Dawson on the cheek and made her exit to the women's locker room to change out of her Spandex shorts and oversized sweatshirt and into her street clothes.

Dawson spotted Locksie walking out of the gym and blew her a kiss. She loved when he made sweet little gestures like that. She loved him, but she didn't love working out, so even though she would have loved to stay in the presence of her man, she'd much rather spend it in the presence of the shoe clerk at Macy's.

After her ten-minute drive from the gym to Eastland Mall, Locksie dug through her purse for her Macy's shopping pass, allowing shoppers twenty percent off purchases when they used their Macy's credit cards. This particular coupon was one with very few exclusions, so that meant designer purses were fair game.

Locksie touched up her face with her bronze 607 dual-coverage powder foundation, which matched her complexion to the tee. She wanted to remove any shine that remained from her strenuous ten-minute workout before heading into Macy's for her real workout—hitting every corner of that store. After tucking away her make-up compact, Locksie put her purse on her shoulder, got out of the car and started her trek through the packed parking lot.

Locksie looked down at her watch. It was five after ten in the morning. It wasn't even lunchtime yet. Locksie wondered why it was so crowded. Didn't anybody have to work today?

Locksie interrupted her own thoughts to say hello to the attractive woman who was heading to her car with Macy's bags in hand. Locksie made it a point not to walk by a person, especially after making eye contact, and not speaking to them. Sometimes just a friendly "Hello" or "How you doing?" from a stranger could make someone's day. Even just a smile. It had done that for Locksie on plenty of occasions, so she decided to return the inexpensive gift to whomever was placed in her path to receive it.

"Hello to you, too, sister," the woman replied with a loving smile. She reminded Locksie of Hannah, only this woman was no doubt 100% Caucasian. "Be careful in there. You see how much damage I did." The woman struggled to raise her four large shopping bags.

"Not to worry," Locksie assured her. "I don't even think my credit limit is that high."

Both women laughed as Locksie kept stepping toward the entrance doors.

"Excuse me, ma'am," the woman called to her. "Do you know that Jesus Christ is your Lord and Savior?"

Caught off guard, Locksie stopped in her tracks and mumbled, "Yes." Locksie didn't know this personally for herself, but at least it's what her aunt Mary had told her.

"Good, then you've accepted him into your heart?"

Locksie forced a fake smile along with her eager head nodding.

"Praise the Lord," the woman said, lifting her

hands to the sky as if now those bags she was carrying were weightless. "A saved woman in God. If I don't run into you again in this lifetime on Earth, I'll see you in our eternal life. Have a blessed day."

"Thank you. You too," Locksie said as she hurried toward the store just as quickly as she had hurried out of the gym. "Ugh," Locksie said once she was safe and sound inside the store.

That woman had ruined her day with all that Jesus and woman of God stuff. On top of that, she had forced her to lie—yet another sin to add to her collection. What else was she supposed to say to the woman? "No, ma'am, I haven't accepted Jesus into my heart, and right now all I care about is getting inside of Macy's before some other unsaved soul snatches up the last pair of eight and a half shoes in my size."

Locksie placed her hand on her head in an attempt to soothe her growing headache. *Remind me not to speak to another soul the rest of my life . . . the ones on earth anyway. Because I'm certainly going to hell now.*

Chapter 9

Hannah splashed a little cologne onto each side of her neck as she stood at her dresser mirror, admiring her brand new negligee. According to the calendar, she was ovulating, which meant her chances for conceiving were at their highest.

Not wanting her husband to feel as though the only reason she wanted sex was for making a baby, Hannah decided to add a little spice to the evening. She hated to admit it, but her ultimate goal for the evening, in fact, was just to conceive. But Elkan didn't have to know. All he had to know was that his wife desired him.

Hannah raced to their nice-sized kitchen and checked on the baked salmon. "Umm, delicious," she said as she inhaled the aroma and turned off the oven. "What next?" She looked around the room. "Oh, yes, the wine," she reminded herself.

She made her way over to the pantry and retrieved a bottle of wine. She then went to the cupboard and pulled out two wine glasses and placed them in the freezer.

"Okay, let's see . . . the salad is made. The lemon meringue pie is ready. I guess that's it."

Hannah took a deep breath and decided to go relax in the television room and wait for Elkan to come home from work. It was already later than he had been coming home lately, so she knew he'd be walking through the door any minute. He'd probably just stopped on the way home to get gas or something.

After about an hour, Hannah tried calling Elkan at the office to see if he had left yet. When she got his voicemail, she assumed he had. She then tried his cell phone and was quite shocked when it went straight to voicemail. "Hmmm, he never turns his cell phone off," Hannah said.

Hannah began to flick through the television channels to keep herself busy—or rather to keep her mind from thinking the worst about where Elkan could be. Eventually she decided on a glass of wine while she waited. By the time another hour had gone by, Hannah was up to four glasses of wine.

After having tried Elkan's cell phone several times to no avail, with a growling tummy, Hannah ate dinner without her husband. By midnight, she was fast asleep on the couch, and instead of caressing her husband, she caressed an empty bottle of wine.

The next morning, when Hannah awoke, still on the couch, she was covered with one of the spare blankets from the linen closet. She grabbed her throbbing head and tried to remember the events of the night before. That's when it hit her that the night before had been quite uneventful.

She recalled waiting up all night for her husband to come home so that they could enjoy a romantic dinner followed by some baby-making lovemaking. Anger swelled up in her as she thought about how he had never made it home. But recalling the blanket on her when she woke up, she knew that he must have eventually made it home.

Rising to her feet, set on going to tell Elkan about himself, Hannah grabbed her head and stumbled. "Get it together, girl," she coaxed before retreating to the bedroom.

The short didn't give her much time to prepare the words she would say to her husband, so by the time she reached the bedroom, she simply yelled out, "And just where were you last night?"

There was complete silence, and soon Hannah realized that she was talking to an empty room. She stomped into the bathroom only to find it empty too. She could hear the shower head dripping. She pulled back the shower door. "How many times have I told him to turn the water off all the way?" Hannah fussed as she tightened the knob to shut off the water.

Hannah went back into the bedroom and looked at the clock. It was after ten o'clock in the morning, so Elkan was probably at work. But one thing was obvious to Hannah, and that was that Elkan had come and gone. He had covered her up and taken a shower. But Hannah wondered when he had taken a shower. Had it been last night or just this morning? Did he even come home last night?

Hannah had enough of wondering, so she picked up the phone and called his office.

"This is Elkan," he answered.

"This is your wife," Hannah replied with a sharp tongue.

"Oh, hey, baby—"

Hannah cut him off. "Don't 'hey, baby' me. Where were you last night? I waited up all night for you. I cooked a special dinner, bought new lingerie, and to top it all off, I was ovulating!"

There was a pregnant pause.

"You done yet?" Elkan said calmly.

"As a matter of fact, I'm not! Why didn't you call? And why was your cell phone off?" Hannah continued her rant.

Elkan knew that Hannah was normally soft spoken, so he concluded that the bottle of wine he had pulled from her clutches when he covered her up was responsible for her sizzling tongue. "Look, there was an emergency with—"

"Let me guess," Hannah interrupted. "A client."

"Well, as a matter of fact—"

"And the battery ran down on your cell phone?"

"Well—"

"And there wasn't any other phone in the gosh darn city that you could have picked up and called your wife, who was worried to death about where you were?"

"By the time I realized how late it was, there wasn't any need in calling. I figured I'd just wake you up anyway, so I decided to drive on home. And besides, you didn't look too worried to me," Elkan shot back. "Looks like that bottle of Zinfandel you were hugged up with kept you company enough."

"Well, if you keep it up, that's not going to be the only thing that keeps me company!" On that note, Hannah slammed the phone down, immediately regretting her last comment. But at the same time, she was furious.

She wanted to believe that everything Elkan had told her was the truth, but it was just so hard sometimes. As far as she knew, Elkan might not have even come in last night, but this morning instead—thankful that she was in a drunken coma, unable to badger him regarding his whereabouts.

She looked down at her new lingerie purchase, on which she had spent almost a hundred dollars. She couldn't imagine what man in his right mind would have seen a girl dressed in that, inebriated and just waiting to be taken advantage of, and simply thrown a cover on her. *Is he not attracted to me anymore?* Hannah thought.

Before another thought could cross Hannah's mind, she found herself bent over the toilet, the salmon not tasting nearly as good coming up as it had going down. "How did I end up here?" Hannah asked herself out loud, wondering if she was referring to where she was at physically, which was hurled over the toilet puking her guts out, or where she was at mentally; once again, doubting her marriage . . . doubting herself.

Chapter 10

"I went online today and priced tickets for Vegas," Dawson said as Locksie sat down next to him on the couch with her dinner plate in hand. She had prepared one of Dawson's favorite light meals; cabbage, candied carrots, fresh string beans and sweet cornbread. He wasn't big on meat, but Locksie was, so her plate had a chicken breast she had prepared on her George Foreman grill.

"Vegas?" Locksie questioned as she set her plate down on the TV tray in front of her.

"Yeah, you remember—" Dawson started before he realized that Locksie had bowed her head, closed her eyes, and was mumbling.

After she finished whatever it was she had mumbled, she opened her eyes and took a bite of her chicken breast. With her mouth full, she then looked over at Dawson, who was looking at her dumbfounded. "Do I remember what?" she asked, catching a piece of food that had fallen from her mouth.

Dawson cleared his throat, now a little embarrassed that he hadn't blessed his own plate of food. But he never had before, unless it was Thanksgiving dinner at his mom's house or something.

"Oh, yeah, like I was saying," Dawson said. *Before I was rudely interrupted by your conversation with God.* "You remember my boy, Daryl? Him and his girl, Angie, are getting married. They're going to Vegas for their honeymoon the first couple days after the wedding, and then the entire bridal party, friends and family and whoever else wants to join them in Sin City for a celebration is invited."

"Oh, yeah. I'm definitely trying to do that," Locksie confirmed.

"Cool," Dawson said as he lifted a forkful of cabbage to his mouth. Before putting the food in his mouth he said, "You are talking about Vegas, right? You trying to do Vegas, not trying to get married?" Dawson winked.

"Boy, you stupid," Locksie said, jokingly hitting him on the arm. Playing, but not so much playing, Locksie shot back. "But actually, I wouldn't mind doing the married thing either," she said nonchalantly, eating one of the carrots and then chasing it with a bite of cornbread.

"Shoot, I think the game is on and I'm missing it," Dawson said, clearly diverting Locksie. He reached for the remote and began flicking the channels.

"What game?" Locksie asked.

"Uh, uh," Dawson stammered, snapping his fingers a couple of times as if he were trying to jog his memory.

"Yeah, that's what I thought," Locksie said, throwing her fork onto her plate.

"Girl, you know I'm just playing with you," Dawson said, pulling her close and kissing her on the forehead. "And I know you just playing too. Ain't nobody really thinking about getting married. I mean, our life is fine how it is. Why go messing it up?"

"Messing it up?" Locksie said, sounding offended. "So, marrying me would be messing things up? You don't see vowing to spend the rest of your life with me as making things better, but instead as messing things up?"

By now, Dawson could see that Locksie was dead serious. The joke, if it ever was one, was over.

"You know I don't mean it like that," Dawson said.

"Then what do you mean?"

"I just mean marriage ain't nothing but a piece of paper and two words—'I do.' But I got three words for you. I love you. That's all that should matter."

"I beg to differ. Marriage is a union. It's you and the person you love becoming one. In Ohio, they don't even recognize common law marriage anymore. So if the law doesn't even recognize what we have, what makes you think God will?"

Dawson closed his eyes and shook his head. He then carefully pushed his dinner tray away from him and stood up. He exited the great room. Locksie could hear his footsteps on the hardwood floors of the foyer. She heard him grab his keys off the table.

"Where are you going?" she called to him.

"To the gym. I'll be back once the words your aunt Mary has been putting in your left ear hurrys up and drips out of the right."

"This has nothing to do with my aunt Mary," Locksie said as she hurriedly moved her TV tray and met Dawson at the front door, which he had opened and was about to exit.

"Like heck it doesn't," Dawson snapped. "Every few months it seems she starts feeding you all this hell and damnation, sin and abomination crap, and then that's when—*and that's the only time*—when you get on this marriage kick. Look, we both agreed in the getty-up that we weren't on that marriage thing. Now, if your mind is changing, let me know, because mine isn't."

Locksie threw her hands up and walked away as she heard the door close behind Dawson. "My mind isn't changing," Locksie yelled as she flopped down on the couch. *It's everything else that's changing . . . and I can't seem to make it stop.*

"Baby, I'm sorry about tonight," soft lips whispered in Locksie's ear, waking her from her sleep.

She hoped the tears she had used to cry herself to sleep hadn't left any traces. The last thing her pride wanted was for Dawson to know his words had affected her so much that they brought her to tears.

Without saying a word, Locksie put her arm around Dawson's neck and brought his face against hers.

"You know I love you, girl," Dawson confessed. "And who knows? We probably will get married some day. It's just that—"

"Shhh," Locksie said as she placed her index finger on Dawson's lips and then replaced her finger with her tongue. Apology accepted.

Before Locksie knew it, her body was rocking back and forth with Dawson's. As they entered the point of no return, they trembled. A few minutes later, Locksie listened as Dawson entered the bathroom and turned on the shower. Water of its own fell out of Locksie's eyes.

In the dark bedroom, suddenly a streak of light came from the bathroom as Dawson cracked open the door and stuck his head out. "You want to join me?"

In hell? Locksie thought as she feigned sleep so that she wouldn't have to reply to her lover's invitation. She knew that stepping into that shower would be stepping into round two of lust, and if she wasn't careful, she might just get knocked out. But there had been weekends when she and Dawson had locked themselves up in the house and done the full twelve rounds. She never worried then, so why was she worried now? *What's happening to me? What's happening to us?*

Chapter 11

"She's just completely trippin' now," Dawson fussed through his cell phone and into his brother's listening ear. "I mean, last week, after we got finished doing the do, I wanted seconds so I invited her into the shower with me and she pretended to be 'sleep."

Drake chuckled. "Man, how do you know she really wasn't 'sleep?"

"Man, I just knew. We close like that. I even know when she's watching me sleep. I feel her."

"Yeah, yeah, yeah, Shakespeare. So, what did you do?"

"Nothing. I just closed the bathroom door and let her be. But I mean, what's really going on here? Am I not good enough for her anymore?" Dawson got real serious. He looked around the living room, knowing that Locksie was at work and he was the only one at home. But for what he was about to say, he needed reassurance. "Do you think I need that stuff they be showing on that commercial? The stuff where the men couldn't keep a woman before they took that little pill, then suddenly their women have smiles on their faces that can't be peeled off?"

"The one where you have to call your doctor if after four hours you still have an—"

"Yeah, yeah, that one," Dawson said, embarrassed.

Drake couldn't contain himself at that point and just exploded with laughter.

"What's so funny? I'm serious," Dawson said, but Drake was laughing too loud to hear him. "Man, I knew I shouldn't have said anything to you. I don't even know why I keep talking to you about this subject matter anyway." Dawson was upset now. "I've been doing just fine without your help."

"Obviously you haven't been doing just fine." Drake continued laughing. But then sensing his brother's frustration, Drake ceased his laughter and calmly told his brother, "Because God sent you to me."

"Huh?"

"God sent you to me to discuss this subject matter because He knew I would understand and be able to minister to you on it."

"But you don't know what I'm going through. You're a . . ."

"But I know what Locksie is going through, and if I can help you understand her, then maybe you'll get a better understanding of yourself."

"All right, all right, I get it," Dawson said in defeat. "It's just so confusing because one minute she's giving it up like she always has, and then the next minute she's got it on lock. I just want my old Locksie back. She's lost somewhere in this new Locksie I share my bed with, and I don't even know where to begin to look to find her. What am I supposed to do?"

Drake took a deep breath. "Some person once said, 'a woman's heart should be so hidden in Christ that a man should have to seek Him first to find her.' Maybe both you and Locksie are seeking out the wrong person to talk to and confide in. Perhaps I'm wrong. Maybe it's not me or her aunt Mary you guys should be talking to."

Dawson thought for a minute, wondering who else there was to talk to. "Oh, you got me twisted. I ain't about to go to no shrink or counselor or anything and discuss my sex life." Dawson shook his head in refusal as if Drake could see him through the phone.

"I'm not suggesting you do that."

"Well then, if not a shrink or a counselor, who should Locksie and I go to?"

"Do I really have to say the answer to that question?"

"Delilah, I'm heading out to meet a potential client, so please forward my calls to your phone and take a message. Voicemail is a blessing, but you know how I am about our clients talking to live people," Drake said as he whisked through the lobby and out the door.

"Yes, sir," Delilah, the receptionist, stated.

As the Moses of his graphics firm, Drake knew he had plenty of Aarons under him whom he could send to meet with clients. He had trained each member of his management team himself and knew they were capable of roping in new clients just as well as he did. But Drake had made a personal commitment to himself to perform the initial consultations with prospective clients. He wanted them to know how much their business meant to him, no matter how big or small the project.

When Drake arrived at the Hilton Hotel at Easton, where he arranged to meet all of his clients because of the elegant atmosphere and the best cook-to-order buffet in the city of Columbus, he still had ten minutes to spare before his client was expected to arrive.

"Mr. Trinity," the hostess said when Drake walked into the restaurant. "Shall I direct you to your favorite table?"

"Certainly, Trina, if it's available," Drake stated.

"How many guests will you be meeting with today?"

"Just one other person."

"Fine," the hostess replied, grabbing one menu. "Right this way." She knew that Drake would be partaking in the buffet, so there was no need for her to give him a menu, but she'd give his guest the option.

Once Drake was seated, his waitress came over and took his drink order. When she returned with his lemon water, following her was the hostess, and behind her was the most beautiful woman he had ever seen.

"Mr. Trinity, your guest," Trina said, moving aside so that the woman could take her seat.

As the waitress placed Drake's lemon water down in front of him, she turned to his guest and asked if she could take her drink order.

"Lemon water will be fine with me also," the

woman stated as both the hostess and waitress walked away. "It's so good to meet you, Mr. . . ." She extended her hand to Drake, who stood up to greet her.

"It's Trinity," Drake told her.

"I'm sorry, Mr. Trinity, it's just that my partner called me last minute to come meet with you because he had a family emergency. Your name didn't stick with me. But thank goodness when I told the hostess I was here to meet someone regarding graphics she knew exactly who you were. When she said your name, it rang a bell. But I feel so rushed and last minute, that by the time I made it over here to the table, it had slipped my mind just that easily." She hated rushing to do things last minute. It always made her feel nervous and unprepared.

"Don't worry about it," Drake told her after shaking her hand. "That explains why the gentleman I set up the appointment with, who had such a deep voice, doesn't fit the face that sits before me." They laughed.

"Yes, Reggie said he tried to call your office, but that you had already left. He sends his regrets for not being able to make it personally."

"Again, not a problem." Drake smiled while saying a silent prayer to God for making whatever events take place so that he could be sitting across from such a beautiful creation and not some huge male ego. He usually got stuck with the type of men who pretended to know more about graphics than he did; although they were, at the end of the day, hiring him to do the job.

For a moment, silence rested between them.

"Your water," the waitress interrupted. "Have

you two decided on what you'd like from the menu, or will you be having the lunch buffet?"

"I'll have the lunch buffet," Drake stated as his guest followed suit.

"Fine, then by all means, you may head to the buffet whenever you'd like."

"Well, shall we?" Drake nodded to his guest as the waitress removed the menu from the table and left.

"Yes, we shall," she replied.

Drake took her hand and aided her in standing up. He then allowed her to go first toward the buffet. After she took two steps in front of him, he already knew he'd have to repent to God for admiring her plump, round apple bottom.

Drake was surprised at himself, not only because he was allowing his flesh to get the better of him, but because never in his life had he been attracted to a woman outside of his own race. But as he lost the battle and kept looking at her rear end, he just knew she had to have some black in her bloodline somewhere in order to have all that junk in her trunk.

"Now I'm the one who is embarrassed," Drake said as the two of them made their way into the buffet area. "I didn't even bother to ask you your name."

"Oh, forgive me," she turned and said. "I let the thought of getting to this delicious food take over my mind. I'm Hannah. Hannah Oxford."

"It's a pleasure . . ." Drake looked at the wedding band on her hand. Disappointed, he stated, "*Mrs.* Oxford." Drake rememberd reading a passage in the Bible that said even if a man looks at a woman with lust in his heart, he is already guilty of adultery. He wondered how in the world he was supposed to have lunch with the lovely woman before him and still talk business.

God, help me! Drake silently cried out. *God, help me.*

Chapter 12

Hannah couldn't believe how well her lunch meeting with Mr. Trinity had gone. She had even managed to get him to knock twenty-five percent off of the standard package he and Reggie had initially discussed. She'd have to look into using him for some of her clients with larger advertising budgets. Hannah knew that Locksie would have a fit if she found out that she was using this new agency instead of Dawson's brother, not realizing that the two were one in the same.

Locksie had mentioned to Hannah that she could connect her to Dawson's little brother, as she always referred to him, but Hannah was comfortable with the smaller agencies she had been working with. Once she had found and been pleased with the companies she used regularly, she simply decided to stick with them. But even though this Mr. Trinity ran a larger agency, he seemed different; more personable and attentive with his clients. Hannah bet that Dawson's little brother wouldn't tear himself away from all of his huge business ventures to have lunch with a little client such as herself. She decided she wouldn't even mention it to Locksie at all. She didn't want to hurt her feelings.

As Hannah sat at the computer in her home office, her cell phone rang.

"Hannah speaking," she answered.

"Hannah, honey, this is Reggie," he said.

"Hello, you. What's going on?"

"I just wanted to thank you so much, sugar plum, for meeting with Mr. Trinity the other day for me. You're a lifesaver, dear."

"Don't mention it. It was a pleasure, honestly."

Reggie and Hannah weren't business partners on paper; they just told people that when they had to cover for one another. Although they worked in the same field of marketing and advertising, they weren't competitive at all. They knew there were enough clients to go around.

"I'm soooo glad to hear you say that, gumdrop, because I need you to perhaps join us, if you could, next week, when I meet with him to finalize everything and sign the contract and whatnot. Something tells me that tight little tush of yours is what got him to knock off another twenty-five percent. So with that said, I need that tush at this meeting for reassurance that he doesn't change his mind."

"Reggie, you are so crazy." Hannah laughed. "Although I'm sure my tight little tush had nothing to do with it, sure I'll meet with you guys next week. But I think you're all wrong about this Mr. Trinity. He was very well mannered and wholesome. Matter of fact, he even invited Elkan and I to come visit his church."

"Don't be fooled, sweet bread. Even a man of God has eyes, and you, pumpkin, are very easy on the eyes. Why, if you were my type, Elkan would have blacked my eye by now for not being able to keep my hands off of you."

"Thanks for the compliment, Reggie . . . I think. Anyway, just email me and let me know when and where, and I'm there."

"Thank you, buttercup. Tah-tah."

Hannah hung up the phone and shook her head before saying to herself, "Why do I always feel like my ears are going to grow cavities after talking with Reggie? Honey this, sweetie that, buttercup this . . ."

Before Hannah could turn her attention back to her computer, her home phone rang.

"Geez. I'm not going to get any work done today," Hannah growled. "Just because I work from home doesn't mean I can just be on the phone chatting it up all day."

Hannah picked up the cordless phone from its cradle and looked at the caller ID. *What does she want?* she thought before turning on the phone and saying, "Hello."

"May I speak to the father of my son, please?" the woman on the other end of the phone asked.

"Peni, you know he's at work," Hannah told her, sighing.

"Oh, yeah, that's right. Gotta work hard for the money when there's child support to pay. Anyway, you can just give him the message for me. I don't feel like dialing another number."

"Sure, Peni. What is it?" Hannah hated when Peni called the house, because she knew it was just to taunt her. She had Elkan's cell phone number and could have just as easily called him and left a message on his voicemail.

"Can you let him know that our son has a little league game next Saturday and afterward they are taking family pictures? Tell him that Little E's uniform is red and blue. I'm going to be wearing red and white, so he should coordinate with us."

Hannah wanted so badly to say, "Why does my husband have to coordinate with you? As a matter of fact, why does he even have to take a picture with you? You can take one with Little E and then he and Little E can take one together." But Hannah didn't bother. She knew Elkan would get upset with her for two reasons: one, Peni would use Hannah getting smart with her as an excuse not to let Little E come over on his next planned visit, and two, Elkan agreed with Peni that they should appear to get along for Little E's sake.

"I will let him know, Peni. By the way, how is Little E?"

"He's good," Peni replied, slurping her lips, "just like his daddy. But you'd know better than me. I only had him once. You have him all the time. Isn't that right, Hannah?" Peni teased, trying to put doubt in Hannah's mind, but Hannah refused to let Peni take her there.

"Look, Peni, that's my other line. I'll be sure to give Elkan the message." Hannah quickly ended the call because she didn't want Peni to be able to squeeze in one more insulting or insinuating word. Plus, she didn't want her to hear the cry that followed just as quickly as she hung up the phone.

Why did Elkan have to cheat on Hannah? Why? And then have a baby with the other woman as a result—as if the affair alone wasn't bad enough. And now Hannah was forced to have a relationship with the baby mama for the sake of her relationship with her husband and for the sake of the child. This just seemed far too much for her to bear, especially when it seemed as though having a child of her own wasn't something that was going to happen. Why would God? How could He? How could He give another woman the honor of bearing her husband's child and dry out her womb?

Tears of anger and resentment—for thinking she was strong enough to handle this situation—strolled down Hannah's cheeks as she shut down her computer and decided to call it quits for the day. She retreated to her bed, where she cried herself to sleep.

But I will give you no more than you can bear. Just hold on, God spoke.

Chapter 13

"Why don't you join my aerobics class?" Mary asked as she and Locksie sat at her kitchen table. Mary reached over and pinched an inch of Locksie's waistline.

"So, what you trying to say, Auntie?" Locksie said, playfully shooing Mary's hand away. "That I'm a big, fat pig?"

Mary giggled. "It ain't like that. You the one complaining how Miss Jane Pitman was at the gym and able to keep up with your man working out more than you could."

"Forget you, Aunt Mary," Locksie said, pushing the half-empty cup of coffee away like she didn't want anything Mary had to offer her.

"I mean, you ain't fat or nothing, but girl, if you just toned up that flesh of yours, you'd be a brick house." Aunt Mary clapped her hands, poked out her lips and did a little dip with her hips as she stood up to go get a refill on her coffee.

"Aunt Mary, you are too much." Locksie smiled and pulled her cup back to her and took a sip.

Mary refilled her coffee cup and sat back down. "Child, I'm pulling a double today at work."

"Then you might need to drink something a little stronger than coffee," Locksie suggested.

"Oh, I got something stronger all right. And his name is Jesus." She took a sip of her coffee. "Besides, could you imagine me drinking something stronger than coffee? Humph. Those folks at Baptist Saints Tabernacle would fit to be tied; probably vote me off the hospitality committee and all."

Locksie laughed as she took a sip of her own coffee.

"You laugh, but I'm serious. With me being a Christian, people put every little thing I do under a microscope. It's irritating, but at the same time, it reminds me of who I am and whose I am, because you never know who you are a witness to."

"Well, wouldn't nobody know but me and you," Locksie playfully pressed.

"And Him," Mary added, looking up at the ceiling. On that note, Mary downed more of her coffee.

Locksie continued to tease. "Sure you don't want a little somethin' somethin' to mix in with that coffee?"

"Now, Locksie, you better quit playing with me. Besides, I get drunk off the Word of God. Speaking of which . . ."

Mary looked up at her crystal cross-shaped clock hanging on her kitchen wall. Her mother, Locksie's grandmother, had given it to her before she passed away of natural causes. It read 8:20 A.M. She had to be at the recreation center to teach her first aerobics class at 9:00 A.M. and Locksie had to be at work at the hair salon at 9:00 A.M. as well. Mary always made sure to read a passage from the Bible before starting her day, and sometimes say a little prayer before she and Locksie parted ways.

Mary reached out her hands for Locksie to hold. The two women closed their eyes and bowed their heads as Mary led the prayer.

"Dear, Lord, in the name of Jesus, I just thank You for today. I even thank You for yesterday, Lord, as I look back to where You brought me from," Aunt Mary prayed. "Thank You, Jesus," she said under her breath as if all He had done for her had just flashed before her eyes and she couldn't do anything but thank Him. "As I stand here holding my niece's hand, Lord, I ask that You work on her to the point where she comes to You willingly, unlike me, Lord, and that You not have to bring her to You on her knees."

One of Locksie's eyes quickly opened. *On my knees? Watch it, Aunt Mary. Don't make me start avoiding you like the plague like I do my own mother.*

Mary ended the prayer with, "So, Father, just watch over us and protect us with the blood of the lamb. In the name of Your Son and our Savior, Jesus Christ, I pray. Amen"

Releasing Locksie's hand, Mary grabbed her gym bag while Locksie opened the front door.

"I'll call you tonight, Aunt Mary," Locksie said as she headed toward her car while Mary locked the front door.

"I got Bible study at the church tonight. Speaking of which, when you gonna come visit my church anyway? You been promising to come visit and ain't made good on your sorry word yet."

Locksie chuckled at her aunt's frankness as she made her way down the walkway. "I know, Aunt Mary, I know. I will. I just need to get myself together first is all."

"And how do you think you gon' do that without Jesus?" Mary asked as she walked up to her car and rested her hands on her hips.

"Aunt Mary, you said it yourself. I'm living in sin and stuff. What would I look like going to church in the condition I'm in?" Locksie raised her arms and let them drop down to her side in defeat. "I need to get right first. You know, get my mind right. I can't see me praying and reading the Bible and stuff. Right now, let you and every other Christian tell it, I'm just this great big ball of sin. Lightning would probably strike down y'all's poor little church building the minute I stepped in the door."

Aunt Mary shook her head and laughed. "Child, you crazy."

"But keep praying for me and hopefully I'll get right so that I can not just visit church, but maybe attend regularly—since God does perform miracles, right? 'Cause you know that's what it's going to take."

Mary's laughter had faded. "But you can't get right without Him." She stared into her niece's eyes and then searched her own brain for an appropriate scripture from the Bible that would back up what she was trying to tell Locksie. "The Pharisees asked Jesus' disciples, in the book of Matthew, why He broke bread with sinners. When

Jesus heard that, He told them, 'They that be whole need not a physician, but they that are sick.'" Locksie put her head down and took in her aunt's words. "The church is a place for spiritual healing, honey. Don't you get it? You got to come to church to get right and stay right." There was a few seconds of still silence. "Have a good day at work, okay?" Without waiting for her niece to reply, Mary got into her car.

Locksie got into her car and pulled off, thinking about her aunt's words. For years Locksie hadn't wanted to hear anything about going to church because she felt that church was the last place someone like her was supposed to be. She fornicated with Dawson. She lied on occasion when she felt Dawson was prodding her. She usually did it not to hide anything from him, but to make a long story short. Sometimes, when she and Dawson were out partying, she drank to the point of inebriation. And whenever she and Dawson got into arguments, she cursed like a sailor. She asked herself what church in the world would want someone like her fellowshipping with them.

Just then it hit Locksie—Dawson played a part in all of her sinning. In order to give up sinning, did that mean that she would have to give up Dawson, since he was the common denominator for everything she was doing that might be displeasing to God? If that was the case, Aunt Mary shouldn't hold her breath waiting for Locksie to walk through those church doors, let alone give her life to Christ. There were just some things in life she wasn't willing to give up—not even for Christ. Dawson was one of them.

Chapter 14

"I need a big favor," Locksie said to Hannah while she shampooed her hair.

"Just how huge?" Hannah asked, opening her eyes as she enjoyed Locksie's fingertips massaging her scalp.

"I need you to be a make-up model for my Mary Kay presentation."

"Girl, you know I don't wear make-up. Now I done already let you talk me into buying all those skincare treatment products from you."

"Which work beautifully on you, might I add. Not to mention that it's the reason you have the beautiful skin that you have, allowing you the gift of not having to wear make-up."

"I know, I know," Hannah agreed. "Which is why I don't want to be a *make-up* model."

"Come on, Hannah. I'm not asking you to wear it on a regular basis. Just for an hour. Come on, I need you. I'd do it for you."

"All right, already. Stop your begging," Hannah said, closing her eyes again. "What day?"

"Friday at six-thirty P.M.," Locksie said as she began to rinse the shampoo out of Hannah's hair.

"Oh, no good. Can't do it. I have an appointment that day."

"You're just saying that to get out of it," Locksie said, not believing her friend.

"No seriously, I have a meeting with . . ." Hannah paused for a moment, almost spilling the beans. Reggie had confirmed their meeting with Mr. Trinity for that same Friday at 5:30 in the evening. Hannah planned on discussing with Mr. Trinity about perhaps doing some graphics work for some of her clients. And again, she didn't want to hurt Locksie's feelings by not using her boyfriend's brother. "Reggie. I have to meet with Reggie on Friday."

"Mm-hmm. Yeah, okay. If you say so." Locksie massaged conditioner in Hannah's hair.

"Girl, now you know I wouldn't play you like that. If I could make it, I would."

"You know I'm just playing with you, girl. It's cool. But I would have given you fifty dollars worth of free products," Locksie said in a singsong voice in an attempt to get Locksie to change her mind.

"Heck, I'll do it," Jem, one of the salon stylists, who was at the shampoo bowl next to Locksie, chimed in.

"Will you really?" Locksie said gratefully.

"For fifty dollars worth of free stuff? Sure, I'm game."

"Thank you." Locksie smiled at Jem and then bent down and stuck her tongue out at Hannah before rinsing the conditioner from her hair.

* * *

Drake arrived at the restaurant fifteen minutes earlier than he had told his client to meet him. Wearing a deep navy Armani suit, he went into the bathroom after being seated at his table to double-check his appearance. This was his first time wearing the suit, and he hadn't had time to get it tailored to a perfect fit.

He wished he had just kept on what he had been wearing earlier as he straightened out the silver tie that lay atop the almost purplish-blue shirt underneath. He was thinking of the nice little business-casual Ralph Lauren hook-up he had been clad in prior to Reggie calling him to confirm their appointment and informing him that his partner, Hannah, would be joining them as well.

"What am I doing?" Drake asked himself, dropping his hands to his side, tired of fiddling around with his tie that wouldn't seem to lay right. "She's married." He looked up. "God, in Genesis 2:18, Your Word says that it was not good that man should be alone. It was You, God, who said that a man needs a wife. But Lord, I know if You were going to send me a wife, it wouldn't be that of another man's. So . . ."

Just then, he heard the flush of a toilet, and the stall door behind him opened. A tall, slender gentleman exited the stall and walked over to the sink next to Drake and proceeded to wash his hands.

Between them lingered the most awkward silence in the world. Drake didn't want this stranger to think that he was a crazy lunatic who hung out in hotel bathrooms talking to himself, so he finally decided to break the silence and clear his name by informing the man, "Oh, I was uh, just talking to God."

With a peculiar look on his face, the man nodded and smiled. He dried his hands and exited the bathroom, looking over his shoulder to make sure the crazy guy who thought God was in the bathroom didn't try anything funny.

Meanwhile, Hannah had arrived at the restaurant and was about to ask the host if two gentlemen were waiting on a third party until she saw a familiar face heading out of the men's bathroom. "Oh, never mind. I see one of them now," she told the waitress as she approached one of her dinner guests. "Reggie, is everything okay?" Hannah couldn't help but notice the strange look he had on his face as he walked toward her.

"Child, there's a crazy man in the bathroom talking to God," Reggie informed her, looking back over his shoulder again.

"Huh?" Hannah looked puzzled.

"Never mind, cinnamon stick. Let's just get a table and wait for our Mr. Trinity to arrive," Reggie said as he grabbed Hannah by the elbow and escorted her back to the restaurant entrance. There were a couple of people being helped in front of them, so they just stood patiently waiting their turn until Drake appeared from the men's bathroom.

"There he is," both Reggie and Hannah said in unison.

"There's the crazy holy roller," Reggie proclaimed at the same time Hannah said, "There's Mr. Trinity." They both looked at each other in shock.

"He's the crazy man?" Hannah asked, confused.

"He's the brilliant Mr. Trinity?" Reggie asked, equally confused.

"Look, forget it. We'll talk about it later," Hannah whispered as she watched Drake walk over to the same table they had occupied the week before. "Come on. Let's go."

Hannah headed toward the table where Drake was sitting as Reggie walked behind her with his head down.

"Mr. Trinity," Hannah said, extending her hand.

"Please, it's Drake." Drake stood and smiled as he gently shook Hannah's hand.

"Drake, this is my partner, Reggie Vineyard, who you have already spoken with over the phone," Hannah introduced.

Drake extended his hand to finally meet the gentleman whom he had only spoken with on the phone as Hannah stepped aside, revealing Reggie's face to Drake.

"Mr. Trinity, it's a pleasure," Reggie said, head still down so that he was looking at Drake's shoes more than his face.

At that moment, Drake wished that for the life of him he knew how to do that *Bewitched* thing and twitch his nose and disappear out of the room, leaving only a puff of smoke behind. Somehow he managed to keep his cool after discovering that Reggie was the stranger in the bathroom who had overheard his conversation with God.

"Reggie,"—Drake cleared his throat—"we finally meet face-to-face." The two men shook hands and that same awkward silence that had stood between them in the bathroom returned.

Hannah cleared her throat. "Why don't we have a seat and order first and then get down to business?"

With that, they sat and proceeded to order their dinners and go over the contract. Drake felt terribly embarrassed inside, but did a wonderful job of acting like his normal, professional self. After all, he couldn't be too embarrassed about the prayer; it had seemed to work as his only focus was the business at hand. And since Drake knew that prayer worked, he said another prayer silently that God would remove any awkwardness and allow them to handle business professionally and without prejudice.

By the time dinner was over and the contract was signed, Reggie had forgotten all about his first impression of Drake. He even gave a verbal commitment that he would be using him for more clients if Drake's work was good.

"Speaking of which . . ." Hannah said. "If you don't mind, Drake, I'd like to discuss some potential projects with you for a couple clients of mine."

Drake looked down at his watch. "Sure. I have time if you do."

Reggie looked down at his. "Um, it's almost eight. I'm going to have to leave you two sweet tarts alone. I promised my wife I'd make it to her parents' house for family night no later than eight. So I must run."

"Wife?" Drake said in an almost shocked tone. He hadn't meant to say it out loud.

Reggie looked back and forth from Drake to Hannah. "Yeah, wife. Why? Is something wrong?"

"Uh, no," Drake was quick to say. "I uh, guess I

just didn't notice the ring is all." He was glad he came up with that one.

"Yep, married five years and loving it," Reggie replied as he stood and reached down into his pockets for his wallet.

"Oh, no, please allow me," Drake insisted. He always paid the tab for his clients, considering their business eventually paid his mortgage. But he also felt guilty for assuming that Reggie, because of his slender build and the way he spoke, using all those cutesy, sweet words, was gay. He was just a male with a genuinely warm spirit that Drake had pegged all wrong. He'd have to repent later for prejudging him.

"Well, thank you Mr.—I mean Drake. I truly look forward to working with you." Reggie buried his wallet back in his pocket and leaned over and kissed Hannah on the cheek. "I'll talk to you later, puddin'."

Hannah smiled as Reggie exited the restaurant. She then looked over to Drake. She was glad that whatever went on in the men's bathroom before the three of them sat down to dinner never came up. But now that Reggie was gone and it was just the two of them, Hannah couldn't resist having a little fun. She cleared her throat, leaned in with her elbows on the table and said to Drake, "So, I hear you know God personally."

Chapter 15

"Jem, you have no idea how much I appreciate you doing this," Locksie said as she and Jem sat in the hotel conference room where the Mary Kay meeting was being held.

"Anytime," Jem replied. "For fifty dollars in products that is." The two laughed.

"Ladies and gentlemen," the regional consultant said as everyone cleaned up the stations where they had been sitting. "This was a marvelous turnout. I just want to let you guys know that next month's meeting will be at its usual location. Somehow, this month the hotel we normally have our meetings at double-booked. But good thing for us, the Hilton Easton location was here to save the day, giving us a tremendous discount on our last-minute use of their facility." Everyone began clapping. "So, if you ever have the opportunity to patronize them, please do so. I hear the food at their restaurant is to die for."

"Mmm, that sounds good," Locksie said to Jem. "I'm starved."

"Me too. You wanna try the food at the restaurant here? We can always just take a look at the menu, and if we don't see anything we like, the Cheesecake Factory is right around the corner."

Locksie, who was never one to wear a watch, pulled out her cell phone and checked the time. It was a little after 8:00 P.M. "Yeah, they should still be open. Let's finish packing this stuff up and head over."

"Cool," Jem said as she helped Locksie pack up the last of the products, making sure she kept aside her hot pink bag full of free goodies.

"This hotel is the smokin' whip," Jem said, pushing her long mircobraids behind her ear once they had gotten on the elevator. Locksie looked over at her, and couldn't help but admire what a wonderful job she had done on Jem's dark chocolate, beautiful skin. Every single shade she was wearing looked as if it were made just for her.

"Yeah, it is." Locksie looked around. "I wouldn't mind just coming here for a weekend alone with Dawson."

"I bet you wouldn't. No offense, but what woman wouldn't? I mean, girl, your man is fee-yiiine. Shoot, I'd want to spend the weekend here with him too."

Just then, Locksie remembered why she never really talked to Jem too often. Her bluntness was just a little too much for Locksie at times. Locksie knew her man was fine, so the fact that Jem said it didn't bother her the least bit; it was the way she said it that sent chills up her spine. It was like what she really wanted to say was, "Watch ya back, girlfriend, or I might steal on ya."

Locksie shook off Jem's comment as they got off the elevator and headed toward the restaurant.

"Seating for two?" the hostess asked them.

"We'd like to look at the menu first, please," Jem told her. "Because if y'all got stuff that we can't even pronounce or if y'all's menus don't have prices on them, we out!" As the hostess handed Jem a menu, Locksie happened to notice a couple cozied up at a table in the back of the restaurant. She couldn't believe her eyes once she realized who the man and the woman were.

An appointment with Reggie, huh? Locksie just shook her head. *Drake, you so-called Christian, out at nine o'clock at night with a married woman. Humph, must be one of them Sunday-only Christians.* Locksie didn't know what was worse, the fact that Hannah had lied to her and was out with a man instead of her so-called appointment with her business partner, or the fact that the man she was out with was her boyfriend's little brother.

"What do you think, Locksie?" Jem nudged her and pushed the menu toward her, interrupting Locksie's thoughts.

"Uh, Jem, I'm sorry. But what I think is that I just lost my appetite," Locksie said as she wondered how she would confront Hannah.

Chapter 16

"Can you believe that?" Locksie said to her aunt as she paced back and forth across the kitchen floor.

Mary sighed, put her hands on her hips and sarcastically replied, "No, I couldn't believe it when you called me first thing Saturday morning to talk about it. I couldn't believe it yesterday when you called me to talk about it again. And now, here it is Monday morning and surprisingly enough, I still can't believe it." Mary shooed her hand at Locksie. "Girl, ain't you got nobody besides me to go running to to put somebody else's business in the streets?"

"Besides you and Dawson, Auntie, you know I don't talk to nobody else. Well, I talk to my client, Hannah, sometimes, but I very well can't in this case, now can I, seeing how she's the topic of discussion."

"Well, what did Dawson say when you talked to him?"

"His brother is the other topic of discussion."

Locksie tightened her lips as if she were fit to be tied. "And I wasn't about to be the one to tell him about that so-called Christian brother of his. I mean, even though Drake is younger than Dawson, Dawson really looks up to him."

"Hold up," Mary said, raising her hand as if taking offense. "Go back for a minute. What do you mean by his so-called Christian brother? You say that like just because the boy is a Christian he ain't human. Like he's supposed to have some superhuman powers that keep him from having an error in judgment."

Locksie stopped pacing, sighed and dropped her arms to her side. "It's not that. It's just that when Dawson and I decided to move in together, Drake started talking all this mess about how much nicer it would be if we moved in together as husband and wife."

"Oh, you mean he said the same thing I told you?"

"Yeah, but you ain't out committing adultery either, now, are you?" Mary was silent. "Are you?"

Not even trying to entertain Locksie's question, Mary said, "Look, Locksie. You are my niece and I love you to death. But I think that right now your focus should be on your own relationship with God and not Drake's."

"Okay, then what about Hannah? I mean *adultery*, Aunt Mary. Do you know how many times she has cried to me about Elkan cheating on her and me thinking that he's just this low down, dirty dog? And here she turns around and does the same thing?"

Mary still wasn't getting why Locksie was in such a huff. "I guess the part where I'm confused is that I don't understand why *you* are so upset about your friends committing adultery, when you, yourself, are fornicating." Mary's tone was gentle because she didn't want to sound condemning. "Baby girl, sin is—"

"Sin." Locksie said, finishing the statement for her. She then slumped down in the chair next to her aunt. "Sin is sin. I know. I've heard that before."

Mary smiled, patted Locksie's hand and then took a sip of her coffee. She pointed to the cup of coffee that sat on the table in front of Locksie. "Go on and drink your coffee before it gets cold."

Locksie picked up the mug and took a sip. "I don't know why I'm so worked up about it. I guess I just hate that Hannah lied to me. The fact that she lied to me scares me because it makes me think that she's not the person I thought she was. I mean, she knows firsthand how it feels to be cheated on. How could she turn around and do the same thing back to her husband? And how could Drake make her do something like this? If he wants to go to hell, fine! But I don't want him taking my friend with him."

"My, my," Mary said. She couldn't believe that last sentence had just come out of Locksie's mouth.

Picking up on her aunt's tone, Locksie said, "What? What's the matter?"

What Mary wanted to say was, "Now you know how I feel about Dawson. Even though you are both consenting adults, you're my niece and I feel like he's taking you to hell with him by allowing you to live in sin with him." But instead she bit her tongue. The Holy Spirit told her not to speak on it right now, so she had to be obedient.

Instead, the Holy Spirit gave her other words to say.

"Locksie, baby, you haven't even talked to them yet; not Hannah or Drake," Mary told her. "So, maybe you shouldn't speak on things that you haven't taken the time to learn the facts about. Believe it or not, sometimes things aren't always what they seem. Take, for example, the one time Brother Will was seen pulling out of the parking lot of that adult book and video store. The news spread across the church like a California wildfire. Come to find out, Brother Will was just trying to go to that little car wash right next to the bookstore, but he passed it. He made the first turn he could so that he could turn around and go back. Well, unfortunately for him, the first turn was the parking lot of that adult store. So, as he sat there waiting to make the turn out of the parking lot, Sister Abram saw him. The next thing Brother Will knows, everybody's gossiping about how he was seen inside the adult store buying perverted items and whatnot, when that wasn't the case at all. Had Sister Abram talked to him first, none of that mess would have jumped off, but instead, she just let those lips get to flappin'."

"So, what are you trying to say, Aunt Mary? That I'm running my mouth?" Locksie took offense at being compared to Sister Abram. Although she had never stepped foot inside Mary's church, she had heard enough stories about the tale-bearing, vicious-tongued, strife-creating Sister Abram, wife of Deacon Abram.

"Plain and simple, what I'm saying to you, Locksie, is that thou shall not bear false witness."

"Ugh! No more. No more about God, Christians,

commandments, scripture. Whatever!" Locksie was truly becoming frustrated as she stood up, walked over to the sink and poured her barely touched coffee down the drain. Religion seemed to be in her face everywhere she went; even in mall parking lots. She was sick and tired of it and just wanted to live her life how she wanted, and not how God, Jesus or the Holy Spirit, whomever He was, wanted her to. *I'm a grown woman*, Locksie fussed in her head. *God can't tell me what to do.*

"You better knock that pitch down a tone or two before I knock you on your a—" Mary caught herself. She wasn't going to let that cursin' demon get the best of her. Besides, she didn't want this to turn into a debate or argument. That would defeat the entire purpose of trying to explain God and Christ's love. She had to show it by action when she couldn't tell about it. So, she closed her eyes, took a deep breath, and then opened them again. "We better go, sweetie." Mary took her mug over to the sink and kissed Locksie on the check. As tears welled up in Locksie's eyes, Mary embraced her.

Mary knew what her niece was going through. She was going through the stages of conviction, and because she only knew of God and didn't have a personal relationship with Him, she didn't understand it nor did she know how to deal with it. So, instead of pointing the finger at herself and perhaps correcting her own life, Locksie wanted to direct the attention away from herself and point the finger at other people. Mary understood because she had been there and done that as her memories went back to when she first gave her life to Christ. Like Locksie, she hadn't wanted to come willingly, so God dragged her. She only hoped that Locksie would see the light before she had to go through the same thing.

After leaving her aunt's house earlier that day, Locksie could hardly even think straight. A client had come in and asked for a relaxer and roller set, but Locksie's mind was so far gone that she took the client right over to the shampoo bowl and began washing her hair. The woman had so much new growth that no way would a roller set have lasted, so Locksie ended up having to flat iron it and not charge the woman.

It was really bothering Locksie how she had behaved at Mary's house. She had never gotten so out of line with her aunt. But standing there in that kitchen, Mary had just reminded her so much of her mother. No matter how sweet a tone and how pleasant Locksie's mother sounded whenever she talked to her, in Locksie's mind, she was simply trying to use honey instead of vinegar to belittle Locksie and remind her what a sinner she was and that if she kept it up, she'd go to hell. Suddenly, it hit Locksie like a ton of bricks, right then and there . . .

"If you keep it up, you will go to hell." Locksie spoke softly, but it was almost as if a ventriloquist act was going on. Like it was Locksie's mouth moving, but someone else's voice was speaking the words to her.

A little shaken by the experience, Locksie stood there and thought, *So, that's what that Holy Spirit Aunt Mary keeps talking about sounds like.*

Chapter 17

"Earth to Drake! Earth to Drake," Dawson shouted as the two sat in a booth at Subway. They had just finished working out together at the gym. Initially, Dawson had a client coming after their workout, but when the client canceled, the two brothers decided to go grab a bite to eat.

"Oh, my bad," Drake replied, snapping out of his daze.

"Have you heard anything I've said all day?" Dawson took a bite of his six-inch tuna sub. "If I didn't know you any better, I'd say you got pu—" Drake gave Dawson a daring look. "I mean, a woman on the brain." Dawson caught himself from almost letting that expletive slip. He had gotten away with one or two around his brother, but he tried really hard to respect the fact that if his brother didn't use that type of language himself, then more than likely he didn't want to hear it.

That was one thing Dawson had noticed about Drake, though. He loved people knowing that he

E.N. Joy

was a man of God. Drake had once told him that people knowing he was a Christian protected him from having to be subjected to foul language or dirty jokes. And if someone at the job was getting married and having a bachelor party at a strip club, Drake didn't even get tempted with an invitation, although he had walked up on a conversation or two at the water cooler about what had taken place at some of those parties. Half the time, he couldn't even attend the weddings because he didn't want to lie by omission when the reverend asked if anyone knew cause why the couple shouldn't be married. He had heard cause enough at the water cooler.

"Well, am I right, little bro?" Dawson asked.

Drake exhaled. "Kinda, sorta." Drake shrugged and then picked at his seafood sub.

"I'll take that as a yes. So, what's her name? Is she fine? Let me guess, she's not saved. Yep, that's got to be it."

"She's married," Drake said without beating around the bush.

"What?" Dawson exclaimed. "She's married?"

"Will you hold it down, for Pete's sake?" Drake attempted to hush his brother. "I haven't known her long, and you know me, I just don't give any ol' woman a second look, but she's . . . she's different."

Dawson could hardly contain himself. He wanted to explode at the thought that his little brother finally had a woman in his life. He hated to admit it, but the last time they were at the gym and his brother told him that he had never been with a woman before, he wondered if Drake was gay and had only dated women in the past as a cover-up. And maybe that was why he was so into God; because he thought God could deliver him from this homosexual thing. *Whew*, Dawson thought as he grinned devilishly at his brother.

"Will you stop looking at me like that?" Drake said to Dawson as he ate a chip from his bag.

"Sorry, man. I'm just shocked. I mean, when you decided to go for it, you really, really went for it, huh? I'm just glad that you went for it, because for a minute there—"

"It ain't even like that." Drake cut Dawson off because he couldn't have him thinking that he had slept with the woman he was referring to. "I ain't went for nothing yet."

"Ah-ha, you said *yet!*"

"That's not what I meant . . ."

"My little brother seeing a married woman. Satan must be proud. That's one point for him." Dawson jokingly patted his brother on the shoulder.

"Will you stop it?" Drake said, pulling away angrily. Dawson could tell that his brother meant business. "I'm not seeing a married woman. I haven't slept with her or anything like that." He paused and shamefully admitted, "I'm lusting after her."

A puzzled look covered Dawson's face. "Lusting? Is that all? You mean you haven't stepped to her? I mean the chick doesn't even know you diggin' her?"

"No, and if God answers my prayers soon, I won't be digging her."

"How can God keep you from feelin' a broad? I mean, if she's hot, she's hot. You're a man. God knows that. He made you, right?"

"I'm just banking on Second Peter, chapter two, verse nine: 'The Lord knoweth how to deliver the godly out of temptation.' " Drake just shook his head as if he was in agony over his internal battle against his attraction toward Hannah. He had even had a wet dream about her the night before. He woke up, and after cleaning himself and changing his bedding, he spent the rest of the night on his knees repenting.

Dawson saw the anguish on his brother's face, yet he felt no sympathy. "See, that's what I don't understand about you Christians. How can you possibly enjoy life when it seems as though you are doing nothing but constantly worrying about God and what Jesus would do and all that crap? It just seems so tormenting. I mean, y'all talk about how much y'all love Jesus. If you love Him so much, shouldn't pleasing Him be the easiest thing in the world to do?"

Drake had to admit that he was a little stumped by Dawson's comment. "You'd think it would be, huh?" He made a mental note to find scripture that perhaps explained why it was easy to talk of one's love for Christ, yet so hard to walk a good walk with Christ.

"You are sitting here beating yourself up over thoughts you are having. Well, stop thinking those thoughts then. If you feel having those thoughts is upsetting God, then stop it." Dawson snapped his finger. "Just like that. Stop thinking them if you want to please your God so bad. I know I love Locksie, and I don't even have to think twice about pleasing her, no matter what the cost. If I can do it for a human, and this God you all worship is so mighty and omnipotent, then why can't you Christians seem to please Him no matter what the cost?"

Once again, Drake remained silent. And on that note, Dawson took a sip of his drink and sat back with a sense of victory as his brother, for the first time since he could remember, had no comeback.

Chapter 18

"How was your day?" Locksie asked Dawson as the two sat cuddled on the sofa watching *CSI*. This was the time, late evening in front of the tube, when the two of them talked and expressed themselves to one another. They didn't go out to dinner much, to the movies or hit the town like a lot of couples did, but the quality time they spent with each other in the home was invaluable to them. They felt the intimate one-on-one time together allowed them to become closer without the outside interference of the world.

"Besides the fact that I lightweight got into it with my brother, it was a pretty good day."

Locksie's ears sprung open at the reference to Drake. Her tiff with her aunt had been weighing heavily on her heart, and she wanted to talk to Dawson about it, but seeing what she could fish out of him about Drake seemed of more relevance to her right now.

"Drake? What did you two get into it about?" Locksie sat up from her previous position, nestled on Dawson's chest. She always loved how she could feel the cut of his body by just pressing up against it. His muscles were a sign of strength, a strength that she felt protected by.

"I don't know if I should say that we got into it, but we kind of ended our conversation on a sour and silent note. It's just that I'm so tired of folks acting like they are so goody-goody when they are human and make mistakes just like the rest of us."

Locksie could feel herself getting a little excited. She hadn't even put any bait on the hook, and already she had a bite. "So, what did he do? I mean, I can't imagine your brother, who should have been a preacher,"—Locksie was sarcastic—"making a mistake."

"He's diggin' on some chick. And she just happens to be married."

Now this was just too easy for Locksie. She thought she was going to explode, but instead she just listened to see how much more information she could get before she confronted Hannah.

Wait until I tell Aunt Mary this. She's always preaching that stuff about waiting on confirmation. Well, here it is!

"So, what's her name?" *Come on, come on . . . bring it home.*

"I don't know. I didn't even ask."

That's not what Locksie wanted to hear. She wanted the nail in the coffin; the smoking gun, more confirmation. But then she had to remind herself that she had seen the two together with her own eyes, and that eyes don't lie.

"I don't even want to talk about it," Dawson said. He stared at the television as if everything was cool, but Locksie could tell that something else was on Dawson's mind.

"Something else wrong? I mean besides what's going on with you and your brother?"

"Nah, it's all good," Dawson said, not even looking in Locksie's direction.

Locksie turned her attention back toward the television and let him be, but after a few minutes of silence, she asked, "Are we okay?"

"Are we? You tell me."

Locksie could tell by his tone that they weren't. She picked up the remote and turned off the television.

"Hey, what's up with that?" he fussed.

"I wanna talk."

"Okay, and what does the TV being off have to do with you talking?" Dawson tried to grab the remote out of Locksie's hands, but she quickly stuffed it down her pants. "Oh, and do you think that's going to stop me?" He grinned. "I look forward to having a reason to get in your pants."

Pushing him away with a chuckle, Locksie said, "Seriously. I think we need to talk."

Dawson released a sigh of defeat and flopped lifelessly back against the couch. "So, talk."

"You go first. Just say what's on your mind, because it's clear to me that something has definitely been on your mind lately."

"Why do you say that?" Dawson stalled. He did want to talk to Locksie. After all, talking with his brother wasn't getting him anywhere. Perhaps Drake was right and he needed to hear from the horse's mouth exactly what was her problem with him.

"Because you haven't been acting yourself lately."

Sarcastically, Dawson mumbled under his breath, "If that ain't the pot calling the kettle black."

Locksie pulled the remote out of her pants and threw it on the table. She then huffed and crossed her arms. "And what's that supposed to mean?"

Finally, Dawson just spit it out. "What it means is that here lately you've been acting like your stuff,"—he pointed to her private area—"is made of fragile crystal, and it's been like walking around on egg shells trying to get near it."

Locksie's mouth dropped open in surprise. "I have not."

"Please," Dawson spat as he stood up from the couch and began pacing. "You don't want me to see you naked anymore, you pretend to be 'sleep just so I won't ask you for none, and on the times you do give me some—which is a lot less than usual these days, might I add—you just lay there like your mind is a million miles away. Afterwards, you either lay in the bed lifeless, staring up at the ceiling, or run and jump in the shower like a rape victim trying to wash my scent off of you."

"Stop it! You stop it right there!" Locksie stood angrily.

Dawson could have kicked himself for that last statement. Although he had expressed those feelings to his brother, he should have been more considerate than to have verbalized it to Locksie, considering what she had been through with her aunt Mary, who years ago had been brutally raped and left for dead.

"Locks, baby, I'm—" Dawson said, reaching for her before she hit his hand away.

"Don't touch me, Dawson." Locksie wiped away the couple of tears that had slipped out and then gained her composure. "Look, maybe I have been acting a little weird when it comes to sex." Now Locksie was the one pacing. "I just, I don't know, I'm just starting to feel differently about it is all."

"Different how?" Dawson was desperate to know. "Is it me? You tired of the same ol' same ol'? Am I getting too big? I mean muscle-wise? I can stop hitting the weights as much and just—"

"Dawson, no. It's not you. It's nothing like that. I love your body. I love your muscles."

"Then what is it?" Dawson was tired of Locksie's soap opera dramatics. Whatever it was that was bothering her when it came to their sex life, Dawson wanted her to spit it out so that they could start repairing it and things could get back to normal.

"It's Him," Locksie said. Her arm was straight down, but her hand and index finger were pointing up. She looked down, almost as if she was embarrassed.

"Him?" Dawson said, trying not to reveal his slight anger. The last thing he imagined Locksie telling him was that another man was coming between their sex life. This he wasn't ready for. "Him who? Who is him, Locksie?"

"Him." Locksie looked upward while slightly nodding her head, still pointing her finger.

"Woman, what the heck are you talking about?"

"God. That's who Him is—God."

Dawson followed with his eyes up to the ceiling. "Oh, geez, you've got to be kidding." Once again, he flopped back onto the couch. He thought about the talks he and Drake had and could do nothing but just burst out laughing. Was it possible that his little brother's assessment of the situation had been on point?

"What's so funny?" Locksie asked, somewhat confused.

Laughing so hard, Dawson could barely speak. "Nothing," he said with a laugh. "It's just that Drake . . ." He continued laughing. "Drake said it was probably something like this. Who knew? I guess my little brother knows more about women than I thought."

Now Locksie was curious as she sat down next to Dawson. "What's this about Drake?" She chuckled a little, only because Dawson's laughter was somewhat contagious. Dawson didn't answer her questions. He was too busy laughing. "What did Drake say?" Once again she chuckled, but on the inside, she was boiling mad at just the mere thought that Dawson had discussed their sexual relationship with his brother.

"Oh, nothing," Dawson said as he got his laughter under control. "It's just when I mentioned to him how you had been acting lately, he mentioned that God might have something to do with it. I just can't believe he's right. I mean, since when do you care about the commandments and what other people think?"

"How could you talk to Drake about our sex life?"

"What sex life?" Dawson reminded her.

Locksie was appalled. "I can't believe you!" she shouted as she grabbed her purse and keys.

"Where are you going?"

"Out. I need to think."

Locksie opened the door, but before she closed it behind her, she heard Dawson yell out, "Well, while you're out, perhaps you can pick me up some lotion or Vaseline . . . and a dirty magazine too. Because with the way things are going around here, that's all the action I'm going to be getting."

Locksie slammed the door so hard that a picture fell off the wall and fell onto the ground, shattering into a million little pieces . . . just like her heart.

Chapter 19

"Ouch!" Hannah yelled as Locksie ran the comb through her hair.

"Oh, my bad," Locksie stated insincerely.

"Are you mad at me or something?" Hannah turned in the styling chair and asked Locksie as she rubbed her sore head.

"No, why do you ask that? Should I be?" Locksie roughly spun her chair back around and continued running the comb through Hannah's hair, which she had just washed and conditioned.

"Ouch!" Hannah yelled once again.

"Sorry." Locksie shrugged. "More nappies than usual today. Guess you are black." Locksie chuckled, but Hannah found nothing funny.

"Excuse me?"

"Oh, nothing. Just trying to add a little humor to the situation. Sorry if I'm hurting you."

"Well, there's no *if* about it. You are hurting me."

"I'm sorry," Locksie said with a huffy attitude. "I'm your friend. I would never hurt you or lie to you." Locksie had to open that can of worms just to see if Hannah would slither out.

Hannah turned in her chair again to face Locksie. "Are you having sex issues with Dawson again? Because if you are, don't be taking it out on me. Unless you plan on losing your regular clients—because they aren't going to have any hair left for you to do if you keep snatching it all out in a comb—I suggest you push aside all those thoughts about sinning and fornication and get laid!" Hannah spun back around in her chair.

"Why, is that what you do, Hannah? When you are having issues you go out and get laid?"

"No, it's not," Hannah replied with furrowed eyebrows.

"Oh, not with your husband anyway," Locksie said as quietly as she could under her breath.

"What? What did you say?" Hannah didn't just turn around in her chair; she rose up out of it.

"Oh, by the way, my Mary Kay facial session went well. I mean it was a lovely affair. We had it at a different hotel this time. We had it at the Hilton Easton. I'm sure you've been there. As a matter of fact, I thought I saw you there." Locksie played stupid and put her index finger to her head. "Oh, but that's right. It couldn't have been you because you had a meeting with Reggie."

"Locksie, what are you talking about?" Hannah looked puzzled. Her meeting at the Hilton was far from her mind.

"You know exactly what I'm talking about. You can play the little dumb white girl all you want, but just remember, I know you're black. And I know when a sistah is getting her swerve on."

"How dare you," Hannah said, snatching off

her cape. "Enough with all the black and white comments. You wanna see black?" Hannah began taking off her earrings. "I'll show you black. Now all I need is a jar of Vaseline . . . that is if Dawson hasn't used it all."

"Locksie, can I see you in the back for a minute? I can't find the Redkin conditioner," Jem said after clearing her throat. She could see that things were about to get ugly, so she had decided to intervene.

Locksie threw the comb down onto her station and stomped off to the back storage room with Jem. "The Redkin conditioner is right there," Locksie said harshly.

"Look, little mama, I know exactly where the conditioner is," Jem said, pointing at Locksie. "What I don't know is where your mind is at. How you gon' act like you up in some ghetto job on the Avenue? You in a chain, remember? A franchise. That means these ol' tattling white folks is probably out there on their cell phones now calling corporate to complain about the mad black woman they got working in their salon. And then you know they gon' follow up with a letter. White folks always write a letter telling on somebody."

Locksie stood for a moment, staring at Jem and realizing how serious she was. "You're right. I don't know what I was thinking."

"And your poor sister-girlfriend out there." She pointed toward the styling area. "You put all ol' girl's business in the street. Who's she cheating on her husband with anyway?"

"My boyfriend's brother," Locksie said without thinking.

"Oooh, no wonder you clownin'. How she just

gon' put you all up in the middle of her mess? Oh, yeah, she had that cursin'-out coming."

"No, she didn't." Locksie sighed and sat down in a nearby chair. "We all do dirt—whether it's lie, cheat or steal—we all do dirt. Who am I to try to judge her?"

"Whateva." Jem shooed her hand at Locksie. "I got to get back out there to my customer. You gon' be all right?"

"Yeah," Locksie said as Jem headed out of the storage room.

Locksie felt as if she had lost control and was losing her mind. *What am I doing?* She cupped her head with her hands and thought about how she had just gone off on Hannah. Locksie couldn't understand why she was so angry at Hannah. Yeah, she was angry that Hannah had lied to her about why she couldn't help her out at her Mary Kay meeting, but for her to stand there and accuse Hannah of adultery in front of everybody was just uncalled for. *As if I'm faultless.*

That's when it hit Locksie that it wasn't really Hannah she was mad at; it was herself. She was mad at herself for the lifestyle she was living with Dawson, yet it was just so much easier to get mad at Hannah for the lifestyle she was living—going out with another man while knowing daggone well she was a married woman. Nonetheless, Locksie wasn't in a position to throw stones at anyone, especially with that glass house she had been living in.

Locksie took a deep breath and then stood up. She knew she had to go back out into the salon and apologize to Hannah. So, she straightened.

herself up and headed back to her station only to find an empty chair, Hannah's cape and towel, and a twenty-dollar bill.

Locksie figured that if she couldn't make amends with Hannah, at least she knew one other person who deserved her apology.

"Come on in," Mary said to Locksie after opening the front door. "I didn't think you were coming over this morning." Mary looked down at her watch. "It's a quarter till. I dumped the coffee pot already."

Locksie walked in like a puppy who knew it had no business peeing in the house and was lucky to even be let back in. She had wanted to call her aunt the night before and apologize, but after her fight with Hannah, she figured she needed to get her mind right. Lately, she had just been an emotional ball of fire.

But last night, Dawson had helped to calm and relax her nerves by preparing her a nice, hot bubble bath, followed by a full body massage that put her in a deep sleep. That was his way of making amends for their fight. She was glad that she had fallen asleep during the massage. She definitely would have felt as if Dawson deserved some nookie for that treat, and sex would have only complicated the feelings she had yet to truly stand and face, but instead ran from.

When she woke up this morning, Locksie felt like a brand new person, ready to face her faults. But by the time she got to her aunt's house, all of her courage seemed to evaporate. She sat in her car for God knows how long before going up to Mary's door. Apologizing just wasn't something Locksie was good at.

"Aunt Mary, I just wanted to say how sorry I am for the way I acted the other day when we were talking about Hannah and Drake."

"Child, you know I don't pay you a lick of mind," Mary said. "Don't even worry about it."

Locksie was relieved that Mary didn't dwell on her getting a tad bit out of line with her during their conversation the other day. Locksie had been stressed about apologizing, and worried her aunt might not forgive her.

"Speaking of Hannah," Mary said, "have you had the time to talk to her yet? You know, give her the benefit of the doubt to tell her side of the story before jumping to conclusions?"

Locksie put her hand to her forehead as if just the mention of Hannah's name had brought on a migraine. "Talked to her; yes. Give her the benefit of the doubt; no."

"So, what did she say?"

Locksie raised her head as something crossed her mind; something Hannah said at Fiesta when Locksie confronted her about seeing her with Drake. Actually, it was something Hannah hadn't said.

"You know what, Auntie? Now that I think about it, Hannah didn't really say much about going out with Drake and lying about it. I mean, she was like O.J. during his trial. You just wanted that fool to shout out one time, 'I didn't do it!' but he wouldn't. He didn't. Well, that's kind of how Hannah was. She never defended herself by rebuking my allegations. So, I guess that clears that up. It wasn't an allegation. It was the truth."

"Now, don't be too quick to come to that conclusion, Locksie. Just because you don't speak up on something doesn't mean you are guilty. Sometimes God won't have you speak up on your defense, but He will make it so that someone else does. Sometimes God will have that person whom you thought liked you least in this world come to your defense. So, like I said, don't bear false witness. Don't speak on something you don't know the whole truth about. 'Cause dang it, if I spoke on half the crap I done seen some of them holy, sanctified, baptized-in-the-water saints do without knowing the beginning, middle and the end, I could stir up all kind of mess."

" 'Dang it? Crap!" Locksie repeated after Mary. "What's up with that? Those aren't the words I'm used to hearing fly out of your mouth."

Mary, who had been gathering her gym bag, purse and keys, stopped in her tracks and looked up at her niece. "You noticed?" She then walked over to the door. "Just something I been praying and fasting on. Guess it's working." Mary shrugged, hiding the proudness she truly felt in her heart as she closed the door and locked it behind her and Locksie.

"Fasting?" Locksie said with a puzzled look on her face. "You say that all the time and I know it means not eating, but why would you not want to eat?" Locksie examined Mary's physique as she turned and stepped off the porch. "But then again, you are looking really good, Aunt Mary. Not that you didn't before. But I can see where you've slimmed down even more. Maybe I should fast and lose some of these few extra pounds I been towing around."

"Then it won't be fasting," Mary was quick to say. "It would just simply be starving yourself, and that wouldn't mean anything to God. Fasting is a sacrifice."

"Why would God care about somebody not eating anyway?"

Mary chuckled. "It's more than just not eating. Fasting is not eating with spiritual communication in mind." Mary observed the confused look that still remained on her niece's face. "Let's see." She thought with her index finger to her chin. "It's deliberately abstaining from food so that you can open up to clear communication with the Father. You deny yourself food as a way of saying that food is secondary to something else—something greater. I wanted God to deliver me from the cursing demon, so I sacrificed food for what I wanted from God to show Him how bad I wanted it. I knew not cursing, although it seems minor to some, would make my walk with the Lord more pleasing. So for me, food was secondary to wanting to better my walk with Christ and honor Him by not having a foul tongue."

"But don't you get hungry doing all that?" Locksie frowned.

"During my fasting, whenever my belly hungered for food, I feasted on the bread—not bread as in a loaf of bread—but bread as in daily bread. In other words, the Word of the Bible."

"Okay, I get it." Locksie nodded. "I think. But I know I'd get hungry if I tried not eating; even if it's just to get in that little red dress I bought on sale at Macy's that I knew I couldn't get into when I swiped my charge card."

Aunt Mary chuckled. "It's not hard when you get to the point where you hunger and thirst for Him only and what He has for you." Mary looked down at her watch. "But anyway, you have a good day, and until you're to the point where you can fast for the things that God has for you and wants you to be, I'll fast for you."

"Oh, Aunt Mary, that's so sweet," Locksie joked as she walked toward her car. "You'd deprive yourself of food all on account of my soul?"

"No, I'd fast and not eat all on account of what I want God to do with your soul." She winked.

Locksie stood outside her car door after opening it. "So, you'd do that. You'd fast and pray—make that sacrifice for me when there's nothing for you to get out of it?"

"But there is something I'd get out of it, Locksie. I'd get the comfort of knowing that when we both have left this earth, we'll meet again in heaven, where we will enjoy eternal life."

Locksie smiled and waved goodbye to her aunt. Tears had formed in her eyes. She managed to catch one on her fingertip before it slid down her face and ruined her freshly applied Mary Kay make-up.

Before she knew it, she burst out laughing as she started her car. "This is crazy. I can't believe I'm sitting here crying over the fact that my aunt is willing to sacrifice food in order for me to get to heaven." Locksie laughed again before pulling off.

But I sacrificed more, Jesus wept.

Chapter 20

"Okay, lemon drop, tell me all about you and Mr. GQ's little meeting after I left the restaurant," Reggie said through the phone receiver.

"Who, Drake?" Hannah replied. She had just returned home from a long day at a marketing seminar when Reggie called her cell phone. She made sure to check the caller ID before answering the call. Locksie had tried calling Hannah several times since their confrontation in the shop, but whenever Hannah saw her phone number, she rejected the call and made a mental note to call up Terri Deal, the owner of Scizzors salon, to see if she could start doing her hair.

"Yeah, Drake," Reggie replied.

Hannah flopped down on her bed and began removing her shoes. "It was *just* a meeting, Reggie. So, what do you mean tell you all about it?"

"Just a meeting my foot," Reggie begged to differ.

"Look, it went the same as any other meeting.

Why would you think this one would be any different?"

"Puhleez. That man was feeling you with everything but his hands. My little raspberry tart, he just wanted to reach out and touch ya."

Hannah laughed at Reggie's concocted misconception. She thought Reggie's observation was far off course. Not once had Drake come on to her or even appeared to have been the least bit interested in her other than businesswise. "You've got it all wrong," Hannah said. "Mr. GQ is all business. So, if he was feeling me, he kept it to himself."

"Humph, he didn't keep it to himself. He kept it between him and God. That was until I interrupted their conversation."

"Huh?" Hannah had no idea what Reggie was talking about.

"Remember now, he's the crazy man that was in the bathroom talking to God."

"Yeah, I teased him about that," Hannah recalled.

"Well, let me tell you, all the stuff he was saying to God makes sense now. He was rambling on about wanting this woman to be his wife, but that the woman was already married. Girl, he had to be talking about you. That man wants you. I heard it with my own two ears. And if you don't believe me, ask God. He heard it too, and you know He ain't gon' lie to you."

"Reggie, you are so crazy," Hannah said as she caught herself blushing at the mere thought that Drake might have been attracted to her. Once she realized that she was blushing, she immediately became embarrassed and straightened herself up.

"I'm not crazy. Granted, I thought your boy was a little crazy at first, but after talking to him, he's cool. Just loves the Lord, I guess." Reggie sighed.

"So, you really think Drake likes me?"

"How can I prove my point?" Reggie paused for a minute. "Okay, I've got it! He gave me a twenty-five percent discount because of you. And let me guess, he gave you a thirty percent discount because of you?" Hannah's slight gasp revealed that Reggie was correct, but she had no idea how he could have guessed. "I knew it."

Hannah slid off her stockings and then lifted her skirt so that she could sit cross-legged on her bed. She couldn't erase the huge smile that was splattered across her face. She looked like a teenager who had just found out that the captain of the football team was going to ask her to homecoming. She had to admit it was exciting to even fathom that another man found her attractive, especially since she had been doubting herself ever since that night Elkan didn't come home. She wanted to hear more of Reggie's perception on how Drake felt about her, but she didn't want him to know that she cared.

"You were so caught up in the contract and your entrée that you didn't catch the way he was gazing at you—like it wasn't an easy effort for him to take his eyes off of you."

Hannah only wished she could have caught a glimpse of the look Reggie claimed Drake was giving her. Maybe he was attracted to her. It had been a long time since Hannah felt attractive. She couldn't even remember the last time her own husband had even said or done anything—even something as minor as just gazing at her affection-ately—that had made her feel attractive.

"The brother is fine," Hannah confessed after picturing Drake in her head again. In all honesty, she hadn't looked at him in that way before. But now there was just something about knowing that he might have a thing for her that made her look at him in a whole different light.

"I ain't no hater. I can give the brother his props. I'd keep him away from my wife, that's for sure."

"Please, my husband has nothing to worry about," Hannah said, trying to convince herself more than Reggie.

"If you say so. But check this out, honey bun. I gotta get ready to go."

"All right then, Reg. I'll talk with ya later."

After hanging up the phone with Reggie, Han-nah walked over to her CD player and turned on D'Angelo's *You're My Lady*. She grooved and crooned to the words as she undressed, preparing to get in the shower. She slid her skirt down her legs and then stepped out of it like she was tip-toeing. She then removed her blouse as she sang along, "You're my lady, such a wonderful lady." She couldn't help but fantasize that a man was singing those words to her in that same deep, smoky tone. His hands were caressing her and he was looking into her eyes as he serenaded her.

Hannah closed her eyes and wrapped her arms around herself. She imagined the arms wrapped around her were those of a man; a man who had thought so much of her to create those words in the song just for her.

She removed her remaining garments and found

herself smiling as she pictured her back to this man, with him pressing up behind her, staring at her every move. She could even smell the cologne she imagined he was wearing. His touch began to overtake her, so she turned to him and opened her eyes to return the stare he had been giving her earlier. For the first time in her vision, the man's face appeared as clear as day.

Suddenly, everything seemed so real as she stood in the middle of her bedroom naked.

"Elkan!" she screamed, startled by his presence. She picked up her skirt and covered her body with it.

Elkan said nothing. He just stood there. Hannah could tell from his body language and the expression on his face that he felt as though he had just walked into the room and caught his cheating wife with her lover. Strangely enough, Hannah felt the same way, and it showed on her face and in her actions as she began to stutter in her speech.

"Uh, uh, Elkan, honey, what are you doing home?" Hannah raced to the closet and grabbed her robe.

"Duh, I live here," he said as he flopped down on the bed and loosened his tie. With all the big cases he had been handling lately, it wasn't unusual for Elkan to put in a fourteen-hour day to bring home the bacon, but today he had put in only ten hours.

"I know that. I meant what are you doing getting off work so early?"

"I worked ten hours. What do you mean early? The average person works eight. You want me to just work an entire twenty-four-hour shift next time?"

"I didn't mean it like that. I know you worked long and hard today. You always do," Hannah said as she nervously tied the belt around her waist, wondering just how much of her striptease Elkan had witnessed. She prayed on everything that Elkan had been unable to read her mind and detect her thoughts about another man. "It's just that you usually get home later. I wasn't expecting you."

Elkan sat silently as he observed his wife's peculiar behavior, then he said, "Not expecting me, huh? What? Did I interrupt something?" Elkan stood and then made his way over to their walk-in closet. He looked around and then came back out and kneeled down to look under the bed.

Hannah watched her husband as if he had lost his mind. "What are you doing, Elkan?" she asked as he got up from his knees. Elkan ignored his wife's question and just continued to look around the room. Eventually Hannah figured out what her husband was up to and became offended. "Elkan Leroy Wells!" Hannah scolded. "Do you think I have a man in here or something? Is that what you're looking for? You think you showed up home early and caught me with another man? You've got some nerve." Hannah's eyes started to water, not so much because her feelings were hurt, but because she was angry. As hard as it was to start trusting Elkan again after his tryst with Peni, she had never as much as looked at another man and he still didn't trust her.

"Well, is there?" Elkan asked matter-of-factly. "Is there another man here, Hannah?" Without waiting for her to respond, he walked into the bathroom to case it. Hannah angrily followed behind him.

"You know what, Elkan? Yes! Yes, there is another man here," Hannah said, letting her arms flop down to her side. Elkan brushed by her as he exited the bathroom, bumping his wife's shoulder. "There is a man in here. Me and D'Angelo. And it seems like D'Angelo is the only man in this room right now."

Elkan stopped in his tracks, turned around. The look her husband was giving her was one she had never seen in his eyes. But then again, she had never insulted his manhood before.

"Sorry," she quickly apologized. "I didn't mean to insinuate that you were anything less than a man. It's just that it's insulting for you to think that I would be in our bedroom with another man. I've never done anything to make you think that I'd ever step outside of our marriage."

Elkan finally spoke. "I'm sorry, too. I don't know what just came over me. I mean, I walk in and you're doing a little striptease thing. You lookin' all good and sexy, and my mind just . . ."

"Never mind, Elkan." Hannah put her index finger to Elkan's juicy lips. "It's okay. But you should know by now that all of this is for you. Just you." Hannah referred to her size eight body. "You never have to go elsewhere, baby." Hannah pressed her lips against her husband's, who in return pulled her against him and began kissing her passionately.

Still kissing her, Elkan took his wife and laid

her on the bed as he began removing his clothing. Once undressed, Elkan rubbed his hands up and down his wife's body like it was his first time ever touching her. Hannah's body began to burn with passion. She took in her husband's touch and kiss. She couldn't remember him ever touching her that way before; kissing her that way before. It all felt so brand new.

Hannah closed her eyes and suddenly the touch wasn't her husband's anymore. The kiss wasn't his. It was the man she had been fantasizing about earlier. It was Drake. Maybe that's why everything felt so different and new to her. She was imagining that it was Drake and not her husband. This time guilt didn't take over as she went along with the fantasy, keeping her eyes closed in order to block out reality.

She couldn't explain her feelings. She hadn't thought twice about Drake since last seeing him, and now, for some reason, she couldn't get him off of her mind—literally. The guilty pleasure of being pleased by her husband while she fantasized about another man had been swept under the rug as Hannah's body burst with ecstasy. She momentarily tried to fight it, but it was too late. Her mind and body had already been taken over by the desires of her flesh. The challenge would be trying to get it back.

Chapter 21

"And she's white? She's not only married, but she's white too?" Dawson shouted through the phone receiver into Drake's ringing ear. "Brother, you might as well turn in your Bible and cross, 'cause you fo' sho' going to hell. 'Cause I'ma knock you into the middle of it when I see you for dating a white woman. Forget about losing your Christianhood or Christianship or whatever it's called. The Muslims won't even let you in now."

Drake couldn't help but chuckle at his brother's somewhat comical outburst. "Oh, so now you could care less if she's married. It's her skin color that bothers you?"

"Now you know I ain't got nothing against white people, but with all these fine sisters out here . . . Negro, please!"

"But God sees us all as his children and He loves us all the same, no matter what our skin color is. You love who you love, and one of the commandments is to love everybody."

"Yeah, but you don't have to go cohabitating with everybody. Look, none of that matters anyway," Dawson exaggerated, shooing his hand at the phone receiver as if his brother could see him. "The original purpose for my call was just to let you know that I'm sorry about how I acted the other day, you know, trying to put down your Christianity. But sometimes people feel like in order to lift themselves up, they have to put other people down. I guess that day was one of those times for me."

Drake smiled as his heart warmed to his brother's words. "Dude, I appreciate hearing that from you. It takes a real man to admit that sort of thing."

"No, problem, bruh. Now back to the married white chick." Dawson couldn't wait to hear more. Sometimes men were just as bad, if not worse, than women when it came to gossip. "You ain't gon' have her chained up and stuff like Samuel L. Jackson had that white woman in that one movie, are you?" Dawson burst out laughing.

"Man, you stupid." Drake chuckled. "Look, me and the white chick . . ." Drake cleared his throat and corrected himself. "I mean me and Mrs. Wells have nothing but a business relationship. Believe me, I prayed on that. Had I not prayed myself up, I probably would have turned her business away."

"Why?"

"Temptation. I put myself to be all up in temptation's face. I should have just referred her to someone else. I mean, I have dozens of people working under me. I could have easily assigned her to someone else."

"But you didn't, which means only one thing."

"What?"

"That you're a Christian, but news flash, you're a man first."

After hanging up the phone with his brother, Drake was in desperate need of prayer. He went into the private bathroom of his office, which also served as his makeshift prayer closet.

Hannah hadn't left his mind since the day she entered it. He felt crazy thinking about someone who hadn't even given him a second thought. It was like he was creating this fantasy in his mind—a fantasy that had no possibilities of becoming a reality. Or did it?

Chapter 22

"Here we were, sitting here talking about all the work I have to do today at the salon with the upcoming audit, and next thing I know, you talking about God," Locksie said, crossing her arms. "How is it you always manage to bring God into everything?"

Mary touched her niece on the chin with her index finger. "Honey, hopefully, before the day I die, you will know the answer to that question for yourself."

"Yeah, yeah, yada, yada," Locksie said, rising up from the table and dumping the remainder of her coffee in the sink.

"Anyway, Locksie, I really would like you to come to Friends and Family Day at church this Sunday. I promise you will be blessed." Mary followed suit and dumped the last of her coffee after taking a sip.

"I'm going to try to make it," Locksie said as if the first thing on her to-do list was to come up with an excuse for not going.

"Promise you'll really come this time, Locksie," Mary said with such sincerity. "It's really kind of important to me that you come."

"I better go to the bathroom real quick." Locksie was bound and determined not to give her aunt a "yes." Her mother had always taught her growing up that "yes" was a commitment. One could change her mind and turn a "no" into a "yes," but to change a "yes" into a "no" gave the person's word very little value.

Locksie rushed off to the bathroom and feigned using it. She and Mary then exited out the door. After locking up behind them, Mary said, "So, Friends and Family Day this Sunday at my church; you'll be there?"

Locksie sighed. "Sure, Aunt Mary, I'll be there." She trotted down the sidewalk to her car in pure defeat. "You'd make a good Jehovah's Witness, you know that?" Locksie commented as she got into her car.

"Honey, anybody who done witnessed what our God can do is a Jehovah's Witness." Mary winked as she got into her car. She rolled down her window and stuck her hand out and waved before pulling out of the driveway and heading down the street.

Locksie just shook her head. She watched Mary's Mustang speed off until the license plate that read GODS FA4 was no longer visible.

Locksie had cramps in her belly as she slipped into her red dress, which was the fourth outfit she had tried on already that morning. The nervous butterflies in her belly just wouldn't seem to let up as she mentally prepared herself for church. She hadn't been to church since God knows when, and wasn't too much looking forward to going today. But there was no telling what her aunt Mary would slip into her coffee Monday morning if she didn't show up.

Locksie had tried her best to talk Dawson into attending with her, but his firm "no" offered no hope for being changed to a "yes." The only time Dawson had been to church was to attend a funeral or a wedding. He hadn't grown up in the church, and neither side of his family were practicing Christians. Of course, almost every one of them had a Bible laying out somewhere in their house for show, as if its mere existence was enough to get them into heaven.

While Dawson simply didn't want to go because church wasn't his thing, churches had always been scary to Locksie, ever since she was little and her mother would tow her to every big church in the city of Detroit. If one church did something her mother didn't approve of, they'd move on to the next church. And if that pastor didn't preach about what Locksie's mother wanted to hear, then they'd move on again. Just when Locksie would make a friend or two in Sunday school, she'd never see them again. It was like changing schools in the middle of the school year—twice. Eventually, Locksie realized that making friends at church wasn't in her best interest. That feeling transferred over to making friends at school as well, so Locksie had always pretty much been a loner. Her relationship with Hannah was the closest thing she had to a friendship.

Locksie walked over to the dresser mirror and

took a look at herself. She gazed into the eyes of
what seemed like that same little girl with her
hair braided up into one big pigtail at the top of
her head. It was that same little girl who wondered if they were going to the old church at
which her mother had last made her way down to
the altar and joined, or the new church where, on
any given Sunday, her mother would join as well.

She smiled in the mirror at the thought of how
she used to use the back wall of her closet, behind
all her pretty little Sunday dresses, to mark with a
crayon the number of churches her mother had
joined. Her intention was to write to the *Guinness
Book of World Records* some day and submit her
mother's name as the person who belonged to the
most churches.

Locksie patted her hands down the dress as she
turned from left to right and then to the back,
looking over her shoulder to make sure she
looked respectable and presentable.

"Yeah, I think this one will do." She sighed, relieved that she had finally found something suit-
able to wear to church. After all, no matter how
saved and holy those church women claimed to
be, Locksie felt that they would be the first to
judge a sistah.

"Ooooh-wee," Dawson said as he entered the
bedroom. "Sexy mama! Lady in red, a brotha
can't wait to get you in bed."

"Oh, great," Locksie said, throwing her arms
up and sucking her teeth as she headed back to
the closet to try on a fifth outfit.

"What? What did I say?" Dawson asked, confused. "I can't compliment my woman?"

"No, baby, it's not that," Locksie said as she

shuffled through the closet. "It's just that I'm going to church. I don't want to walk up in there looking sexy, having them women think that their husbands are thinking what you just said—that they want to take me to bed."

"Oh, God, Locksie, it ain't that serious." Dawson threw himself on the bed and folded his arms.

"Don't be using God's name like that."

"Like what?" Dawson raised his voice an octave and said with furrowed eyebrows. "Jesus." He flopped his head back down.

"Dawson, stop it," Locksie snapped.

"Dang, if going to church makes you all funny-acting like that, I sure hope your aunt Mary don't ever invite you again." Dawson got up out of the bed and headed for the bathroom.

His Sunday morning had been going just fine. He had gotten up and worked out fifteen minutes longer than he normally did, working off some of his pent-up sexual frustration, and he was feeling good. He didn't want to change his mood by hanging around for a brewing argument with his girlfriend. "I'm going to take a shower."

"Look, Dawson, I'm sorry," Locksie said as she came out of the closet with a black pantsuit draped across her arm. "It's just that I haven't been to church since I was a little girl and I'm nervous. I'm scared. I don't know what to expect."

"Then don't go." Dawson made the most obvious suggestion. "Why would you want to go be with people you have to be nervous or afraid around? If that's what being a Christian is about, then they can keep that mess." Dawson went to close the bathroom door.

"Wait!" Locksie stopped him. She took a deep

breath before making a suggestion. "You see what a nervous wreck I am, baby. Will you please just go with me?" She folded her hands and made a puppy-dog face.

"Naw, I'm straight," Dawson said then closed the door behind him, leaving Locksie standing there nervous, afraid . . . and alone.

Locksie sat in the church parking lot for about five minutes, waiting on her aunt Mary to pull up before she realized that Mary's car was already there. Good thing, too, because Locksie had no intention of going into that church not knowing a single person. She was hoping to beat her aunt Mary there so that when she did pull up, Locksie would already be there and they could go inside together. Now she'd have to go inside alone, looking around for her aunt, making it even more obvious that she was a lost outsider.

After taking a deep breath, Locksie looked up and said, "Lord, please let this church thing go smoothly." She opened the car door and stuck one leg out before looking back up to say, "Oh, by the way—my name is Locksie." It had been so long since she had last been to God's house that she didn't know if He still remembered her.

That might not have been the best introduction in the world, but right now the last thing she wanted to do was walk into church late. So, she'd have to properly introduce herself to God later.

As Locksie made her way to the church door, she looked down at the royal blue top she had chosen to wear underneath the black pantsuit. Used to wearing the top three buttons undone on her blouses, she quickly buttoned it up all the way to the top. Before entering the church, Locksie pulled a tissue from her fall jacket pocket and blotted her lips.

"What was I thinking going with this apple berry lipstick?" Locksie mumbled to herself. She told herself that she shouldn't have chosen a red, even if it was a soft red. She should have worn downtown brown. Just then, Locksie saw two people coming up the walkway and decided to keep stepping on into the church so that she could get out of the oncoming saints' way.

Standing at the door was a young girl holding a stack of papers. Locksie smiled at the girl as she extended her hand to accept one of the programs the girl was offering. Locksie's smile quickly faded once she realized that the girl wasn't going to smile back.

She felt like such an idiot, realizing that church was supposed to be serious and here she was smiling all up in the girl's face. Locksie swiftly straightened up and reminded herself not to smile, but instead to appear serious about the Lord.

Locksie looked around as she made her way down the center aisle. She wanted to sit down right there on the back pew, but then she remembered her aunt Mary saying something about how the folks who used to come to church regularly, then backslid only to start coming back to church again, always sit in the back, hiding from man or God. She didn't know which. But Locksie didn't want them to think she was one of those people. A backslider she wasn't. Heck, she had yet to even slide forward. So, against her quivering legs' wishes, Locksie walked closer to the front of the church.

She pretended like she knew exactly where she was going and exactly where she wanted to sit. She put on an air as if she had been there a thousand times. She tried hard not to let on that she was looking for someone. But little did Locksie know, it was obvious to some that she was, in fact, looking for someone . . . she was looking for *Him*; she was looking for God. And boy, had she come to the right place.

Five rows from the front and still no sight of her aunt Mary, Locksie decided to take a seat on the left side of the church. The decent-sized sanctuary had rows of long pews, fifteen on the left and fifteen on the right side. At the head of the church was a three-level setting that consisted of a carpeted stage at the first level, a platform with a shiny wooden podium as the second level, and behind that was a level that held a tier of four pews.

"Excuse me," Locksie said to the people who were already seated in the pew where she was trying to sit. Although they had seen her coming and it was obvious she was attempting to join them on the pew, not one of them voluntarily bothered to stand and let her by until she had made her verbal request.

Guess that's what they mean by lifting your voice in the sanctuary, Locksie thought. One woman even looked up at her and rolled her eyes.

Locksie sat down and took off her jacket just as a man walked on the stage with microphone in hand and said to the congregation, "Let's begin to give Him some hand praise." People stood and clapped their hands.

"Hallelujah," a couple of people shouted.

"Thank You, Jesus," the woman next to Locksie clapped.

Not wanting to stick out like a sore thumb, Locksie stood and began to clap. She felt silly because she had no idea why she was clapping.

"Come on and stand to your feet and give our God some praise," the man shouted. A few of the people who were still seated stood to their feet and began to clap. "I don't know about y'all, but I came here today to praise the Lord. I didn't come here to sit on God. He's done too much for me to come here today and sit on Him."

Locksie looked around at the few people who were still seated in their pews. She knew the man with the microphone was referring to them. A couple more stood and began to clap. The few remaining seated were hell-bent on staying that way because they had just been called out, put on Front Street by the man who was doing the exhortation.

The words "Humph, we'll show him," were written all over their faces, as well as "He ain't gon' tell us what to do up in here. I can praise God sitting the same way I can praise Him standing."

Just as if the man was reading their minds, he replied, "Don't sit there and be mad at me. I'm just the messenger. The message came from God. He told me to tell you that He wants you to stand to your feet and praise Him."

"That's right, Brother Wilkersen. You tell 'em," someone called out.

"Praise Him!" Brother Wilkersen said with a little more bass in his voice, as if he was spiritually angry that not everyone could find it in their hearts to stand and praise God. "Give Him what you owe Him, church. Stand and praise Him!"

"Thank you, Jesus. You are an awesome God. We magnify you. We glorify you," members began to shout.

"If it wasn't for Him, I wouldn't be here this morning. I wouldn't even be awake this morning. Yeah, the alarm clock went off this morning, but that ain't what woke me up, or should I say *who* woke me up," Brother Wilkersen declared.

"Hallelujah! Thank You, Jesus!" members exclaimed.

Locksie smiled at the man's clever words. For years she had given that annoying alarm clock credit for waking her up each morning. There stood a man before her telling her that it was God who had been waking her up.

"That's right," he stated. "Through His mercy and grace, He allows me to wake up each morning. Some of us know darn well from the things we did last night that we didn't even deserve to be woke up this morning."

"Amen!" one of the last few people who had been seated stood and shouted.

"Some of us were at the club drinking our brains out. Some of us were laid up with our *boo*, who we ain't even married to. Some of us were laid up with our boo who someone else is married to," the man said with a stomp. "I know I ain't gon' get too many *hallelujah*s or *amen*s on that one." Brother Wilkerson, along with a few members of the congregation, giggled. "But God said that He still loves you and that the blood of the lamb has already paid for your sins . . . Oh, but what good it would do God's heart if you would just obey His Word. Won't you stop taking for granted that Jesus died for your sins? Y'all know what I'm talking about. Some of y'all walk around talking about, 'Since Jesus died for my sins, why should all His suffering be in vain? Let me get in a few good sins,'" he mocked.

Locksie shook her head and smiled because she had heard Dawson say that before. As a matter of fact, that's what he had told her the night he finally talked her into giving up her virginity.

If Locksie learned anything at all from the dozens of churches her mother dragged her to, she learned that they all agreed on one thing: fornication was just as great a sin as any. No man or woman should lay down with another person sexually unless that other person is their partner in marriage. Sex outside of marriage was forbidden. So for years, Locksie had kept her mouth open and her legs closed in declaring such—not because she believed it herself, but because it had been instilled in her with a fear of going to hell. But eventually she threw that concept out of the window; and not soon enough.

By the time she met Dawson, she had dated two boys. The first had been her high school sweetheart from back in Michigan. They started dating their senior year, which was when Locksie was allowed to start dating boys. Although most of her friends were allowed to date at age 16, Locksie didn't miss it because she didn't have time for a boyfriend anyway. Her mother had kept her busy with school activities such as cheerleading and volleyball, and church activities such as the youth choir. Last time she counted, she had been a member of five choirs. Still involved in each of these activities once she started dating Ishmael, Locksie never had enough time to have sex with him even if she had wanted to.

The day the letter from The Ohio State University arrived, informing Locksie that she had been granted an academic scholarship along with the volleyball scholarship she had already earned, she couldn't wait to pack her bags and get away from her church-hopping mother and church itself.

Locksie's mother couldn't stand that her daughter would be leaving home, but there was a sense of security knowing that her sister, who had also moved to Columbus, Ohio, years ago to attend OSU and still remained there, would be able to watch over Locksie.

Locksie hated leaving Ishmael behind, but felt that since they were only a four-hour drive away from each other, they could see one another a few times a month. Plus, there were always cell phones and the Internet. But after the first year of their long-distance relationship, the two realized that it wasn't going to work, especially when Locksie found out that Janelle, a girl who used to be on the cheerleading squad with Locksie, had been satisfying needs that Locksie had never taken the time to realize Ishmael had.

After that, Locksie was so hurt and confused that she buried herself deeper into her college work and volleyball. She cut off the few friends she had, and since then, never really trusted other women enough to have them around her—or her man, for that matter. By her senior year, Locksie met Samson, a young professor from another university who had come to one of her classes as a guest lecturer. In this relationship, Samson seemed to be the busy one. Later, Locksie would find out that it was his wife and two kids that kept him so busy. Fortunately for Locksie, she found out the night before she planned to have sex with him, but not before spending what little funds she did have on what she called her "sex me" kit from Victoria's Secret. It was a couple of jazzy pieces of lingerie and some bath and body products all stored in the cutest overnight bag she had also purchased. Needless to say, Locksie returned it all to the store and substituted it for what she would soon call her "poor me" kit. Unlike the "sex me" kit, this one consisted of all of her favorite snacks and desserts in a brown paper bag.

Locksie spent months of depression and burying her troubles in one too many "poor me" kits. She was trying to figure out why the men she chose had chosen someone other than her to please them sexually. This was the reason Locksie ended up joining the gym where she met Dawson.

With Dawson's well-built physique, Locksie couldn't keep from getting moist as she worked out, and it wasn't from the sweat of five sets of twenty stomach crunches he had her doing. It was from the touching of her body Dawson would have to do every now and then to position her to do a specific exercise. She often found herself having to hit the cold shower after her training with Dawson.

It wasn't that Locksie didn't want to have sex. She had left behind most of that mess about sin and fornication when she left Michigan. She wasn't about to become as mixed up as she felt her mother was when it came to religion. This was one reason why she had always been so quick to turn down her aunt Mary's previous invites to church. But after dating Dawson for a few months, Locksie found herself, after an hour of heavy petting, dry sex and a bunch of trash talk in each other's ear, in a position to finally go all the way. Right at the last minute, though, she got scared and tried to throw up all the things she could remember about what the church used to say regarding sex outside of marriage. Of course Locksie couldn't have cared less about the church's opinion, but she felt better using that instead of the truth. The truth was that after seeing Dawson's manhood in the flesh, she was scared out of her mind to let something of that size enter her.

Dawson countered her preaching and concerns about sinning with, "But you said it yourself; Jesus died on a cross for your sins. Don't you at least want to commit one sin so that his dying wouldn't be in vain?"

Now, as Locksie sat in her aunt Mary's church, she chuckled at Dawson's persistence, followed by a quiver at the thought of how good he had felt inside of her the first time they had sex, and the many times to follow.

Locksie thought that she was going to hell for sure as she looked around the church, wondering if there was anyone there who could read her mind . . . one of those prophet people. She had to be the biggest sinner of the bunch, sitting there in church reminiscing about sinning . . . with a smile on her face, no less.

"Before we go into praise and worship," Brother Wilkerson said, interrupting Locksie's thoughts, "Evangelist Jonna is going to come forth with our mission statement, followed by Sister Brown with scripture."

Brother Wilkerson handed the cordless microphone over to a woman dressed in a purple satin skirt suit with purple snakeskin pumps to match. She asked the congregation to repeat the church mission statement after her, and proceeded to recite it. After that, she handed the microphone over to another woman, who asked that everyone turn to Ecclesiastics 12:13.

"Fear God, and keep his commandments: for this is the whole duty of man," she read. She then informed the congregation that it was time for praise and worship. The keyboard player, who had been playing softly throughout the recital of the mission statement and the reading of the scripture, was joined by a drum player and an electric guitarist. As the musicians began to play, the church choir filed in from the double doors on the side of the sanctuary and into their places in the choir stand, which was the third level of the pulpit area.

"God has been so good to me, I praise Him," they sang as they clapped their hands and stomped their feet.

Pretty soon, the entire congregation was on their feet, joining in on the tune that was sung to the beat of George Benson's "On Broadway." Locksie subconsciously began to sing along as if she had been singing the song her entire life. She couldn't remember the last time she had sent praises up to God, but it sure felt good.

Locksie hated for that song to end, but was happy when the choir immediately went into another upbeat song of praise. Next a male soloist led them into a song of worship that brought tears to Locksie's eyes. At first she was embarrassed to be standing there crying like a big baby, but then she looked around and noticed that no one was paying her any attention, and that other folks were crying too. Some people even had their eyes closed as they extended their arms up in the air.

Tears poured down her face as she began to witness how the same thing that was moving inside of her was also moving in others as well. She wished she had put a tissue in her purse. She remembered seeing a box of tissues on one of the pews and another in the hands of an usher, but neither box was made available to her, so she wiped her tears away as best she could with her hands. By the time the song ended, Locksie had managed to regain her composure, but that was before the lady in purple introduced the dance ministry.

Locksie stood to her feet in awe at the sight of her aunt Mary exiting from the same doors the choir had come through. She was followed by three other women wearing silky white skirts that flowed down to the floor, and matching shirts with sleeves that flared like an angel's wings. Each woman wore a sky blue sheer sash around her waist.

"Ask the person next to you: Will you still say

yes?" The words hummed from the speakers as the women began to move in sync.

"Auntie," Locksie mumbled softly as she covered her mouth with her hand. Locksie realized that she had been so wrapped up in the praise and worship that she had forgotten all about looking for her aunt.

The liturgical dancers couldn't have been thirty seconds into the song before more than half the church was on their feet, being questioned as to whether or not their hearts, spirits, minds and souls would say "yes" to the Lord.

Locksie watched as her aunt gracefully danced from one end of the sanctuary to the other. It was just absolutely beautiful. All the tears she had managed to wipe away somehow returned. She had no idea her aunt could dance like that; that anybody could dance like that, for that matter. All of the women were like one, dancing with such conviction on their faces. It was so powerful that before Locksie knew it, by the middle of the song, she was shouting out, "Yes, Lord, yes!"

"All God wants is *yes*," the vocalist assured Locksie.

So a heartwrenching, "Yes!" is what Locksie gave the Lord as she cried out and fell to her knees. Locksie had no idea what she was experiencing, and wished someone would have just come and wrapped their arms around her, but they didn't. Instead, she just stayed on her knees, crying until the song faded out, hating that she had missed seeing her aunt and the dancers minister the remainder of the song.

When Locksie finally felt a warm embrace, she

knew it was her aunt Mary. She smelled the Michael Kors perfume she always wore long before she felt her touch.

"Let Him have his way," Mary told her niece as she wrapped her arms around her.

Locksie could hear others crying out, "Yes!" and Jesus' name as the church remained in the presence of the Lord. After what seemed like forever, the pastor finally took his place behind the podium.

"I wanted to move on earlier, but I couldn't." He apologized for the delay in the delivery of his word. "I couldn't move until the Holy Spirit said it was time to move. And, saints, you know that we'll never interrupt worship for anything."

"That's all right, Pastor Clevens," someone called out.

"Yes!" the pastor began to yell. "Yes!"

Once again, the church was in an uproar with cries of "Yes."

"Yes!" Pastor Clevens continued to yell out as folks fell out.

By now, Mary had helped Locksie up off her knees and to a sitting position on the pew. She kept her arms around her, rocking as they tuned in to the pastor's message.

"Like the song says, when you say yes, you might have to give up some things you hold dear to you. You might have to give up some relationships."

"Oh, God." A woman rose up out of her seat and began running back and forth across the front of the church.

"I dare you to just run around this place and say yes to the Lord!" the pastor shouted. Upon his command, a few others leaped up as if they had no control over their flesh and just let the spirit move them. One woman even ran around the entire church.

"Dance ministry, that couldn't have been a more perfect selection for today's message," Pastor Clevens said, wiping his forehead with a cloth the woman in purple had handed him. "Because this Sunday, the Word from God to you is 'when.' " He looked around the sanctuary. "Oooh, I see some confused faces and I see some faces trying to hide because you know I'm about to drive down your street."

There was some subtle laughter amongst the congregation.

"When are you going to stop trying to live the life you want to live and live the life God wants you to live? When?" the pastor shouted. "When are you going to stop trying to get all the materialistic things the world has to offer and start seeking after what God already has for you? Can I get an *amen*?" Pastor Clevens stomped, after only receiving only a couple of *amen*s. "Aw, I knew I wasn't going to get too many *amen*s on that one," he chuckled. " 'But, Pastor, I worked hard for my big house and my big car and this fine jewelry. I deserve it.' Ain't that right, Sister Washington?"

"You right about it," Sister Washington answered, raising her hand.

"I'm not saying you shouldn't have nice things. God don't want you to have no junk. God wants you to have a nice car . . . so that you can drive to church in it and pick up a few folks along the way." *Amen*s rang out. "Remember back in the day when your neighbor went out and bought a new car, typically a Cadillac, which was referred to as their Sunday car because they only drove it to show off for church? Well, guess what? You might have thought they were showing off for church, but they were really showing up for God and showing out by showing others what God had done for them. He made it so that they could afford a vehicle that nice. If you drive a hooptie, you better start believing in bigger things because He's able, church! He's able!"

"He's able," members echoed, jumping to their feet.

"Faith is the belief in things hoped for but not seen, says the Bible," the pastor continued. "So, when are you going to start having faith that the Lord can use you? When are you going to start letting the Lord use you? When? When are you going to make a conscious decision to get right with God? I know, I know. Y'all saying, 'But pastor, I got to get right with myself before I can get right with God.' The devil is a liar! Because guess what? You can't get right without Him!"

The church began to shout out in agreement with the pastor. His words struck a chord with Locksie, seeing how she had used that very same excuse with her aunt Mary.

"So again, I ask, when? When are you going to say 'yes'?" the pastor asked.

"Yes," could be heard from every corner of the sanctuary.

By the time the pastor finished delivering his message, Locksie felt as if she was alone in the sanctuary and that the pastor had been talking to her and only her. She was moved beyond words.

She felt as though God had truly sent her a word through the man in the pulpit.

The pastor wiped his mouth with his cloth and then took a deep breath. "I don't ever want to take it for granted that everyone in the room is saved," the pastor said as the keyboard player began a soft tune. "So, I need every head bowed and every eye closed." He paused for a moment. Obviously not everyone in the sanctuary had done as they were instructed because he then said, "Come on, saints, be obedient. There's nothing to see. I need every head bowed and every eye closed." The pastor waited until everyone obliged. "If there is anyone in the room today that is not saved and would like to get saved, please raise your hand. If you didn't know before, but now believe that Jesus Christ is your Lord and Savior—that the Son of God died on a cross to wash away your sins and was then resurrected from the grave—if you now want to accept Jesus Christ into your life, raise your hand. If you want to say 'yes,' raise your hand." After asking that same question a couple more times, the pastor said, "Now, for those of you who raised your hand, I ask you to make your way down to the altar."

Locksie looked over at her aunt Mary. Although she hadn't raised her hand, at that moment, that day, that hour, that second, she wanted nothing more than to accept Jesus Christ into her life. She wanted nothing more than the power she had just witnessed the Lord give her aunt to minister His Word through dance and the glory that shone all over her while she did it. She wanted nothing more than to allow God to use her the way He had used the man in the pulpit—to touch someone else's life. She wanted it bad.

So, without even confirming verbally what Mary knew she saw in her niece's eyes, she said, "I'll go with you."

Locksie reached for the hand that Mary held out to her, and they both stood and made their way down the aisle.

"Hallelujah," the woman next to Locksie shouted, grateful that another soul was being saved.

"Thank You, Jesus," someone else called out.

When Locksie joined the other two people at the altar, the pastor asked them to raise their hands in surrender. "Romans 10:9 says that if thou shalt confess with thy mouth the Lord Jesus, and shalt believe in thine heart that God hath raised Him from the dead, thou shalt be saved." The pastor noticed the puzzled look on Locksie's faced and answered the question that it asked. "Yes, that's it. You didn't know getting saved was that easy, huh?"

Locksie's eyes welled up with tears. Once again, it was as if the pastor was reading her mind, reading her life.

"It's okay, daughter. I know what you're thinking. Jesus had to go through and to hell, and all you have to do is say *yes*. All you have to do is to believe that he did it and that he did it for you."

Locksie's knees gave out. Immediately, the members of the altar ministry, along with Mary, held her up. They weren't about to let her go down without first seeing to it that her soul was all right.

"Repeat after me," the pastor instructed, and

those at the altar for salvation did just that. "I accept Jesus Christ as my Lord and Savior. I believe that the Lord Jesus Christ died at Calvary for the remission of my sins. I believe in thine heart that God hath raised Him from the dead."

After the three individuals at the altar repeated what the pastor had recited, the pastor said to them, "Your souls are now saved. You have the promise of eternal life."

As the sanctuary clapped and praised God, Mary walked Locksie back to her seat and then whispered, "Your new walk with Christ isn't going to be easy. You've just pissed Satan off. But stay in God's Word and pray the devil under your feet. In Jesus' name he has to obey you." Mary kissed Locksie on the check. "I'll talk to you after church." She went and sat with the other three dancers while the benediction was given and church was dismissed.

Locksie sat in her seat while she watched Mary try to make her way through the people stopping to tell her what a wonderful job she and the other dancers had done setting the atmosphere with their praise dance.

"All glory be to God," Mary would say.

As Locksie waited, the churchgoers just brushed by her, anxious to get home and take their chickens out of the oven or be the first in line at the Country Buffet. She felt weird and out of place as she waited for her aunt. She had just gotten saved. Didn't that make her one of the saints too, now? Still, no one seemed eager to welcome her into the Christian family. After a few more moments of awkwardness, Locksie decided to go wait in her car. Noticing Locksie's exit, Mary hurried out, still in her dance garments, and met up with Locksie at her car.

"I know you weren't going to leave here without saying good-bye," Mary scolded as she ran up behind Locksie.

"Oh, no, Auntie," Locksie said as she turned around, right before opening her car door. "I was just going to wait in the car for you."

Mary held Locksie by her shoulders and just stared at her and smiled. "Oh, Locksie, you don't know what it does to my heart to know that you are saved."

"Aunt Mary, I've never felt this way in my life. I can't even explain it. I don't even feel the same anymore."

"And you're not supposed to. You are renewed. The blood of Jesus has washed away your sins and you've accepted it. You have died to the things of the world. The old you is gone. Just keep believing it, baby." Mary pulled Locksie against her for a tight embrace.

"And you, Miss Thing," Locksie said, pulling away and nudging Mary. "Why didn't you tell me you were doing praise dancing? You were awesome."

"All glory be to God," she replied. "That's where I've been heading out to during my favorite show." She winked. "One Sunday, actually, a couple months ago, I had a breakthrough and it was in the form of dance. The praise and worship team was singing 'Praise is What I Do.' I was deep in worship, and the next thing I knew, I was on my feet and the Holy Spirit was guiding my steps. I had no idea it was my calling, but when He called me, I had to answer with a 'yes.' "

"I hear you." Locksie smiled.

"A few of us are headed out to eat." Mary turned around and pointed to a group of folks chatting. "Would you like to join us? Get to know some of the church members?"

Locksie looked at some of the people her aunt was pointing to. One was the usher, who didn't seem too friendly, and another was one of the people in the pew who wouldn't move out of her way when she was trying to sit down. For some reason, they just didn't seem like people she would enjoy dining with.

"I'll pass," Locksie said. "Dawson and I are supposed to be going to Best Buy to get a movie and grab some take-out. I don't want to be too late getting home."

"Okay, well, I'll see you in the morning then," Mary said, kissing her now-saved niece on the cheek and walking away.

"Bye, Auntie," Locksie said before climbing into her car and starting the engine. All of a sudden, the joyful smile Locksie was wearing just seconds ago faded. "Dawson." His name rolled off of her lips as if it was just dawning on her how, if she was going to start a walk with the Lord, there was no way she could walk in the world with him . . . or could she?

Chapter 23

"So how did church go?" Dawson asked as he and Locksie perused the DVD aisle of Best Buy. Dawson preferred to purchase DVDs instead of renting them. He figured by the time he finished paying all the late fees when he forgot to return them, he could have owned them in the first place.

For some reason, Locksie had been avoiding discussing church ever since she had gotten home. How was she supposed to tell her boyfriend that she had gone off to church and fallen in love with another man . . . Jesus?

"It was, uh, okay. It was good," Locksie replied after he asked her yet again.

"Did you catch the Holy Ghost?" Dawson joked as he held his arms up over Locksie as if he were a ghost hovering over her.

At first she just let out a little chuckle, but then she cleared her throat and said, "Uh, actually I did."

"Girl, you crazy." He laughed it off.

Once again, Locksie chuckled, but then said, "Seriously, I, uh, I did. I got saved today."

"Saved? You mean you let the preacher man splash you with some water? Put a little holy oil on ya?" Dawson nudged her playfully, but as she stood stiff in her position, staring up at him, he could tell she was serious.

"Splashed with water? I got saved, not baptized." She sucked her teeth and rolled her eyes. "I gave my life to the Lord."

"Oh," is all Dawson could manage to say. What was he supposed to say? Congratulations?

Locksie observed the blank look on his face as he fingered some DVD cases. "You okay with that?"

"Yeah, I mean, sure. Why not? I ain't got no problem with you giving your life to the Lord." He turned and kissed Locksie on the forehead. "As long as you still give your body to me." He winked and continued perusing the aisle with Locksie lagging behind him.

This was going to be harder than Locksie thought.

"How about this one?" Dawson held up the movie *Smokin' Aces*.

After reading the cover, Locksie turned up her nose. "Nah, I don't want to sit and watch a movie with nothing but cussin' and violence in it."

"You're kidding, right? That's coming from the girl who not too long ago sat and laughed her tail off at the movie *Harlem Nights* with Eddie Murphy, Red Foxx, Richard Pryor, and Della Reese; the most filthy mouths in movie history ever."

"That was then, this is now," Locksie reasoned. "Look, how about this one?" She held up *Pink Panther* with Beyoncé and Steve Martin.

"Girl, you trippin'. Put that back and let's get this one and go." Dawson took the DVD out of his girlfriend's hands, put it back on the shelf and headed toward the counter with *Smokin' Aces* in hand. "I'm sure you ain't gon' go to hell just for watching an R-rated movie."

Locksie thought that perhaps Dawson was right. It was just a movie. Besides, God didn't expect her to change everything and be perfect overnight, did He? On that thought. Locksie joined Dawson in line as they purchased the DVD.

After leaving Best Buy, Locksie and Dawson stopped and picked up something to eat and then headed home to enjoy their flick.

"Man, this movie is wild," Dawson exclaimed as he licked the garlic sauce from the chicken off his fingers.

He was enjoying the movie far more than Locksie. For some reason, she felt as though she should have been watching *Passion of the Christ* or something. Now that she was saved, she just didn't feel as though she should do some of the things she used to do, watch some of the movies she used to watch, say some of the things she used to say. She just felt different—new. Now if she could only convince the old her that it had been replaced, and even then, she could only hope that it would pack up and leave willingly.

*   *   *

"You all right in there?" Dawson asked from the other side of the bathroom door. "You've been in the bathroom all night."

"Oh, yeah, I'm fine," Locksie answered nervously, startled by Dawson's pounding. She had been sitting on the toilet the last half hour. She wasn't using the bathroom; just sitting on the toiled lid, hoping that if she stayed in the bathroom long enough, Dawson would fall off to sleep and she wouldn't have to worry about him trying to get sex from her. If the rated R movie hadn't reserved her a seat in hell, the act of fornication would definitely get her in the VIP section.

"You sure?"

"Yeah, I'm sure. I just don't think the chicken agreed with me is all."

"Aw, come on out here, baby, and let me rub your belly."

Great! My plan backfired. Now he wants to rub on me. "Just a minute, honey."

"All right. I'll go downstairs and see if we have any sick pop," Dawson said, referring to ginger ale.

Locksie gave Dawson a half-hearted, "Thank you."

She flushed the toilet and ran some water as if she was washing her hands. She then climbed into the bed. Dawson returned with a glass of ginger ale in hand. He climbed into the bed next to her and handed it to her.

Locksie faked a moan and then took a sip of the pop before setting the glass down on her night stand.

"Feel better?" Dawson asked.

"Yes, thank you."

The room was lit only by the glow from the television that was turned down near mute, which was how the two always fell off to sleep.

"I know how to make you feel better." Dawson grabbed the remote and turned the television off so that they were now in complete darkness with the exception of the moonlight slipping in through the curtain cracks. The last thing on Dawson's mind was falling off to sleep.

Locksie laid stiff on her side as she felt Dawson's hand crawl up her leg. She had deliberately worn her cotton two-piece pajama set that she normally wore when it was that time of the month, instead of the cute little nightgowns she preferred to wear. She was hoping her choice in wardrobe would send up a red flag to her horny toad of a boyfriend, but it did no such a thing.

"You feel so soft," Dawson moaned in her ear. His lips against her lobe sent chills up her spine. The next thing she knew, his hand was in a warm place. A moan of her own escaped her lips, and it wasn't a fake one this time.

"Dawson," she whimpered as her eyes closed.

He continued to caress her. "God, you feel so good."

Suddenly, Locksie's eyes snapped open. She thought about God and how she had forgotten all about Him just that quickly. Earlier she had said "yes" to God and now she was saying "yes" to sin. That couldn't be right.

Before Locksie realized it, she had pushed Dawson away from her and sat up in the bed. "Dawson, I . . . I . . . I can't."

He looked her up and down. "Oh, snap. The pajamas. It's that time of the month?"

Locksie could have easily played along with it and pretended to be on her period. That would have given her at least five to seven more days. But she knew it wouldn't get any easier, so she decided to just get it over with.

"No, I'm not on my period." Locksie sighed, looking away from Dawson.

"What is it then? Oh, wait, let me guess. You're saved now?" Dawson spit venom with his words.

She tried to think of words to calm Dawson and make this transition more comfortable for him, but then she realized that this wasn't about him. "Yes, it's because I'm saved," Locksie said proudly, laced with a little bit of authority. "I'd think you'd be happy for me, not angry at me."

"I am happy for you. You want to change for the better. That's cool, but where does that leave me? Where does that leave us?"

Locksie was speechless. She hadn't included Dawson in the equation when she made the journey down to the altar to get saved. All she could think about was living for God.

"Well, I tell you where that leaves me tonight—on the couch!" Dawson got out of the bed and angrily snatched the top cover, grabbed a pillow and then stormed out of the room, slamming the door behind him.

Locksie's eyes watered because not only did she feel as though Dawson had slammed the door closed on her, but it felt as if he was slamming his heart closed on her as well.

This was too hard for Locksie, this being saved

stuff and changing her life. Instructions should have come along with being saved, Locksie thought as she caught the first tear that dropped down her face. Then she realized that there were instructions. She hurriedly turned on the lamp on her nightstand and then pulled open the nightstand drawer.

It was there, just where she had last seen it. Locksie pulled out the Kings James version of the Bible her mother had given her when she had sent her off to college. She had never even opened it—not once.

After fluffing up her pillow and crawling under the sheets, Locksie sat with the closed Bible in her lap.

"Where should I even start?" she asked herself. She opened it up to the book of Genesis, chapter one, figuring she might as well start at the beginning.

For I already know your ending, God spoke.

"Ten more, nine more, eight more, seven more . . ."

Drake watched from the piece of exercise equipment he had been working on as his brother huffed and puffed, pushing himself to extremes. "Dude, don't overdo it."

"Three, two, one . . . ahhhhhh!" Dawson screamed as his overexerted biceps roared with pain after pushing that last set of presses.

"Killing yourself trying to tone up your body ain't gonna get you laid," Drake just came out and said. "If anything, you're going to strain yourself and it's not going to work anyhow."

"Is that all you got to say? Oh, wait a minute. I almost forgot—you're saved too. That means you're on Locksie's side. Guess I won't bump into either one of you in hell." Drake ignored his brother's sarcasm. "So, I'm right. You don't have nothin' to say?"

"Dawson, it's not like I don't have anything to say. It's just that it's difficult to try to explain the war to someone who hasn't even fought in a battle. Walking with Christ is a journey that unless you are involved in that same journey yourself, you can't possibly understand it."

"But dig, li'l bro. I think she's taking it a step too far, like hearing voices or something, because one minute she was all into it—you know, moaning and carrying on—and then out of nowhere she just jumps up talking about 'No, I can't. Stop it.' Man, that's crazy."

"It's crazy to you, but what is happening is that the Holy Spirit is convicting her for even thinking about committing sin. So, in a sense, she is hearing a voice; the voice of God."

Dawson just sat there shaking his head. "I can't believe she ran off and got saved. She didn't even ask me or take my feelings about this into consideration. I mean, if I wanted a church girl, I would have gone out and got one."

"It's not about you, bro. It's about—"

"Look, man, it's almost time for my ten o'clock," Dawson said to Drake as he got up from the bench press. He wasn't trying to pick up what Dawson was about to put down. "I'm funky as I don't know what. She's liable to fire me for offending her with such an odor."

"All right then, man. I'ma go home and shower

up before I go into the office." Drake gave his brother some dap and then pulled him in for a quick hug. "P-U. You right." He waved his hand in front of his turned-up nose. "You do need to shower."

"Oh, and believe you me when I say I'm going to take one. A cold one."

It was ten o'clock A.M. on the nose when Dawson exited the men's locker room, and just like clockwork, his client was walking through the gym door.

"Dawson, my own personal body sculptor, don't go easy on me," his client greeted him. "I think I gained a pound or two over the weekend." She patted her flat tummy after removing the jacket to her sweatsuit.

Dawson had never noticed before just how sculptured his client's body was becoming. Her firm breasts, small waist and tight buttocks were near perfect. For lack of more diplomatic words, she was looking darn sexy to Dawson. Before now, Dawson couldn't recall if he had ever thought that any of his clients were sexy. He always looked at them as the product of his craft . . . the same way a writer would look at their finished book—a masterpiece. But not once had he ever looked at one of his clients sexually. But then again, before now he never had a reason. Looks like a lot of things were about to change due to Locksie being saved. But Dawson's sex drive wasn't one of them.

"You ready to get started?" Dawson asked, clearing his throat in the embarrassment of his client catching him stare at her figure.

She smiled at the unspoken compliment. "Ready? Humph . . . I thought you'd never ask."

"Well then, Peni, let's get warmed up." Dawson turned and headed for the indoor track.

Warm? Peni thought as she followed behind Dawson, gazing down at his rear end. *Feels to me like it's already hot in here!*

Peni had been utilizing Dawson's services faithfully for three months now. From the moment she laid eyes on him, she thought he was the hottest man she had ever met since Elkan, but Dawson had never even given her a second look. He had never even attempted to flirt with her by throwing out sexual innuendoes like some men tried to do. For a minute there she thought he might even be gay, or a down-low brother at the very least, but after catching him nearly drool over her—and that knot in his pants he tried to hide by quickly turning away—she knew the real workout was just about to begin.

Oh yeah, Peni thought, licking her lips. *We'll burn a few calories your way for now. But I got a much better idea on how to burn off some of these calories of mine.*

Chapter 24

Locksie could hardly sleep on Saturday nights anymore. For the last three Saturdays, she had tossed and turned like an anxious kid on Christmas Eve. Going to church every Sunday morning was now the highlight of her week. She had been doing everything she could to set the schedule so that she was off on Sundays or could trade days with another stylist. She woke up every Sunday morning with an expectation. And she knew exactly just what to expect—something from God.

Locksie had to admit, the fellow saints of the church weren't the nicest bunch, but she figured once they got used to seeing her attend regularly, they'd warm up to her. She could only hope. But in the meantime, she was hungry for the Word that the pastor, who was a wonderful man of God, preached every Sunday.

"Do you have to make so much noise?" Dawson said as he slammed his hand down on the clock to turn off the ringing alarm.

"Sorry," Locksie apologized as she stood up

out of bed. Prior to the alarm going off, she had been lying in bed, staring over at the clock every few minutes to see if it was time to get up yet. She didn't know why she hadn't just gone ahead and got up and turned off the alarm anyway. "I'm sorry, Dawson. I was trying to get over there and turn it off before it woke you up."

"Looks like you didn't make it, now, doesn't it?" Dawson sighed and rubbed his eyes. "I got a right mind to think you do that mess on purpose every Sunday, trying to send me a message. Well, you can forget it. I ain't going to church with you, Locksie. When you met me I wasn't going to church, so don't trip 'cause I ain't going now. The only reason why you go is because your aunt nagged you to death."

As badly as Locksie wanted to respond to Dawson with an attitude just as nasty as he had, she knew God wouldn't be pleased, so she pushed her flesh aside. "You wouldn't be so crabby about me getting out of bed and leaving you for a few hours if you'd just join me," Locksie said as she headed toward the closet. "And you're wrong. I'm not going to church because of my aunt. I'm going to church because of God." Locksie entered the closet and began searching for something to wear.

"Well, I ain't about to spend my only day off listening to some man stand in the pulpit delivering his interpretation of the Bible and telling me I'm going to hell for buying a lottery ticket." Dawson got up and went to the bathroom, leaving the door open while he did his business.

Locksie shook her head and chuckled at his comment. "Trust me, I used to think the same thing," she called out, "but it ain't about that. God is using Pastor Clevens to deliver the message he has for the congregation. Pastor Clevens sits down so that God can stand up. Pastor Clevens shuts up so that God can speak up through him. It ain't about the carnal man in the pulpit, Dawson. God is just using him."

"Well, since God is so good at using people, then I'll let God use you to come back and tell me what He told Pastor so-and-so to tell us." The toilet flushed. "What difference does it make who tells me, as long as I get the message, right?"

Locksie just chuckled and shook her head again, deciding she should probably just go ahead and accept that her efforts to get Dawson to go to church with her would always be a lost cause.

Last Sunday she had also tried to convince Dawson to go to church with her, but he had declined her offer. She could tell that her new interest—something he had no interest in whatsoever—was starting to bother him even more. She felt that maybe if she could get him to participate with her, he wouldn't be so disdainful of her attending. Because if Locksie wasn't mistaken, Dawson was jealous of her new relationship with God.

"Why you laughing?" Dawson asked, exiting the bathroom after doing a 'quick three-second splash of water on his fingertips' hand wash.

"Because of you," Locksie said, exiting the closet with a long navy blue dress with white polka dots on it. "You are too much."

"And so is that dress." Dawson chuckled. "I

forgot you even had that thing. I remember when your mama sent it to you for Christmas. You said you wouldn't be caught in hell in that thing. I mean, look at it. Looks like something Pollyanna would wear." Dawson exited the bedroom, heading for the kitchen, laughing.

Locksie gave the dress a once-over and then turned her nose up at the garment. Dawson was right. It wasn't the most attractive dress in her closet. Locksie returned to her closet and began digging through some other dresses. Most were too short, while others were long but had even longer slits practically showing her thighs. Right when she thought she had found a nice, simple white one, she realized the neckline was dang near down to her belly button. Anything decent enough to wear to church, she had already worn the last few Sundays. She couldn't even repeat an outfit because she hadn't gone to the dry cleaners. Some of the excitement Locksie felt when she had awakened was beginning to disintegrate.

"I ain't got nothing decent to wear," she mumbled under her breath. "I can't go to church if I can't find anything to wear."

A month ago, Locksie thought everything in her closet was sharp and had her name written all over it. But now she couldn't believe she had even left the department store with some of the revealing and provocative pieces, let alone worn them in public for the world to see parts of her body her own mama hadn't seen.

The ringing phone interrupted Locksie's clothing dilemma. "Hello," she answered.

"You up and getting ready?" Mary asked.

"Yes, Aunt Mary," Locksie said, rolling her eyes in her head. "You don't have to call me every Sunday to check and see if I'm going to church."

"I know, I know. Just making sure you didn't oversleep or anything. You'd be surprised at the stunts Satan will pull to keep you from going to church."

"I'm up, Auntie. But I'm discovering that my wardrobe isn't conducive to what one would wear to church. I should have gone shopping. Matter of fact, I think that's what I'm going to have to do. Maybe this Sunday I'm going to have to just pass on going to chu—"

"The devil is a liar!" Mary shouted, cutting Locksie off. "Don't you fix your lips to say what I think you are about to say. That's just the devil trying to give you an excuse not to go praise and worship the Lord. What did I just tell you? He got some dirty, sneaky little tricks up his sleeve, that Satan. You just put on some jeans and a T-shirt if you have to and I'll meet you at church."

"I ain't wearing no jeans and T-shirt," Locksie spat. "Look, I'll find something. Let me get off this phone and see what I can come up with."

Locksie hung up the phone and retreated to her closet, although everything in her, instead of going church, wanted to take the afternoon to go shopping for some decent church-wear. But she was not trying to hear her aunt's mouth, so she continued picking through clothing, deciding that she would definitely go shopping first thing after church.

A few moments later, Locksie came out of the closet with a purple one-piece pantsuit with an attached belt. She fingered the large flap collar, noticing there was still quite a bit of a dip down the cleavage area. *But this will have to do*, Locksie thought after looking over at the steadily ticking clock. *I'm running out of time.*

She laid her outfit down on her bed, went into the bathroom to get washed up, and then returned to her bedroom to slip into the pantsuit. "Now for my make-up," Locksie said as she scurried back into the bathroom. She began to apply light, smooth mounds of foundation onto her skin until it was spread evenly and just right. She had already applied her powder, rouge and all of her eye make-up; but she was mid-way through applying her lipstick before she had a sudden thought. *I ain't going to the club, I'm going to church.*

Here Locksie had been going to church Mary-Kay-cosmeticed-down like she was about to kick it. Maybe that's why some of the members had been acting the way they had been toward her. They probably took her for that wayward woman the men are being warned about in that one book of the Bible she had heard pastor talk about.

Although Locksie had enjoyed receiving the Word these past few Sundays, she hadn't equally enjoyed the reception of the members of her aunt's church. It seemed like there was a clique going on and one had to be the holiest of holies to get in. It appeared to Locksie as though no one smiled at her, and even when Pastor Clevens would ask the congregation to hug three people, she had to practically chase people down in order to get a hug. Maybe this was why—her appearance. Perhaps she had been going about this church thing all wrong. She hadn't been looking the part.

Locksie immediately turned on the faucet and began to scrub the make-up off her face. Once it was all removed, she simply applied a light coat of powder and some clear lip gloss. She raced back into the bedroom and retrieved her large silver hoop earrings from atop her dresser. After putting them into her ears, she admired herself in the mirror with a smile. But the smile soon faded.

"Who do I think I am, J-Lo?" She snatched the earrings out of her ears and replaced them with some dainty pearl ones. "Much better. Now I'm all set."

The night before Locksie had hot-curled her hair all over with beautiful ringlets that reminded her of that sexy Janet Jackson picture where Janet's hair was spiral-curled all over with her hands resting above her head and a man's hands covering her breasts. On that thought, Locksie made her way back into the bathroom and fumbled around in a drawer for her brush. She fanatically brushed each and every curl out of her hair; afterwards swooping her hair back into a tight ponytail and then twisting it into a bun.

"Now I'm all set." Locksie gave herself one last once-over in the mirror. "I hope this is what a Christian is supposed to look like," she said out loud as she headed out to church.

"Praise the Lord, saints," Locksie heard as she entered the sanctuary, two minutes after service had started.

The usher gave her a look of dismay for her tardiness and then held her hand out sharply, stopping Locksie from taking any further steps.

"You have to wait," the usher snapped. "Gotta let the Holy Spirit operate in the church without folks coming in late and interrupting."

Locksie became flushed with embarrassment. She could have understood if prayer was taking place and the usher didn't want her brushing by people trying to find a seat, but church was just now getting started.

The usher held Locksie at bay a little longer before dropping her arm and letting her by. *I could have worn my make-up and kept my hair curly had I know their attitudes up in here wasn't going to change any*, Locksie thought as she spotted her aunt Mary sitting in the pews amongst the congregation. She was dressed in her regular church clothes, which meant the dance ministry wouldn't be ministering today. Locksie made her way toward her aunt.

The pew where Mary was sitting was slightly full, but not to the point where room couldn't be made to accommodate Locksie. But the woman and her husband sitting next to Mary acted like they didn't want to scoot over and let Locksie sit down next to Mary. Finally Locksie had to whisper to them, "Do you mind scooting down just a tad? I would like to sit with my aunt."

The woman sucked her teeth and the husband sighed, but they scooted down—just a wee bit. Locksie looked at them as if to say, "You can't scoot down just a few inches more?" But the woman shot back with a look that said, "If your big behind can't fit in between there, then you straight out of luck."

By now, the first lady, who was sitting in the front row directly in front of them, turned around

to see what all the ruckus was about. After noticing that the latecomer was having people move
out of her way so that she could sit next to someone she knew, the first lady sharply said to Locksie, "We save souls around here, sister, not seats.
We come to be seated in the presence of the Lord,
not next to our sistah-girlfriends." She turned
back around and began praising the Lord with
the same mouth she had just hurt somebody's
feelings with.

Mary rolled her eyes and shooed her hand at
the first lady, telling Locksie to pay her no never
mind, but to go right ahead and sit down next to
her. By the time Locksie sat down, it was time to
get back on her feet again anyway, as one of the
ministers under Pastor Clevens began to set the
atmosphere by cheering on the saints, asking
them to give God some praise. Service was awesome as usual, and afterward, Locksie did just
what she promised herself she would do. She
headed to the mall.

Locksie drove to her favorite store, Macy's.
Once inside, she had no idea where to even start
as far as picking out church clothing. A rack with
a bunch of bright orange, yellow and green colors
caught her eye, so she made her way over there.
She found a couple nice pieces that she knew
would compliment her figure, but then she realized that perhaps that shouldn't be her goal when
shopping for "holy wear."

After about twenty minutes of deciding on one
thing only to place it back on the rack for one reason or another, Locksie was frustrated. A clerk
who had been on duty straightening up racks and
working the counter noticed Locksie's frustration

and decided to see if she could be of some assistance.

"Hello," the clerk said to Locksie, who had just slammed back on the rack a really nice-looking long black dress. She thought she had a winner until she turned it around and saw that it was cut so low in the back that her bra strap would probably show. "Hello," the clerk repeated again after getting no initial response from Locksie. "My name is Naomi. Are you looking for something in particular? Perhaps I can help you."

Locksie sighed, then realized the woman chattering about next to her had been chattering to her. "Oh, I'm sorry. Were you talking to me?" Locksie looked up at the clerk, who seemed a little familiar to her. Perhaps she had done her hair before or something.

The clerk smiled. "I was asking if I could help you find something in particular. You just seem so frustrated, like you're trying to find the perfect dress for the perfect occasion and aren't having a bit of luck."

"Well, you're partly right." Locksie thought about taking the clerk up on her offer, but then she realized the clerk would ask her what was the occasion. Locksie would have to tell her about her dilemma, being a new creature in Christ and not knowing what type of clothes to wear to church. God forbid this complete stranger find out that up until a few weeks ago, Locksie had been a sinner all her life. "But I think I'll be all right."

"You sure?" the clerk said with furrowed eyebrows. "You haven't seemed to be doing all right thus far."

Locksie giggled. "You noticed, huh?"

"I noticed." the clerk giggled too. "Really, I don't mind. So, where exactly do you need to wear the outfit you're looking for?"

"Wellllll . . . I'm not really looking for just one outfit. I, uh, well-uh . . . I guess you could say that I'm looking for an entire new wardrobe."

"Let me guess. You just lost a ton of weight and you're celebrating by treating yourself to a new wardrobe?" The clerk clasped her hands together with excitement.

"Well, uh, no. Not really."

"Oh?" The clerk seemed a little disappointed. "Okay, well then . . . You just got you a new man and want to show off a little for him, aye?" The clerk became cheerful again.

"Nooo," Locksie said, then she thought for a moment. "Well, actually, I guess you're partly right."

"I knew it. Where'd you meet him?"

"Uh, well, at church."

If the clerk hadn't been excited for Locksie before, she sure was now. "Church? That's great. The women that come in here shopping to look good for their beau usually met him at some club. I always say that's the last place I ever want to have to tell my children that I met their father when they ask me, 'Mommy, where did you and Daddy meet?'"

Locksie began to finger a cream pantsuit on the rack next to her. "Oooh, this is nice."

"Yes, it is. Your man of God is certain to adore you in that. Forgive me for getting off track there a moment ago. It's just that it's not too often I get to talk about church and God in the workplace. Anyway, back to you and your beau."

Locksie felt the need to tell the clerk the truth, not allow her to go on thinking that she was in some wholesome relationship with some man she had met in church.

"He's not really my beau," Locksie told the clerk.

"Huh?" The clerk had a puzzled look on her face.

"The man I met at church. He's not really my beau."

"Oh, I see."

Locksie couldn't really read the look on the clerk's face, but just in case she was thinking something freaky—like Locksie was dressing up for the preacher man, trying to get his attention—she wanted to nip that thought in the bud. "He's Jesus." Locksie's words were barely audible.

"Excuse me?"

"It's Jesus." Locksie further explained. "I just started going to church a few weeks ago and most of the clothes in my closet aren't really, you know, church appropriate. I haven't been to church since I was a little girl back living with my mama, so I just don't know . . ."

The clerk smiled and shook her head. "Mm-hmm. Well, not to worry because I've met your kind too."

"My kind?" Locksie was confused.

"Yep, women who were used to dressing for a man and now want to dress for the Lord. Well, amen, hallelujah."

Locksie smiled and relaxed her shoulders. She felt as if the weight of the world had been lifted from her shoulders.

"First of all, I understand where you're coming

from. I've been saved for the last fifteen years, and I was once in the same boat. But don't think for one minute that a Christian looks a certain way. God knows your insides no matter what you're wearing on the outside. Now, I know churches like that saying, 'come as you are.' And I believe in that, but I also believe in giving God your best. So, when you were in the world and you gave the devil your best by dressing to the nines to go out to the bars, then I think you should give God that same best." The clerk looked over at the counter and noticed a woman ready to check out. "Let me take care of that customer over there and then I promise I'll be back to help you pick out some things I think you'll really feel comfortable in."

"Thank you."

After the clerk returned, she and Locksie picked out four really nice outfits. Locksie was glad that this particular clerk just happened to be working and able to not only help her, but relate to exactly what she was going through.

"I certainly appreciate all of your help," Locksie said as the clerk finished checking her out and handed her her bags of merchandise. "I know you guys don't make commission or anything, so I really thank you for going that extra step."

"No problem."

"Well, thanks again." Locksie hesitantly waved goodbye and turned to walk away. She didn't know why, but she felt as though her business with this clerk named Naomi wasn't finished. She couldn't explain the connection she felt she had with Naomi after only spending forty-five minutes in a department store with her.

"By the way," Naomi called out. "What church are you a member of?"

"Well, actually, I'm not a member. It's my aunt's church."

"Oh, I see. Well, if you're willing to visit any other churches, I'd love to invite you to mine one Sunday. Matter of fact, I wrote and produced a play and my church is putting it on next Sunday afternoon. Maybe you could visit my church for morning service, we could do lunch or some-thing, and then we could go back and watch the play."

"That sounds great. I would love to come see you act in it."

"Oh, no, I'm not acting. God didn't anoint me to do that; just to write and produce. We have to know the limits of our gifts, you know."

"God has given my aunt the gift to dance."

"Oh, she does praise dance, does she?"

"Yes. I had no idea she had it in her. She never once mentioned that she was interested in danc-ing."

"Well, you know it's not always about what we want to do or what we are interested in. When God gives us a gift, we better use it or He'll take it back just as quickly as He gave it to us. Anyway . . ." The clerk took out a slip of paper and pen and began to write down her church information. She handed it to Locksie.

"Thank you." Locksie stuck the piece of paper down in her purse and then paused for a minute. "Just one question. The same thing I wear to your church service I can wear to the play, right? Or do I have to go home and change? I mean, you know I'm new at this fellowship thing. I'd know what to wear to a Tyler Perry play in a minute, but a church play . . ."

Both women laughed.

"No need to change or anything. You'll be fine." The clerk paused and smiled before saying, "You know, God is so divine. I usually don't work on Sundays because I'm in church. But the girl scheduled to work, her flight got canceled and she got stuck in New York. As a result, the airline is giving her a voucher for a free trip, and me . . . well, I got to meet a special woman of God. So you know what? I was supposed to be here today. You were supposed to be here at this very time."

Locksie shook her head and smiled. "Yeah, you're right."

Just then a customer came up to the counter ready to check out. "See you next Sunday, Locksie."

"Okay, Naomi," Locksie said as she turned away, but then she stopped in her tracks. As far as she could remember, she hadn't told Naomi her name. Locksie turned back around. A mischievous grin covered Naomi's face as she winked at Locksie, then proceeded to wait on the customer.

Chapter 25

"So, is my leg going to be okay, doctor?" Peni cooed as her bubble-gum-colored nails molested the bandage that had been tightly wrapped around her knee.

"Well, uh, um, yes, Mrs. Uh . . ." the doctor stammered as he got sidetracked by yet another one of Peni's flirtatious moves.

"Givens. *Miss* Givens," Peni enunciated as she squirmed on the examination table, the tissue paper scrunching beneath her.

The doctor cleared his throat. "Excuse me, Miss Givens. Uh, yes, you are going to be just fine. Try to stay off of it as much as possible. Keep it elevated and keep it iced."

"Stay off it for how long? It's Friday night and my girls are expecting me to meet them out at our spot later on." Peni used her best rehearsed whining tone, the one she always used on Elkan. The screech of it annoyed Elkan so much that he was always quick to give in to Peni's requests. It annoyed him because it was that same pleading whine that had landed him on top of her doing things to her body that he had never even done to his wife's.

"Well, if a night out with the girls includes any dancing, you might want to call them up and take a rain check. There'll be no dancing on this knee."

"Pooey," Peni pouted. "Oh well, another Friday night alone."

Just then the doctor's pager went off. "Well, Miss, uh, Givens, I've got to go," the doctor said after looking down at his pager. "The nurse will be back in with your discharge papers and your pain medication prescription. I'm going to suggest that you follow up with your family doctor in about a week or so. But if after a couple days the swelling doesn't go down and you're still experiencing pain, you should come back to the ER and let us check it out."

"Will do, doctor. And thanks for everything." Peni extended her hand to the doctor, taking his into hers and stroking the back of his hand with her thumb.

"Uh, well, uh, that's my job." The doctor turned to open the door and exit, but his palms were so sweaty that he couldn't turn the knob. Embarrassed, he looked back over his shoulder at Peni, who was watching him fumble, wiped his hands down his coat and finally made his escape.

"Dang it," Peni said under her breath. "I must have come on too hard and scared the little Doctor McDreamy off. He didn't even ask me for my number or anything." Peni made a mental note to tone down her advances next time so that she didn't come across so dominant. Today's men were often intimidated by a strong-willed woman who knew what she wanted. She'd have to play the coy little Paris Hilton role next time.

Peni waited a few minutes before the nurse finally returned. She went over the doctor's instructions one more time with Peni, and explained the dosage of her prescription.

"All right, Miss Givens," the nurse said, handing Peni a copy of her discharge papers. "That knee will be back to normal in no time."

"Thank you," Peni said as the nurse helped her off the table and into the waiting wheelchair.

"Oh, and your husband went to pull the car around for you, so he's waiting out front," the nurse said chart in hand.

Husband? Peni thought as a candy striper rolled her down the hall and out the hospital doors. *Oh yeah, I almost forgot,* Peni thought as she saw Dawson waiting for her at the exit.

Once he saw her, he got out of the car and ran to her aid, opening the passenger door and helping her out of the wheelchair and into the car. Peni had been so caught up in trying to rope in a fella with a PhD, that she forgot all about her other prospect. A smile crept across her face as Dawson gently released her down into the seat.

"Is that comfortable?" he asked with such care and attentiveness in his voice. After all, he felt responsible for Peni's trip to the emergency room.

After twenty minutes on the treadmill and thirty minutes of weight training, Dawson had Peni warm down with her usual lap around the track before a set of stretches. She had been doing so well that he pushed her for a second lap. It was during that second lap when Peni's knee gave out on her and she went down.

Dawson immediately scooped up the tearful damsel in distress and rushed her to the emergency room. He apologized the entire way for pushing her to do that extra lap. His guilt had kept him waiting for her at the hospital and now making sure she got home.

"I'm fine," Peni moaned in agony.

Dawson closed the door and then walked around the car and got into the driver's seat. "Make sure you turn over all of your doctor's bills to me," Dawson said, pulling off.

"Oh, that's so sweet of you, but you don't have to do that. My insurance covers one hundred percent of ER visits, and I don't have a deductible, so there's no out of pocket expenses. But thank you anyway. You are such a dear." Peni stroked the back of her hand up and down Dawson's cheek.

"Are you sure? I just feel so bad. If I hadn't pushed you to run that extra lap . . ."

"Dawson, honey, it's not your fault. I probably just lost my bearing trying to put an extra little twitch in my hips because I knew you were watching." Peni winked as Dawson looked over at her.

"Woman, you are too much."

"More than enough, maybe, but not too much." Peni looked down at her watch. "Oh, no!"

"What is it? You in pain?"

"No. I'm late picking up my son from the sitter. I called my job when I knew I wouldn't make it back from lunch, but I forgot to call the sitter. She's probably worried sick. I knew I shouldn't have used my lunch hour to work out."

"You had no idea you were going to get injured. Look, just calm down and tell me what time you were supposed to pick your son up."

"Over an hour ago," Peni said. "At five-thirty."

"Where does the sitter live? I'll drive you straight there."

Peni gave Dawson directions to her sitter's house. Just as they pulled up, Hannah was coming down the walkway holding Little E's hand. Peni opened the car door.

"I'm so sorry," she called out to the sitter, who was still standing in the doorway. Peni slowly slung her leg out of the car so that they could see her injury. "As you can see, I got into an accident."

"What happened? Are you okay?" the sitter inquired as she came out of the door and onto the porch.

"I'm fine. Just a sprained knee is all. I had to go to the ER. Sorry I forgot to call you."

"It's okay," the sitter assured her. "I left several messages on your cell and when I didn't hear back from you, I called his dad." She pointed at Little E.

Peni always left her cell phone in her car whenever she went in the gym to work out. Since Dawson took her to the ER in his car, she didn't have her cell phone to hear it ringing when the sitter was calling.

"Your leg is broke, Mommy," Little E said as he released Hannah's hand and walked over to Peni.

"Oh, baby, Mommy is going to be fine." She kissed him on the cheek.

"Since it's his weekend with his father anyway, I can go ahead and take him," Hannah chimed in as she walked over to the car and leaned down to speak with Peni.

"Could you? That would be great. I don't think

I'd be able to drive him over anyway, especially after I get my pain medicine in me."

"I don't mind at all," Hannah replied. "Come on, EJ. Tell Mommy good-bye."

Elkan Junior did what he was told then placed his hand back in Hannah's, and they walked away.

"Handsome little guy you got there." Dawson smiled as he watched them walk away.

"Yep. He takes after his father. You don't have any, do you?"

"Huh? What?" Dawson said, turning his attention back to Peni.

"Kids? You don't have any . . . but you want them."

Dawson looked back to Little E. He shrugged. "Yeah, I guess I do."

Locksie and Dawson had never really talked about having kids before. In all actuality, Dawson could have easily given or taken kids in their relationship. After seeing Little E, though, he could picture playing catch with a little Dawson. But at the rate of his and Locksie's sex life, he was having a hard time getting to first base, and everybody knows that it takes a home run to make a baby.

"I'm sure raising kids is hard work. You're lucky to be able to have a sitter and a nanny."

"Nanny? I wish. But don't think I haven't asked his father to include money for one in the child support."

"So, who's she? The white woman?" Dawson pointed to Hannah, who had just buckled Elkan Junior in and was getting into her car.

Peni burst out laughing. "Oh, her. She's his

dad's wife. And trust me, she can be black when she wants to. You know the saying that there is two sides to every story?"

"Yeah." Dawson nodded.

"Well, literally, there's two sides to her." Peni winced from a sudden sharp pain through her knee.

"You okay?"

"Yeah, but I think I'm going to need that pain medicine."

"I'll tell you what. Let me go ahead and take you home so that you can get comfortable. I'll run out and get your prescription filled and have one of the guys at the gym help me bring your car back to you."

"Dawson, I would really appreciate that." Peni touched his face and smiled.

"It's no problem, really," Dawson replied, staring into Peni's eyes.

Hannah, blowing her horn as a means to say good-bye to Peni, interrupted their moment. Peni turned to see the top of Little E's head and his little hand waving good-bye as Hannah pulled off.

"Point me to your place," Dawson said as he pulled off behind them.

Peni was more than happy to oblige. After all, if she could help it, she was going to get more than just a sprained knee out of her trip to the ER. She was going to get a man—Dawson, to be more specific. She knew that Dawson had this little girlfriend, but he rarely talked about her. But Peni had taken someone else's man before, so she was convinced she could do it again.

Chapter 26

Hannah sat at the desk in her home office, reading the email on her screen for the hundredth time, debating whether to hit the send button. It was an email to Drake, asking him to meet with her to go over some graphic ideas for one of her clients; at least that's what it appeared to be on the surface. But Hannah knew doggone well that she simply wanted to be in Drake's presence to see if she could see what Reggie saw, confirming his attraction for her.

"I can't believe I'm doing this," she said to herself as she rested her elbows on her desk and planted her head in her hands. She had wanted to send the email an hour ago when she had first typed it, but something was telling her not to.

She got up and began pacing as she continued talking to herself. "It's just a meeting—a business meeting. I mean, we'd have to meet again eventually. Better sooner than later. I mean, if we're going to do business together, we have to communicate." On that thought, Hannah plopped back down in her burgundy leather office chair and hit the send key before she could talk herself out of it again. "There. All done. It's just business."

Hannah's ringing cell phone interrupted her thoughts. "This is Hannah," she said into the phone.

"Hannah, hey," Drake's voice rang from the other end of the phone.

Wow, that was fast, Hannah thought. A smile crept over her face at the thought that Drake had just been sitting there waiting by the computer or the phone for her to contact him again. It boosted her ego to know that she could have that effect on a man.

"Drake, hi," Hannah said into the phone. "I didn't think I'd hear from you so soon."

"Soon?" Drake was confused, considering it had been more than two weeks since they had last seen each other. He knew because he had been marking his calendar as to when to call her again. He didn't want to contact her too soon and have her thinking that he wanted anything out of her other than a business relationship. Heck, deep down inside, he was still trying to convince himself of that.

"Well, yeah . . . so soon after the email."

"I didn't get any email. When did you send it?"

"Dang it," Hannah lipped, removing the phone from her ear. She knew that had she waited just five more seconds, he would have contacted her first. She wished she had listened to that little voice in her head that told her not to send the email. Hannah placed the phone back to her ear. "Oh, I just sent it about five minutes ago."

"Oh, yeah, well I'm sitting right here at my computer and—oh, wait a minute. It just popped up." Hannah could hear Drake mumbling the email. "Oh, that sounds great. Sure, we can get together. Actually, I was just calling to ask you a couple of things, but if you need to meet, I can oblige."

I didn't say that I needed *to meet*. "Fine. When and where?"

"Is this afternoon too short notice? My week is crazy busy and I think today is the only time I'll be able to fit you in so that I can give you the time that you need."

Hannah wondered what it was with this "need" thing. Had she come across as needy to him? Maybe Elkan saw her as needy too. Maybe that's why he cheated on her. Hannah's mind started going all over the place until Drake brought it back to their conversation at hand.

"Hello, you there?"

"Oh, yeah, Elkan, this afternoon will work fine." Before she realized what she had said, the words had already spilled from her lips. She had just been thinking about Elkan, so that's the name that came out of her mouth.

"Elkan?" Drake was puzzled.

"Oh, sorry. That's my husband."

"I see." Drake tried to hide the drop in his excitement at the mention of Hannah's husband's name. Once again, he wouldn't want to give her the wrong impression. "Well, uh, I'll see you this afternoon." He ended the call.

Before Hannah could beat herself up anymore, her phone rang again. "This is Hannah."

"And this is Reggie. How are you, apple juice?"

"Ugggggghhhh," Hannah screamed.

"I take that as a 'not so good.' Talk to me, Almond Joy."

Hannah proceeded to tell Reggie about the email to Drake and their phone conversation.

"Sugar cane, if you're already calling him by another man's name, that's not a good start for y'all's relationship." Reggie laughed.

"What relationship?" Hannah became very defensive. "This is just business. How many times do I have to say that?"

"However many times you need to say it to convince yourself. Calm down, cherry butter. I was just joking, but looks like I hit a nerve."

"I'm sorry, Reggie." Hannah exited her office and walked across the hall to her bedroom and flopped on the bed. "I don't know what's gotten into me."

"I must confess. It's me that's gotten into you. I planted a seed in your head and now the devil is watering it."

"Huh?"

"Me putting the whole idea in your head about Drake being attracted you. I'm sorry, lollipop. I shouldn't have been playing devil's advocate. You and Elkan have the perfect marriage now. He adores the heck out of you. And why shouldn't he? Sir Mix-a-Lot said it best. You got an L.A. Face with an Oakland booty." They both laughed.

"Reggie, you are crazy. I see why your wife loves you so much. You are like her husband and best girlfriend all rolled into one. No offense." Hannah knew how many times Reggie had been mistaken for gay.

"None taken. Just like you, vanilla swirl, being

able to pass in two different worlds has its advantages. Half my income comes from the gay community because they think they are supporting one of their own. They think I'm one of them down-low brothas or something—along with all these other people who judge me from the outside looking in."

"Does that bother you?" Hannah got serious for a moment. "Being judged by people from only what they see on the outside?"

"Not really . . . Well, yeah, sometimes I guess," Reggie confessed. "I get discriminated against by people who are homophobic or by the so-called Christians who judge me from the outside without getting to know me; without getting to know that I'm a happily married heterosexual man. Instead, they think I'm part of the abomination just because I'm not afraid to show my sensitive side. I grew up the youngest of five with four older sisters. They taught me how to cook, clean and dress coordinated and neat. They also taught me how to fight, so of course I knew how to windmill, honey." Again the two laughed, then Reggie got serious again. "Even the elders at the church I grew up in used to warn my mother that they felt I had a little sugar in my tank. That's why I stopped going to church in the first place." Reggie was silent for a moment.

"You okay?" Hannah asked.

"Yeah. I was just sitting here thinking. All the whispering the church did about me; if I did have a homosexual spirit in me, not one of them ever brought me up to that altar and tried to pray it out of me or help me get delivered from it. They never laid hands on me and rebuked the spirit.

Imagine if the church wasn't so quick to act like their minister of music or deacon wasn't gay and had the holy boldness to rebuke it. Kids wouldn't have to grow up subjected to the prospect of going to hell or the awful discrimination—especially the black ones. I mean, we're already discriminated against for our skin color. Why add something else on top of that, like being gay?"

"Wow, that's deep," Hannah said.

"Yeah, well. It's nothing like what you and Sarah Jane had to go through, I'm sure," Reggie said, referring to the little girl in the movie *Imitation of Life*.

"You know what, Reggie? You stupid and I gotta go. I gotta get ready for my date with Drake.

"All right, Tootsie Roll, I'll holler." Reggie hung up the phone, deciding not to call Hannah on her reference to her and Drake's meeting as a date, since she had been so adamant about describing their communications as just business.

Yeah, it's business for Hannah all right, Reggie thought. She was making it her business to finally pay back Elkan for his affair by having one of her own.

Chapter 27

"Don't even ask," Dawson said before Locksie could say a word. He had just come from the living room, where he had slept on the couch and flopped into his bed, knowing Locksie was no longer in it, but getting ready for church. It was too hard for Dawson to sleep in the bed with Locksie without trying to get some. On a couple of occasions, he had convinced her to do some other intimate things that brought him to that same climax, but lately his body was craving more; it was craving the real thing. He couldn't wait until Locksie got off of this religious kick so that things between them could get back to normal.

"I didn't even say anything," Locksie replied as she put on her earrings.

"Yeah, but you were going to. Every Sunday you ask will I go to your aunt's church with you, and every Sunday I decline."

"I wasn't even going to ask you to go to Aunt Mary's church, so now." Locksie playfully stuck out her tongue. "I was going to ask you to go visit this other church with me."

"See, there you go." Dawson chuckled, pulling the covers over his head.

"Come on, D . . . Okay, how about you just come to the play afterwards with me?"

Dawson peeped his head from under the cover. "Is Madea going to be in it?"

"Dawson!"

"Then nope." He covered his head again.

"All right, be that way," Locksie said, stomping off into the bathroom. "You can hide from me under those covers all you want, but God will be the first to pull the covers off of you."

Dawson slowly slid the cover halfway down his face. "What's that supposed to mean?"

Locksie shrugged. "I don't know. I've just heard the pastor say it a couple times.

Dawson sucked his teeth. "See, you don't even understand half of that 'thee, thousest and say-eth' crap and you want to drag me into it. No thanks." Once again, Dawson was hidden under the cover.

"And hurry up back home." Locksie heard his muffled voice. "It gets lonely without you," he teased as a last ditch effort.

Locksie smiled and shook her head. She had to admit, as eager as she was to get to church, a part of her was just as eager to return home to her man.

"Oh, welcome, my sister," the greeter at the church door said to Locksie while embracing her with a warm hug.

"Thank you," Locksie said, returning the embrace. At first she was a little thrown off. The greeters at her aunt Mary's church had never once made her feel that welcome.

"Can I have a program?" Locksie asked the woman.

"Oh, baby," the woman said, "we used to pass out programs, but not anymore. We learned that it was a waste of paper because service never went how it appeared in the program. The Holy Spirit runs this show." She smiled and passed Locksie onto the arms of the usher, who greeted her with an even tighter and more loving hug.

"Welcome to God's house," the usher said. "Do you like to sit in the front, middle or back?"

"Anywhere is fine," Locksie informed him. At her aunt's church, the ushers just sat her where they wanted to. But this church obviously realized that no matter where the sheep sat, they would be able to hear the shepherd's voice.

"Good morning, sister. Oooh, I just love you," the little old lady the usher had led her to sit by greeted Locksie.

Although Locksie had never seen this woman a day in her life, when she told her that she loved her, Locksie believed her. She believed her because she felt it in her heart. "I love you too," Locksie replied from a place in her heart that she didn't even know existed; a place that had love for strangers.

With Naomi being white, Locksie had just assumed that the church was going to be filled with white people, but it was just the opposite. There were people of all races and nationalities there;

predominantly black, but still enough of a mixture to make a rainbow.

"Surely the presence of the Lord is in this place." The church began to sing at 11:00 A.M. prompt, the time service was scheduled to begin. During the song, folks still continued to file in, being greeted by the loving and serene tune. The spirit realm in the atmosphere was so thick that no one noticed the latecomers being ushered in, and they weren't disturbed and bothered by them.

As the words to the song Locksie had never even heard before began to fall from her lips as if she had written the lyrics and melody herself, she felt a tap on her shoulder. She looked up to see Naomi smiling. Just that quickly, Locksie had forgotten all about the fact that this was Naomi's church and she probably should have been looking to sit with her. But as far as Locksie was concerned, it was God's church, and she felt right at home in her Father's house.

After the song ended, morning prayer was said by one of the church leaders, there was a scripture reading, and then visitors were welcomed and asked to stand and have words. There were about ten visitors in all, and Locksie's turn to speak was last. As a child, Locksie had always dreaded this part of visiting a new church, having to stand and speak, but not today. She felt as if she was amongst long lost family members that she had been in search of all her life, and she couldn't wait to introduce herself to them.

"My name is Locksie, and I was invited by Naomi." She pointed to Naomi. "But I'm here visiting the Lord."

"Amen! Hallelujah," members said.

"Well, it's an honor to have you all here this morning," the leader, who was a middle-aged black man, stated. "I just love it when folks invite their friends to come get the Word. After all, when we were in the world, we didn't have no problem calling up all of our homeboys and homegirls talkin' 'bout, 'Meet me at the club, partner, and I'll pay your way in.' "

There were a few chuckles.

"Now, don't get religious up in here on me now. All y'all who ain't been saved all your life know what I'm talking about. Well, if we did all that for the devil, then we should be able to outdo ourselves for the Lord. Amen?"

"Amen," some shouted.

"On Saturday night, the same way y'all used to call up Quita, Becky, Maria, Tom, Pedro and Rayshawn and dem, y'all need to be calling 'em up inviting them out to church. Tell 'em to meet me at the church—it's going down." The younger members laughed at how the older gentleman had taken one of their hip-hop lyrics and flipped the script with it. "And to make it sound even better, make sure you tell them that there ain't even no cover charge to get up in here because the price has already been paid!"

Most of the congregation stood to their feet and gave up some hand praise.

"That's right," the gentleman continued. "The price has already been paid by the blood of Jesus. And tell 'em if they thirsty for the Word, drinks are on the house!"

Now the entire congregation was on their feet, and tears were even flowing from many eyes.

"Thank you, Jesus!" Naomi said. "You did it for me. You paid that price for me. You didn't have to do it, but you did."

Locksie wiped escaped tears after watching Naomi and hearing her words. Naomi had said them as if there was something about her life that she had been brought through that nobody knew about but Jesus. There was such intimacy in her tone. Locksie wanted that. She looked at Naomi and wanted in her heart for Christ what Naomi had in hers. Locksie wanted it, and she felt in her spirit that right there at that church was where she could get it.

It was Locksie's staring at Naomi that jarred her memory back to where she recognized her from. She was that same woman Locksie had met in the parking lot of Macy's a few months ago, who had asked her if she was saved. Now, once again, God had placed Naomi in her path again. Locksie was convinced that there was no such thing as coincidence in life. God wanted her to connect with Naomi, and He made sure that it happened. Perhaps God even had something to do with Naomi knowing Locksie's name before she had even told her what it was. Locksie reminded herself to ask Naomi about that before the day was out.

By the time Locksie made it back home Sunday night, Dawson was nowhere to be found. She felt so bad. It was after ten o'clock. She had lost track of time and hadn't thought twice about calling Dawson to tell him that she would be home late and that he should probably go ahead and grab himself something for dinner.

After church, Locksie had lunch with Naomi before she had to head back to the church to set up for the play. Since Locksie would only have about forty-five minutes to spare, she decided to go back to the church, but instead of waiting inside, she sat in her car in the church parking lot, talking to Mary on her cell phone, going on and on about her beautiful experience at Naomi's church. Mary didn't have too much to say, but then again, Locksie was talking ninety miles per hour, not really giving her a chance to get a word in edgewise. Before Locksie knew it, it was time for the play to start.

Locksie couldn't believe that Naomi was responsible for such a wonderfully orchestrated and anointed production. Deliverance took place during the play, and souls were saved afterwards when the pastor allowed Naomi to have words and invite audience members who had not yet dedicated their lives to Christ to do so. Many of the souls saved were young ones. Locksie had watched in awe as Naomi used the power God had given her and had instructed her to use that night.

Afterwards, when people came forth and began to give Naomi praises, just like Mary would do, she humbly said, "All glory be to God!" She wouldn't say thank you or take credit for anything. Her eyes would just gleam at the thought of what her Father had just done with such a vessel. Locksie knew right then and there that she wanted to follow Naomi. She wanted to follow her to the throne of the God that she worshiped.

Before heading home, Locksie had a question for Naomi. "How was it that you knew my name before I ever told you?"

Naomi smiled. "I was wondering if you had figured that out yet or if you were ever going to ask me."

"Well?" Locksie waited curiously.

"You used your charge card. Your name was on it." Both women laughed. "See, sometimes God makes stuff real easy for us."

"I suppose He does, doesn't He?"

"By the way, how did you get a name like Locksie?" Naomi inquired.

"My mother named me that. She said that when I was born and the doctor handed me to her for the first time, when she looked down, all she saw was jet-black, curly locks of hair, so she named me Locksie."

"Well, it's original, and it fits you just fine."

Before saying good-bye, Naomi reminded Locksie that the doors to the church were always open and that she was welcome to come anytime she wanted. That went without saying for Locksie because she had every intention of returning to that same church the coming Sunday and as many Sundays as God would allow. Heck, Locksie figured she could even wear as much Mary Kay make-up as she wanted to this church. She could do so without one person looking at her cross-eyed. She felt that the folks at this church had their eyes on the Lord instead of each other. As far as Locksie was concerned, she had possibly found her church home, and with all the weekly programs and ministries they offered, it could very well become her second home.

Speaking of home, Locksie was surprised that Dawson wasn't there. It was late, and he had work the next day. It was unusual for Dawson to be out this late on a Sunday night. She couldn't help but wonder where he could be.

Chapter 28

"All I know is that at least that heifer is out of my hair," Hannah said as she sat in the salon chair while Locksie flat-ironed her hair.

"Well, I know you are glad. You haven't stopped talking about it since you walked in the door," Locksie said.

Locksie was happy that Hannah had finally returned her phone calls and accepted her apology for the terrible way she had acted and for the accusations she had made about her cheating on her husband. Actually, Locksie never really gave an official apology. Hannah just called her up and made nice. From what Locksie could tell from the conversation, Hannah still had no idea just what incident Locksie had been referencing when she accused her of cheating, so Locksie didn't even bring up the fact that she saw Hannah with Drake that night at the Hilton. She was just grateful that they were on speaking terms again; even though she wasn't one hundred percent certain that Hannah really wanted to make amends, or if she just wanted someone to gossip to. Nonetheless, Locksie had to worry about being delivered from her own sins before she worried about ministering to somebody else about theirs.

How Locksie saw things, it was just like the stewardess's instructions on an aircraft—when she tells the passengers that if they're in an emergency and need to put on their oxygen mask, put on their own first before trying to help somebody else get theirs on.

Hannah, on the other hand, was feeling brand new and excited about the fact that perhaps the thorn in her side, that baby's momma of her husband's, had possibly turned her attention away from making Hannah's life miserable to making someone else's life miserable. Hannah was on cloud nine.

"Can you re-do that piece right here?" Hannah asked, grabbing a lock of her hair that didn't appear to be as straight as the others.

Locksie took a step back and eyeballed Hannah up and down. "Excuse me? I wasn't finished yet. Now, how long have I been doing your hair? You know I always go back over it if I see a hair out of place." Locksie playfully popped Hannah on the head with the comb.

"Sorry, girl, I know . . . it's just that . . ." At that moment, Hannah decided against telling Locksie why it was that she was so concerned about making sure a hair was not out of place. Her friend had already accused her of the unspeakable act of adultery once. She didn't want to give Locksie the wrong idea by mentioning that she was on her way to meet a man other than her husband and wanted to look her best.

"It's just that what?" Locksie asked. Before Hannah could reply, the salon phone rang. "Excuse me for a minute." Locksie took the call while Hannah sat in the chair, admiring herself.

Hanna looked down at her watch and saw that it was 2:40 P.M. She was supposed to meet Drake at 3:00 P.M. She had lost track of time, running off at the mouth about Peni and the mysterious man she had seen her with in the car. The man had obviously been keeping Peni occupied because she hadn't been bugging Hannah or Elkan half as much.

Hannah had made a mental note a long time ago that whenever she was in a hurry, she wouldn't hold a juicy discussion with Locksie because sometimes Locksie would get so engrossed in the conversation that she would stop doing Hannah's hair to listen intensely or add her own two cents.

"Look, I gotta go," Hannah said, rising up out of the chair as she pulled off her cape.

"But I didn't get to go back through your hair," Locksie said as she walked back over after hanging up the phone.

"I know, girl. It's okay, though." Hannah grabbed her purse and pulled a fifty-dollar bill out and then handed it to Locksie. "Keep the change."

Locksie watched as her friend darted out of the salon as if it were on fire. Little did Locksie know, there was a firing burning all right, but it wasn't in the salon.

Chapter 29

"Hello there," Hannah said to the PYT that was manning the reception desk at Drake's firm.

The girl was so busy with the paperwork in front of her that she hadn't even noticed Hannah enter the office. Upon hearing Hannah's voice, without even looking up, she plastered the warm and welcoming smile on her face that she used to make every client or prospective client feel right at home.

"Oh, hello to you too. Sorry I didn't see you come in," the receptionist said.

"Oh, that's quite all right," Hannah assured her with a playful laugh and the shooing of her hand. She didn't know why she was acting that way. Perhaps the receptionist's mandated actions were contagious. "Anyway, I'm here to see Drake."

The receptionist's smile became more forced than ever, as if she really wanted to brush the smile off of her face, but knew she shouldn't. Hannah noticed the change in her facial muscles and thought maybe the girl had a sudden case of gas and was holding in a fart or something.

"Uh, Drake? You mean Mr. Trinity, don't you?" It was obvious that the girl simply did not like the way Drake's name so easily escaped Hannah's tongue—like she knew him all like that or something.

It was even more obvious that not only wasn't the girl feeling the fact that Hannah had called Drake by his first name, but she wasn't feeling Hannah. Hannah quickly recognized this and figured she had shown a lack of respect towards the girl's boss, so she quickly tried to recover. "I mean Mr. Trinity. Yes, that's what I meant."

In a matter of seconds, both women's smiles had gone from fake to forced. This wasn't going to be pretty.

A fake laugh was a prelude to the girl's next words. "I'm sure you did." The girl pointed to the black leather couch. "Why don't you have a seat right there, Miss . . ."

"Wells," Hannah finished. "Hannah Wells."

"Miss Wells, have a seat and I'll let Mr. Trinity know that you are here." She picked up the phone. "Oh, I forgot to ask. You do have an appointment with him, don't you?"

"Yes, of course. Drake is . . . I mean Mr. Trinity is expecting me."

The girl went to push a button, but then she looked down and realized that the light on Drake's phone line was lit up. "He's on a call right now. I'll buzz him when he gets off."

"Thank you," Hannah said. Just then her cell phone rang. As she pulled it out of her purse to answer it, she made a mental note to turn it off so that it wouldn't ring during her meeting. "Hello," she answered. "Oh, hi, honey, what's going on?" Hannah asked at the sound of Elkan's voice on the other end.

"Honey, I need you to—" Elkan started before the phone cut off.

"Hello? Hello, Elkan." Hannah removed the phone from her ear and then looked down at it. "Darn it! I meant to charge this phone." She looked up at the receptionist, who rolled her eyes as if to say, "Oh well, since you didn't, looks like you won't be talking."

Hannah put her phone down in her purse, hesitated for a moment and then asked the receptionist, "Do you mind if I use the phone to call my husband?"

The girl's eyes lit up at hearing that Hannah had a husband. Hannah figured that the receptionist must have thought that she could have been talking to one of her kids or something. Hannah noticed the receptionist's eyes wander down to Hannah's platinum wedding ring set, confirming her married status.

"Sure," the girl said. She opened her desk drawer and pulled out her cell phone. "You can use my cell phone. Mr. Trinity is funny about tying up the business phone lines for personal calls. I'm sure you understand."

This girl is a trip, Hannah thought. *Guess good help is hard to find.* Hannah accepted the girl's offer by taking the cell phone and dialing Elkan back on his cell phone. "Sorry, honey, my battery died," she said into the phone. "What did you need me to do? . . . oh, okay . . . sure . . . no problem . . . Okay then . . ."

At that moment, Drake came through the doorway behind the receptionist's desk. Hannah's eyes immediately locked with his. "Yeah . . . uh . . . you too," Hannah said, quickly ending her phone call with Elkan.

The receptionist looked at her strangely as Hannah handed back her phone. Hannah wondered if it was obvious to the girl that Elkan had told her that he loved her, and a lousy "you too" was all she had given him in return.

"Mr. Trinity," the receptionist stood and said, having not missed one beat of the way Hannah had ended her call with Elkan. "I tried to buzz you, but you were on your other line. "Hannah Smells,"—she looked at Hannah with her nose turned up—"has been waiting to see you," she said, deliberately mispronouncing Hannah's last name.

Hannah was going to correct the girl, but then decided to do what she had pretty much done her entire life when someone did or said something she didn't care for. She brushed it off.

"Hannah," Drake said. His eyes had a sparkle in them so bright that he seemed to look down and not directly into Hannah's eyes for fear he would blind her with them.

"Mr. Trinity." Hannah shook Drake's hand. They forgot that anyone else was even in the room as they just stood there shaking hands, Hannah staring at Drake and Drake staring down and past Hannah.

The receptionist was busy observing Drake act like a shy little boy who had found himself alone in the same room with the girl he had a crush on.

She knew the look. She'd possessed it herself the first day on the job.

"Oh, please, how many times do I have to tell you? It's Drake. Call me Drake. I insist," he finally said as the two still stood there, now holding hands—the shaking had stopped.

"Okay, Drake," Hannah accepted. As badly as she wanted to look over at the receptionist and toot her nose up at her, she didn't. She simply followed Drake's lead behind the cherry wood door.

"Oh, and Delilah," Drake said to his receptionist.

She stood with a huge smile on her face as she patted down the short little number of a skirt she was wearing. "Yes, Mr. Trinity."

"Hold all of my calls. I'm going to be busy with Hannah." Drake, along with Hannah, then disappeared behind the other side of the door, out of Delilah's view.

"I bet you are going to be busy with Hannah—gettin' busy," Delilah mumbled to herself as she began slamming papers around once Drake and Hannah were out of sight. "You think I didn't see that stupid little look on your face when you walked into the room and looked at her? Huh? And you're on a first-name basis with her?" Delilah continued by thinking all the words she wanted to say to her boss.

Delilah had been hired as Drake's receptionist when he first started the firm. As a matter of fact, it was only the two of them. He'd hired her through one of the local high school's Cooperative Office Education programs as a senior intern in order to save on salary. After she graduated, she stayed on permanently and began taking on the duties of a secretary. Eventually, she began to wear many other hats as well, and although she remained at the receptionist's desk, her duties varied and her paycheck reflected her true worth to Drake. Delilah never cared about her title with the firm. All she ever cared about was being close to Drake.

It became obvious to Drake after only a few months of working with Delilah that she had what seemed to be a little crush on him. But like all high school crushes, Drake knew that the sparks Delilah thought she was feeling for him would fizzle down and die out. In Drake's eyes, they had, but in all actuality, Delilah had just turned the flame down to an invisible simmer.

The phone rang and Delilah answered it, informing the caller that Drake was tied up for the rest of the afternoon. That call only reminded her of the fact that her object of desire was behind closed doors with a woman he was obviously attracted to—doing God knows what. Once again, she began slamming papers around while talking to herself out loud.

"It's just like a black man to reach a certain status on the corporate ladder and then go out and get himself a white woman. I thought Mr. Trinity would be different. Turns out he's a Mister Charlie just like the rest of 'em. For five years, I've been working like a Hebrew slave for him. Not once does he notice me. But Cameron Diaz walks up in here and he's all over her. With all these good sistahs out here, not to mention the one right up under his nose, and he's interested in a white girl? It's about time someone let these so-called brothas out here know that this jungle fever thing is played out. And who better to do it than me?" A sinister smile crept across Delilah's face.

Although Drake had never once shown any interest in Delilah other than businesswise, Delilah still held on to the one-sided infatuation with Drake, hoping that he'd come around eventually and take her on as a partner in his firm and his life. And she didn't care how long it took. Drake was worth waiting for. But now with this Hannah girl entering the scene, there were one too many chefs in the kitchen, and somebody was about to get burned.

"I'm so sorry for being late," Hannah said as Drake pulled out her chair at the conference table so she could sit down.

"Oh, don't worry about it. I was on a call anyway until I looked up at the clock. I came out to let Delilah know that I was expecting you." Drake pulled out his chair and sat away from the table so that he was almost sitting directly across from Hannah.

"You could have finished the call. I wouldn't have minded waiting. I'm sure Delilah would have kept me company."

Drake thought that he detected a hint of sarcasm in Hannah's comment. "Yeah, well, actually, it was just my brother. He's having woman issues."

"You have a brother? For some reason I took you as an only child."

"No, I have a brother. He's a bodybuilder." Drake didn't know why he always used the term bodybuilder instead of personal trainer. But in a sense, Dawson was a bodybuilder. He helped people build healthy bodies.

"So, he's the good-looking one and you are the brains." Hannah winked, not realizing she had this look in her eyes that put her comment on the verge of flirting.

Drake blushed. "I guess you could say that."

"I was just joking." Hannah crossed her legs. A little thigh fell out of her tangerine-colored skirt.

Drake tried to ignore it. "So, the lady has a sense of humor." But he couldn't. "I like that in a woman." He wondered where that comment came from. "Will you excuse me for a sexy . . . I mean a second?"

Drake darted out of the conference room, closing the door behind him. When he looked up, Delilah was standing there. "Oh, snaps!" Drake expressed his surprise.

"I uh, was uh, about to knock and see if I could get you and Mrs. Wells something to drink." Delilah tried to play off the fact that only two seconds had passed since she had placed her ear up against the conference room door to eavesdrop. The only thing she had a chance to hear was what sounded like her boss calling Hannah sexy. But for her, that was enough. More than enough.

"Yeah, uh, that would be nice, Delilah." Drake could feel the sweat beads his forehead had started giving birth to. "Excuse me." Drake brushed by Delilah and made his way into the men's bathroom next to the conference room.

Drake grabbed a paper towel and dabbed the sweat from his forehead. He then did what he had come into the bathroom to do in the first place. He closed his eyes, bowed his head and began to pray.

"Father God, I just thank You for the position You have placed me in; to be able to come into contact with individuals that will allow me to be prosperous and successful in this life You have blessed me with. Father God, I thank You for allowing me self-control in the relationships that might be formed as a result of these contacts. I thank You for allowing me to see the purpose of these relationships from Your eyes, God. Thank You for magnifying Yourself in situations so that my flesh may become microscopic. Right now, Father God, in the name of Jesus, I declare that my flesh has no control over my spirit man and that anything that is not of You be bound and sent off to a dry place, never to return again. In the name of Jesus I pray. Amen."

Drake opened his eyes, wiped his palms down his slacks and then took a deep breath before exiting the bathroom. As he was coming out, Delilah had just exited the conference room and was heading back to her desk.

"Hannah, are you okay?" Drake said, entering the conference room and finding Hannah wiping tears from her eyes. "What happened?"

Chapter 30

Although Locksie still enjoyed her morning coffee with her aunt Mary, ever since Locksie had joined Naomi's church two months ago and had managed not to miss a Sunday since, their relationship felt a little distant. When Locksie called Mary from the church parking lot that day after service, excited by the wonderful new church she had visited, she didn't really think about disappointing her aunt. Now she realized maybe she should have.

Mary felt the distance between her and her niece and thought that it might be hindering their relationship, so she decided that it was finally time to address the situation with Locksie.

"Can I ask you something?" Mary started. "And I don't want you to take this the wrong way. But I was just wondering . . . I mean, I'm so happy to see you into church and all, but I was just wondering why you didn't choose my church to worship at," Mary said, trying not to take it personally. But she had. She loved The Baptist

Saints Tabernacle. That's where she had given her
life to Christ ten years ago after her rape. It had
taken a near death experience for God to get
Mary's attention, but she hadn't looked back
since. Every now and then she thought about the
night she was beaten, tortured and raped for nine
hours. Locksie had even left her home in the middle of the night a couple of times when her aunt
had called her up afraid and crying after a night-
mare. But she knew that by the grace of God she
was alive. She'd watched Court TV enough times
to know that some women don't make it out of
those situations alive, and had it been up to the
perpetrator, she wouldn't have. But it hadn't been
up to him; it had been up to God, and He spared
her.

Pastor Clevens had heard about the incident on
television and went up to the hospital and prayed
with Mary. She got saved right there in that room,
not knowing if she'd ever make it out of the hospital. But Pastor Clevens and other church members of The Baptist Saints Tabernacle showed up
every day and prayed for Mary's healing until
she began to walk in it.

Mary knew that sometimes the church folk
there could be a little difficult at times, but as long
as God kept showing up at that church, so would
she. She'd hoped Locksie would have the same
outlook.

"You said yourself you enjoyed the service,"
Mary reasoned with Locksie. "You talked about it
for days."

Locksie pretended to take a sip of her coffee
even though she had already guzzled it all down.
This gave her time to think of an excuse for why

she chose not to go to her aunt's church. But then she realized that she didn't need an excuse. She should be able to worship God wherever she wanted to. "I did enjoy the service. It was excellent; truly wonderful. Your church is beautiful, Aunt Mary. I mean, whoever designed the building deserves an award. It truly is beautiful." Locksie beat around the bush until finally blurting out, "It's the people that were just ugly." Locksie took another pretend sip of her coffee as Mary waited for her to explain herself. "Don't get me wrong. I don't mean ugly in the literal sense— like their outside appearance. I mean ugly as in the way they were acting. The girl at the door acted like she was mad that I wanted one of the programs she was supposed to be handing out. The usher acted like he didn't want to take the few more steps to seat me a few pews closer than the one he had picked out for me. And during the welcoming of the visitors, them heifers only half wanted to look at me, let alone welcome me."

Mary shook her head. "Umph, umph, umph. I guess I've just been so caught up in getting the Word and doing what I'm supposed to do, that I didn't even think about how things might look to anybody else, especially visitors. I guess I'm just used to all them heifers by now." Mary tried to laugh it off, but Locksie could tell she was a little disturbed.

"I'm not trying to talk about the people you fellowship with, but it's just not for me. They didn't make me feel at home or welcomed. And they seem to get it honest."

"What do you mean?"

"That first lady; her tongue is like a knife. Trust

me, I don't know too much about the Bible. I've only read a few books, but I read the book of Ruth. And that first lady is certainly no Naomi that I'd want to follow."

Mary sat silent for a minute as certain situations that had taken place in church began to resurface in her head. She thought about the time one of the ministers told a choir member that she had a voice that only God could love. She thought about another time when the first lady had run off one of the members of the church by belittling her and talking to her like she was some chick on the street. And that was just one person. No telling how many other members the first lady had run off with that sharp tongue of hers. Because of some of the things Mary had endured in life, she was tough-skinned, and there wasn't too much the first lady, or anyone else for that matter, could say to hurt her feelings. But perhaps she should have considered other people who didn't have skin as thick as hers.

Mary knew God's Word and that it said to turn the other cheek. She couldn't help but reason, though, that in His house, perhaps some things were just unacceptable and should have been rebuked.

Up until now, Mary had turned the other cheek and a blind eye to some of the not-so-Christ-like characteristics of some of her fellow members. She figured that was just the way they were and that God would deal with them accordingly. But now that she realized there was a possibility that their actions were keeping members from coming back to God's house, possibly keeping souls from being saved, she knew it was time to do something about it. With the church meeting coming up, that would be the perfect time.

Mary couldn't get into the church quick enough for the 7:00 P.M. monthly church meeting. She marched in ten minutes early and sat right in the front pew, not the back pew where she usually sat after creeping in ten minutes late.

"Well, Sister Mary," First Lady Clevens said as she entered the sanctuary from one of the side doors that led to the church offices. "I'm surprised to see that you are the first one here. The mall close early or something?" She snickered. "By the way, that's a cute little number you're wearing. Shows every curve."

The first lady had always accused Mary of trying to purposely outdress her. She had even suggested to one of the Deacon's wives, who she had under her thumb, that perhaps Mary wanted to take her place as the first lady.

Usually Mary just brushed off the first lady's snide remarks, flattered by her jealousy instead of hurt by it, but this time, her flesh seemed to be dominating, and so she fixed her mouth to reply. Just then, several other members of the church started to file in. First Lady Clevens quickly turned her attention away from Mary to go entertain them and perhaps slice up one or two of them with her tongue.

"Hello, First Lady," someone said and then coughed.

"If you pray to get delivered from those cigarettes, you can lose that cough," First Lady replied. "Besides, how you gon' be up here waving your hand shouting 'holy-holy' knowing you 'bout to use the same hand to puff on a Newport? Anyway, sweetie. Hello, and I'm glad you could make it out to the meeting." She gave the woman a hug before all of her body parts fell to the ground after being sliced up like a character on *Kill Bill*.

The first lady thought that every skirt at the church wanted to bed her husband, therefore she had to break them down with words to make them feel like they weren't worthy of a man of his stature. No telling how many verbal battles she had with the women of the church in front of visitors or people who might have been considering becoming members of The Baptist Saints Tabernacle. Matter of fact, had a new visitor overheard the comment the first lady had just made, it might have affected their decision to ever come back again.

Before Mary knew it, the sanctuary was near full and the meeting was about to be opened in prayer. "Everything okay, Sister Mary?" Sister Aisha asked as she sat down next to Mary. "Your mind looks a million miles away."

"Oh, no, Sister Aisha. I'm just thinking about some things I need to speak on and asking for the Holy Spirit to give me the very words I need to say."

"Oh, Lord, if it's something you need to keep your flesh out of, then it must be good."

"Everything that's of God is good, Sister Aisha." Mary winked as the pastor instructed everyone to rise for opening prayer.

For the first hour, Mary just sat back watching the members go at it, unable to even agree upon the menu for the church anniversary dinner. No matter what subject was brought up, someone always had something to say about it. And then there was always somebody else who had something to say about what that other person had said. It all became a ball of loud noise and confusion until finally Mary couldn't take it anymore.

"Pastor?" She raised her hand. "May I speak?" she asked once he acknowledged her.

"Certainly, Sister Mary," he said, hoping she was volunteering to referee this fiasco of a meeting.

Mary stood up from where she sat and asked to no one person in particular, "How would you like to be remembered after your death?" She looked to her left and then to her right at the blank stares. "Has anyone in here thought about what the epitaph on your gravestone is going to read once you are dead and buried?" Mary turned around and faced the congregation. "Sister Aisha, is your gravestone going to read: here lies a woman who would lay down her life for anyone?" Mary looked out into the congregation. "Sister Beverly, would yours read: here lies a woman who was warm and loving to all she came in touch with?" She walked over and put her hand on the first lady's shoulder. "First Lady, would yours read: here lies a woman who had a kind and ministering word for everybody?"

The first lady cleared her throat and tried not to show the embarrassment on her face. She knew her gravestone would say anything but that.

"I'm not trying to call anybody out," Mary explained in a loving tone. "I guess what I'm saying is that we have to be careful of the things we do to each other and the words we speak to each other, especially in the house of the Lord."

"Amen," Aisha affirmed.

With her hand still on the first lady's shoulder, Mary said, "We are brothers and sisters." She looked down at First Lady Clevens, who stared back up at her. "You are my sister. I don't care what your birth certificate says. We have the same Father—our Father in heaven."

"Praise the Lord, woman of God," the pastor said. "Speak into their lives this evening."

"I love you all because my Father loves you. Because you belong to Him—and just like I was telling sister Aisha a minute ago, anything of Him is good. So, we have to begin to treat each other good. We have to do better, saints. We have to make our Daddy proud."

"Amen and amen!" a couple of people shouted.

Mary removed her hand from the first lady's shoulder and started back to her seat on the pew. Before she could get there, all of a sudden she felt a gentle tug on her hand. A warm, gentle spirit, almost childlike, was released from the hand. She didn't recognize the touch at all. When she turned to look, it was the first lady's hand she held in her palm.

"Thank you," the first lady mouthed to Mary as tears fell from her eyes. She tugged Mary closer and then stood up as the two embraced.

Not once had the first lady ever initiated an embrace with a member of the congregation. Never once had she just broken down and allowed room for deliverance. Half the time, members thought she felt that she didn't have anything she needed to be delivered from. While Mary and the first lady hugged, members prayed out, cried out and shouted out, for God had just moved up in there. A couple members still had the look of disbelief in their eyes that the first lady had actually been convicted and moved by Mary's words.

Mary, on the other hand, wasn't in disbelief at all. She had showed up at the church expecting something that would seem impossible to some and short of a miracle to others. Mary had believed God for it. *Nothing is too impossible for my God. Nothing at all!*

Chapter 31

"What time is it?" Locksie yawned as she looked over at the clock on the nightstand.

"It's almost eleven. I didn't mean to wake you," Dawson said after having just crept in the bedroom door. He began removing his clothes as he made his way into the bathroom. The door closed behind him and Locksie heard the shower come on.

Locksie sat up in the bed. "No, he didn't . . ." She immediately snatched the covers off of her. "Oh, I know this fool don't think he's just going to come waltzing in the house at eleven o'clock at night without even the courtesy of a phone call to say he was going to be home late," Locksie mumbled as she climbed out of the bed and walked straight into the bathroom.

"Don't you knock?" Dawson snapped. "I mean, you knew I was in here. How you just gonna bust in like somebody wasn't even already in the bathroom?" Dawson clenched his towel around his waist.

"Don't try to be funny." Locksie pointed, realizing that Dawson was simply throwing her own words back in her face. "It's almost eleven. I didn't mean to wake you," she mocked. "You act like it's eleven in the morning and not at night."

"And you act like you're my momma."

"Oh, now I'm acting like I'm your momma, huh?"

"Yeah, like you checking up on me. I ain't got no curfew."

Locksie took offense. For years she had made it a point not to be like some of those women who were always riding their men's backs; questioning their comings and goings and calling them on their cell phones trying to detect background noises so that they could confirm that their men were exactly where they said they would be. She had trusted Dawson, and now he was doubting her trust that she had worked so hard to make evident.

"I'm a grown man," Dawson spat.

His tone was one he had never used with Locksie. "Why are you talking to me this way, Dawson? You act like you don't owe me an explanation. You never come in this late, and if you do, you call. I was worried sick."

"So worried that you couldn't sleep, and that's why you were sound asleep when I walked through the door? So worried that you blew my cell phone up calling to see if I was okay?"

"I did call your cell phone. It kept going straight

to voicemail so I figured you had it off because you were still at the gym or something."

"If you thought I was at the gym, then why you trippin'? I was at the gym. There, happy?"

"I don't deserve this, Dawson." With hands on hips, Locksie cut to the chase. "Where were you? Who were you with? You're supposed to be my man."

"Oh, so now I'm acting like your man? Step off, Locks." Dawson brushed up close to Locksie. "The role of the jealous girlfriend isn't becoming."

"I'm not trying to be a jealous girlfriend."

"You got that right. The last few months you really ain't been that much of a girlfriend at all." He dropped the towel, making sure his manhood brushed up against Locksie before he got in the shower, closing the door in Locksie's face.

"I get it. It's the sex thing again."

"What sex? And I mean that literally. What sex?" Dawson began to lather and wash his body.

"So, is that what brings you home at night to me? What's between my legs?"

Dawson sucked his teeth. "Don't flatter yourself. I can count on one hand how many times I've been between your legs in the last few months. So if that was the case, you would have filed a missing person's report on me by now."

Locksie knew Dawson was just trying to hurt her. It was his flesh talking, not him, she told herself. "I love you, Dawson."

"You've got a funny way of showing it, babe."

"Let me show you in other ways. Right now . . . where I am in my life . . . I just can't . . ."

"Can't what? Make love to your boyfriend . . . whom you live with?"

"It's not that simple, Dawson. I'm afraid."

"Of what?" Dawson yelled out of frustration as he rinsed the soap off his body.

"Of God! I'm afraid of God! What He'll think! What He'll do!" Locksie confessed as tears streamed down her face. There. She had said it. Now she could stop dodging Dawson's sexual advances toward her or faking sleep when he got out of the shower. Now no more lies. She was a saved woman now and no longer wanted to have sex outside of marriage. "Dawson, I gave my life to His Son, and that's a big deal. I may look the same to you right now, but I'm changing. I can't say some of the things I used to say. I can't even read some of the books I used to read. I can't go some of the places I used to go, and I can't do some of the things I used to do. And premarital sex with you is one of them."

It hurt Locksie to say those words to Dawson. She didn't want to hurt him, but she didn't want to hurt God either. She walked over to the shower, opened the door and rested her hands on each of Dawson's cheeks. "Baby, even when I just think about you inside of me and how good you feel . . . it's like this voice begins to convict me. And no matter how bad I want you, I just can't—"

"Stop it!" Dawson pushed Locksie away and closed the shower door.

"I'm sorry, D," she cried.

Suddenly, the shower door flung back open. "You're sorry? You're sorry? So where does that leave me?"

Locksie shrugged. She wished she knew what to tell him, but she was a babe in Christ herself. She could barely make sense of it, so how could she convince Dawson?

"I love you, Dawson. That's all I know." Locksie gave him one last plea, hoping her words would melt him and he would try to see where she was coming from.

"Well, I love you too, Locks. But sometimes love ain't enough."

"What's that supposed to mean?"

Dawson turned off the water, exited the shower and grabbed his towel. "Figure it out." He stormed out of the bathroom.

"I'm sorry to come over so late, and without calling, at that," Locksie said as she brushed by her aunt and headed straight for the living room couch. "I just don't know what to do. I had to leave. I had to get out of there."

"What, baby? What's wrong?" Mary said, closing and locking the door and then joining her niece on the couch. "Is everything okay?" Suddenly, she became very serious. "Wait a minute. Did that fool put his hands on you?" Mary looked down at Locksie's pajamas and flip-flops. "Did you have to run for your life?" She stood up and began to walk away in a haste. "Well, I got something for him. Madea ain't the only somebody that believes that a piece of steel can keep the peace. You know what I'm saying?"

"Aunt Mary, stop it! No, Dawson didn't hit me. He would never do that."

Mary paused and slowly made her way back over to Locksie. "Then what else could a man have done to make a woman leave the house in pajamas and flip-flops?"

After swallowing hard a couple of times, Locksie burst into tears as she exclaimed, "Dawson's seeing someone else!"

"Oh, honey." Mary sat and put her arms around Locksie. "Oh, baby. It's okay. It's okay. Your auntie got this too." Mary eased Locksie from her arms and then stood up.

"Where are you going?" Locksie snorted.

"To get the other steel. My bat. The other woman don't deserve to be shot, but the tramp still needs her knee caps busted so that she don't go sleeping around with another woman's man."

"Aunt Mary!" Locksie said. "You're a saved woman."

"Yeah, but I ain't been saved all my life. I still know how to take it to the streets." She looked up. "God forgive me," she said as she headed toward her hall closet.

"Aunt Mary, stop it!" Locksie exclaimed. Just then Mary turned around to face her, stared at her for a moment and then winked. They both burst out laughing.

Mary rejoined Locksie on the couch and kissed her on the forehead.

"Point taken," Locksie said, feeling embarrassed by the way she had just stormed into her aunt's house in the middle of the night.

"Yeah, the same way I just overreacted on purpose is the same thing you're doing—overreacting. That man ain't even yours to be cheating on you.

I done told you that already. Here he's got you out in the middle of the night in your doggone pajamas."

"I know, Auntie. And trust me, I feel really silly now. But it's just that . . . I love him. And I can't believe he would do this to me."

"How long has Dawson been cheating on you?"

"I don't know."

"What's her name?"

"I don't know."

"Did he confess?"

"No."

"Did you catch him in the act?"

"No."

"Then how do you know that he's cheating on you?"

"I just do."

"Oh girl, get the H-E-double-hockey-sticks out of my living room before I go get my steel and use it on you."

"I know he's cheating on me. He didn't come home until just an hour ago. He didn't call. He didn't answer the phone when I called him. And the first thing he did when he did get home was take a shower."

"Locksie, the man is a personal trainer in the gym all day. He's supposed to take a shower when he gets home."

Locksie buried her face in her hands. "Auntie, I don't know if I can do this."

"Now, now, baby." Mary put her arms around Locksie. "It's going to be okay."

"I'm going to lose him. I'm going to lose Dawson."

"Dawson loves you."

"He just told me that love ain't enough. In so many words, he just told me that if I can't perform my girlfriend duties, if you know what I mean, then he's going to find someone who can. So, if he isn't cheating on me already, he will be. And I don't know what to do." Locksie began to weep, her shoulders heaving up and down.

Mary hated to see her niece crying, but she had to admit, she felt good knowing that Locksie was taking steps toward living the life God would want her to live. But she wanted to be sure that Locksie was saying what she thought she was saying, so she asked flat out, "So, you and Dawson have stopped having sex outside of marriage?"

"Yes. But don't go giving me too much credit because I tried to do it. My flesh wanted to do it. But I realized that no matter how many showers I took, I just couldn't wash away the sin."

"Oh, baby, that's because only Jesus' blood can wash away our sins."

"I know that now. But for so long now, like you said before, I've lived trying to please Dawson. Well, now I want to live to please God." Locksie began to cry even harder as she spoke. "Auntie, I just can't explain it. It's like He's everything to me. God is everything to me." A tear fell from Locksie's eye. "He's everything I touch. He's everything I see. He's everything I feel. He's everything to me. I want to live for him, Auntie. I love Dawson, and I would die for him. But I want to live for God."

Pulling her niece in close to embrace her, Mary said, "See, you've just answered the question."

"What question?" Locksie said, pulling away, wiping away her tears.

"You once asked me how is it that I always manage to bring God into everything."

Locksie thought for a moment and then said, "Because He is everything."

Mary nodded her head as tears fell from her eyes, joyous in her niece's revelation.

Locksie put her arms around her aunt and hugged her tight. Mary squeezed her arms even tighter around her niece. Then God embraced them both.

Chapter 32

"His receptionist had me laughing so hard, tears were falling from my eyes," Hannah told Reggie as they sat in Chipotle's having lunch. "Poor Drake thought she had done something wrong to me and that I was crying. You should have seen his face when he ran into the conference room and saw me wiping the tears from my eyes." Hannah began to laugh as she reminisced about that day in Drake's office.

Delilah had brought in some refreshments while Drake was in the bathroom praying. Out of nowhere, Delilah began telling Hannah some of the most embarrassing stories about Drake. Of course, Delilah was hoping to turn Hannah off from Drake and at the same time humiliate her boss, but Hannah found the stories quite amusing and cute. Especially the one about one of Drake's clients thinking he was gay because he had never seen him with a woman or known him to have a girlfriend for all the years they had dealings with each other.

The client, beating around the bush and hoping Drake would read between the lines, invited him out for business cocktails. Turns out, the meeting spot Drake's client invited him to happened to be a spot frequented by gays. Drake took what some might have seen as a bad and awkward situation, and turned it into good. One hour and two cranberry juices later, Drake found himself circled at his table and ministering to some of the homosexuals. He even invited one to his church, and eventually the man was delivered from homosexuality altogether. Of course, Drake lost the client's business because the client was too embarrassed to ever face him again. He just happened to be one of Drake's largest accounts. But in Drake's mind, he might have lost some money, but he saved a soul.

"That sounds like some fine mess I'd find myself in," Reggie said as he crunched on a tortilla chip. "Well, it sounds like that Drake sure does know how to turn lemons into lemonade."

Hannah gazed off as she sipped her drink. "Yeah, he does."

"Hello, Earth to Hannah. Earth to Hannah."

"What?" She smiled mysteriously as she continued sipping on her drink.

Reggie simply shook his head and said, "Umph, umph, umph."

"What?" Hannah demanded to know.

"You can try to fight it and deny it all you want, but cherry puddin' cake, you've been bitten." Reggie took a sip of his drink.

"Bitten?"

"Yes, bitten . . . and not just by any old bug."

"You mean the love bug?"

"Nope, by something for more dangerous and deadly." Reggie got in close and said in a serious whisper, "You've been bitten by the lust bug."

After lunch with Reggie, Hannah headed to Fiesta so that Locksie could do her hair. During the entire drive there, she couldn't help but think about what Reggie had said to her. Had she really been bitten by the lust bug? Was it possible that the thought of someone other than Elkan being attracted to her had her acting brand new? Could she be deliberately playing into it? Or even worse than that, was there a chance that she could act on it?

"Beep-beep!" The car behind Hannah, honking its horn to let her know that the red light had turned green, brought her out of her thoughts. She continued on to the salon, where she had to wait twenty minutes before Locksie could begin her hair. Fiesta was a walk-in only salon and didn't take appointments, and when Hannah arrived, Locksie was finishing up another client's hair. But as soon as Locksie got Hannah to the shampoo bowl, she gave her an earful on the current details of her and Dawson's relationship.

"Girl," Hannah said to Locksie, "did I hear you right? You're not going to give that man no more puddin' tang, ever?"

"Shhh," Locksie said, putting her index finger over her lips. "You heard me right. No more fornicating for me," Locksie said confidently, not backing down from her stand.

"But what if he cheats on you?"

"What if Dawson cheats on me?" Locksie snapped. "What if I cheat on God?"

Once Locksie realized that she had drawn the attention of a couple other stylists and customers, she cleared her throat and plastered on a fake smile.

"Sorry, I didn't mean to make you go off or nothing," Hannah apologized. "It's just that you been screwing Dawson for all these years, and now all of sudden you just wanna stop. And on top of that you want him to be okay with it?" Hannah sucked her teeth. "Girl, I wish I would try some mess like that with Elkan."

"Well, you don't have to. You and Elkan are married. He made an honest woman out of you."

"Still, Locksie, I don't know. Like I said, y'all been doing the do for this long . . ."

"Hannah, if I was a crack head deciding I didn't want to use crack anymore, is that what you would be telling me? Well, you been doing crack for all these years and now all of a sudden you just wanna stop?"

Hannah thought about it for a moment and then sunk down in her chair as Locksie began to rinse her hair. "I guess I never looked at it that way."

"Sit up," Locksie ordered, wishing she had never brought it up.

"Okay, dang. Don't take it out on me just because you ain't getting any." Hannah smiled. "Girl, I'm just joking. Don't get mad." Hannah held her hands up in defense. "I don't want you burning my hair on purpose or nothing like that."

"Girl, you crazy. You know I wouldn't do that."

Locksie began to lather Hannah's hair for a second wash and rinse. She watched the shampoo rinse down the drain as she silently prayed. *Jesus, help me. Cleanse away my sins and give me control over my flesh so that I may not commit them again. Jesus, please help me.*

Those were the only words Locksie could think to pray. Prayer was new to her. She hoped she was doing it right. She hoped that just simply crying out to Jesus was enough.

I hear you, daughter, God spoke.

Chapter 33

When Locksie rolled over and opened her eyes the clock read 8:22 A.M.

"Oh, my Lord," Locksie said as she jumped up. "I forgot to set the daggone alarm again."

That had been one of the perks of having Dawson lying next to her in bed. He had to be at work an hour before she even rolled over out of bed. She was a deep sleeper and sometimes never even heard him moving up and about in the mornings. So, once he had rolled out of bed, he would always re-set the alarm clock for her.

Locksie knew that she was going to be late for work today as she pulled off the covers. She did not want those girls standing outside the door waiting for her to unlock it so they could call the regional office first chance they got, trying to get her job. "Devil, you is a liar!" Locksie shouted to the air, determined to beat her co-workers to the salon.

She got out of the bed and headed toward the bathroom and then stopped in her tracks. "Aunt

Mary," she said out loud. "Let me call her and let her know I'm not going to make it over for coffee this morning." Locksie quickly picked up the phone from its cradle and dialed Mary's number.

"Aunt Mary," Locksie said into the phone receiver after Mary picked up.

"Yeah, sweetie," Mary responded, sounding a little groggy.

"You still 'sleep? You better get your tail up before you late to the rec."

"That's if I make it," Mary said. "My throat is killing me. It started hurting last night."

"That's what you get for not keeping your butt under that dryer yesterday, running out of the salon with that wet hair."

"I know, but I couldn't be late for Bible study. You know, if we can be on time for when man wants us to be somewhere, we can sho' nuff be on time for the Lord." Mary coughed.

"You sound bad."

"I know. I just took some medicine. The directions called for two tablets, but child, I took three. This vessel needs to be back up and working. We ministering in dance this Sunday and got practice this weekend." Mary coughed again. "I'm about to go put on some water for some tea and see if that helps. I'll still put on coffee for you, though."

"Oh, no, that's okay. That's why I was calling you. I'm running late this morning. I overslept. Unfortunately, I was late for Bible study. I had to clean up my station after you left. But it ended up going over anyway. Reverend Franklin got to preaching, we got to praising and then the Lord invited us into worship and we stayed there for I don't know how long. It was awesome."

"I know that's right." Mary coughed again.

"Well, you go on and make your tea and I hope you feel better. I love you."

"I love you too."

After hanging up the phone, Locksie got ready for work. She then grabbed her things, along with a couple of magazines she had purchased to place in the salon for clients to read, and headed out the door. Once in her car, she realized that she hadn't said a formal word to God that morning.

"Dear Lord, I just want to thank you for waking me this morning and giving me breath. Thank You for allowing every limb on my body to still function. Thank You for giving me a job that I can be late to. Dear Lord, I just thank You for being You. In Jesus' name I pray. Amen."

And God don't like quickies either. Locksie remembered her aunt's words. Although she felt her prayers were becoming more heartfelt, she knew that God deserved more than a microwave prayer. She made a mental note to spend her lunch break praying in her car.

Locksie put on one of her favorite gospel CDs and headed for work. She was playing Tye Tribbet's, "You're Everything to Me," so loud that she didn't hear the sirens of the fire truck coming up one of the streets on her right. Locksie made it past the intersection by the skin on her nose. The car behind her obviously hadn't heard the sirens either because the fire truck came inches from hitting it.

"Thank You, Jesus." Locksie sighed after turning off the music, stopping her car close to the curb and witnessing the almost deadly collision behind her from her rearview mirror. Locksie looked around to make sure no more trucks followed. She then quickly pulled off. Locksie hoped to get a head start before the fire truck that had to wait for the stunned driver to move his car out of its way went back in motion again.

"See ya, Aunt Mary," Locksie said as she passed the street she would have turned down to get to Mary's house if she had been going over for coffee this morning. In the next few hours, Locksie would regret missing her morning cup of coffee with her aunt.

"Dawson, what are you doing here?" Locksie smiled as she looked up at the clock in the salon that read 12:15 P.M. Perhaps he was there to surprise her by taking her to lunch. Three weeks with him sleeping on the couch as punishment to her for not giving in to his sexual cravings had put a strain on their relationship. Locksie had no idea where the two of them were headed, but she prayed to God every day that He would order her steps and direct her path when it came to Dawson. Perhaps today God was speaking to her situation by having Dawson show up at the salon. Perhaps he had come to his senses and realized that what they shared, and being obedient to God, was more important than sex.

"Hey, baby." Dawson's tone was somber, his eyes unable to meet Locksie's.

Her smile disappeared. "What is it?" Negative thoughts like Dawson coming there to tell her that he had found someone else crossed her mind.

"Locks, I, uh, was in the gym when the twelve

o'clock news came on. I rushed here as soon as I saw it."

All of a sudden Locksie's spirit became very disturbed. Dawson was speaking, and with his words, visions began popping into Locksie's head. She heard the siren. She saw the fire truck. Then everything rewound and she was having coffee while her aunt sipped tea. She saw the alarm clock that read 8:22 A.M. She saw herself placing the phone call to her aunt telling her that she wasn't going to make it over that morning. Lastly, she saw herself driving by her aunt's street waving good-bye.

"No," was the only faint word that managed to escape from Locksie's lips. "No," she repeated, each time louder than the last. "NOOOOO!"

"Locksie, baby," Dawson said as he tried to control his girlfriend, whose arms were flailing wildly out of control.

"Noooooo, not my auntie . . . Noooo . . . Noooo." Locksie began to swing at Dawson and hit him, pounding on his chest. She hated him right now. She hated him for the cruel joke he was playing on her by telling her that her aunt was dead. "Liar! Liar!" she yelled. "I hate you! I hate you! Don't you say that! Don't you say that my aunt is dead."

Dawson's emotions couldn't be described. Tears spilled from his eyes at the sight before him. Never had he seen Locksie in so much pain. It was a pain so sharp that when she touched him, it seemed to transfer into his body. He didn't feel her punches and blows. He felt the anguish and pain Locksie released at hearing that her aunt had passed away.

"I'm sorry, Locksie. I'm sorry," Dawson said as he continued to tousle with her until he was finally able to overpower her and lock her in a bear hug. "It's going to be okay, baby," he comforted her, kissing her atop her head as she fell limp in his arms.

It seemed like forever that Dawson stood there holding a weeping Locksie, who kept verbalizing that she didn't understand why; why her aunt had been taken away from her. Dawson didn't understand either, but he hoped that whomever this God was that his girlfriend had been chasing would provide her the answer.

Chapter 34

"All the guests are leaving. You sure you are going to be okay, sweetie?" Locksie's mother touched her shoulder. "You sure you don't want me to stay with you for a little while? I can see about taking off work."

"Yeah, I'm sure, Mom. I'm going to be okay," Locksie sniffed as she lay on her bed, resting her head on her tear-soaked pillow. "You go on and head back home."

The fire responsible for Mary's death actually wasn't that bad; damaging mainly the kitchen, not the entire house. With her bedroom being right next to the kitchen, smoke had quickly filled Mary's bedroom and that had caused her death. Locksie figured those pills Mary told her she had taken probably kept her from hearing the smoke detectors going off.

Since Mary's body had not been injured in the fire, she could have very well had an open casket funeral. But she had always voiced the fact that she didn't want money wasted on some drawn out two-day mourning fest. She didn't want family viewing her body, followed by a wake for the public, a funeral service and then a burial. She definitely didn't want the KFC bucket-toting mourners coming back to the church afterwards to continue mourning over an original recipe leg and thigh. Locksie granted her aunt's wishes by arranging for a cremation and a brief memorial service.

It was short, sweet, simple and memorable. The Baptist Saints Tabernacle praise dancers danced to Psalm 23 as a vocalist sang the words. The pastor read the obituary while a couple of church members said a few kind words. Hannah and Elkan were unable to attend because they were on a week-long cruise that they had scheduled almost a year ago, but they did send some lovely flowers.

After the memorial service, a few mourners stopped by Locksie and Dawson's place. Now that the handful of guests were departing, Dawson, Locksie and her mother were the only ones remaining in the house.

"Yes, child, God is surely going to keep you now," Martha said.

Locksie put her hand up. "Not now, Ma. I don't want to hear nothing about God right now." Locksie's tone was laced with anger. As a matter of fact, she had been feeling nothing but anger since hearing of her aunt's death. She was angry at God. She was angry at her aunt for leading her to this God who would do something so cruel as to take her aunt away from her.

Locksie's mother slowly removed her hand from Locksie's shoulder. "But, honey, Mary told me that you had been getting quite close to God lately. She said you found you a nice church home and everything."

Locksie sat up. "When did you talk to her?"

Martha chuckled as if Locksie's question was farfetched. "I always talked to her. Well, not always. At least twice a month, though. A few months ago, when she called to tell me about you, we started talking a little more."

"Hmm. She never mentioned it to me."

"Why should she have?"

"Well, as far as I was concerned, you two were sort of . . . I don't know . . . estranged. Just not as close as one might think two sisters ought to be."

"Well, some might say the same about you and me. That we're not as close as one might think mother and daughter ought to be."

Locksie cleared her throat and lay back down, defeated by her mother's comeback.

"Anyway, baby, I know how you must feel right now, being a babe in Christ and all, you don't under—"

"Ma, don't. There is no time length that I have to be a Christian . . . or to know God . . . to know that this whole religion thing is a joke. It's like, if I didn't know any better, I'd say the devil had something to do with tricking me into thinking that God was good—that He was real. Well, I see now that He's no more real than when you used to drag me from church to church looking for Him." Locksie sat up. "Is that what you were doing, Ma? Church-hopping, looking for God? Well, I get it now. I get it now, Ma, and I'm not going to get tricked the same way you did. I almost got caught up, but not now."

"Honey . . ." Martha reached for her daughter, but Locksie jerked away.

"No, Ma. Please, go. Just go. I know you want to sit here and tell me that God has His reasons for taking Aunt Mary, for taking my best friend from me, but there is no reason in the world I can comprehend. God's a joke!"

As Locksie's mother's eyes watered, she had no words for her daughter, so she did the only thing she knew how. She began to pray. "Heavenly Father, I just ask that You send the comforter right now to caress and keep Locksie during this time of mourning, and God, that you—"

"Stop it, Ma!" Locksie cried. "What part didn't you understand? I don't need you here right now, and I sure don't need you summoning down some man in the sky you've been chasing all your life. I'm surprised you haven't chased him away like you chased Daddy aw—"

"Locksie! That's enough," Dawson interrupted as he stood in the bedroom door. He walked over to a crying and trembling Martha and helped to lift her off the bed. "Ms. Winters, thank you for coming."

Taking Dawson's cue, Martha grabbed her purse off the floor next to the bed and allowed him to escort her out of the room. She stopped in the doorway, looked over her shoulder at her hurting child and whispered, "Lord, help her. Apprehend her heart."

"I apologize for how Locksie was talking to you," Dawson told Martha. "She's just hurting so bad. She feels guilty about not going to have coffee with your sister the morning of the fire. She feels that if she had been there, the fire would never have happened."

"No need to apologize," Martha assured him. "That's just the devil trying to take over her. Satan waits for a time like this in a person's life, a time when he thinks they believe God has forsaken them. The devil finds that opening, then creeps in and whispers lies in their ear."

Dawson looked at Martha as if she was a nutcase. Did this woman actually have the nerve to be standing in their living room trying to tell him that his woman was possessed by the devil? If this was the type of conversations Locksie had to put up with all her life, he could almost understand why she liked to keep her distance from her mother.

"Have a safe drive. You sure you'll be okay driving straight back to Detroit by yourself?"

"Oh, it's only three hours—four hours at the most. God will keep me." Martha hugged Dawson and went on her way.

Another car pulled into the drive as Martha's pulled out. Dawson didn't recognize the woman who got out of the car carrying a plant and a Bible under her arm. She walked up to the door and greeted him.

"Hi, I'm Naomi. I go to church with Locksie," she said.

For some reason, Dawson had just assumed Naomi was black. Locksie had never mentioned her being white. "Oh, yes, Naomi. I've heard about you." Dawson attempted to control his tightening jawbone and his furrowed eyebrows.

So, this was the woman who had tag-teamed Locksie along with Mary, convincing her that her life with Dawson would land her in hell. "Come in."

What Dawson really wanted to do was take the plant that he assumed was a token of sympathy for Locksie and tell the holy homewrecker that Locksie was asleep. Dawson hated that it was taking something like the death of her aunt to make Locksie see that God wasn't all that He was made out to be, and he didn't want this Naomi chick coming in trying to change her mind about it again.

As far as Dawson was concerned, he had been the one there for Locksie during this time of sorrow. He had been caressing her and holding her while her shoulders heaved as she wept. He and Locksie had even been sharing the bed together again. Although Dawson wasn't completely inhuman and insensitive to try to get any from Locksie, he knew that it would only be a matter of time before things would be completely normal between them again.

"Thank you," Naomi said, stepping inside. "You must be Dawson."

"Yes." *Who else would I be?*

"It's good to finally meet you."

Oh, yeah, a sinner like me? "Good to meet you too. Uhh, Locksie's in *our* bedroom. It's straight ahead." Dawson pointed.

Naomi proceeded to the door Dawson had pointed her to. Even before she got there, she could hear Locksie cursing God. Naomi smiled. Just as she had expected. She was walking into the situation the Holy Spirit had told her she would be and had prepared her for. She creeped into the bedroom and set the plant down on the nightstand without Locksie being aware of her presence. She opened the Bible to Psalm 6.

"Father God, hear my prayers as I stand in proxy for my sister, as I intercede on her behalf, God. These are her words that I speak on her behalf with my voice. *O Lord, rebuke me not in thine anger, neither chasten me in thy hot displeasure. Have mercy upon me, O Lord; for I am weak.*"

Locksie suddenly ceased her tearful fit and took in Naomi's soft, gentle voice as she continued. *"O Lord, heal me; for my bones are vexed. My soul is also sore vexed: but thou, O Lord, how long? Return, O Lord, deliver my soul: oh save me for thy mercies' sake. For in death there is no remembrance of thee: in the grave who shall give thee thanks? I am weary with my groaning; all the night make I my bed to swim; I water my couch with my tears."*

Naomi sat down next to Locksie and continued reading. *"Mine eye is consumed because of grief; it waxeth old because of all mine enemies. Depart from me, all ye workers of iniquity; for the Lord hath heard the voice of my weeping. The Lord hath heard my supplication; the Lord will receive my prayer.* In Jesus' name. Amen." Naomi closed the Bible then looked over at Locksie. She spoke no more words. She simply opened her arms wide and allowed Locksie's weak body to fall into them.

"I hear what you're saying, Naomi. honestly, I do," Locksie cried, still angry and full of confusion. She had received the scriptures Naomi had read to her, but she still had just one question she needed answered before she could even think twice about allowing God back into her heart. "I just don't understand one thing that I need you to help me gain some clarity on," Locksie said as she pulled away from Naomi and began wiping her tears away.

Naomi looked into Locksie's eyes as she waited for her to pose the question.

"Where was God when my aunt died?" Locksie said, returning Naomi's gaze.

With a loving smile on her face, Naomi sighed. *That's an easy one*, she thought before she kissed Locksie on the cheek and replied, "The same place He was when His Son died."

Her words were like a revelation to Locksie. It was just the answer she needed to hear in order to soften her heart and remove all doubt that God had not forsaken her. Tears, once again, flooded Locksie's eyes. "I get it," she told Naomi as she fell back into her arms. "I get it now."

Naomi held and rocked Locksie for the next hour, instilling scripture in Locksie's heart and soul, renewing her love for God.

Chapter 35

It had been two weeks since her aunt Mary's death, and Locksie's spirit was no longer weak and vexed. She missed her aunt dearly, but whenever she got to feeling down, she would remember that Mary was with the King of kings and the Lord of lords. She was in that place that Jesus had prepared for her. Before Locksie knew it, her grief would almost turn to jealousy. It gave her the strength to continue her walk so that someday she could be seated at His feet, praising and worshiping Him twenty-four hours a day with her aunt Mary.

After relaying to Naomi her interest in wanting to be a part of the praise and worship services, but not having the gift to sing or dance, Naomi had suggested Locksie join the flag worship team that one of the church members had just recently formed. Today would be Locksie's first day waving the flag. It wasn't anything rehearsed. She, along with the two other members thus far, would simply wave however the spirit moved through them during the praise and worship song selections.

The flag team waved the gold and purple metallic flags through the air to the melody of the songs. Locksie found the spirit taking over her as she went from just standing still while waving the flag to doing spins and turns with the flag.

It was during the second song when Locksie turned with the flag in hand only to see Dawson coming through the church doors. She was completely surprised. Her and Dawson's relationship had seemed so distant lately. They barely even said two words while in the same room together. To see Dawson walk through those church doors was an unexpected blessing for Locksie.

Although Spirit of Life Christian Center wasn't the type of church that made a big scene when someone showed up late to church, some members couldn't help but turn their heads at the late-comers, causing a domino effect for others to do the same.

When Dawson noticed Locksie in the front of the church, a huge smile crossed his face. He waved at her. Locksie couldn't help but be a little embarrassed that her man had showed up late and was waving her down, but at the same time, she couldn't help from smiling huge and flagging harder, now with something even greater to give praise and thanks to the Lord for.

After Locksie and her team flagged to three praise songs, a member of the dance ministry did a prophetic dance to "Conversation" by Quan Howell. After that, Reverend preached like it was the last sermon he was ever going to preach in his life. He preached hard. He opened up so many hearts and touched so many lives with his message on relationships.

"When you get into a relationship with someone and they already have children," Reverend Franklin preached, "it becomes a package deal. In order to have a relationship with that person, you must now have a relationship with their children as well." Reverend Franklin noticed a few puzzled faces among the congregation. "Just stay with me here for a minute . . . I promise you this thing is going to go somewhere." He continued. "For example, I'm gonna pick on one of the single sisters. Sister Lipsey, say you wanted to get into a relationship with a man of God that already had a ready-made family. You would have to have a relationship with his children. It would be pleasing to the children's father, and even help him and you to have a better relationship, if your relationship with them was a good and cordial one. Wouldn't you agree?"

Sister Lipsey nodded her head in agreement.

"Well, then I have just one question for you: Who's yo' daddy? I'm not talking about in the biological sense. I'm talking about the real creator of all men—the Father of all fathers. The one who is never delinquent on child support. The one that shows up at every graduation, function and event."

"That's right! Preach," members shouted.

"I think it's about time we all come to realize that if we claim to be the children of God, the one and only almighty Father in heaven, then in order to truly have a relationship with Him, we need to also have a relationship with one another. Like I said before; it's a package deal. You want a relationship with my daddy? Then you have to have a relationship with me. If you want to have a relationship with me, then you have to have one with my daddy, which is our Father in heaven.

"Let me say that again just in case some of you missed that one. If you want to have a relationship with my daddy, then you have to have a relationship with me. It works both ways, saints. If you want to have a relationship with me, then you have to have a relationship with my daddy! You can't have one without the other. So, if someone claims they want to be in your life, but they don't want to deal with the godly part of you, then you better reconsider that person's role in your life."

Locksie couldn't help but look over at Dawson, who happened to be looking at her as well. He had a look on his face that said, "I get it now." She hoped he had. She hoped that Reverend Franklin had managed to find just the right words to get through Dawson's head—his heart—that she hadn't been able to.

The way the reverend continued preaching, it was as if he was saying everything Locksie had been trying to tell Dawson, only she hadn't been able to articulate it in such a moving manner as Reverend Franklin. Coming from her, it sounded like fussing, complaining and nagging. Coming from the reverend, it sounded like gospel. But how in the world did the reverend know? How did he know Dawson would be in church that day and would need to hear those words spoken? Locksie was in awe. She could tell by the look on Dawson's face that he was too, as she caught him nodding in agreement with the pastor, allowing some *Amen*s to escape his mouth and even a tear from his eye.

If seeing all this transpire in Dawson wasn't enough for Locksie to shout about, she thought she was going to fall out when Reverend Franklin opened the doors of the church and Dawson stood up from where he sat.

"Won't you come?" Reverend Franklin asked. "If you don't already have a church home and you want to get closer to the Lord, won't you come?"

Locksie watched as Dawson's feet seemed to be mounted in cement, disabling him from moving. But every time Reverend Franklin said, "Won't you come?" it was like he couldn't control his feet anymore. They just began to make their way down to the altar where he joined church so that he could learn more about and get closer to the Lord, prayerfully, his next step being turning his life over to the Lord.

"Hallelujah," Locksie shouted out as Dawson reached the altar. "Thank You, Jesus! Thank You!" Naomi grabbed hold of her to help her balance on her feet.

At that moment, it didn't matter that Dawson had arrived late for church. Sometimes it's better to come to church late than never. As long as God is right on time, that's all that matters.

The following Sunday, Locksie was extremely excited to be attending church hand in hand with Dawson for the very first time. She got up an hour earlier than usual to prepare a nice breakfast of scrambled eggs, bacon, toast and hash browns.

She knew how sometimes if a person went to church on an empty stomach, the devil would use that to distract them from getting the Word, having them worrying about what they were going to eat after church or cook for dinner. She didn't want that to be a problem for Dawson.

"Get up, sleepy head," Locksie said as she walked into the bedroom. "Breakfast is ready."

"Breakfast?" Dawson said, surprised as he stretched his arms and yawned.

"Oh, shut up," Locksie said, hands on hips. "It ain't like I've never cooked breakfast before."

"Yeah, but I can't remember the last time you did."

"Just hightail it on out of the bed and come and eat."

Dawson got up, went to the bathroom, and then joined Locksie for breakfast at the kitchen table.

"This is good, baby," Dawson said as he shoveled down a forkful of eggs after Locksie had blessed the food.

"Thank you," Locksie said as she took one more bite of toast and then took her plate over to the sink. She had barely touched her food. She was far too excited to eat. Her prayers were being answered. Her and Dawson's relationship had a chance after all. *God is so good!* she thought as she scraped her plate into the garbage disposal.

"Hurry up so we won't be late for church," Locksie told Dawson as she rinsed her plate and put it in the dishwasher.

Dawson almost choked on his food. "Huh? Uh . . . what?" he said, scoffing down the last of his hash browns.

"I said hurry up so we aren't late for church, boy." Locksie kissed him on the cheek before she started off toward the bedroom. "This time you gon' be on time."

"Oh, baby, you go ahead without me," Dawson said as he rubbed his belly.

Locksie stopped in her tracks. Surely she hadn't heard what she thought she heard. Surely Dawson had been just as excited to go to church as she was after last week's awesome sermon. Of course, during the week they hadn't discussed going to church this Sunday, but Locksie didn't think they had to. She just assumed it was a given. They had discussed his first visit and how wonderful he thought the sermon was; how he felt Reverend Franklin was talking directly to him. Based on that alone, Locksie just knew he was going to return. Now she understood how disappointed her aunt Mary must have felt when she decided not to come back to her church.

"What do you mean, go without you?" She walked back toward Dawson.

"I think I'm going to pass. The game is coming on." Dawson stood with his plate in hand. "But check this out. Why don't I make dinner since you whipped up such a great breakfast?" He kissed her on the cheek, trying to save face as he set his plate down on the counter.

"You're kidding, right? I mean, Dawson, what about last week? You just joined church and all. What's it going to look like if you don't even come today?"

He shrugged. "I don't know. I mean, what? Do y'all take attendance up in there? Am I going to get suspended after I miss so many days?" Dawson joked.

"Dawson, this is not funny. I'm serious. Now stop playing and come get ready." Locksie started off again back toward the bedroom. She soon realized that Dawson was not behind her. She turned around to find him still standing in the kitchen, looking down. "You're really not going, are you?" The look on Dawson's face said it all. "I can't believe this." Locksie threw up her arms and let them drop lifelessly to her side.

"Believe what?"

"You! How you just gonna make your way down the altar to join church and then not even have the decency to show up the following Sunday after you join? Now, what's that gonna make you look like?"

Dawson paused for a minute. "I don't think the problem here is what it's gonna make me look like, because I don't care. I never have to see any of those people again, for that matter. I think the real issue is what it's gonna make *you* look like." Dawson pointed at Locksie.

She didn't deny his correct observation of the situation. "You're right about that! I mean, if I'm going to be made to look like a fool, I would like to do the honors myself."

"How am I making you look like a fool by not going to church?"

Locksie put her head down as tears began to well up in her eyes. She couldn't explain it to Dawson. She couldn't explain how many times she had taken their situation to the altar for prayer. She couldn't even explain all the praying she had done that he, too, might share in her joy of loving the Lord and going to His house to praise and worship Him and to fellowship with the body of Christ; that he, too, may learn the Word of God and know that there is only one way to live, and that it is by His will. She couldn't explain it. So, instead of trying, she wiped her tears and got dressed so that she could head out to church . . . alone.

Chapter 36

Locksie felt just awful as she pulled into the church parking lot without Dawson. All those congratulations and praises and prayers she had received for her mate, who she had been praying for and had put on the prayer request list to come to church, let alone join, were now all in vain. She had failed her church. She had failed God. She knew Naomi had led strangers in the streets to Christ. Locksie hoped God didn't expect her to perform such works, because here she couldn't even lead a person to church, let alone to Christ.

On numerous occasions, Locksie had prayed to God that He would bless her life in such a way that Dawson would line up with her and begin to seek God. She thought those prayers were starting to be answered when he joined church last week. But now she was beginning to think that it had nothing to do with God at all, but that the devil had played a dirty trick on her. What Locksie needed to understand, though, as she grew in her Christianity, was that a blessing delayed didn't always mean a blessing denied.

She parked in the very rear of the church parking lot, and turned the car off with a sigh. She didn't know what she was going to tell those people when she walked in there without Dawson. She thought about telling them that he got sick, or that he hurt himself working out at the gym and that's why he was not in church. She was immediately convicted for just thinking about telling lies. Then Locksie thought that maybe she should just go back home and try again next Sunday. That would give her an entire week to talk it up. That way, Dawson would know that he was expected to go to church with her. Perhaps that's where she went wrong this past week. She didn't mention going to church or even ask Dawson to go to Bible study with her because she didn't want to be pushy. But now she could see that wasn't the proper route to take. So, she convinced herself to come back to church next week, and this time with Dawson in tow.

Locksie started her car up and prepared to creep off, but then one of the brothers of the church tapped on her window and waved hello to her as he, his wife and two children made their way into the church. She had been outed; now there was no turning back. She cut off the car engine, and with her head down from shame and embarrassment, she headed inside the church.

"Good morning, Sister Locksie," the door greeter said as she hugged Locksie tightly. "God bless you, my sister."

"God bless you too." Locksie waited for the greeter to look over her shoulder as if to say,

"Where's that boyfriend of yours who took up space down at the altar to join church last week?" But that look never came.

Locksie took a seat toward the rear of the church, rather than in her usual second-row seat. She knew if she walked down the aisle to the front by herself, she would probably catch on fire with all the eyes burning her back. As one of the ministers began to exhort, Locksie silently thanked God that the flag ministry didn't have to flag this week. No way would she have wanted to stand in front of the church while everyone whispered about her.

Praise and worship was just as awesome as ever, but humiliation kept Locksie on her butt instead of on her feet. She figured the less attention she drew to herself, the less people would be reminded that just last Sunday she was hoopin' and hollerin' down at the altar about the man she was living in sin with possibly turning his life over to the Lord. Locksie had seen Dawson's joining church as a step closer to him eventually learning how wrong their lifestyle was. Then he'd surely propose to her and make her an honest woman. But somehow, the scenario just didn't seem so likely anymore.

After Reverend Franklin's sermon, "Removing the Mask of Guilt and Shame," Locksie sneaked out of the sanctuary and into the bathroom during altar call. That part of the program was just too much of a reminder of the cruel joke Dawson had played on her and God last week. At first she was just going to leave church altogether, but she knew the benediction sealed the service, and she wanted Reverend's message to be embedded in her spirit so that she could go home and meditate on it. Besides, she wouldn't leave the movie theatre without seeing the ending, so she wanted to show the head of the church, and the Lord, that same respect. She would get up during the movie and go potty, though; so that helped with some of the guilt she felt by hemming herself up in a stall until she thought altar call might be over.

Locksie had entered the last stall of three, put the toilet lid down, sat down and then put her head down as well. Everything was down, including her spirit. She wanted to pray. She wanted to talk to God, but she couldn't bring herself to do it. She knew the devil was right outside that bathroom door doing the victory dance, and when man gives Satan the victory, that's a point he could have given to God instead. Locksie was certain that she was the last person on earth God wanted to hear from anyway. The Bible says that Jesus wept. So did Locksie.

After wiping away her tears and making her way back into the sanctuary, Locksie lifted her hands to receive the benediction, then grabbed her purse and Bible to quickly head out the door. Thus far she had managed to remain somewhat invisible, now if she could just make it to her car without incident, all would be well. But that would have been too much like right.

"Sister Locksie!"

Locksie heard her name being called.

"Sister Locksie," the voice called again.

Locksie turned to see Reverend Franklin waving her down. *I couldn't even talk to God. What makes him think I want to talk to him?* Locksie thought as she dropped her shoulders and shuffled over to him. She made her way through several of the same ol' folks who always made their way down to Reverend after service, as if the benediction alone wasn't enough to seal in his word, but they needed to touch him—shake his hand or something—to confirm it.

"You gave a great word today, Reverend Franklin," Locksie complimented once she was finally able to get to him.

"I'm blessed to be used by God," he told her as he grabbed her softly by the shoulder and began toward his office. This was his sign to the others still waiting around to talk to him that he was no longer available. "Can I talk to you in my office for a moment?"

"Sure," Locksie agreed as they entered his office, where he went to close the door behind them. Before he could get it closed, his wife stopped it with her hand and poked her head in.

"Honey, may I?" First Lady smiled at her husband.

First Lady Deborah was a very fair and petite woman; totally opposite of her husky, dark-complected husband who stood at least six feet tall. She had a class about herself that exuded elegance. She always wore a nice suit, nothing too flashy in color, but instead something with more of an earth tone. Her naturally wavy locks hung just below her ears in a bob cut. Only when she pushed her hair behind her ears could one see the dainty little gold hoops with diamond chips she wore. Her nails were natural, none of that fake acrylic stuff, with only a clear shade of polish.

The only ring she wore was a solid gold wedding band. Her theory was that if she was going to be ministering to someone, she didn't want anything she was wearing to distract them from receiving the message; not clothes, not jewelry, not wigs and hair weave or big fancy hats—not anything. Granted, every now and then she did have to show off her latest shoe purchase from Nordstrom.

Pastor returned his wife's smile and nodded as if there was some unspoken secret between them.

Locksie looked from the reverend to his wife. "What's going on here?" Locksie asked as Reverend Franklin sat down in his desk chair and pointed for Locksie to sit on the brown-and-tan fabric couch across from his desk. First Lady Deborah remained standing. Locksie knew something was up just by that secret little grin of theirs.

Here it comes. I knew I wasn't going to make it up out of here without somebody saying something about Dawson.

"Locksie, you're naked," First Lady Deborah said ever so bluntly.

Locksie's eyes bulged as she crossed her legs and folded her arms across her chest. She looked down at herself. Yeah, the little tan top that she wore was sheer, but she had deliberately worn a black camisole under it just to be certain that it couldn't be seen through. Perhaps the lighting in her bedroom had deceived her.

The reverend chuckled at Locksie's physical insecurities. "What my wife means, Sister Locksie, is that you were transparent today. We could see right through you."

"Huh?" Locksie was confused.

"From the moment you walked through the church doors, you came in wearing nothing but the spirit of embarrassment, shame and guilt," Reverend said. "Heck, the Holy Spirit even made me change my sermon because of you. I had four pages of notes for another topic." He chuckled.

Locksie slumped down on the couch. All her dipping and dodging had been in vain.

"You probably barely got today's message because you were so worried about what other folks were thinking," First Lady Deborah said.

Locksie decided to give dodging the ball one last shot as she allowed a look to cover her face as if to say, "I don't know what you're talking about."

"Dawson, the young man you brought last Sunday who joined the church," Reverend Franklin refreshed her memory after seeing the bewildered look her face.

"Honey, trust me when I say that it is neither your burden nor battle," First Lady Deborah said as she sat down next to Locksie on the couch. "Take it from me, I know firsthand what you're going through."

"You do?" Locksie asked, her misery desperately seeking company.

"It happens at every church," Reverend told her. "The man of God delivers a powerful word. Folks get caught up and moved in the moment, or even by a song or praise dance. They join the church or profess giving their life to Christ, then they walk out of the sanctuary and back into the world, sometimes never to return to that church again."

"It's what Reverend and I like to refer to as a crime of passion." First Lady Deborah winked at her husband.

Locksie knew that playing dumb was useless. Her reverend and first lady could see through her charades. "I couldn't believe when he told me he wasn't coming to church this morning," Locksie decided to confess. According to First Lady Deborah, she was already naked; might as well take off her earrings and shoes too. "I mean, you saw him last Sunday. He had that same look on his face the first Sunday I came here—it felt like home." Locksie began to weep. "All that praying I did. I just felt so rejoiced. I kept telling the devil, 'I told you so. I told you God would answer my prayers.' Now it's all like some big joke."

Reverend Franklin spoke. "You can lead a horse to the river, but you can't make him drink the water," he told her. "Dawson is going to have to thirst for God. It's going to have to be a thirst so strong that he can't help but drink."

"Reverend is right," First Lady Deborah said, grabbing a tissue from the reverend's desk and then wiping Locksie's tears away. "Like I said, I know firsthand what you're going through." First Lady Deborah got comfortable before she began her story. "I was born on the church pew. So, when you hear folks say, 'I ain't been saved all my life,' . . . well, I have. Daddy was a pastor, Mama was a minister. Me and my brothers and sisters only had three friends growing up; the Father, His Son, and the Holy Spirit."

They all chuckled.

"So, when this fine little New York boy came strolling through the city on business, if you know what I mean, and caught the eye of a preacher's daughter, you know my folks, family and friends were fit to be tied. But I wasn't trying to hear it. And me, knowing the power of God, was just convinced that after a month of Sundays in my daddy's church, my little New York beau would be speaking in tongues in no time, getting my folks', family and friends' approval and change his lifestyle altogether."

"Did you get him to go to church with you?" Locksie was on the edge of her seat.

"Well, I did manage to finally convince him to come to my daddy's church. And let me tell you that Sunday was fire. My daddy's message from God had my New York stallion, on his knees, crawling to the altar, repenting in tears. Girl, I mean snot running out his nose and everything. I was like Shug Avery on *The Color Purple*. Running up to pastor talkin' 'bout, 'See, Daddy. Sinners have souls too." Once again they all laughed. "My folks saw something good in that New York boy of mine that day at the altar—an anointing on him is what they said—a calling on his life. And I was proud." Suddenly, a sad look came across First Lady Deborah's face.

"Then what happened? He didn't even bother to come back to church that following Sunday, did he?" Locksie sucked her teeth. "Figures."

"No, he sure didn't. And I was so embarrassed. So humiliated. Here I had walked around bragging and boasting, shouting 'hallelujah' and 'praise the Lord' and yet had to walk through those church doors the very next Sunday without him. 'Where's your so-called saved, little dope-slinging boyfriend now? Girl, he probably only put on that show last Sunday at the altar thinking he could get in your panties.' "

Locksie put her head down in shame. She, in fact, had given in to Dawson this past week. She hadn't had intercourse with him, but she had engaged in oral pleasures with him. He had convinced her that giving him some oral action wasn't actually sex. But now that she thought about it, she felt so stupid. She was a grown woman and fell for that little teenage crap. The devil had used Dawson to get her to go back on her word to God.

First Lady Deborah rested her hand on top of Locksie's. "It's okay," she told Locksie, almost as if she had read her thoughts.

"So, what happened to the New York boy? What was his excuse for not coming back to church?" Locksie asked.

"Seven to ten years," First Lady Deborah replied.

"What?"

"His excuse was a seven-to-ten-year prison sentence. That Sunday night after church, when he tried to tell his people that he was getting out the game, they didn't take too kindly to that. There were some deals that needed to be finalized. He was going to mess up a lot of people's money. But he refused to put off God for the game. The people he was dealing with told him that they'd rather see him dead. So, they tried to kill him. They shot and missed. He shot back and killed somebody. He got sentenced to seven to ten years."

"Oh, gosh," Locksie said.

"Do you know what ever happened to him?"

First Lady Deborah chuckled. "Do I know?" She leaned in close to Locksie. "Girlfriend, I married him."

Locksie looked over at Reverend Franklin, who was grinning from ear to ear. He stood up from his chair and walked over to Locksie and his wife. "So you see, Sister Locksie, you do what is right for you, and what is right for you is what God tells you to do. The good Lord ain't gonna steer you wrong. Pray and wait on God. Then you do what He instructs you to do in this situation. Just be obedient and trust in God to do His will in your life. Okay?"

"Yes, Reverend Franklin." Locksie smiled and exhaled. Reverend and First Lady's words were so comforting.

First Lady Deborah stood and pulled Locksie up with her. "Now, the next time you come into the house of the Lord, you come with your head held high, knowing that right now, you are only accountable for yourself. What another person does has nothing to do with you; that is unless you allow that other person to pull you away from the Lord."

"And that thing that separates you from the Lord is called sin," Reverend added. "What is in the middle of the word *sin*; spelled S-I-N?"

Locksie thought for a minute. "I."

"And that's the worst part about sin; that 'I' am usually in the middle of it." Reverend chuckled. "Don't be that 'I' in the middle of sin, sister."

Locksie's eyes watered. She could feel the Holy Spirit dictating to the reverend and first lady everything she needed to hear. "I won't, Reverend. *I* won't be in the middle of sin."

"Understand, Sister Locksie, that in this walk there is a cost," Reverend told her. "You might not always like what God says once you hear from Him. He might ask you to give up some things, and there should be nothing in this world you're not willing to give up for God, including your life." Locksie nodded. "So, you stay in the Word. Stay in prayer and allow God to direct your path. Allow Him to show you what goes and what stays. Who goes and who stays. And once He reveals this to you, be obedient and oblige Him. Do you understand?"

"Yes, Reverend," Locksie answered. "I understand."

She gave both Reverend and First Lady Deborah a hug and then made her way to her car. On the way, she thanked God for such a wonderful and powerful reverend and first lady. She thanked God for them taking her in like she had been a member of that church since it had been built, and for sharing their testimony with her. While she had God's attention, she prayed that He would do just what Reverend Franklin told her He would do; show her what and who goes and what and who stays. On the drive home, she couldn't help but wonder if Dawson would be who stays.

Chapter 37

"Thank you for coming in on your off day," Hannah said to Locksie as she finished up her hair by spritzing her cornrows.

"Oh, it's no problem. I had to come in today anyway to do a little inventory. I hadn't planned on doing any hair today, though. But this is cool. I know you are in Elkan's cousin's wedding and all."

"Yeah, and his cousin's stylist was supposed to do everybody's hair, but as I sat in that shop waiting on my turn and seeing all the jacked-up heads she had done before me, there was no way I could let her put her fingers in my hair."

Both women laughed.

"Was it that bad?" Locksie asked as she began to spray the Redkin Fresh Curls curl boost on the back of Hannah's hair, which she had left down to show off her naturally curly hair as the neatly parted corn rolls decorated the front.

"It was that bad." Hannah snapped her finger as if she had just remembered something. "Let me grab my purse. The rhinestones we are supposed to wear in our hair are in it." Hannah picked up her purse from off the floor and pulled out a small package and handed it to Locksie. "They have the Velcro thingies on them, so you shouldn't need any glue or anything."

"Thanks, girl."

"By the way, how are things going with your aunt's house and everything?" Hannah got cozy back in the chair.

"Oh, everything is going good. She had an insurance policy that paid off her house in case of her death, plus had another twenty thousand on top of that. We're using that twenty to repair the kitchen and the other areas in the house that have smoke damage." Locksie tore the package open with her teeth after unsuccessfully trying to open it with her slippery fingers; greasy from all the sprays she had been using in Hannah's hair.

"Elkan has an uncle that works on houses. I can get him to come by and take a look if you want me to," Hannah offered.

"Oh, that's okay. A member from the church she went to owns his own building company and they've already started working on it." Locksie turned Hannah around in her chair to face her and began placing the rhinestones in her hair.

"Well, that's good. What are y'all going to do with the house once they get it together?"

"Auntie, left it to me. Of course I already have more house than I need, so I'm going to put it on the market."

"You know my mother does real estate."

"I already have somebody lined up for that too. Girl, the bereavement committee at the church

Aunt Mary used to attend is on top of everything. They have somebody in place for any situation you can imagine deriving out of the loss of a loved one. They may not have been the nicest folks the few times I visited their church, but they are definitely about their Father's business."

"Girl, I'm glad everything is working out."

"Thank you."

"Is everything working out just as good with you and Dawson?"

Locksie sighed. "Girl, I'm praying and praying, waiting to hear from God like Reverend and First Lady told me to, but He ain't said a word." Locksie sighed again and leaned against her station. "He's back to sleeping on the couch."

"Does that mean you and him aren't . . . you know. He ain't gettin' no boom-boom." Locksie shook her head. "I hate to say it, Locks, but he's a man. He ain't into God's Word and praying for strength to practice celibacy like you are, which means only one thing."

"Hannah, I try not to even think about it. I try to keep my eye on the prize."

"Which is? Because the last time I checked, I thought Dawson was the prize."

"Pleasing God is the ultimate prize." Locksie placed the last rhinestone in Hannah's hair.

"Tah-dah," Locksie said as she turned Hannah around in her chair to face the mirror.

"Oh, it's beautiful, Locksie." Hannah turned from side to side, admiring her 'do. "I feel like I'm the bride. You did a great job."

"Thank you."

Locksie and Hannah walked over to the cash register, where Locksie rang Hannah up.

"And that's for you," Hannah said, handing Locksie her regular tip of five dollars.

"Thanks, girl," Locksie said, very appreciative. She always loved it when customers felt she had done such a good job that she deserved a tip. On the other hand, there were still those handful of customers who didn't know that it was good etiquette to not only tip your waitresses and bell hops, but your hair stylist too. "So, what time do you have to be at the church?"

Hannah looked down at her watch. "In about a half hour. But we're not meeting at the church. We're meeting at his cousin's parents' house. She spent the night there last night because she said that she wanted to stay in the old room she grew up in. She wanted to experience one last night as her parents' little girl before she became her husband's woman."

"Awww, that is so sweet and symbolic," Locksie cooed.

Hannah looked out the window. "I took my shower and everything already and I have my dress and stuff in the car. Her parents live way out in Pataskala. Peni is supposed to meet me here to drop off Little E, since he's the ring bearer, so he can ride with me. That way she doesn't have to drive him all the way out there. She should have been here already. Knowing her, she's trying to make me late on purpose."

"Or she's with that guy she's been seeing; the one she was with that day you had to get Little E from the sitters."

"Well, I'll tell you what; somebody has been keeping her busy, because as you've noticed, I haven't been complaining half as much as I used to about her evil self." Hannah looked out the window again. No Peni.

"Little E is supposed to go with me so that the women can get him dressed and all. After what I heard was the wildest bachelor party in history, the men probably won't even be able to put on matching socks, let alone dress the ring bearer." Hannah sighed and flopped down in one of the waiting chairs. "I called and left Peni a message on her cell phone to bring him here instead of that salon of horror she was originally going to drop him off to me at." Hannah chuckled. "I hope she got the message. Let me try calling her again."

Just as Hannah took out her cell phone to dial Peni's number, Locksie interrupted.

"Isn't that her?" Locksie said, pointing to the pearl-colored Chrysler that had just pulled into the parking lot. Locksie recognized the car from Hannah's description when Elkan had first paid the down payment and co-signed for Peni to get the car; not to mention the notorious license plates that read: BBY MAMA Hannah and Elkan had had a huge falling out over him helping Peni with the purchase of that car.

"But you didn't even help me pay the down payment on my car," Hannah had complained to her husband.

"Yeah, but you don't have a child to tote around either. Peni's old car broke down and the mechanic said it's dead, and she has my son to take care of," Elkan had reasoned. "I ain't gon' have my son walking and riding public transportation if I ain't doing it myself."

"But why can't her man help her buy a car?"

"I don't want my son riding around in some car another dude done bought."

"Are you sure this is about your son, or you just don't want Peni riding around in some car another dude bought? Perhaps this is your way of continuing ties with Peni."

"Continuing ties? Now how stupid does that sound? Peni and I have a son together. Automobiles come and go; our connection to our son will last forever."

And it was Elkan's connection with Peni that ate away at Hannah. But she never once took it out on their son. It wasn't his fault he was born into an ungodly mess. The actions of his parents didn't make him a bad child. Still, Hannah, deep within her heart, wished that the child had never been born, at least not to Peni. She wished he had been born through her; after all, she was Elkan's wife. She was the one who was supposed to bear children for him and continue his family name.

"Hannah," Little E said as he burst through the salon doors.

"Hey, E, what's up?" Hannah replied in a hip tone, giving Little E a high-five. Initially, Little E had thrown his arms up as if he was going to embrace her like he usually did every time his father brought him home for the weekend. But looking toward the window, remembering that his mother was outside, he decided that a high-five would suffice. He didn't want to hurt his mother's feelings by giving a motherly hug to someone who wasn't his mother.

"My mom said to meet her outside and she'll take my stuff out of her car and put it in yours."

"Sounds like a winner," Hannah said. She turned her attention to Locksie, who was standing their admiring Hannah's interaction with the love child. "I'll talk to you later."

"Mm-hmm. Have a good time," Locksie said to Hannah. "And you too, little Elkan."

"I will, Miss . . ." Little E started before looking up to his stepmother for some name assistance.

"Miss Locksie," Hannah helped him out.

"I will, Miss Locksie." Little E smiled as they headed out the door.

Hannah walked outside and waved to Peni, who was parked right next to Hannah's champagne pink Sebring. Peni didn't wave back. She just got out of her car after popping the trunk.

"You all are going to take this tux back on Monday, right?" Peni asked as she walked to the trunk and pulled out a garment bag.

"Yeah, Elkan's going to take it back when he returns his," Hannah replied as she opened her car door. Little E climbed straight into the backseat and buckled himself in.

"Good, because I am so forgetful, which is how Little E got here," Peni joked, and then in a slight whisper said, "Forgot to take that darn jagged little pill."

Hannah swallowed hard as she walked to her trunk and lifted it, trying to force down the knot that was stuck in her throat. Her attempt was unsuccessful as she remained silent, with a fake smile on her face.

Taking Hannah's silence as a sign of weakness, Peni continued with her taunt. "Lucky for you that you don't have to worry about taking a pill. I mean, if you forget, chances are you still probably

won't get pregnant. Elkan told me you and him
been trying to have a baby. I told him you two
should go get checked out to see which one of
y'all is the problem." Peni thought for a minute.
"Then again, I guess it's obvious who has the
problem considering Little E was conceived. The
women in my family can just look at a you-know-
what and get pregnant. Girl, you don't know how
lucky you are."

Don't do it. Don't do it, Hannah told the tears
that were about to well up in her eyes. *Don't cry.*
She had endured Peni's taunts for years, but
never once gave her the pleasure of thinking her
words had gotten to her. Unbeknownst to Peni,
though, Hannah had cried a river of tears, lost
sleep and even missed a few meals over some of
her nasty words and actions. This time, like all
the others, Peni's tongue was seasoned.

Peni extended her arms with the garment bag
in them and Hannah accepted it, laying it flat in
her trunk. Right before Hannah closed the trunk,
Peni noticed that she had lain the garment bag on
top of a box with a baby walker in it.

"Oh, my goodness," Peni said, pushing the
garment bag to the side so that she could make
sure she was seeing what she was actually seeing.
"Maybe I spoke too soon. Is Little E going to be
having a little brother or sister after all?"

Perhaps Hannah had actually been the one
who spoke too soon, when she told Locksie that
Peni hadn't been bothering her; now here she was
at her best. "Uh, no," Hannah said, swallowing
down that knot, finally able to speak. "One of my
clients is having a baby shower next week. I-I

had, uh, just picked that up for her." Hannah's heart sank.

"Oh, well, it'll happen." Peni shrugged. "I mean, God performs miracles every day, right? I mean, at least that's what Little E is to me and his father; a true miracle."

Hannah closed her eyes and slammed the trunk closed, not knowing or caring whether Peni had been able to move her hands out of the way in time. When she didn't hear a piercing yelp, she knew Peni had. Opening her eyes, Hannah turned to Peni, who looked as though she wanted to kick, scratch and bite Hannah for almost taking her fingers off.

"Yes, God does perform miracles every day. If He did it for you," Hannah said, looking over Peni from head to toe, "then I know He'll do it for me." Hannah let out a chuckle and got in her car, leaving Peni standing there with a clenched jaw.

Taking a deep breath, Hannah looked at Little E through the rearview mirror. "You ready, little fellow?"

"Yep," he replied anxiously. Hannah backed out of her parking space while Little E waved good-bye to his mother, who had walked over to the driver's side of her car.

Hannah felt a tear drop down from her cheek. "Can You, God? Can You do it for me?" she whispered as she turned up the radio and drove away.

Chapter 38

"Where are you going?" Locksie asked as she entered the living room with her late-night snack, a bowl of cereal, in hand.

Dawson was slipping on his jacket. "Out." he answered flatly as if Locksie had no darn business asking him where the heck he was going.

"Out where?"

"I got some business to take care of."

"At nine-thirty at night?"

"If that's what time it is, then yes."

"How long are we going to play this game, Dawson?" Locksie asked

"You tell me."

"I don't know, because I'm not playing games."

"You full of games. Just because you all into church and I'm not, you act like you're better than me. Like you can't even lay with me or else some of my sin cooties are going to rub off on you. I thought we were better than that. I thought you loved me. But I guess I was wrong."

Locksie quickly set the bowl down on the coffee table and walked over to Dawson. "Is that what you think? That I don't love you anymore? Dawson, baby, please. I love you. How many times do I have to keep telling you that?" She placed her hands on his face. He removed them.

"Actions speak louder than words." Dawson grabbed his keys. "And trust me, you ain't even up for an Oscar nomination as far as acting is concerned."

Dawson knew his words were hurting Locksie, but he was hurting, and hurting people hurt people. It's their so-called way of transferring the pain. Studies show that it doesn't work. But still, Dawson decided he would exhaust his efforts; after all, how dare the woman he had loved as his solitaire all of a sudden deny him all of her and then blame it on God? She could have come up with something better than that. Maybe it was just a cover-up because she was cheating on him; had another man on the side. Dawson wouldn't be surprised if it was the preacher. Yep, all sorts of crazy thoughts ran through his head.

Although Drake tried to convince Dawson that Locksie denying him sex had everything to do with Locksie's love for God and nothing to do with him, Dawson wasn't buying it. Like he had told Drake, Dawson felt that holding out on sex was just Locksie's twisted way of trying to get him to marry her. Well, he would marry her when he was good and ready, and not because he wanted her to remove the lock from her chastity belt. Heck, there were plenty of women out there who would love to have sex with him. Matter of fact, for the past month, he had been with one.

"So, what are you trying to say?" Locksie really

didn't want to know the answer to that—or rather, she didn't want to hear it. She already knew the answer. She could just feel it. For the past few weeks, there had been periods where, for hours at a time, Dawson was MIA; wouldn't call home and would turn off his cell phone so that whenever Locksie tried to get in touch with him, his phone would go straight to voicemail. Even if her women's intuition hadn't been screaming on a bullhorn that Dawson was cheating on her, she would have known.

At that moment, Dawson wanted to tell Locksie all about him and Peni, how Peni was filling the void she had left. He wasn't in love with Peni or anything; matter of fact, he hardly liked her. Although she was a beautiful black woman, some of that beauty turned ugly once she opened her mouth. She was a bit more loud and outspoken than Dawson was used to, but when it came to her performance in the bedroom, her over-the-top characteristics were quite beneficial.

His fling with Peni started after her knee injury. He felt so bad about it that he had gone by her house to check on her a couple of times to make sure she was okay; taking her a card and flowers on two different occasions. On the third occasion, he took her himself. Bad thing about it, Dawson knew exactly what he wanted when he went to Peni's house that third time. Locksie had rejected him, so he went where another woman would gladly accept him.

Dawson thought that maybe if he told Locksie about the affair, it would remove all of the guilt he was carrying around. Perhaps she would realize how seriously bad things were between them;

how he had needs too, and that a compromise needed to be made if their relationship had a chance in hell of surviving. The verdict was in; Dawson did love Locksie with his heart and soul. But his body was the jury member that was holding out. His flesh needed to hear a little bit more evidence before the final judgment could be made.

Chapter 39

"Sorry, but I'm just not going to be able to go. I have to close at the salon that night. I don't have a choice. You know my assistant is out on maternity leave." Locksie, with great disappointment, had to turn down Dawson's invitation to an event they were having at the gym. A new company had bought out the gym, and they were having a grand re-opening in the form of a happy hour. Dawson had called to invite her to go.

Dawson was equally disappointed by her response, and wished he'd never taken his brother's advice only to be let down now. His brother had convinced him to focus more on the mental aspect of what he and Locksie had; not the physical.

"Try courting her," Drake had suggested. "That's what's wrong with black people. We don't know how to date and court. Folks, mostly Christians, look at that reality show called *The Bachelor*, and they judge it, talking about that's just trying to get society to think that type of thing is okay. But look at the Book of Ester in the Bible. Isn't that what King Ahasuerus did to find his queen? Date? It doesn't mean that you have to sleep with every woman you date.

"But a relationship needs to be formed. And you can't have a relationship without a courtship. Just like when God wants us to have a relationship with Him; He courts us first. We need to learn how to court each other again."

Maybe Drake was right, but still, Dawson's efforts to court Locksie were in vain as she, once again, rejected him. "Fine," Dawson said, slamming down the phone after Locksie gave him her excuse for why she couldn't attend the grand reopening with him. Dawson was willing to bet that if the church was having an event, she'd make a way.

Just then his cell phone rang. Maybe it was Locksie calling back. Perhaps she had changed her mind and was calling to accept his invitation. Now he'd have a date after all. He looked down at his caller ID. He smiled. It was, in fact, his date for the event. But it wasn't Locksie.

"Your brother called while you were on the other line and left a message reminding you of the event at his job tomorrow evening." Delilah held the piece of paper on which she had just written the message.

Drake smacked his forehead. "Oh, shoot, that's right. I almost forgot."

"He also said,"—she read the paper—"bring a date. L-O-L. Laugh out loud."

Drake laughed at his brother's inside joke. The day Dawson invited Drake to the event, he had told him to bring a date, just in case some of the guys from the locker room were there and had overhead Drake the day he confessed to never having been with a woman. He didn't want anybody getting any ideas about his brother.

"All right. Thanks, Delilah." Drake took the note from her hand and headed back to his office. He stopped in his tracks and turned around and looked at Delilah.

She could feel his eyes on her. She turned around excitedly. "Yes, Mr. Trinity?" *Could it be?* she thought. Could it be that the moment she had been waiting for since she could remember was about to take place? She swallowed hard as Drake stood there thinking.

"Would you mind doing me a favor?"

Oh, God, yes! Delilah shouted in her head. *Yes, I'll go to your brother's event with you.*

"Sure, Mr. Trinity. What is it?" Delilah said calmly, as if her insides weren't screaming out.

"Get Hannah Wells on the phone for me. Would ya?" On that note, Drake disappeared behind the door.

The tears formed in Delilah's eyes so quickly that she was immediately blinded. *How could he?* she asked herself. *What's wrong with me? What's wrong with me?*

Delilah wiped her tears away as she began having a conversation with herself in her head. *I thought for sure all those embarrassing stories I told that little tramp about Drake would turn her off. Especially the one that was meant to instill the possibility of him being gay.* Delilah shook her head. *Guess I was wrong. Looks like Barbie is still holding on by a strand of her blonde hair. She wants herself a black man whether he be single, straight or gay. Just like a white woman.* All of a sudden, Delilah's hurt turned to anger. Her anger then turned to thoughts of revenge.

"Oh, I'll get Miss Thing on the phone for you," Delilah said to herself as she picked up her desk phone. "I'm sure she'd love to go to your brother's event with you." After Delilah flipped through the Rolodex for Hannah's contact information, she called Hannah and put her through to Drake. She then pulled out her cell phone, which Hannah had used that day at the office to call Elkan. She scrolled through her electronic phone book until she got to the number she had saved under "Her Husband." She knew that number would come in handy someday. A wicked grin spread across her thin lips. "I hope you two have fun out on your little date. I just hope you guys don't mind if her husband joins y'all."

Hannah logged off her computer when she heard Elkan enter the house. She went downstairs to greet him. "Hey, honey," she said with a kiss. "How was your day?"

"Excellent," he replied, returning her affection. "Settled a big case today."

"Umm, then let's celebrate. Speaking of which, what are you doing tomorrow evening?"

"Oh, babe, something just came up. I got a phone call today and there's an event I have to—"

"Darn," Hannah whined before Elkan could even finish.

"Don't be sad, baby. All that means is that it looks like we're going to have to celebrate tonight." Elkan lifted Hannah and carried her to their bedroom.

Just that quickly, as her husband loved up on her, she had forgotten all about her disappointment about him being busy tomorrow evening. Drake had called and invited both her and Elkan to the event at the gym. He thought it might be a good opportunity for them to come network and possibly pick up some new clients. New owners always meant the opportunity for new business.

Unbeknownst to Hannah, Drake had also invited Hannah for some selfish reasons of his own. He had been praying to God to deliver him from that spirit of lust he had been feeling for Hannah. He thought it might help to see her happily joined with her husband. If that didn't work, though, he knew what he had to do; cut off his relationship with Hannah altogether. It brought in decent business, but he was willing to give up all of that if it meant not jeopardizing his walk . . . of course, a little part of him hoped that he didn't have to.

The next day at work for Locksie was productive—until a semi-truck carrying deadly gas fumes turned over and the salon, as well as surrounding businesses, was forced to evacuate. There were four customers in the salon at the time. One was a woman under the hairdryer with a roller set, one was a girl utilizing the tanning bed, a gentleman waiting on a haircut, and a lady in Locksie's chair getting her long hair blow-dried so that Locksie could flat-iron it.

The fire department wouldn't allow the woman under the dryer to stay there until her hair was completely dry. They wouldn't let Locksie flat-iron the other woman's hair, which she had already blow-dried. Fortunately for the girl tanning, she was exiting the tanning bed when the fireman entered to evacuate them.

Locksie gave the woman under the dryer permission to leave with the rollers in her hair if she promised to return them the next morning. The hair of the woman in the chair was so straight from the combed blow-dryer that Locksie decided against a flat-iron anyway and was content with just a little sheen. All worked out well. Locksie even told the gentleman who had been waiting on a haircut that if he came back tomorrow for his cut, she'd give him fifty percent off. There were no displeased patrons. And Locksie was more than happy to be getting out of there early.

It wasn't until Locksie got home that she realized that now she would be able to attend Dawson's event at his job. She immediately raced to call him up on her cell phone to tell him the good news. Perhaps they could even stop and pick up a DVD afterwards.

Just as Locksie picked up the phone to dial Dawson's number, she changed her mind about calling him. "Why don't I just surprise him instead?"

Locksie hung up the phone and headed to the shower so that she could get cleaned up and dressed and head to Dawson's job. Little did she know, the evening was about to be full of surprises.

Chapter 40

"I'm so glad you could make it," Dawson said to Peni as they stood by the refreshment table in the gym, drinking one of the power drinks a sponsor had supplied for the grand reopening.

"Who, me? Decline an invite from the most beautiful man in the world?" Peni flirted. "Not to mention the best . . ." She whispered the rest in his ear.

Dawson blushed at the sexy compliment. Just then he spotted Drake coming his way. "Wait here," he told Peni. "I just spotted someone I know."

Drake spotted Dawson at the same time. He put up his hand to wave and started heading toward Dawson and Peni, but then he heard his name being called. He turned back around and saw Hannah coming in the door behind him. Dawson watched the woman at the doorway flag down Drake as he turned around to go greet her.

"Oh, just a sec," Dawson said as he turned

back to face Peni. "Looks like his date just arrived."

"Who?" Peni said as she began to scan the room.

"My brother." Dawson turned and pointed as Drake and Hannah came walking in their direction.

"I was expecting your husband to show up," Drake told Hannah as they walked, Hannah smiling at him the entire time.

"I know. I wanted him to come too." Hannah had a disappointed tone. "But something came up at the last minute. Some event he had to go to. He felt bad. I told him not to, that Reggie was going to come with me."

"Oh, yeah?" Drake said as he slowed his pace, looked back at the door and around the room. "Reggie's coming?"

"Well, he said he would, but then something popped up on his schedule, too, so he can't join me either." There was that disappointed tone in her voice again. "Looks like all the men in my life keep standing me up."

"Not to fret, my dear. You've got me." Just as Drake said those words, he grabbed Hannah's hand and they stood in front of Dawson and Peni.

"Well, introduce me to this lady with you," Dawson said to his brother.

With Hannah's hand still in his, Drake opened his mouth.

"Hannah!" Peni shouted out before Drake could speak a word.

"Peni!" Hannah replied after finally looking up and noticing that other people were in the room besides Drake. "I uh, uh, didn't see you . . . recognize you," Hannah stammered.

"I bet you didn't." An evil smirk was plastered on Peni's face.

"You two know each other?" Dawson asked, looking from Peni to Hannah.

Just then, Hannah recognized Dawson as the gentleman who was in the car that day with Peni.

"My date asked you a question," Peni said, looping her arm through Dawson's, still with a wicked grin on her face. "Answer the man. How do we know each other?"

"Your date?" a voice erupted. "Your date?" Locksie looked to Dawson for an explanation as she approached the foursome.

"Locksie, baby," Dawson said as his heart dropped to his knees.

"Dawson, what's going on?" Locksie demanded to know, not paying attention to anyone but Dawson.

"Dawson," Hannah mumbled. She knew there was something familiar about him. She had never met Dawson in person before, and the only picture of him she had seen was the one that Locksie had sitting at her station when he had hair and a goatee. She didn't recognize him with his bald head and no facial hair.

Upon hearing a familiar voice speak Dawson's name, Locksie turned her head. "Hannah?" She looked to Drake and shook her head. "Oh, my God. I can't believe this. Hannah, you are supposed to be my friend and yet here you are on a double date with my boyfriend and his ho."

"Wait, Locksie. It's not what you think. I'm

here with Drake only." Hannah looped her arm through Drake's in an effort to show Locksie that she had nothing to do with whatever was going on between Dawson and Peni. She was just about to further explain how she came about attending the event with Drake, until a baritone voice boomed from behind her.

"So, you are, are you?" Elkan chimed in. "You're here with Drake? Drake only?" Elkan looked to Hannah with menacing eyes. "I thought you were going to some business function with Reggie tonight."

"Elkan, honey." Hannah loosed her arm from Drake's. "Let me explain."

"Yeah, I think a whole lot of explaining needs to be done," Locksie stated, her lip trembling while her heart ached. She was trying hard to keep on a game face. "I now know, Hannah, why you lied to me a few months back about going somewhere with Reggie and then I see you and Drake at the Hilton. Heck, you were probably waiting on the other half of your double date to show up."

"The Hilton?" Elkan said, grabbing Hannah's arm.

"And I'm the ho?" Peni spat.

"Peni, what are you doing here?" Elkan had just noticed her.

"Peni!" Locksie stated. "*The* Peni?"

"Well, my date was about to introduce his brother and his date to me until—" Peni attempted to answer.

"See, Locksie—introduce," Hannah reasoned. "Did you hear that? She said Dawson was about to introduce us. I have never even been in the presence of these two before except for that day at the babysitter's house when they were together in his car . . ."

"What?" Locksie yelled, becoming even more angry. "And you didn't tell me?"

"I didn't realize—" Hannah tried to explain.

"Hey, honey muffin," Reggie called out as he walked up. "What's going on over here? All eyes are on you guys, so I couldn't help but spot you."

"Reggie," Hannah said in relief. Now he could explain to Elkan how he was actually supposed to be there with her and how he had been at the Hilton but had to leave. But before he could explain, not even noticing Elkan, he extended his hand to Drake.

"Drake, my man," Reggie stated. "It's good to see you again. You been taking care of my girl here?" He pointed to Hannah.

"Yeah, he's been taking care of her all right," Elkan snapped. He turned to Reggie. "So, you've known about the affair too?"

Locksie chimed in. "Looks like everybody knew about our mate's affairs but us."

Elkan wasn't interested in Locksie's misery-loves-company antics. He turned to her. "You're just as bad. You see my woman at a hotel with another man that you know is not her husband . . . What kind of friend allows another friend to make such a mistake?"

"Whoa, hold up, hey!" Reggie said, holding up his hands. "I feel like Larry from *Three's Company* and I've walked in at the end of a bad episode." Reggie chuckled, trying to ease the tension in the atmosphere.

"Dawson, is everything all right here?" The

new owner of the gym suddenly appeared. The group kept getting louder and louder, so he felt the need to intervene. "Are you and Peni okay?" The owner had taken the time to come into the gym often and get to know the employees. The day he met Dawson, he just happened to be training Peni, so the owner had remembered her from that day.

"So, how long have you been screwing Peni here?" Locksie spat, poking Dawson in the chest with her index finger.

"That's no way for a Christian to act," Dawson replied. "Is it, Drake?"

"Who is a non-Christian to tell a Christian how they should act? You ain't read the rule book," Locksie spat back.

"There ain't no rule book," was Dawson's comeback.

"There is so. It's called a Bible, fool!" Locksie poked him again.

"Come on now, Locksie." Drake tried to calm her by gently taking hold of her arm. "The last thing I want to see is my sister in Christ lose her religion."

Locksie snatched away from Drake. "Sister in Christ my foot! You runnin' around with a married woman."

"Locksie, that's not true!" Hannah shouted. "If you'd just let me explain . . ."

Elkan grabbed Hannah's arm. "Well, you can explain to me at home. Let's go." His grip was tight. Hannah winced.

"Man, all that ain't necessary," Drake said as he reached for Hannah in an attempt to release her from Elkan. The next thing Drake knew, he was resting in darkness. He could have sworn he saw stars; he thought he might be on his way up to heaven. But after coming to and seeing punches being thrown, hair weave and earrings flying and the sounds of police sirens, he knew heaven could wait. There was still a whole mess on planet Earth that needed his attention.

Chapter 41

It had been a week since the outrageous incident at the gym. The work on Mary's house had been completed, and Locksie was now living in it. After not getting home from the gym that night until after midnight, thankful that no one had been arrested or taken to jail, Locksie immediately began packing her things. As she packed, Dawson unpacked, begging and pleading with her to just hear him out.

"I just want to know one thing," Locksie said to him. "Did you sleep with her?"

"Locksie, it's not that easy—"

"Oh, trust me, Dawson. I know just how easy it is. I ain't been saved all my life, remember?"

"Locks, that's not what I mean."

"Then just answer me. Did you sleep with Peni?" There was silence. Dawson lowered his head. "That's all I needed to know."

That night, Locksie, without allowing Dawson to explain anything else to her, loaded her car with all that could fit and moved into the house her aunt had willed to her. Two days later, Two Men and a Truck made sure the rest of her belongings were moved as well.

Dawson was suspended from work for a week after a hearing to determine whether he should lose his job altogether for being involved in the fight at the gym. Normally, Dawson wasn't a violent person, but when he saw Elkan deliver such an explosive blow to Drake, he had to intervene with a power punch of his own. When Hannah saw her husband get hit, she immediately jumped on Dawson's back. Angry at him or not, Locksie wasn't about to stand there and let some other chick scratch up her man; she felt she was entitled to that privilege herself, so she began to pull at Hannah, trying to get her from around Dawson. Next thing she knew, Hannah released Dawson, and both Locksie and Hannah went flinging into Peni. It was a mess.

Officers arrived at the scene and interviewed each party involved individually. After hearing what everybody had to say, the officers decided not to arrest anyone. They felt that if they did haul them off to jail, their superiors wouldn't believe the story anyway. They further concluded that the judge would probably bust his gut laughing at the entire scenario. So, they were all given a warning and told to seek counseling . . . and if counseling didn't work, to write a story about their lives; it was sure to be a bestseller.

It was the first Saturday Locksie had off in months, and she sat at the kitchen table sipping on a cup of coffee. She pictured her aunt Mary sit-

ting across from her, sipping on a cup of her own,
like they had done for years. Tears formed in
Locksie's eyes, but before they could fall, the
doorbell rang.

Locksie wondered who could it be. She knew it
wasn't Dawson because the night at the gym, the
officers had also suggested that the couples give
each other some space—time to cool down—and
if they got a single complaint about one person
bothering another, there would be an immediate
arrest; no questions asked. That threat had kept
Dawson away from Locksie and from calling her
on her job, where there were witnesses who could
attest to his harassment. Getting her cell phone
number changed had stopped his phone calls.

Locksie got to the door and looked out the
peephole. She sighed, debating whether to open
the door for the unexpected visitor. After a few
more moments and now a knock, she decided to
open the door.

"Hey . . ." Locksie said, for lack of a better
greeting.

"Hey," Hannah replied.

There was silence.

"Would you, uh, like to come in?" Locksie
moved aside and gestured for Hannah to enter
her home. Hannah nodded and proceeded.

Locksie closed and locked the door behind
them. The two women just stood in silence; one
not knowing what to say to the other. Hannah
and Locksie hadn't spoken since the night of the
fight. Hannah had been too busy trying to save
her marriage. By the time she finally did get
around to calling Locksie, her cell phone number
had been changed. She had thought about calling

up at the salon or stopping by, but enough drama had already taken place at Dawson's place of work. The last thing she wanted was to cause a scene at Locksie's job and risk her livelihood too.

She had never called Locksie at her home before, but remembered that Locksie had given her the number one time. It was on an occasion when Hannah had come into the salon, but Locksie had so many clients waiting that she couldn't service her. It just so happened that Locksie was going to be off the next day; therefore, she couldn't do Hannah's hair then, either. So, Locksie told Hannah that she would do her hair at her home. Hannah wrote down Locksie's address and phone number. The next morning, one of the girls at the salon called off work and Locksie had to go in anyway, so Hannah ended up being her first client that day.

When Hannah called up the home number she had written down for Locksie, she was surprised when Dawson told her that Locksie no longer lived there; that she was staying at her aunt's house. Dawson gave Hannah the address, asking her to call him and let him know how Locksie was doing after she talked to her.

Locksie looked at Hannah and shrugged as if to say, "Well?"

Hannah swallowed and then softly uttered, "I'm sorry." She put her head down as tears began to fall.

Locksie's heart was softened. She looked away, trying to keep her own tears from falling. Hannah continued.

"I'm so sorry for everything." Hannah broke down in tears. "I'm sorry for everything I've done—

everything you thought I did—just everything."
She hunched over and her shoulders began to
heave.

Locksie stared at her for a minute. She pitied her
estranged friend. She wanted to go over and comfort her, but another part of her remembered that
she was the woman who knew about Dawson's
affair with Peni and hadn't peeped a word of it.
But no sooner than that thought had entered her
mind, a sermon Reverend Franklin had preached
titled "Forgiveness" popped into her head. "How
do you expect God to forgive you when you can't
forgive others?" Reverend had said.

Locksie thought about all the mistakes she had
made and sins she had committed that God had forgiven her for. She thought about all Jesus had to
endure for the forgiveness of her sins. Just then,
she felt blessed; she felt blessed that in order for
Man to wipe away wrongdoings against each
other, all one had to do was say, "I'm sorry." And
all the other person had to say in return was, "I
forgive you." It was that easy. No beatings, no
being spat at, no nails.

"I forgive you," Locksie said as she put her
arms around Hannah.

"I feel so ridiculous, Hannah," Locksie said as
the two sat on the couch after Hannah finished
explaining to Locksie how she met Drake and
why she hadn't told her about doing business
with him. She had no idea that Drake was Dawson's little brother. She also told her how she hadn't
realized who Dawson really was until that evening at the gym. "And just think, I thought you

were cheating on your husband with Drake and double-dating with Dawson and Peni." Locksie hugged her friend again. "I wish I had just let you explain it all to me before now."

"Yeah, me too." Hannah pulled away and put her head down. "You and Elkan both."

"You and Elkan still haven't straightened things out?"

"No, but how can we when I've been living in a hotel room for the last two weeks?" Hannah confessed.

"What do you mean?"

"He put me out that night after the fight. He wouldn't let me explain. He was so angry, so mad. Locksie, I swear I thought he was going to hit me. He packed my stuff up and threw it out the door and sent me on my merry way. I've tried to talk to him; been calling him every day, but—" Hannah broke down.

"Oh, Hannah." Locksie took her hand. "I can't believe you've been going through this. What hotel have you been staying at?"

"Country Inn Suites on Broad Street."

"Well, come on." Locksie stood, pulling Hannah up with her.

"What? Where are we going?"

"To get your things." Locksie grabbed her purse and keys. "You're moving in with me."

Chapter 42

"She won't even talk to me," Dawson confessed to Drake as they sat in Drake's living room eating pizza and watching the game.

"Have you told her that you've broken things off with Peni?"

"No, man. She won't give me a chance. I haven't talked to her in over a month; since she packed up and moved her things out. This whole thing is just one great, big mess; a mess she caused in the first place, matter of fact."

"Whoa, hold up," Drake said. "The last I checked, you were the one who slept with her client's husband's baby mama."

"Yeah, but I wouldn't have had to if she had been doing what she was supposed to do in our relationship to keep it right."

"Pardon me for saying, but she was doing what she was supposed to be doing in y'all's relationship. She was keeping it holy."

Dawson slapped his slice of pizza back down in the box. "Don't start, Drake."

"I'm not gonna start, big brother. I'm going to finish; and you're going to shut up and listen!" Drake said with authority. "You have control over your flesh, not Locksie or any other person. You can't even blame it on the devil. You have control over your flesh. Nobody made you sleep with that woman. You made that choice, and now you are reaping what you have sown. You were a man when you were rolling around in the sack with Peni, but now you don't want to man up and admit that you made a mistake. Well, how do you expect Locksie to forgive you for a wrongdoing that you won't even confess to? Even worse, how do you expect God to forgive you for something you won't even confess to?"

Dawson sat for a minute, taking in his brother's words, which had a ring of truth to them. He hated the truth. The truth hurt, so his only reply was, "Man, I should have just let dude knock you out cold, because that's exactly what I feel like doing; blacking your other eye."

Drake rubbed his hand across his left eye, which was still just slightly bruised from the blow he had suffered a month ago at the hands of Elkan. "Well, I forgive that man for hitting me in the eye, and I'd forgive you too."

Dawson realized that the fight he was looking for, Drake wasn't going to give him. "Look, man. I'm going to head home." Dawson stood up. "There's some thinking I've got to do."

"Well, before you go, can you do me a favor?"

"Yeah, sure man. What?" Dawson said, willing to do anything just to hurry up and get out of there so that he could go get his mind together.

"Let me pray for you." Drake extended his hands to his brother.

Reluctantly, Dawson reached out and held hands with his brother. "Man, this feels gay."

Drake ignored his brother's comment and just proceeded in prayer. "Dear Heavenly Father, first and foremost, I just thank You for the person whose hands I hold, and ask that You just give him a clear mind to be able to make the right decisions. Lord Jesus, I thank You for the woman in his life who You have reached out to and are preparing a place for in heaven. I just ask that You begin to operate in their relationship and that Your will be done in their lives. I ask that they each let go of trying to handle this thing on their own and let You. Move them out of the way, Father God, and You take over. In Jesus' name I pray. Amen."

"Amen," Dawson repeated. There were a couple seconds of awkwardness for him. "Well, I guess I better go."

"All right, man. Drive safely," Drake said as he walked his brother to the door.

As he was cleaning up the mess from the pizza, words he had just spoken to Dawson came to mind: *I forgive that man for hitting me in the eye.* Drake had forgiven Elkan for knocking him out because he knew he had no business inviting Hannah to that event in the first place, whether or not he had invited her husband also. And when Hannah showed up without her husband, the devil, for a minute, tried to tell Drake that it was a sign meant for him. Drake should have proclaimed that the devil was a liar and either sent Hannah on her way, letting her know that he thought it might be a little compromising to been seen together like that, or he should have left. He couldn't help but look back and think of how so much could have been prevented. But thank goodness that God is a forgiving God.

Speaking of forgiving, Drake knew he had to release Elkan by confessing his apologies for anything he had done to provoke the situation through the bad decisions he had made; and forgiving him for his violent act as a result of the situation. They needed to release each other, but he had no way of getting in touch with Elkan.

He thought about how Delilah used to do those Internet searches where she could find out contact information for almost anybody in the country. Thing was, Delilah didn't work for him anymore. She had upped and quit a couple days after the incident at the gym.

Drake headed toward his home office, where he juiced up his computer. He sat down and logged onto the Internet, thinking it couldn't be too hard to track down a person.

Chapter 43

Locksie and Hannah had been roommates for a few weeks now. Hannah's time apart from Elkan had given her time to really look at some things in their relationship that needed repairing, so that if they did get back together, they could have a better marriage. She didn't want to get back with him just to have to face some of the same jacked-up issues in their marriage; issues that Elkan probably knew bothered Hannah, but that they had never really laid out on the table and talked about.

Locksie, on the other hand, enjoyed the freedom of just keeping her head buried in the Bible for as long as she wanted. Before, Dawson would suck his teeth or sigh as a signal to her that he was tired of always seeing her spending more time in the Word than with him. So, whenever he entered the room and she was reading the Word, she would stop. But now, she would feed off of the Word until she was plenty full. She had to admit, though, at night, after she had said her evening prayer and gone to bed, she couldn't help but to think about Dawson. For some reason, she just couldn't turn the love switch to "off" mode no matter how badly he had hurt her.

Together, the two women had been leaning on each other, offering support over the break-up and separation from their mates. Most of the time they found themselves crying and overdosing on cartons of United Dairy Farmers ice cream. But then one Sunday, Locksie invited Hannah to church. Hannah declined, opting to stay home and feel bad. Locksie knew, though, that if she'd just go to church, she wouldn't leave that place feeling the same. Locksie wanted nothing more than to stand there and try to talk to Hannah until she was blue in the face, but then she remembered how her mother's preachy-ness had pushed her further away from the bosom of God rather than into His arms, and the last thing she wanted was to do that to her friend. Trying to scare someone into heaven by constantly preaching hell and damnation and making them feel convicted was no way to win a soul.

During that week, Locksie prayed feverently that God would put it in Hannah's heart to want to come to church with her. That following Sunday, Locksie didn't even have to ask Hannah if she wanted to come; Hannah asked Locksie if she could tag along with her. Hannah enjoyed the service. She went to the altar for prayer, and the mothers of the church covered her in a mighty-mighty prayer.

After service, Naomi offered to take Hannah and Locksie to lunch. It was then that Naomi suggested that perhaps the two women should meet with First Lady Deborah to get some godly advice on their circumstances.

"The Lord has really given that woman some insight on relationships through trials and tests of her own," Naomi informed them.

Locksie already knew firsthand and wished she had thought about speaking with the first lady earlier. But it was better late than never as Locksie and Hannah sat in First Lady Deborah's office one evening.

After the first lady began with prayer, Locksie and Hannah each relayed their current situations to First Lady Deborah. She sat listening intensely until the last word was spoken. Then she sighed a huge sigh. "Hold on, ladies. I gotta grab me a bottle of water. And after hearing those stories, if I wasn't a Christian, I'd be getting something stronger. Can I grab you two a bottle?"

Locksie and Hannah declined as First Lady Deborah grabbed a bottle of water from the mini refrigerator in her office. She took a sip and then proceeded. "Isn't God good?"

The excitement in the First Lady's voice didn't echo the stories the two women had just told. And although they didn't feel First Lady Deborah's excitement, they each agreed that God was, indeed, good.

"Locksie, do you know how many women drive themselves crazy trying to find out what their men are doing? What they're up to? If they're running around cheating on them?" First Lady Deborah asked. "Girl, I've seen 'em lose weight, gain weight, lose hair, break out with bumps, lose sleep, get ulcers—you name it. But you didn't have to go through any of that. You didn't have to go looking for nothing by going through his pants pockets, wallet or trying to break his voicemail code to listen to his messages or even sneak into his email account. God revealed it all to you, didn't he? Hallelujah!"

Locksie nodded. She had never looked at it that way. Leave it to First Lady Deborah to see the good in what Locksie saw as nothing but a bad situation. Some of First Lady's excitement was now beginning to brush off on her. *Thank You, Lord*, Locksie said silently as she thought about some of the horror stories she had heard in the salon of women who had gone so far as to hire private investigators to follow their mates. She knew one who had even contacted that show, *Cheaters*. And though Locksie was embarrassed that all those strangers in the gym found out her boyfriend was a cheat at the same time she did, at least millions of folks hadn't seen it on national television. Oh, yes, God is good!

"And you . . ." First Lady Deborah turned to Hannah. "God stopped that spirit of lust in its evil tracks, didn't He? The devil was going to use the fact that your husband had been unfaithful to try to convince you to pay him back by doing the same thing to him. But God blocked it! Praise the Lord!"

Hannah had never really looked at the situation like that before. Might something in her have pursued a physical relationship with Drake? Was the devil maybe even trying to use her to test Drake?

"Don't you feel awful that your husband just *thinks* you cheated on him?" First Lady Deborah asked Hannah.

"Yes," Hannah replied.

"Imagine how you would feel if you actually had cheated on him."

Hannah thought about it. "I wouldn't be able to live with myself, I don't think."

First Lady reached out and grabbed Locksie's and Hannah's hands. "Ladies, believe me when I tell you God has a blessing in every situation. That's how He speaks to you."

"Then why can't I hear him?" Hannah cried. "I love my husband. Why won't God tell me what to do?"

First Lady Deborah released the women's hands and sat back in her chair. She rubbed her chin and then asked Hannah, "Well, did you ask Him?" Then she looked at Locksie. "Have you asked Him what to do about your situation?" Back to Hannah. "Did you even ask God if Elkan was your husband before you said 'I do'?" Back to Locksie. "Did God say Dawson was your husband?"

The women sat in their chairs, dumbfounded, then Locksie admitted, "I just keep telling God how much I love Dawson and how much I want to be with him."

Hannah added, "I've only really been talking to God and learning how to pray since I've been staying with Locksie. I, too, just tell God how much I love Elkan and how much I want to be with him."

"But have you women asked God what He wants for you? And when you asked, did you wait for an answer?" The women's blank faces let First Lady Deborah know their answers. "Prayer is a conversation with God. It takes two people to converse. Once you have said to God what you need to say, be silent—and listen. He will always answer when you call."

"Can I ask you something, First Lady?" Locksie asked. "Is that how you knew Reverend Franklin was your husband? Is that one of the reasons why you waited for him all those years to get out of jail?"

"That's the only reason why," First Lady Deborah confirmed. "And folks thought I was crazy, too. 'He's my husband!' I'd proclaim to them. Because Lord knows I prayed over my situation with my New York Boy, aka Reverend Franklin." She chuckled. "When I first laid eyes on him, I knew he wasn't a bit more saved than the man on the moon. But there was this connection—not physical—but like I was on assignment from God. You know, kind of like in the book of Hosea.

"So, I prayed and I waited to hear from God. All I kept hearing was that this boy was my husband, so that's what I'd tell folks. 'Oh, that's just the devil talking to you, trying to trick you into thinking it was God,' my mama would say. 'Un-huh,' I'd tell her. 'His sheep know His voice. It was God Himself who declared him as my husband.' "

"But why in the world would God be telling you that a drug dealer was your husband? You were a saved woman," Locksie commented.

First Lady Deborah told Locksie, "I asked myself why my God would have me unequally yoked in a marriage. And He told me to lean not on my own understanding. So, I waited and endured. I ministered to Reverend Franklin back then through jailhouse letters. Never once went to visit him, though. God didn't tell me to do that. He just told me to feed him the Word and to help him grow. We basically did a five-year written Bible study course."

"But I thought you said he got sentenced to seven to ten years," Locksie said.

"God showed him favor to get out early." First Lady smiled big. "Must have been because all of those souls he brought to the Lord while in there."

"That's an awesome story," Hannah said. "But why go through all of that for a man?" she asked. "Couldn't you have found another man that was already saved and into church?"

"I could have," First Lady Deborah assured her. "But my New York boy was fee-yiiine!" She flailed her arms up in the air like she couldn't stand how fine he was.

The women high-fived and laughed. "On a more serious note, ladies," First Lady Deborah said, "it wasn't like Reverend got out of jail and it was happily ever after. Oh, we went through some things. But guess what? I went through what I went through so that you wouldn't have to." She pointed to them both. "What I went through wasn't for me; it was for you—to be able to share it with you so that you will know that if God did it for me, then He'll do it for you. Amen, sisters."

Hannah and Locksie looked at each other and smiled. "Amen," they said in unison.

"Now, let's pray," First Lady Deborah said as the women held hands and bowed their heads. "Heavenly Father, oh gracious merciful Lord, I just thank You for the Holy Spirit joining us in this room and giving me the words needed to help these two women whose hands I hold. Lord, I ask that they receive these words and take them to heart and begin to converse with You, Lord. That they begin to wait on You, Lord, before they do anything.

"God, I ask that You hear these women's prayers and answer them. That You show them if the men they are anguishing over are the men You would have them have as their husbands. If not, Father, God, then I ask for You to give these women the strength to walk away and walk toward what You have for them. I say this prayer in the sweet-sweet name of Your Son and our Savior, Jesus Christ. Amen."

"Amen," the women repeated as they embraced First Lady Deborah, each shedding tears on her shoulder. After what seemed like hours of First Lady Deborah just sitting there holding the hurting women, they finally released themselves from her.

"Now what do we do?" Hannah asked as she and Locksie prepared to leave the office.

First Lady Deborah looked at them and smiled. "You wait."

Chapter 44

Hannah and Locksie were prayer warriors in the making as they prayed faithfully and diligently for the past week; ever since talking with First Lady. They had even committed to a three-day fast, where they prayed through their hunger pains. As a matter of fact, they were just finishing up a soft, quiet prayer together, after Locksie had finished flat-ironing Hannah's hair.

"We touch and agree. In Jesus' name, amen," Locksie said.

"Amen." Hannah smiled.

Just then, Hannah's cell phone rang. She pulled it out of her purse and looked at the caller ID. She looked at her watch. "Girl, let me get out of here. This is Reggie; probably calling to give me grief. I have to meet with him today. I called and told him I might be a little late because I had to come here and get my hair done, since your lazy tail didn't do it last night like you said you would."

"I know, girl. I'm sorry. I was just too tired by

the time I made it home from doing all that hair up in here."

"It's okay. I'm just messing with you. But anyway, I ain't trying to hear Reggie's mouth. That's why I ain't even answering that call."

Feeling a stare, she looked up at Locksie, who was making a crazy "yeah, right" face. "I really do have to meet with Reggie this time." They giggled.

"Girl, I know. I was just teasing," Locksie said as she removed the cape from around Hannah's shoulders and they headed to the register.

"Here you go, girl." Locksie handed back the credit card that Hannah had given her to charge her services. While Hannah signed the credit card slip, Locksie looked out of the salon window and happened to catch a glimpse of a familiar face.

"Here you go," Hannah said, handing Locksie the slip. Locksie wasn't paying her any mind. She was too busy trying to figure out if the person she was looking at was actually who she thought it was. Just then, Hannah's cell phone rang. She looked down at the caller ID. It was Reggie again. She figured she might as well answer it just to let him know that she was on her way so he would settle his britches. "I'm on my—" she answered before Reggie quickly cut her off.

"Butter rum cakes, I'm sorry, but the man came up to my office and asked me if I knew where you were. He seemed happy and excited, but the last I saw him he had laid a cat out like a rug—and I'm way too good looking to be walking around with a busted-up mug," Reggie hurriedly explained. "So I told him where you were."

"Slow down, Reggie. What are you talking about?"

"Elkan," Locksie said after staring long enough to confirm the identity of the man standing outside next to Hannah's car.

Hearing Elkan's name, Hannah followed Locksie's gaze to the parking lot. "Reggie, let me call you back." She hung up the phone and laid down the credit card slip. "Locks, I'll see you this evening," she said as she made her way toward the door.

"You want me to come with you?" Locksie offered.

"No, I'll be okay. I'll see ya tonight at home."

"Hannah, baby," Elkan said as soon as he saw her come out of the salon. He went to meet her halfway up the walk. "I've been looking for you all day."

"Then why didn't you just call me?" Hannah asked, not even an ounce as excited as Elkan was. For weeks, she had been sick not hearing from him. She had tried to call him several times the week after the incident at the gym, but then she realized that as long as technology consisted of caller ID, she'd never get through to him; she'd have to wait until he was ready to talk to her. It had seemed like forever, but now here he stood as if he had just talked to her yesterday.

"Baby, I know I should have called you before. But now that I know everything; now that I know what I need to say, I wanted to see you in person."

"What do you mean, now that you know everything?"

"Drake; he called me and explained everything. He said that he had been trying to track me down for a minute and that he finally . . . Well, never mind about all that. I'm just so glad to see you. I'm so glad to finally know the truth. I can't believe I actually thought—"

"Oh, so it took somebody else calling you up and telling you the truth? You just couldn't listen to little ol' me, your wife?" Hannah interrupted.

Now even Elkan's excitement was starting to dwindle. He couldn't understand why Hannah had an attitude. He was there to take her back. "Look, Hannah, you're lucky I'm even here. Any other woman—"

"Any other woman like who? Peni? Is that why you got so upset? Is that why you were so quick to think I was cheating on you, because you were so quick to cheat on me? Well, I'm not like you, Elkan." Hannah pointed at him.

Through the clear glass, Locksie, as well as the other two stylists in the salon and the customers inside, tried their best to imagine what Hannah and Elkan could possibly be saying. But all they could see was a lot of finger-pointing and head-bobbing.

"I know you're not like me, Hannah," Elkan stated. "In a lot of ways."

"What's that supposed to mean?" Hannah snapped.

Elkan was dumbfounded. Hannah was coming out of left field as far as he was concerned. She had never been so forceful with her tone. She was usually a passive person. Any other time if he had come running to take her back, no questions asked, she would have simply fallen in his arms. That's what he thought was going to happen. Obviously he had thought wrong.

"It's not supposed to mean anything, Hannah. Just that we're different in a lot of ways."

"Oh, who are you kidding, Elkan? When you mean different, you mean our blackness."

"See, you're trippin' now," Elkan said.

"Am I, Elkan?"

"Yes, you are."

"Yeah, right. I see how uneasy you get when sistahs walk by and give you the evil eye. You still get embarrassed that they think you're hugged up with a white girl." Hannah felt so powerful for the first time in her life with Elkan. Things that she had wanted to say before but never had the courage to were just flying out of her mouth. "It was never enough for you that my mother is black; that I am African American in spite of what I look like on the outside. Well, I got news for you; I may not be one hundred percent black, but some of my ancestors came over here on the same boat as yours did, and don't you ever forget it, nigga!"

Just then a black woman and what looked to be her teenage daughter had gotten out of their car and were heading into the salon. They hadn't heard anything Hannah had said except for the "N" word.

Elkan's head dropped in complete embarrassment. As the two women walked closer, they looked at him in disgust. They looked as though they wanted to personally revoke his brotha-hood card for standing there allowing his white woman to use the "N" word.

She's the one who said it, he thought about saying to the women. *So, why y'all looking at me like y'all want to beat me up?* But he knew why they considered him to be the culprit. They thought that he was sleeping with the enemy. In their book, that was just as bad as being the enemy.

"See, there it is; there's that look again," Hannah said. "You're embarrassed by me."

"Yeah, but not your skin color, or what anybody else thinks, but because you just said the 'N' word."

"If my skin was a little darker and my hair wasn't blonde and pressed straight, would you be embarrassed?"

"Well, no, but . . ." Elkan searched for words and found none. "Where is all this coming from anyway?" He grabbed Hannah's arm to lead her toward the car. "Come on, let's just go home and we can talk about it. We can talk about everything. I just want you to come home with me."

"No." Hannah snatched away.

"Come on, baby. Little E misses you. I miss you." He grabbed her arm again.

"I said no!" She snatched away again. "Locksie's been letting me stay with her at her aunt's house. I need some time to think about things. I need to hear from God."

"What?" Elkan snapped. "What's God got to do with it? This is about me and you."

"He's got everything to do with it. Look, Elkan. I need to go. I need time."

He grabbed her again, this time somewhat forcefully. "I need you."

As far as Locksie was concerned, Elkan had grabbed her friend one too many times. She thought about Hannah telling her that the night after the gym fiasco, Elkan had been so angry that Hannah thought he was going to hit her. Locksie wasn't taking any chances. With broom in hand, as if she had been inside sweeping, Locksie exited the salon. "Is everything okay, Hannah?"

"Yeah, everything is okay," Elkan answered for her with an attitude. "Why you storming up out of there like you coming to her rescue or something; like you her man? Do you think I would hurt my wife?" He looked at Hannah. "Do you think I would ever hurt you?"

Hannah looked into Elkan's eyes. "You have, baby," she said softly, touching his face. "More than you'll ever know." On that note, she got inside her car and drove away. This time, he let her go without a fight.

Chapter 45

The following Wednesday, Hannah and Locksie were pulling up to the house after Bible study only to see Elkan's car parked in front.

"Elkan, what are you doing here? How did you know where the house was?"

"Never mind all that," Elkan said. "I just need to talk to you."

Hannah looked at her husband, from whom she had been separated for two months now. He looked nothing like the strong, handsome, confident man she had known for years. He was unshaven and sported some khaki pants, an untucked T-shirt and dress shoes with no socks.

"Please," he pleaded. "Just five minutes."

Hannah sighed. "Okay, Elkan. Just five minutes." She turned to Locksie, who definitely had her back. "I'm cool. I'll be in in a minute."

"You sure?"

"You heard her," Elkan jumped in.

Locksie began to mumble a prayer as she walked into the house, giving Elkan a look that told him he better keep his flesh under control while on her property or she wouldn't hesitate to call the police.

"What do you want, Elkan?" Hannah asked him once Locksie was in the house.

"I want you. Let's talk . . . for real this time."

Elkan and Hannah talked for the next two hours. They discussed everything, right down to Peni, the affair and how he always made her feel that even though she was his wife, because Peni had given him a child, Peni held a higher place in his heart. Hannah expressed how not being able to give Elkan a child ate away at her.

"But you have me," Elkan had tried to comfort her. "Isn't having me better than having ten sons?"

Hannah went on to explain to him how she was blessed to have Elkan, but that childbearing, to her, was like a badge of womanhood that she might never achieve.

Hannah confessed her feelings about Drake to Elkan; how just the idea of another man finding her attractive boosted her confidence. And of course, they discussed the touchy subject of race, which got so loud that Locksie had to come out of her prayer closet to see what the heck was going on. Aunt Mary used the back den as her prayer closet; her quiet room where she could pray and be in sweet communion with God. Locksie had kept the room that way for her own use.

"Is everything okay out here?" Locksie opened up the door and asked after hearing all of the commotion.

"I'm fine, Locksie," Hannah assured her. "Everything is fine." Hannah stood there with her arms folded, looking down.

"You sure, now?" Locksie said, not completely convinced.

Still a little fumed from Hannah continuously accusing him of being embarrassed of her, Elkan snapped at Locksie, "You heard her! What are you, her watchdog or something? She said she's straight. Now, take your behind back in the house while I have a discussion with *my* wife—or do you think she's your wife now just because she's livin' up in here with you?"

Hannah's mouth dropped open as she looked at Elkan, who was glaring at Locksie with disgust.

"Huh? Is that what's going on here?" Elkan questioned. He looked from Locksie to Hannah. "Your man done left you for another woman so now you trying a different flavor?"

At first Hannah thought that Elkan might just have been trying to get under her skin with his outlandish insinuation, but the look on his face showed that he couldn't have been more serious as he waited on an answer that he never got. He looked at his wife. "You screwing your hairdresser now? Is that why you don't want to come home with me? You into wome—"

Before Elkan could finish his last word, the palm of Hannah's right hand had connected with his left cheek. His instincts were to ball a fist and retaliate. Seeing the balling of his fist, Hannah protected her face in her hands.

"Elkan!" Locksie's voice brought Elkan to his senses right before he could land the intended blow to Hannah's face. Immediately, Locksie rushed out the door and grabbed Hannah out of harm's way. Hannah was shocked by the fact that she had put her hands on her husband and shocked that he was only inches away from putting his hands on her.

"I think you better go now," Locksie said to Elkan as she pulled Hannah into the house and closed the door behind them; locking it and putting the chain on the door.

"Oh my God, Locksie," Hannah said, putting her hand over her mouth as tears formed in her eyes. "I hit him. I actually hit Elkan. I hit my husband. I can go to jail for domestic violence. But besides that, he's my husband. I can't believe I put my hands on him like that. I feel awful for hitting him."

"Hannah, just calm down," Locksie told her.

"Hannah!" They could hear Elkan yelling from the other side of the door. "Just let me talk to you, baby. Look, it's okay. I'm sorry. This is all my fault; not yours. I don't blame you for hitting me. I deserved it. Please, just talk to me. Let's go somewhere and talk."

Elkan began pounding on the door. Hannah jumped and began crying. What was going on? What was happening to her life? It had gone from a dream come true, her meeting a handsome, wonderful man who had treated her well and had been good to her—with the exception of his one forgiven mistake of adultery—to a complete and total nightmare. She needed help, but she had no idea where it would come from.

Out of nowhere, Hannah just began calling out the name of Jesus. "Jesus!" she wept. "Jesus."

"It's okay," Locksie said as she tried to comfort her by bending down and wrapping her arms around her.

"No," Hannah said, pushing Locksie's hands away as if to say that it wasn't Locksie she needed to comfort her. "Jesus!" she yelled out again. "Jesus, help me! Oh my God, in the name of Jesus, help me!"

Locksie pulled away and watched as her friend experienced what was either a breakthrough or a breakdown.

"Jesus!" Hannah called out as she looked around, hoping that the person whose name she was calling would suddenly appear. "Jesus!"

Locksie ran to the linen closet and grabbed a large bath towel. She placed it over Hannah's trembling body. She had seen people do this in church; place a scarf-like material over someone who had fallen out at the altar. Locksie didn't know the significance of it, but she felt that it seemed fitting at the moment. She had prayed over the towel from the closet to the living room; hopefully by covering Hannah with the towel, she was covering her in prayer.

Upon returning to the living room, Locksie realized that Elkan's knocking, ranting and raving had ceased. She hadn't even noticed when, but it had. He was gone.

After placing the towel on Hannah's body, which was stretched out across the floor in front of the door, Locksie stepped back and watched as Hannah wept. She wanted so badly to go and comfort her hurting friend, but her spirit told her that it wasn't the time and to just let her be. Being in control of her flesh and not having a disobedient spirit, Locksie slowly backed away into her bedroom. She knew that Hannah would be okay. Jesus had kept her when she and Dawson broke up and she was going through the motions. *If He did it for me,* Locksie told herself, *then I trust that He'll do the same for Hannah too.*

And believing such, Locksie pulled out her Bible and walked over to the chair where her Aunt Mary used to sit and read the Word. She opened up the Bible to no particular book or chapter and just began to read. She didn't know how she was supposed to help her friend whose life as she knew it was about to change; but she was certain that the answer was somewhere between those pages.

Chapter 46

The evening Elkan had showed up on their doorstep, Locksie and Hannah, in their separate spaces, had prayed into the midnight hour for God to speak to Hannah's situation. To this day, as Hannah sat in her and Elkan's favorite restaurant attempting to have a civil conversation, she still had not heard from God. She didn't want to just completely write Elkan off as she waited to hear from God, which was why she agreed to have dinner with him. But God had not told her to move, so moving back in with Elkan right now was out of the question, even though Elkan's intended purpose when inviting his wife out to dinner was to get her to come back home.

"I just can't come home yet, Elkan. Not until I hear from Him."

Elkan couldn't believe that he was sitting there listening to his wife tell him that another man was to be the determining factor. He couldn't help but wonder if this other person was Drake. Even though Hannah had assured him that nothing had ever gone on between her and Drake, he still couldn't shake the thought. Just when his blood began to boil and he wanted to snap, he got himself under control. In their past conversations, he realized that his high temper hadn't gotten him anywhere. He had made a mental note to try a new approach.

"So, what does this other man have that I don't?" Elkan calmly asked. "Why do you respect what he says so much?"

Hannah grinned and shook her head. She had to admit, Elkan being jealous was a sign that he cared. But how much did he care? "It's not what you're thinking, Elkan," Hannah tried to assure him. "Right now I'm at a place in my life where it's all about me and Him. And you know what, Elkan? He doesn't care if I'm white, black, Hispanic, Japanese, Chinese, Vietnamese, or whatever else. All He cares about is what's in here." Hannah pointed to her heart. "My soul."

"So, it's like that? It's over?" Elkan asked, defeated.

Hannah shrugged. "I don't know, Elkan. It all depends."

"On what?"

"On what He tells me to do." Hannah was about to explain exactly who *He* was, but Elkan's temper got the best of him.

"Ugggh, here we go again!" Elkan tried to hide the aggravation that came over him, but the tone of his sudden loud pitch was a dead giveaway. "You mean you gon' let another nigga decide whether or not you gon' be with me or not?"

Elkan's use of the "N" word had definitely got some patrons' attention. A few began to shoot him evil looks while others rolled their eyes and whispered. For a moment, Hannah just sat there looking at Elkan as if he'd lost his mind. But then, once she couldn't hold it in any longer, she just burst out laughing.

Elkan began to look around and notice the glares. They weren't glaring because of Hannah's loud laughter either. They were still stuck on the fact that he had just used the "N" word. Right then, he realized that no matter what color the person was who said the "N" word, it was still offensive; and he had offended many. Hannah's laughing didn't help matters any.

"And just what is so funny?" Elkan said between clenched teeth.

"Oh, nothing." Hannah laughed. "I was just thinking; God has probably been called a lot of things, but never the 'N' word."

"What? Who? What are you talking about?" Elkan asked.

"Nothing, sweetheart," Hannah said as she removed the napkin from her lap and placed it on the table. "I think I'm going to pass on dessert, Elkan." Hannah stood as she managed to take control of her laughter.

"But . . . I don't understand," Elkan stammered.

"Me either, but He'll help me to. And like I said, I don't know what's going to come of our marriage. I got a lot of praying on it to do, you know."

Elkan buried his face into his hands and sighed. He looked up at his wife, not knowing whether she was soon to be his ex-wife. "I guess, Hannah. I mean, what can I do? Obviously, this he-him-or-whoever has got control of you. And you know what? I ain't mad. I mean, maybe this is your way of paying me back for Peni. But I love you, Hannah. And I know I may sound like a punk, but if spending time with *him* means there is a chance of us getting back together, then it's a chance I'm willing to take. Who knows? Maybe me and him can be cool; kick it someday."

Hannah chuckled. She rubbed the back of her hand down Elkan's face. "Yeah, Elkan, maybe someday I will introduce you to *Him*. Matter of fact, I think you just might like Him." Hannah kissed Elkan on the forehead and then exited the restaurant.

Although Hannah's dinner with Elkan hadn't gone as planned, it could have been worse. Hannah unlocked her car door and got inside. She sat there for a moment before she burst out laughing again just thinking about the fact that Elkan had no idea that the *Him* she had been referring to was God. Maybe Elkan not knowing would keep him on his toes.

"Well, Lord,"—Hannah looked up and prayed—"You see what I'm working with, right? I mean, that's my husband. I met him before I met You, so I'm not sure if my flesh chose him or if You chose him for me. But, dear Lord, as much as I love Elkan, I'm going to put it in Your hands to show me whether or not this is the husband You had for me that I am supposed to stay married to and spend the rest of my life with.

"I love him with all of my heart, even though there are some ways about him that I dislike. But, God, I know You can turn anyone's life around. I know that You would want the man You have for me to love You just as much as I do, and Elkan really doesn't know You like that. But it says in the Bible, somewhere in the book of Corinthians, that the unbelieving husband is sanctified by the wife, and the unbelieving wife is sanctified by the husband.

"Now, Heavenly Father, I know I said I love Elkan with all my heart. I want to keep him as my husband if we can repair and work on some things. But if he is not who You have for me, Lord—because I only want what You have for me—then I'll give him up in a heartbeat. So, Lord, I just ask that You speak to my situation and show me the way. If You lead me, I'll follow, no matter where or how far. In Jesus' name I pray. Amen."

Hannah started up her car and pulled out of the parking lot and onto the road. Spiritually, she was headed down a road with no idea where it might lead her, but she knew that no matter what, she'd end up in that place which was prepared just for her.

Chapter 47

Hannah lay on the floor, crying and shaking. She had woken up that morning prepared to spend her day working on her laptop, but something in her told her that instead, she needed to spend it with God. After having coffee with Locksie and seeing her off to work, (something Locksie suggested the women do along with prayer, of course; just like Aunt Mary would have wanted.) Hannah borrowed a stack of Locksie's gospel CDs that she had inherited from her aunt Mary and allowed praise music to fill the air.

Hours later, Hannah was still in His presence as she sang, danced and worshipped Him. She had no idea how many hours had passed. Time seemed to have stood still in God's glory. She had recently rededicated her life to Christ at Locksie's church and was scheduled to be baptized along with Locksie. Hannah just couldn't imagine how she had gone through life all of this time without acknowledging and having a relationship with God.

When the CD Hannah had been listening to went off, that's when she dropped to her knees and just began to cry out unto the Lord. She cried out for her marriage. She cried out her forgiveness for anything Elkan had done in their marriage that hurt her. She even cried out forgiveness for Peni. When she was finished, she was about to stand up, but she felt the need to just be silent and listen . . . and that's when she heard it; the voice of God!

"Hey, girl," Hannah said, entering the living room after she heard Locksie come through the door.

"What's up?" Locksie said, looking down at her mail. For some strange reason, a dark feeling came over her. She looked up into Hannah's eyes and knew that the words that would soon be spoken by her friend had everything to do with that feeling.

"I'm going back to Elkan," Hannah announced.

Locksie didn't know what to say. She knew she was supposed to be happy for Hannah; no one wants to see her friend go through a divorce. But at the same time, a spirit of envy crept up on her. If Hannah was going back to Elkan, that meant she was leaving Locksie. Misery loves company, and although Locksie hated to admit it, she enjoyed not being the only somebody who was miserable and had issues. So at first, instead of being happy for Hannah, she felt sorry for herself. She was jealous.

"But, Hannah, what happened?" Locksie started. "Just the other day you were complaining about having not heard from God on what to do yet. You said that not hearing from God was probably His way of telling you that you're not supposed to be with Elkan."

"Like the saying goes, and I guess it applies to Him too,"—Hannah pointed up—"no news is good news."

"But you said it yourself that even if you did go back to Elkan, you don't know how things would work out with you having rededicated your life to Christ and all. That would mean a lifestyle change. You saw what I went through with Dawson. The man was jealous of God, for Pete's sake. You think Elkan was jealous of Drake, huh? You just wait and see—"

Hannah put her hand up to cease Locksie's tongue. She knew how her friend was feeling. The Holy Spirit had warned her that not everybody would be happy about her decision. Hannah knew deep down inside that Locksie didn't want to see her unhappy, but that sometimes it's hard for people to rejoice over somebody else's blessing, especially if that blessing is something they, too, had been waiting on for themselves.

Despite Hannah suggesting that she talk to the hand, Locksie continued. "I mean, you were sold out to Jesus one minute, and now you're going to go back into a situation that hasn't been healed yet. The Bible says, II Corinthians 6:14: *Do not be unequally yoked together with unbelievers. For what fellowship has righteousness with lawlessness? And what communion has light with darkness?*"

"And I understand that, Locksie," Hannah told her. "But the Bible also says that a person can be saved through their spouse." Hannah walked over and held Locksie's hands in hers. "Besides, and even more importantly, I heard from God, Locksie. This is not my flesh sending me back home with Elkan. If that was the case, as badly as I've been missing my husband and craving him, I would have long been back home by now. God assured me that Elkan is the husband He has for me. And I know things might be rough between Elkan and me at first—heck, probably even get worse before it gets better—but I'm going to believe and trust in God. Yes, Elkan and I have a lot to overcome, but I'm going to keep praying for strength, and I'm going to need you to keep praying too."

At that point, Locksie remained silent—against her will. Oh, her flesh had a few more words that it could have mustered up, but in her spirit, she knew that if Hannah had heard from God, there was nothing else she could do or say. She had no authority over Him, and arguing with Hannah would have been like arguing with God; she couldn't win.

"So, when are you leaving?" Locksie asked.

"Elkan's on his way to help me lug all my things back to the house."

"It'll be dark soon."

"I'll turn the porch light on. We'll be fine."

"So, what were you going to do," Locksie joked, "leave me a Dear Joan letter telling me you were gone?"

"Girl, no. You know I wouldn't have left until you got home. After all you've done for me." Hannah walked up to Locksie and hugged her. "You saved my life—literally, girl. You saved my soul. If it wasn't for you, I wouldn't have gotten back into church. I wouldn't have rededicated my life to Christ." Hannah paused for a minute, deep in thought.

"What is it?" Locksie said, pulling away and wiping the tears that were running down her face.

"As crazy as it might sound, I think everything that has happened, happened just to get me here; at this place, at this time. God brought me here to get me closer to Him." Hannah got excited as if she was having a revelation. "Think about it, Locksie. Think about the chain of events that have taken place in our lives. Think of the timing of everything. None of this is an accident. It's all God's will. It's like a big game of chess. We're the pieces that God moves around to get everybody positioned where they need to be. It's destiny. In the end, everything works for our good."

Locksie began to smile. "You know what? I think you're right."

"You do?"

"Yeah, I do," Locksie said.

Hannah began pacing with excitement. "Just think; before, you were just my hairdresser. Now you're my sister in Christ, my prayer partner, my Bible study buddy. Look at God! And now, He wants me to take what I've got and give it to my husband—the husband He has for me." Hannah ran back over to Locksie and hugged her. "Thank you, friend. Thank you so much. Because of your obedience, I'm changed for the better."

Locksie couldn't explain the elated feeling that had come over her. Until that moment, she had never realized how her submissiveness to God affected other people's lives. She was experiencing what she thought was a little taste of what Ester must have felt when she saved her people by being obedient.

Just then, there was a knock on the door.

"I'll get it," Locksie said.

"You sure?" Hannah asked, knowing that it was Elkan and that the last couple of times he and Locksie had an encounter, it wasn't pretty.

"Yeah, I got this." Locksie winked, deciding to be the bigger person and make amends with Elkan. But Elkan beat her to it.

"Hey, Locksie," Elkan said after she answered the door. "These are for you." He handed her a beautiful bouquet of roses.

"Uh, well, uh . . . thank you." Locksie grinned, accepting the roses from Elkan and then inhaling the scent. She was about to ask Elkan what they were for, but he answered before she could ask.

"Thank you for taking care of my wife."

"Anytime," Locksie told him. "Anytime."

Hannah was glad to see Elkan make peace with Locksie. After all, he would be seeing a lot more of her prayer partner now. All Hannah wanted anyway in their lives was peace. She had even gone as far as calling Peni up to clear the air between them. Hannah simply told her, "You can have the baby and you can have the child support, but you can't have my husband." Surprisingly, Peni received what Hannah had to say, promising that she would try her best not to be such a witch anymore. Besides, she didn't have the time to dedicate to tormenting Hannah anymore.

Supposedly, Peni's attention would soon be focused on her own husband. Evidently, she and some doctor had enjoyed a whirlwind romance and were going off to Hawaii to be married. Elkan had done his homework on the doc because he wanted to see what type of man was going to be helping to raise his son. The doctor turned out to be very well respected and seemed like a pretty decent man. Hannah thanked God for finding Peni a man of her own so that now she didn't have to ruin so many other lives and relationships trying to snag one. If God could bless Peni with a good man, then He could bless any woman.

After Locksie put her roses in water, the three of them loaded up all of Hannah's things into her and Elkan's cars. Once they were finished, Elkan and Hannah gave Locksie a good-bye hug.

"Uh, before we go," Elkan said as he fumbled his hands in his pockets and looked down. "I know you've already done so much." He looked to Locksie. "But can I ask you to do one last thing?"

Locksie looked puzzled. "Yeah, sure. What is it?"

Hannah stood waiting to see what it was that Elkan wanted.

"Can you pray for us? Pray for me and my wife."

Locksie's shoulders relaxed and she smiled. "Of course I will keep praying for you guys."

Elkan cleared his throat. "I mean right now." He could see the shocked look on Locksie's face, so he felt the need to explain himself. "See, my wife finally explained to me who *He* is."

Locksie had no clue what Elkan was referring to.

"She said she couldn't come back to me until He said so. Well, on the phone today when she called me to tell me she was coming home, we talked for a while. She confirmed my thoughts that another man was in her life—and that man is God. She told me about all the praying you two did for us. And truthfully, if I never believed in prayer before, I believe in it now. My wife expressed to me that just because God has answered her prayers, she's not going to just forget about Him. She said that He's a part of her now, and she said something you told her about a package deal . . ."

Locksie and Hannah smiled at each other. Locksie had told Hannah the story about Dawson's visit to her church, when Reverend Franklin preached on relationships; how he had said that relationships were a package deal. If a person wanted to be in a relationship with one of God's children, then they had to have a relationship with God as well. Obviously, she had shared the sermon with Elkan.

"Well, anyway," Elkan continued, "I would pray myself right now, but I really don't know how. So, I was wondering if you and my wife can keep praying for us." He looked to Hannah. "Until, that is, I get the hang of it and my wife and I can pray together."

Hannah put her hand over her mouth as tears ran down her face. She was so elated that she dropped to her knees and began to shout right there on Locksie's front lawn. Then all of a sudden, words that Elkan didn't recognize came out of Hannah's mouth. It was almost as if she was speaking a foreign language. Elkan went to help his wife up, but Locksie stopped him.

"Let her be," Locksie told him. "She's talking to God." Locksie briefly explained to Elkan that his wife was speaking in tongues. She took Elkan's hands into hers. "Come on, let's you and I pray. Heads bowed, eyes closed."

Elkan bowed his head and closed his eyes as he and Locksie prayed, while Hannah continued her conversation with the Lord.

"Dear Lord, you are so awesome and worthy to be praised," Locksie said. "I just can't thank You enough for all You do and all You've done, and, Father, all You're gonna do. First of all, Father God, I'd like to thank You for what You're doing right now at this very moment. I thank You for not being a temporary fix in our lives, Lord, but instead, the path to eternal life.

"I thank You for putting it into Hannah's heart to know that she's just not to just call on You when she's got a mess, but to call on You always in order to be blessed. God, we know that You are not just some Vegas slot machine who has a lever we can pull on to get what we want when we want it; but, God, You are an all-the-time God, an every-day God who we must seek a relationship with.

"Father God, I just ask that You bless Hannah and Elkan's lives with an overflow; an overflow of love, communication and understanding. Make them rich with happiness, dear Lord, keep them humble, surrendering to each other, but more importantly, always surrendering to You. Father God, I thank you in advance for the mighty move You are about to do in their lives. In Jesus' name I pray . . ." Locksie then shook Elkan's hands, signaling him to go ahead and give prayer a try.

He opened one eye. "Who, me?" he asked. Locksie nodded with a smile. Elkan cleared his throat, thought for a minute and then prayed, "The Lord is my Sheperd, I shall not want. Amen." Unfortunately, the only time Elkan had been in church and heard prayer was at a funeral, and that scripture was pretty much what every pastor recited. He opened his eyes for Locksie's approval. "How was that?" he asked.

She chuckled. "Well, it's a start," she told him. "It's a start."

The Final Chapter

"I expect a miracle!" Locksie shouted over the Byron Cage and J-Moss collaboration that was ringing through the speakers. She loved songs that allowed her to experience both praise and worship at the same time. Most songs were either songs of praise or songs of worship, but when the artist used the praise portion of the song to allow God to invite them into worship, it was felt by the listener's soul; therefore pulling the listener into the presence of the Lord as well.

As the song ended, Locksie was all set to go hit the repeat button on the CD player. She had been blasting the music to make sure that the sounds of praise hit every corner of her house, blessing each and every room. She had been cleaning up Hannah's former bedroom, turning it back into the original guestroom that her aunt Mary had had it set up to be.

As the song faded, and right before her finger hit the repeat button, she heard a loud banging at the door. What followed was a voice shouting, "Locksie, open the door!"

She could tell it was Dawson's voice, and the first thing that came to mind was that he was there to finish what Elkan had started; acting a fool out in her front yard. Surely the neighbors would call the police this time if she didn't spit on the spark before it turned into an uncontrollable blaze.

Locksie ran to the door, tripping and falling down on the way. She got up off the floor and quickly limped over to the door and flung it open before Dawson could do any more banging or any more shouting. "What, man? What do you want?" Locksie said, out of breath and frustrated from the fall in which she had hurt her knee, which was now throbbing.

Although more angry at the floor than at Dawson, she was still angry at him. How dare he show up out of the clear blue sky after four months? She probably would have refused to talk to him, but the very least he could have done was try.

"What are you doing here? You get tired of Peni?" Locksie spat. That's what Locksie had been assuming all of this time; that the reason Dawson wasn't trying to get her back was because he had been off gallivanting with the other woman.

"What's wrong with you?" Dawson said in response to Locksie's greeting that was full of attitude.

"You bangin' on the door like the po-po; that's what's wrong," Locksie spat as she rubbed her aching knee.

"You okay?" Dawson was concerned.

"Yeah, I just fell on my way trying to get the door that you were out here beating on like a lunatic."

"I rang the bell and knocked for ten minutes. I even called your phone. But I guess you couldn't hear it over your gospel jubilee."

"Oh, yeah, the music was kind of loud, wasn't it? But I wasn't expecting anyone, so . . ." Locksie's words trailed off.

"Anyway," Dawson looked down at Locksie's injured knee and then deep into her eyes. "I didn't mean for you to get hurt. I really didn't."

Locksie could tell that Dawson's words were directed at more than just her knee. They were meant for her heart. His sincerity immediately chipped away at some of the ice that was sealing her heart.

"Well, I did get hurt, Dawson. And I'm still hurting. So, why don't you just go back to Peni and—"

"Peni and I are through." Dawson cut her off. "We haven't seen each other since the night at the gym. I tried to tell you, but you wouldn't talk to me."

"So you just gave up?" Locksie's arms flailed and then dropped to her side. "You gave up on us just like that."

"What was I supposed to do? I could have gone to jail if I harassed you. I really thought you were done with me, Locksie. I didn't know what to do."

"So, why now? Why now after all of this time?"

"I need closure," Dawson confessed.

"So, this is about you and your getting some closure?"

"I just don't understand why you have to make this so hard." Dawson sighed.

"Me making this so hard?" Locksie replied defensively. "I just don't understand why *you* can't see that you are the one who is making this hard, not me. All I ever wanted us to do was to live right."

"Who's to say we are not living right? Living right by whose standards? Society's?"

"By God's!" Locksie shouted, then caught herself and toned it down. "By God's standards; the only standards that matter."

Dawson threw his hands up. "Here we go again. If it ain't you, it's Drake. I'm so sick of talking about God. I don't want to talk about God anymore."

Locksie couldn't explain the anger that erupted in her body. God was her father who was doing great things. How could anyone not want to talk about Him? Instead of letting her anger be quick to speak, she dipped into the "the gap" that was mentioned in a book she had read titled *God Speaks to Me* by Valerie Love. The gap was that slight period of time that allowed her to think about her response to Dawson's words that had angered her. She could either fly off the handle by retaliating with angry words, or she could be Christ-like. She decided to go with the latter.

Taking a deep breath, Locksie stood in the doorway and replied, "You've been my best friend for years now. I've always been able to talk to you about everything; a really good movie I saw or a really good book that I've read. Now here there is the one thing that I love talking about the most in my life, and we can't have a conversation about it."

Dawson took each one of Locksie's hands into his. "But you can. You can talk to me about anything."

"But you just said you don't want to talk about God, so evidently I can't. Besides, I don't want to just talk. I want to have a conversation. I want you to talk too, but how can you talk about something you don't know anything about?"

Dawson released Locksie's hands. "You saying I'm the devil or something? Locksie, I believe in God."

"Believing in God isn't enough, Dawson." Locksie put her hands to her temples as her eyes watered. "This is just so frustrating. Why can't I get you to love Him like I do?"

"Him, Him, Him. I'm so sick of hearing about Him as if God's a real person that's walking the earth."

Clearing her mind and choosing not to proceed with the topic of their conversation, Locksie asked, "Was there any other reason you stopped by? I need to get back to cleaning."

For a minute there, Dawson had forgotten the initial purpose for his visit. "As a matter of fact, I did come by for another reason. I came by to just . . . to just tell you I love you, girl. I ain't cool with this. I ain't cool with us being apart. I don't want this."

"I don't want this either," Locksie assured him.

"Then you need to choose, Locksie."

"Choose what?"

"Choose if you're going to just give up on us completely, or try to work this out."

"In all honesty, I think a choice needs to be made by you. I'm heading in a certain direction in my life. My walk in life has changed, Dawson. I have to live for God."

Dawson's jaw tightened. "Then my walk is going to change, too, in a direction that leads me away from you forever."

Locksie felt her heart drop to her feet. She had been the one doing all the walking away, in hopes that Dawson would see the light and follow. But to see him stand there and say that he was going to start walking all right, but in a direction away from her, was a huge blow.

Dawson continued. "You need to sit down and say to yourself, 'Is it going to be Dawson and me, or Him?'"

"Him?"

"Yes, Him; God, who you've all of a sudden fallen in love with and out of love with me at the same time. How can God be so greedy and take all of your love?"

Locksie shook her head, and she was the one who now took Dawson's hands into hers. "No, baby, you've got it all wrong. When I found my love for Christ, Dawson, I didn't stop loving you."

"Like heck you didn't!" Dawson snapped. "You wouldn't even let me touch you anymore." Dawson fought back his emotions. The last thing he wanted to do was stand there and cry in front of the woman for who he was trying to be every man in the world.

It hurt Locksie to see Dawson so emotional. "I

love you, baby. But you can't ask me to choose between you and—"

"And some supernatural being that doesn't even have a shape or form? I mean, yeah, I believe there is a God and all, but come on. It's not like God is a person. Someone you can see. That you can touch. I mean, I could see if I was up against some pretty-Ricky, rich millionaire dude or something. But for some so-called—"

"Dawson, don't . . ." Locksie put her hands up as if they were a barricade whose only purpose was blocking Dawson's words from landing in her ear.

"You don't have to choose right now, Locks. I'm gonna give you some time to think about it and then tell me the choice you've made. As a matter of fact, I'm going to let you show me the choice you've made." He turned and picked up the tweed, flower-print carry-on bag that he had set down next to the porch during all of his knocking. Locksie had left the bag under the bed at Dawson's place, their former house together. Since she hadn't been on any overnight stays, she hadn't needed it and therefore hadn't missed it. She also hadn't even noticed it sitting next to the porch.

"Our Delta flight to Vegas leaves next Thursday at 6:00 P.M.," Dawson informed her, handing her the bag.

Oh my God! Is he asking me to marry him? was the first thing that popped into Locksie's mind.

"We need to be checked in at least an hour before the flight departure time. I'll be at the Delta check-in counter at 5:00 P.M. If you're there, too, then I'll know what that means."

Locksie shrugged. "And what would that mean?"

"That you chose me; that you chose me and you. That you can stop playing this stupid little game and sell this house and move back into our home. The home we made together. The home that when we picked it out, you said heaven made just for us. Now, heaven can't be wrong, can it?" Dawson said sarcastically.

"I'm not going against God and living in sin with you, Dawson. What part of that don't you understand?"

Words couldn't begin to describe how torn Locksie was. She was so certain that because her heart wanted to be with Dawson so much, God would make a way for them to be together. That God would assign some of His angels to get all up in Dawson's heart and make him begin to seek and love God, so that the two of them could be equally yoked. After all, she could have sworn that she had read somewhere in the Bible that God would provide her with her heart's desires. Well . . . Dawson was her heart's desire, but here he stood on her doorstep, talking about throwing in the towel.

The more the reality of losing Dawson forever set in, Locksie began to waver. She thought that there was no way she could lose this man. This was the man she had vowed to love to eternity on the first night they ever told each other that they loved one another. Before now, she hadn't really thought about it. Hannah had been there to keep her company, and with all the praying those two had done, she was just certain that things would turn out the way she wanted. After all, God saw to it that everything turned to Hannah the way she wanted. Wouldn't He do the same for her? But now here was Dawson, planting doubt.

Dawson could see that his heartfelt words were starting to persuade Locksie, so he better keep chipping away while the heat seemed to be melting the ice. "I love you so much, Locksie, and I know you love me. We've been nothing but good for each other. I make you happy. You mean to tell me that God wouldn't want you with a man that makes you happy? That takes care of you? That's never called you out of your name, and disrespected you or any of that? A man that wants to be with you for the rest of his life? A man that can own up to his mistakes and apologize? Because I am sorry, Locksie. I'm sorry for ever hurting you, and I promise I will never hurt you again . . . ever. Wouldn't God want that kind of man for you?"

Dawson's last query opened up a can of worms that Locksie couldn't help but push him into. "So, if all that is true and you want to be with me the rest of my life, then why don't we confirm and commit to that by just getting married?"

Dawson rolled his eyes up in his head. *Great . . . I asked for that one.* After thinking for a minute, his comeback was, "So what if I was to say, 'Okay, Locksie, we'll get married while in Vegas, not because I want to, but because you said I have to if I want to be with you'?"

Of course that's not the type of proposal Locksie had dreamt of as a little girl. She twisted her face a little bit as if she'd just eaten a sour grape. "Then I'd have to pray on it and see—"

"That's what I'm talking about." Dawson cut her off in a frustrated tone. "You'd have to go pray on it and see what God gives you, right? No matter what, it's never going to be about me anymore. It's never going to be about just us."

"You're right!" Locksie said, stepping out the door and walking close to Dawson. She'd had enough of his tantrums and blatant disrespect for God. "It's never going to be about you or me, because in this life, it's not about us. It's not about anybody on this earth. It's all about God. And if you had a closer relationship with Him, you'd know exactly where I'm coming from. I can't explain it to you any better than that, Dawson. I just can't explain it." Locksie slumped her shoulders and put her head down as she began to cry.

Seeing her in so much pain made Dawson reach out to her. "Can't you see what this is doing to us?" he said, putting his arms around her. "It's tearing us apart. We can work this out. Let's just give it some time. You didn't change into the person you are overnight, so don't condemn me."

Locksie began crying harder in Dawson's arms. She had never wanted him to feel as though she was condemning him. She just wanted him to be saved. How could she tell him that she loved him so much that she wanted to spend life and afterlife with him? Maybe Dawson was right. Maybe she had gone about this entire thing all wrong. Maybe God had spoken, but she just hadn't heard Him. Maybe God had placed Dawson on her doorstep today out of nowhere because Locksie hadn't been taking heed. After all, with the exception of the Peni situation, which she might have driven him to, Dawson had been nothing but good to her. So why wouldn't God want her to be with him?

So there Locksie stood, weak and confused and left with a decision to choose the man she had vowed to love to eternity versus the love for the one who promised her eternity.

"Sir, the system shows that there should be another traveler in your party," the man at the Delta ticket counter stated as Dawson checked in for his flight to Vegas.

"I know. She should be here any minute," Dawson said with confidence before looking down at his watch that read three minutes until five o'clock.

Dawson had arrived at the airport around a quarter to five. Originally he was just going to wait for Locksie before checking in so that they could do it together. As he waited, the line seemed to get longer and longer, so he decided to go ahead and stand in it, figuring by the time she got there, it would be their turn. By the time Dawson was next in line, he remembered that Locksie preferred curbside check-in anyway, so he went ahead and checked in without her.

After the check-in process, Dawson was instructed to take his bags over to luggage security. As he turned away from the counter, he searched the doorways for any sign of Locksie. There was none. Slowly, he proceeded over to luggage security, the entire time looking over his shoulder for Locksie.

By the time Dawson turned his luggage over, and after informing security that he didn't have any film or disposable cameras of any kind that could possibly be ruined by the X-ray used to examine luggage, Locksie still hadn't showed up. Dawson decided to cop a seat and wait a few more minutes before heading through passenger security and heading to his departure gate. Just as he sat down, his heart skipped a beat at the sight of Locksie, who made her way through the parting doors. With a huge smile on his face, he rushed over to her.

"Thank God you showed up," Dawson said, setting down his carry-on bag and embracing her.

"Oh, so now you thank Him?" Locksie asked with sarcasm that was obviously well hidden because Dawson didn't catch on.

"Where's your bags?" he asked as he looked down, noticing that she didn't have any with her. "Oh, that's right. You always do curbside check-in. Shoot, not me. Why waste the tip dollars?" He chuckled.

"You're so crazy," Locksie told him with a slight chuckle of her own, but it seemed somewhat forced.

Dawson noticed. "Baby, what's wrong?"

Locksie looked down. Dawson slowly released her from his embrace. He lifted her face so that they were now eye to eye. "You aren't coming to Vegas, are you?"

Locksie didn't say a word. She didn't have to. It was written all over her face.

"Baby, don't do this to us," Dawson begged, looking around, feeling like everyone in the airport was witnessing him being dumped.

"If there's ever going to be an 'us', the kind of 'us' I want, then I have to," Locksie told him. "I came because I wanted to tell you personally. I didn't want to just not show up."

Dawson looked unimpressed. "You could have just called me on the phone and told me this."

"But I wanted to pray on this up until the last hour—the last minute. I even prayed the entire drive to the airport. My luggage is even in the backseat of my car just in case God told me something different on the way here. But He only confirmed what I already knew in my spirit anyway."

"So that's that?" Dawson shrugged, not knowing what else to say.

"That's that."

"Then I guess He won. That God sure is a lucky man to have a girl like you. You're loyal, that's for sure." Dawson tried to hide his true hurt and pain with some comic relief.

After a few seconds of awkward silence, Dawson looked at his watch and said, "Well, I better get going. You already left me; I wouldn't want the plane to do the same thing." Again, more failed comic relief.

"Take care, Dawson," Locksie said sincerely.

"Yeah, take care, kid." He kissed her on the forehead, winked and then walked away.

Locksie watched him. He never looked back. Had he, he would have seen her standing there in a hurtful tremble of tears and pain as she watched someone who she had held truly dear to her walk out of her life.

I don't understand, God, Locksie couldn't help but pray. *You gave Hannah her husband. Where's mine?* She tried to be strong, but she wasn't happy with God's decision for her.

"You okay, honey?" a concerned woman stopped and asked Locksie. Locksie, unable to speak, nodded. "You'll be just fine. Jesus loves you," the woman added. "It might sound crazy to you right now, but sometimes it don't hurt to just let people know that Jesus loves 'em."

"I know," Locksie said as a smile crept on her face, but the woman had already walked away and didn't hear her response. "I know Jesus loves me." Being reminded of and filled with the love of Christ somehow instantaneously took away Locksie's pain. Now her tears were of happiness and joy.

Wiping her eyes, Locksie exited the airport proud of herself for not only following her heart, but for being obedient to God.

As Locksie got into her car in the airport garage, looking at her luggage in the backseat, she didn't regret her decision at all. She knew that even if she had stood in that airport and talked to Dawson until she was blue in the face, he still wouldn't have understood.

After paying her parking fee, Locksie exited Columbus Metropolitan Airport and hit I-270, still thinking about Dawson. He would never understand the love she had for God until he, too, was overcome with that same love. And it was at that moment, for the first time ever, that Locksie finally knew exactly how her mother felt.

Excitedly, Locksie dug down in her purse for her cell phone. She skimmed through her digital phonebook and then selected the number she wanted to dial. As the phone rang, she felt ashamed that she hadn't dialed the number enough times to have memorized it.

"Praise the Lord," the voice on the other end of the phone greeted.

"Ma," Locksie said.

"Baby, is that you?" her mother said, almost unable to believe that it was her only child on the other end of the phone, the one who usually only called on Mothers' Day and a couple of other holidays throughout the year. The daughter she hadn't seen since Mary's funeral.

Locksie broke down in tears, almost impairing her vision while she was driving. She quickly wiped them away. Her mother said nothing. Her spirit of discernment must have informed her that she needed not to speak, but to allow her daughter to release.

After a minute of whimpering into the receiver, Locksie finally spoke. "Ma, Dawson and I broke up—for good."

"Well, I'd only met him one time; that time you guys just happened to be driving through this way to get to your final destination. I take that back. Twice—I saw him again at the funeral too. But he seemed like a decent man."

"He is, Ma. He's a good man. He's a fine man, too. But like that one Christian fiction book asks, 'Is he saved?' And the answer in this case would have to be no."

"So, you had to let him go?"

"Yeah, Ma." Locksie began to cry again. Although she knew that Jesus loved her and God would see her through while the Holy Spirit comforted her, she still knew there would be some rough patches. "It hurts, too, but I know it's what I had to do."

"Well, baby, sometimes God gotta move things out of your life—sometimes the things you want—so that He can make room for the things He wants in your life."

"I know, Ma. I know," Locksie said. "But look, Ma, I was thinking about taking my vacation next month. Would it be okay if I came there and spent it with you?"

"Child, you ain't got to ask me that," her mother exclaimed. "I would love for my daughter to come visit me." She was on the verge of tears. Her daughter had finally found her way back home—not just to her home in Michigan, but her home in the Kingdom. She thought about Proverbs 22:6: *Train up a child in the way he should go: and when he is old, he will not depart from it.* How true God's Word is.

"It took years of praying and standing on God's Word for this day to come," Martha proclaimed. "Glory! Glory! But diligently I continued to pray." By now, both Locksie and her mother were rejoicing. "This is just a reminder that God doesn't answer prayers overnight. But if you ask Him to do something and you have faith and believe, stand in His Word and wait in desperate desire, 'cause He's gonna do what He said He's gonna do, then you'll get your result."

Locksie smiled, because she believed just that. She knew in her heart that when God told her she couldn't be with Dawson, He didn't necessarily mean never. He meant "not now." So, that's just what Locksie decided she was going to do when it came to her and Dawson; keep praying and keep waiting. She would pray for the day that

Dawson would come to her as a saved man, ready to walk with the Lord and live life according to God's commandments.

And just then, Locksie realized that Aunt Mary, may she rest in peace, might have been wrong about one thing: God is into threesomes. Because when two people are joined together, it takes God being right there in the midst to keep them together. That's the way Locksie wanted it to be with her and Dawson.

But for now, Locksie thought to herself, *it's just going to be me, myself and Him.*

Reader's Group Guide Questions

1) What character could you most relate to?

2) Did the actions and reactions of the characters in this novel seem believable to you? Were there any characters you could have done without, or do you think each one played a significant role?

3) How big a role did Locksie's aunt Mary play in Locksie deciding to give her life to Christ?

4) Initially, Locksie's mother came across as a holy roller. Did learning about her past change your opinion of why she was the way that she was when it came to expressing her love for the Lord?

5) Do you think there is a fine line between loving the Lord and expressing it on a daily basis versus one wearing religion on one's sleeve? Even if someone resists the issue of going to church or becoming saved, should the person trying to convince them of the benefits be persistent? Why or why not?

6) Although Drake didn't physically commit adultery with Hannah, he thought about it. Do you think God is requiring too much of Christians by asking them to control their thoughts? Do you sometimes catch yourself having negative or sinful thoughts? How

difficult is it to have complete control of the mind?

7) Drake remained a virgin throughout high school and college. Do we as Christians find it hard to believe that Jesus gave Drake strength and kept him even when Drake didn't know it? Do we as Christians find it hard to believe that a man can call upon the strength of Jesus to have such control and that Jesus will deliver? If so, what does that say about our faith in Christ and what He can do for us?

8) Locksie decided to become a member of a church other than her aunt Mary's. What are your thoughts on church membership? Is a member of a church any better than a regular attendee? If your answer is no, then why have the act of membership at all? Do you think it matters where a person goes to church? Should they be committed to one church, or should simply being committed to God be enough?

9) Think back to some of the negative comments Dawson made about God. Did his comments ever anger you like they did Locksie?

10) Dawson's negative statements about God never upset Drake like they did Locksie. Why do you think that is so? Did it mean that Locksie loved and felt more strongly about God than Drake did?

11) Do you agree that sometimes God doesn't answer our prayers with a "no," but instead with a "not right now"? If so, do you believe that waiting period is a test from God?

12) By the end of the story, Hannah had a theory when it came to Elkan and the fact that he had an affair with Peni, resulting in a child. She said to Peni, "You can have the baby, but you can't have my husband. You can have the child support, but you can't have my man." Do you believe that women who deal with this type of infidelity, instead of being so quick to divorce, should take this stand as part of being a virtuous woman? Why or why not?

13) When Hannah heard from God and He blessed her to go back to Elkan, Locksie found it hard to be happy for her. As Christians, is it sometimes difficult to be happy for someone else's blessing?

14) Do you think when a couple marries and both are unsaved, if one decides to dedicate their life to Christ and the other doesn't, that they are unequally yoked? If a married couple is found to be unequally yoked, should they divorce, or do you think it is the other spouse's duty, or even test, perhaps, to lead the unsaved mate to Christ?

15) As a babe in Christ, do you think Locksie's new journey of a walk with the Lord is going

to get easier, or is she going to become more challenged?

16) If you are currently walking with Christ, what have been some of the challenges and tests you've faced? If you haven't decided to dedicate your life to Christ, are some of the same things holding you back that were, at first, holding Locksie back? For example, the infamous *I got to get right first*.

If this book didn't end quite how you wanted it to or if you could have seen something else taking place in the characters' lives that didn't, use the space below to write an alternate ending.

_____

_____

_____

_____

_____

_____

_____

_____

_____

_____

_____

_____

_____

_____

_____

_____

_____

About the Author

Although she is the editor of the anthology titled *Even Sinners Have Souls*, this work, *Me, Myself & Him*, is E.N. Joy's very first Christian fiction novel. Formerly writing secular novels under a different name and pseudonym, when E.N. Joy stood still long enough for God to speak His calling for her into her ear, she immediately replied with, "Yes, I'll do it, Lord." So she began using her pen to glorify God.

"For an individual writing Christian fiction who truly sets out to minister God's Word, it's like taking dictation from the Holy Spirit," E.N. Joy says. "Every message that God wants to be delivered is sent to me that way. When I used to write secular novels, I always wrote my endings first because then I knew exactly what my characters had to do and say, and what type of situations had to take place, in order to get my desired outcome. But now, I have absolutely no idea how God is going to have my stories unfold. I, too, am like an anxious reader, sitting on the edge of my seat to learn the final outcome."

E.N. Joy's next work is about a woman who goes from one extreme to the next in life, and then finally into God's glory. Be sure to look out for her sophomore Christian fiction work titled *I Ain't Me No More*.

You can visit the author's website at *www.enjoywrites.com* or email her at *enjoywrites@aol.com*

Coming Soon

She Who Finds a Husband

BOOK ONE
of the *"NEW DAY DIVAS"* series

By E.N. Joy

Chapter 1

"So just how long had he been sleeping around on you anyway?" Paige asked, almost in a whisper, as if the other women who were in the room weren't already tuned in to the conversation. Paige intensely sat on the edge of her chair in anticipation of Tamarra's response.

"Fifteen years," Tamarra responded through gritted teeth. If the evil expression that was taking over her usually kind and inviting oval shaped face wasn't proof that her flesh was rising up inside of her, then her hands that slowly curled into fists sure were.

"Fifteen years?" Paige repeated. "Oooh, child, the devil is a liar."

"The devil ain't have nothing to do with it," Tamarra begged to differ. Her oak with a gloss finished complexion began to turn red. "Unless devil is another name for that thing down his underwear that he couldn't seem to keep in his pants."

After holding back a chuckle, Paige asked,

"How did you find out? I mean, how in the world does a husband tell his wife that he's been cheating on her for fifteen years?" It wasn't as if Paige didn't already know the story. It was just that the more she pressed whenever Tamarra was telling it, the more new pieces of information she'd always learn.

"Oh, it wasn't that coward who told me. It was his fourteen year old daughter who showed up on our door step one day looking for her daddy. Her daddy who just happened to be my husband. And there was no denying that she was Edward's child. The girl was his spittin' image. So if this was my husband's fourteen year old child, and we'd been married for fifteen years, then surely that meant I was her mother, right?" Of course that was a rhetorical question that Tamarra didn't expect anyone to answer.

The women in the room looked at one another in disbelief. If what Tamarra was saying was accurate, then that meant that Tamarra's husband had been cheating on her for practically the entire fifteen years of their marriage.

Tamarra looked around the room and could read the expression on the women's faces loud and clear. "Yep, that's right. That sucka had been cheating on me for the entire fifteen years of our marriage. The mother of this daughter of his happened to be his high school sweetheart, of whom which he'd had a relationship with for years. It was supposedly one of those on again, off again and then back on again things." She folded her arms and rolled her eyes. "Looks like I must have hooked him when they were off, and just as soon as I said 'I do,' they got it on again . . . I mean they were on again."

"Unbelievable," Paige stated, making a tsk sound. Although upset, due to her deep dimples that donned her cheeks whether she was smiling or not, it was hard to tell just how upset she really was.

"I mean, at first I thought I was going crazy when that child stood at my door telling me that she was my husband's fourteen year old daughter," Tamarra said. "I really thought I had lost my mind; that I'd had a child all these years ago and couldn't remember. For a minute there, I could vouch for the feelings Mary must have felt when she learned she was pregnant with Jesus. Only in my case, there was no immaculate conception. I knew how I would have gotten pregnant and who the daddy was, but I just didn't remember being pregnant." Tamarra paused for air, shifting her size twelve bottom in her chair. "I stood in that doorway pondering, trying to recall the nine months of carrying this child in my womb and the hours of labor. But then reality set in and I realized that this was no more my child than the man on the moon."

"I just can't believe after all those years the child got the courage to show up on your doorstep like that," Paige said.

"Oh, Little Bo Peep didn't just make her way there on her own. Her mother put her up to it I'm sure. Yeah, I'm sure that wench orchestrated the entire thing. I'd bet the farm she was probably parked around the corner somewhere watching the entire scene play out; taking me for the fool I was. A fool who had no idea that not only had her husband fathered a child by another woman, but had been playing an active role in the child's life. Paying child support. Going to school functions and dance recitals."

"Lord, have mercy." Paige shook her head in empathy. Her slicked back ponytail bobbed with each turn of her hair. Hadn't her skin been so chocolate brown, she might have even turned red with anger. She had never been cheated on by a man, not that she knew of anyway. Neither had she ever been married. But she could only imagine the pain her friend sitting next to her must have felt to find out that the man she had been so faithfully committed to for all those years had been living a lie.

"Oh, the Lord had mercy alright. He had mercy when I waited at the door for Edward with a big, black frying pan and got to wailing on that no good husband of mine." Tamarra shook her head in disbelief. "I still don't know how he came out of it with only a mild concussion. I mean, I'd watched *Madea's Family Reunion* enough times to know how to swing that frying pan just right to put him in a three day coma at least. Yeah, the Lord had mercy on him alright; that rotten, dirty, son of a-"

"Sister Tamarra!" Doreen shouted as she stood up from her chair that nearly tipped over from her abrupt movement. "Now I know you're hurt and all about what your ex-husband did to you, but child, need I remind you that you are in the Lord's house?"

Tamarra looked around the room as if to re-familiarize herself with her surroundings. For a minute there, she had forgotten that she was in the church class room where Wednesday night Bible study was held. Perhaps it was the fact that it was Friday and not Wednesday, or the fact that they were in the church classroom instead of the modest sanctuary that made Tamarra forget that she was in God's house.

Doreen, affectionately called Mother Doreen by the members of New Day Temple of Faith, sat back down as she profusely tried to fan away the sweat beads that were now forming on her forehead. Her olive colored skin was now shining like the North Star. She pat down her salt and pepper ear length hair that she wore in a roller set as if Tamarra's near slip up had caused it to stand up straight on her head.

Mother Doreen was a petite, calm and passive woman, always the voice of reason, so even just the hint of any negative drama or excitement got her girdle in a bunch. And the first sign of Mother Doreen's uneasiness was always the sheet of perspiration that showed up on her forehead like a pimple the day before prom or school picture day.

"Oh, I'm sorry, Mother Doreen." Tamarra accepted the tissue that Paige handed her and quickly wiped away the lone tear that rested in the bottom lid of her eye before it could even think about falling. "It's just that it hurts so bad. I mean, I know it's been almost a year since my divorce was final, but it still hurts just like it all happened yesterday." Now tears weld up in both her eyes, but she was sure to blink them into the tissue, leaving no evidence that tears were ever threatening to flow from her eyes.

"Now, now, sweetheart." Mother Doreen stepped

away from her chair and walked over to Tamarra. Tamarra was five feet and eight inches tall compared to Mother Doreen's four feet and eight inches. So Mother Doreen was practically eye to eye with Tamara even though she stood and Tamarra was seated. "I know it hurts, but you got to let go. You got to let go and let God. All this pain, hurt, and anger you're carrying around is bounding you up. And anything that bounds you is intended to keep you from God. We don't want that, now do we?"

"I know, Mother Doreen, but I swear on everything I want to be angry now and repent later," Tamarra sniffled. "The sun goes down, but my anger doesn't go down with it. I just don't know what to do."

"Then it sounds to me like I need to pray for you. You know what the word says; the prayer of the righteous availeth much."

"You can pray for me if you'd like, Mother Doreen, but I've been praying for myself, and it still hurts." Tamarra didn't sound too confident in the power of prayer right about now, although whenever she was called on by the Pastor to come up and pray for church members during altar call, she could pray down the wall of Jericho. Yet she felt as if her personal prayers regarding her own situations never made it to God's ears.

"I know how you feel, baby, but prayer works," Mother Doreen assured her, very confident in her ability to pray for others. She wasn't the church intercessor for nothing. "I'm a witness that prayer works. I was married to my Willie for almost thirty years. We had a strong, loving marriage, but we also had our share of marital issues as well. And it was prayer that brought us through till death do us part." She looked up. "God rest my Willie's soul." She drew an invisible cross across her heart with her index finger and then continued. "I had to pray through the lying. I had to pray through the cheating. I had to pray through the gambling, the drinking . . ." with each issue Mother Doreen called out, for the first time ever, the women could see the flesh rising up in her. And once she noticed that her hands were now balled into fists, she could see it too. "Oh, dear." Mother Doreen began to fan herself again. "Maybe somebody else should pray for you," she said while patting Tamarra on her shoulder and then walking back over to her seat and sat down. "And maybe they should pray for me too while they're at it."

Not being able to take much more of the scene that was playing out before her, Deborah Lucas rose to her feet. "Oh, for Pete's sake," Deborah said under her breath while throwing her hands up. She then said out loud, "I'll pray. I'll pray for everybody . . . God help us all." Deborah sighed heavily.

It wasn't that Deborah didn't want to pray, it was just that she was tired of always ending up being the one that had to pray. This was usually because the women had made themselves weary with reflecting on their past relationships, versus looking forward to the future relationships God may have in store for them. But Deborah should have been used to it by now. The New Day Singles Ministry's first Friday night of the month meetings always ended up being more of an ex bashing session in which the women ultimately found themselves praying and repenting for their words and thoughts. But it was easy for the conversations to stray from words of encouragement to discouragement regarding men, namely the men the women had been in a relationship with. This was because there were no men in the room to object.

In the Singles Ministry's nine months of being in existence, there had been no male members to join as of yet. This left an ample amount of time for the women to share their relationship war stories and compare their battle scars; to determine whose wound was the deepest and yuckiest. They discussed things they more than likely wouldn't have discussed had there been men present.

Although Deborah had a few relationship war stories of her own, she never put her business out there like some of the other women did. She didn't want to make herself look stupid, or in her opinion, let the other women know that she was stupid. She had to be stupid in order not to suspect that the last three men she'd dated had been cheating on her. But in hindsight, she could see everything just clearly now. Clear enough to know a cheat when she sees one a mile away, or let her tell it, "smell one" a mile away. Because in her opinion, she could smell a dog before she could see it. And according to the fictitious Book of Deborah, verse 1 . . . all men were dawgs! So with that belief buried in her heart, she always expected the worse from men. But with that same belief system in place, it was up in the air whether or not she'd know a good man if she saw one, or better yet, if God sent her one.

Deborah stood, all five feet seven and a half inches of her medium build frame, at the front of the class room. She was positioned beside the podium that Pastor taught at every Wednesday. "Everybody please stand." After the women did as they were asked, Deborah began to pray. "With heads bowed, eyes closed and all minds clear, Saints, let's pray."

Deborah led the dozen or so women into an anointed prayer. She asked God to forgive the women for any impure or unrighteous thoughts and comments, and to touch the women's hearts that they may be able to forgive the men in their past relationships that might have hurt them. She also asked God to place a man of God in the women's lives that was after His heart first, and then the women's. After she closed the prayer, the women clapped and then hugged before sitting down and resuming their meeting.

"Now, ladies, can we get back to the business at hand?" Deborah said as she went and pulled her notebook out of her Bible bag; then went and stood behind the podium. She flipped through her notes from the previous meeting. "At the last meeting we discussed having a singles dinner, but we ran out of time before we were really able to discuss it in detail. I personally like the idea, and I'd like to suggest-"

"No offense, Sister Deborah, and I don't mean to cut you off," one of the women spoke up, "but look around." Deborah's light brown, slanted eyes looked around the room that was full of women. "What good is it to have singles events when there ain't anybody but us women there? I don't know about the rest of y'all, but I'm going to tell the truth and shame the devil. I joined this ministry to meet me a single man. Heck, that's what I thought a Single's Ministry was all about; the singles hooking up and connecting. If that's not the case, shoot, I wouldn't have canceled my membership to that online dating network."

The woman sat back down to a crescendo of "Amens."

"She's got a point," Paige added. "We plan stuff and then it's just us women who participate. The last time I checked the Bible, that sort of thing was an abomination, if you know what I mean." Paige's comment was followed by some laughter and comments of agreement. "Besides, a dinner? Come on, do I look like I miss that many dinners that I need to put one down on my calendar." Paige was making refernece to her plus size figure.

When Mother Doreen saw that Deborah was starting to become agitated, she interjected before any drama could jump off. "Now, ladies, the entire purpose of this ministry is for the support of the singles in this church. Which reminds me, I need to get the bylaws typed up so I can give you all a copy. Then the purpose and vision will be clear in black and white. But in the meantime, remember that the church is not and has never been a place where you come to find a man."

"And just where was it again that you and the late Willie met?" Paige asked with her thick, long eyelashes fluttering over her big, brown eyes. She knew darn well she recalled the story Mother Doreen had told about how she and her now deceased husband had met.

"Well . . . uh . . . at church," Mother Doreen stammered. "But when I went to church. I didn't set out to find no husband. I set out to find the Lord. I just got blessed with both. Because spite all the issues me and Willie had to endure in our marriage . . ." She looked up. "God rest my Willie's soul." She drew an invisible cross across her heart with her index finger and then continued. "My marriage with that man was a blessing. I wouldn't trade those years of my life for the world." She looked at Tamarra. "And I know if you look back on your fifteen years of marriage, your good outweighed the bad and you wouldn't trade it for the world either."

"No, not the world," Tamarra partly agreed, "just a little island off the coast of Mexico with enough tequila for me to forget that low down dirty dog of a man ever existed." Tamarra shook her head. "And thank goodness we never had any children together to remind me of that dirt bag."

The comment Tamarra had just made stung Deborah for her own personal reasons. Reasons that were between her and God. She quickly recuperated and just shook her head, her shoulder length sisterlocks dancing with every movement. She wondered if she'd be needing to pray for these women all over again.

The women began to murmur and mumble, mostly in support of both Paige and the other woman's earlier remarks about what they perceived as failed singles events.

Deborah cleared her throat to get the women's attention. "If you ladies would have let me finish, I believe my suggestion would have covered your concerns regarding male participation in the singles events." Deborah was able to keep from shooting daggers at the women with her eyes before proceeding. "I was going to suggest that even though we can't seem to get the single men at New Day to join the Singles Ministry, we can still invite them to the dinner. That might break the ice and even get a few of them to become members."

The women began to nod and chatter in agreement of Deborah's suggestion. *Finally, a breakthrough,* Deborah thought a moment too soon.

"Where were you thinking we should have the dinner?" another woman asked.

"Oooh, The Olive Garden has that bottomless salad," Tamarra suggested.

"But Red Robins has those bottomless fries," Paige countered.

"Weren't you the one who just made a comment referencing your weight?" Tamarra reminded her friend.

"Yeah, and now I can't *wait* to eat," Paige chuckled. She was never one to diet, and complaints about her weight were far and few in between. She knew that if she didn't like her size, she could do something about it. But being big boned pretty much all her life, she'd accepted the fact that she was a life time member of the big girls club with a platinum membership.

"How about we have the dinner at . . . .." The women in the room spoke amongst themselves, throwing out the names of their favorite restaurants as suggested locations to hold the dinner.

"Excuse me," Deborah interrupted, once again clearing her throat. "I was thinking that we could have the dinner right here at the church, in the fellowship hall."

The women eyeballed one another and nodded.

"Hmm, now that doesn't sound bad either," Paige said. "My cousin has her own catering business, Integrity Catering. I know she'd give us a good deal on catering the event."

"Now you know good and darn well I do catering for a living," Tamarra huffed. "You just trying to be funny. Besides, why would you want to have someone outside the church cater when God has everything we need already in this house?"

"I wasn't trying to be funny," Paige stated. "I just figured you'd want to relax and enjoy the dinner instead of preparing it." Paige rolled her big eyes.

Those all too familiar sweat beads began to dance about Mother Doreen's forehead. It was now Deborah's turn to intervene before these meetings ended up giving the sixty something year old woman a heart attack before it was all over.

"I was thinking us women would prepare the food and invite the men," Deborah explained.

An instant hush swept over the room and the women stared at Deborah as if she was standing naked before the Lord . . . literally.

Tamarra stood up and put her hands on her hips. Her fingers wrapped around her toned waist. "I wish I might even think about slaving in the kitchen for a bunch of men who don't even find us worthy enough to come fellowship with us for a night. And it's just one evening out of the month. Oh, but I'm sure they'd come out to eat our food."

"Yeah, I bet if that mini skirt, low cut shirt wearing Lorain was a member of this ministry, the men would flock here in droves," one woman added. "The way they dang near be salivating over the woman is just shameful."

"Guess our skirts ain't short enough and v-necks ain't v enough, like that jezebel spirit possessed Lorain's," another complained. "Guess we all can't be spiritual divas like good ol' Sister Lorain." Her tone was laced with sarcasm and a hint of jealousy.

"Then she be having the nerve to run to the altar every dang on Sunday and fall out in the spirit, showing every ounce of her-"

"Ladies," Deborah interrupted. "We're getting off track again. And in addition to that, we're starting to sound like the children of Israel with all this murmuring and complaining. We always talking about how we want the Lord to use us, but now we won't even let Him use us to cook a meal for some members of our own church."

"Not just members; the men," Tamarra corrected.

"Ya heard?" a young twenty-something woman stated. "And my momma told me don't cook for no man but my husband. That's almost just as bad as giving up the milk for free without making him buy the cow."

"And the men at this church probably wouldn't appreciate it anyway," Tamarra continued, rolling her eyes. "Trust me, I've been a member for nine years. I know how these New Day men are."

"Let them cook for us," Paige suggested. "Ain't nothing wrong with a man cooking for a woman. Besides, just in case one of these men at New Day is my future husband and God just ain't revealed it to me yet, I don't even want him to get the impression that I'm going to be cooking for him all the time. I need me a man who's gonna take me out to dinner. I ain't trying to always be in no kitchen."

"You could have fooled me," a woman said under her breath, just low enough so that Paige didn't hear her, but the woman next to her could. The two of them shared a private chuckle.

Mother Doreen just shook her head. Listening to these women talk, it was no wonder they were all single. It may not have been scripture, but Mother Doreen was a strong believer in the saying that the way to a man's heart was through his stomach. Seeming as though these women weren't trying to lift a finger in the kitchen, they might never find their way to a man's heart, which explained all their war stories.

"How about a compromise?" Mother Doreen suggested. She had everyone's attention. "The women cook the meats and maybe some main dishes, and we have the men bring beverages, rolls, desserts and side dishes like potato and macaroni salad; you know, things they can buy from the grocery store deli, since I'm sure most of the men don't cook." Mother Doreen bit her tongue in adding her thought, *Because most of y'all women don't even cook.*

"We can have a sign up sheet," Deborah added, in full agreement with Mother Doreen's suggestion. Somehow, her and Mother Doreen always managed to end up on one accord. This ultimately led the others to follow suit.

The women now spoke amongst one another in more lively tones, nodding their heads in favor of the direction in which the Singles Dinner was heading.

Finally, there was a consensus. Deborah was relieved. She stood in the front of the room, wondering how she'd been unofficially put in charge of the Single's Ministry anyway. After all, it was Mother Doreen who God had given the vision to and who had taken the idea to Pastor for approval. But after the first few meetings, it was evident that these pack of women needed someone who would come before them boldly, so to speak. And although Mother Doreen was the Singles Ministry Leader appointed by the pastor of New Day, Deborah pretty much took charge. This was to both Mother Doreen's approval and appreciation.

After ripping a sheet of paper from her notebook, Deborah passed around a sign up sheet. The women bragged and boasted about their specialty dishes as they signed the sheet.

"I'll get with the church secretary and check the church calendar," Mother Doreen said, "and then I'll run a couple dates by Pastor in order to get approval on everything."

"Sounds good to me," Deborah said. "Sound good to you, ladies?" she asked the women.

"Sounds good," they all replied.

Deborah smiled with satisfaction. It looked like this Singles Dinner was going to turn out just fine after all. But just like everything else in life, looks could be deceiving. Very deceiving.